PRAISE FOR BARBARA TAYLOR

THE LAST INNOCENT HOUR

"This is a plot worthy of Daphne du Maurier . . . a compelling tale of innocence lost."

—*The Houston Chronicle*

"Sissel's writing is strong and the characters and their motivations clearly drawn."

—Bev Vincent, author of *The Road to the Dark Tower* and
The Stephen King Illustrated Companion

"A taut psychological suspense thriller, exciting and quite dark with no light in sight adding an almost gothic feel."

—*Midwest Book Review*

"Sissel's first novel is a worthy achievement . . . along the lines of Iris Johansen. Frightening . . . poignant. Sissel's strength lies in her multi-dimensional characters . . . that make the reader react—with fear, with relief, with anger, with tenderness."

—*Book Browser Review*

"*The Last Innocent Hour* will ensnare you in a web of family secrets and suspense, powerful crisp writing and characters so real you'll think you've met them."

—Colleen Thompson, bestselling author of *The Salt Maiden* and
Phantom of New Orleans

THE NINTH STEP

"Barbara Taylor Sissel crafts a sure-handed, beautiful garden of a novel on ground tilled by Jodi Picoult and Anita Shreve . . . Sissel's vibrant voice, rich characters, and deft plotting draw the reader in and keep pages turning to the gripping, unexpected end."

—Joni Rodgers, *New York Times* bestselling author of the novels *Crazy for Trying* and *Sugarland*, and a memoir, *Bald in the Land of Big Hair*

EVIDENCE OF LIFE

"The . . . pace of Sissel's novel allows readers to savor the language and the well-drawn characters . . . Enjoyable and insightful."

—*RT Book Reviews Magazine*, four stars

"A chilling mystery with a haunting resolution you won't see coming."

—Sophie Littlefield, bestselling author of *Garden of Stones*

SAFE KEEPING

"Past secrets contribute to present-day angst in this solid suspense novel, and the even pacing keeps the reader's interest until the captivating conclusion."

—*Publishers Weekly*

"Impressive writing and affecting subject matter."

—*Kirkus Reviews*

"A gripping read . . . perfect for a book club."

—*Library Journal*

"A book you need to set aside time for because you will not be able to break away."

—*Suspense Magazine*

FAULTLINES

"An in-depth portrayal of how one moment—and one mystery—can crack a family open. These compelling characters will stay with you long after the final reveal. Sissel's fans will not be disappointed."

—Catherine McKenzie, bestselling author of *Hidden* and *Fractured*

"This is that rare sort of book that grabs you from the very first line and refuses to let go. Beautifully written, intricately plotted, and perfectly executed, *Faultlines* is an intimate look at the unraveling of a family after a tragic accident. Sissel weaves a clever web of emotional fallout as she alternates seamlessly between two storylines that converge in a devastating way. An atmospheric, emotional, suspenseful journey that will stay with you for a long time after you've finished the last page."

—Kristin Harmel, international bestselling author of
The Sweetness of Forgetting

"Barbara Taylor Sissel brilliantly weaves a compelling, suspenseful, and emotional family drama . . . As the parent of a teenager, I immediately connected with the story and the characters, and was hooked from page one. Ms. Sissel is a masterful storyteller when it comes to suspense and an exceptional writer. It's a definite page-turner!"

—Kerry Lonsdale, bestselling author of *Everything We Keep*

"A gripping tale of secrets and obsessions in which nothing is quite as it seems. After tragedy and accusations of blame rip a family apart, Barbara Taylor Sissel masterfully unravels the shocking truth."

—Barbara Claypole White, bestselling author of *The Perfect Son*

"I was completely sucked into *Faultlines*. Told with great skill and compassion, *Faultlines* had me feeling for so many of its flawed but very human characters, each of them struggling toward the grace that can only come of forgiveness. My favorite of Sissel's many fine books, *Faultlines* kept me reading long past midnight . . . and the powerful, yet hopeful, resolution will stay with me for a long time."

—Colleen Thompson, author of *The Off Season* and *Fatal Error*

THE TRUTH WE BURY

"Once again, Barbara Taylor Sissel has kept me up into the wee hours of the night with an unputdownable masterpiece that explores family, love, and the ramifications of the decisions we make. The perfect blend of mystery, danger, and the type of secrets people kill for, *The Truth We Bury* will keep you reading furiously until you reach the perfectly executed end."

—Kristin Harmel, international bestselling author of
The Sweetness of Forgetting and *When We Meet Again*

"What would you do if your grown child was implicated in a brutal murder? . . . As family secrets, lies, and betrayals are revealed, they also find the strength to take ownership of their own mistakes. A gripping book club read!"

—Barbara Claypole White, bestselling author of *Echoes of Family*

"Engrossing murder mystery . . . Sissel's characters are all too real, their harrowing devotion and blind love for their children not far from what every parent feels. As their choices play out, and the consequences and truth unspool, you will be riveted until the very last page."

—Emily Carpenter, author of *The Weight of Lies* and
Burying the Honeysuckle Girls

"Barbara Taylor Sissel ratchets up the suspense . . . Rich with beautiful prose, compelling characters, and questions about the imperfect nature of family relationships, this is one of those books that will stay with me for a very long time."

—Colleen Thompson, author of *The Off Season*

"Beautifully written . . . the perfect emotional storm of family secrets, regret, and revenge. *The Truth We Bury* will keep you guessing until the final shocking reveal, all while making you wonder which of your own little buried truths could come back to haunt you."

—Jenna Patrick, author of *The Rules of Half*

"Compulsively readable and gorgeously written, Barbara Taylor Sissel's *The Truth We Bury* had me enthralled from the first page to its stunning conclusion. Readers will love the blend of suspense, mystery, and family drama, and book clubs will find much to discuss. This is a novel you won't want to miss."

—Karen McQuestion, bestselling author of *The Long Way Home* and *Hello Love*

"Part riveting mystery, part moral dilemma, *The Truth We Bury* is a beautifully written exploration of the depths of a mother's love."

—Robyn Harding, author of *The Party*

WHAT

LIES

BELOW

ALSO BY BARBARA TAYLOR SISSEL

Safe Keeping
Evidence of Life
The Last Innocent Hour
The Ninth Step
The Volunteer
Crooked Little Lies
Faultlines
The Truth We Bury

WHAT LIES BELOW

BARBARA TAYLOR SISSEL

LAKE UNION

PUBLISHING

Published by Lake Union Publishing, Seattle

www.apub.com

Amazon, the Amazon logo, and Lake Union Publishing are trademarks of Amazon.com, Inc., or its affiliates.

ISBN-13: 9781503950115
ISBN-10: 1503950115

Cover design and photography by Faceout Studio, Derek Thornton

Printed in the United States of America

For and in celebration of those who take time to whisper to a child: you can do it.

1

Zoe Halstead wouldn't go missing until Thursday, the day after Gilly made her a breakfast pancake in the shape of an elephant's head. Zoe ate the ears first, then worked her way up the long trunk, but when she got to the eyes—chocolate chip–dotted mini marshmallows—she balked.

"Daddy," she said, "if I eat its eyes, how will it see?"

Gilly, doing coffee refills at the adjacent booth, glanced at Jake over Zoe's head, interested in how he'd answer.

He didn't miss a beat. "Those are pretend eyes. They're made to eat."

"But what if a monster comes and eats my eyes?"

"Can't happen, snickerdoodle. All the eyeball-eating monsters are gone. Ask Miss Gilly."

"It's true." Gilly came to their table, not missing a beat either, although had she been summoned by any other man wearing untidy smears of glittery blue polish on his fingernails she might have lost focus. "One night, very late, those monsters were out hunting for eyeballs, and they got lost in the woods."

"The woods by my school? We aren't supposed to go there."

"Well, the monsters didn't follow the rules. That's why they got lost."

"Are they still there?"

"No," Gilly answered. "They got very tired from hunting and being lost; they fell asleep under the trees, and the next morning a fairy found them."

"Did they eat her eyes?" Zoe's own eyes were worried.

"They couldn't." Gilly looked at Jake, waiting for his nod, his smile of approval, before she continued.

She wasn't sure how it had happened, but in the six months since she'd started waitressing at Cricket's Café the storytelling had become ritual like the pancakes. At first Gilly had related short versions of the old standards, fairy tales she knew from her own childhood. "The Twelve Dancing Princesses" was a favorite of Zoe's. Eventually, though, she had branched out, making up stories on the fly. Eyeball-eating monsters was the latest, and most far out, if Jake's dubious, one-cornered grin was any indication.

Gilly looked back to Zoe. "You see, the fairy put a magic spell on those monsters while they were sleeping, and when they woke up, they weren't monsters anymore. They only wanted to eat pretend eyes like the marshmallow ones on your elephant."

Zoe looked at her plate, and quickly, not allowing time to reconsider, she popped a marshmallow into her mouth, looking from Gilly to her dad, clearly pleased with herself. "When I come next time, will you make a g'raffe pancake?" She tipped her glance at Gilly. "With his neck this long?" Zoe spread her hands apart over her head, and her delighted smile made Gilly's heart turn over.

"With blueberries for eyes?" Gilly asked.

"Yes! And a Blue Moon smoovie?"

"Yep. I can do that." It was another of Gilly's online discoveries in her quest for kid-friendly recipes. She combined blueberries with bananas, a dollop of plain yogurt, and a splash of apple juice and whirred the concoction up in the blender. Zoe loved it. But as she had explained once in detail to Gilly, she liked blueberries because they were blue. She liked blue potatoes, too, and Blue Bell ice cream, and she carried a tattered length of blue satin ribbon, or at least Jake claimed it had once been blue. She wore it looped around her wrist, or sometimes tied in her hair or pinned to her shirt. But often, she just carried it in her hand.

There was a story behind the ribbon, Gilly was certain of it, but while she had gotten to know Jake a bit over the six months she'd worked at the café, she didn't feel comfortable asking about it.

"Did you see mine and Daddy's polish?" Zoe spread her fingers wide, making Gilly think of blue-tipped starfish, lovely and plump. "I let Daddy pick the color this time, and he chose my very favorite." She turned her hand in the warm bar of sunlight that striped the table. "It's real glittery, see? Like stars at night. Show her, Daddy."

Jake spread his hand as if wearing nail polish was the most natural thing in the world for a man. And Gilly guessed it was for him. It seemed to her he wore a different color every few weeks.

She bent to inspect the latest shade, minding her expression, keeping it earnest for Zoe's sake. She'd intuited the first time she had spotted Jake's polished nails—alternate shades of yellow and green that week—that it was serious business. It was hard, though, not smiling—Jake's hands were a workman's hands—solidly made, square, big knuckled, and so obviously masculine—and the exuberantly applied strokes of girly polish looked funny, and silly, and endearing. That he would do that—let his little girl paint his nails. It got to Gilly every time. "Just gorgeous," she said. "I really liked that shade of rose last week," she added, "but now, I think this blue is my favorite."

Zoe bounced excitedly. "I could paint yours like I do Daddy's. Want me to?"

"Oh." The moment turned awkward. Regretting it, and the flush she felt warming her face, Gilly glanced at Jake. He had stopped in at the café occasionally when she'd happened to be on a break, and they'd sat together over coffee, but they'd never met outside Cricket's.

"Maybe sometime, ZooRoo," he said. "But right now we have to go. You have to get to school, and I've got to go to work."

He ran a concrete company. Gilly had heard he'd inherited it when his dad died suddenly of a heart attack two years ago. She knew he'd been close to his dad. He was close to his mom, too. His affection for his folks showed in his voice whenever he mentioned them. Gilly envied him.

She hefted the coffee carafe. "Let me refill the guys at the counter, and I'll meet you at the register."

Jake thanked her, and that quickly their routine was restored. They had the same conversation every Wednesday morning.

Wednesday was Zoe's day. If asked, she would tell you she'd been "borned" on Wednesday, and she was its princess—the Princess of the Wednesday Kingdom. By her imperial order it was also Pancakes for Breakfast Day.

Gilly refilled coffee mugs down the length of the counter, and Jake helped Zoe out of the booth. Her strawberry-blonde hair was in pink-ribboned pigtails that curled to her shoulders. Painting fingernails wasn't Jake's only talent. He did Zoe's hair, too. Braids were a specialty, although he complained that Zoe's hair was slippery; he had trouble getting the braids to hold.

But he was careful in so many ways with his daughter. Gilly had heard folks call him Mr. Mom. Sometimes the older ladies teared up when they talked about him, and Zoe, his poor motherless child. Mandy Bright, the stylist at A Cut Above, who cut Gilly's hair, had given Gilly an earful about Jake's ex-wife, the infamous Stephanie, citing details that had made Gilly feel bitter against her, too—a woman she'd never met. But Stephanie had abandoned Jake and Zoe, who would be four in July, almost two years ago, around the time of Zoe's second birthday.

"What kind of mother does that?" Gilly had asked Mandy.

"An alcoholic one," she had answered.

Had Stephanie never heard of Twelve-Step? Gilly hadn't asked. For herself, she attended meetings up in Greeley. She didn't want folks in Wyatt knowing she had her own issues.

Gilly set the carafe on the burner and joined Jake and Zoe at the cash register. "So are we all set?"

Jake was patting his pockets, looking worried.

"Daddy can't find his wallet," Zoe said. "I have some money," she told him, and squatting on the floor, she opened her backpack, a facsimile of Nemo, the cartoon clownfish from the movie *Finding Nemo*. She'd been aghast, as only a three-going-on-four-year-old can be, when Gilly had confessed she'd never seen it.

"Here!" She shot straight up now, brandishing two one-dollar bills. "I have 'leven dollars."

"Where did you get that money?" Jake asked.

"Grammie gave me it yesterday when I weeded her garden."

"Ah. Well, it's only two dollars, ZooRoo."

She wrinkled her brow, perplexed. Jake explained. Gilly wasn't sure when he was done if Zoe was any clearer on the issues of high finance.

Jake met Gilly's glance. "I must have left my wallet in my truck. Can you hang on and let me look?"

"Sure," Gilly said. "I'll keep Zoe in lieu of payment. If you don't come back, she can wash dishes. Want to, Zoe?"

"Okay, but I'll have to have a stool so I can reach," she answered somberly.

Gilly laughed. "Just teasing, kiddo."

After settling Zoe at the counter, Gilly rang up another customer's tab and made change. She filled Clint Mackie's thermal mug with hot coffee. He was local law enforcement, the police captain, and got all the coffee he wanted for free. He would likely get his coffee free anyway, given he was married to Cricket, Gilly's boss. "Where's Sergeant Carter?" she asked him. "Doesn't he want a refill, too, before you go out on patrol?" Looking around for the sergeant, she caught sight of him at the back of the café.

"He's talking to Liz Ames," the captain said at the same time Gilly caught sight of her.

She gave Liz a small glad wave when their eyes met. "I didn't know she was back in town."

"She's from Dallas, right?" the captain asked. "Ken told me she's a pharmaceutical rep?"

"That's right," Gilly said. "She's based out of Dallas now, but her territory is changing, or maybe it's expanding." Gilly couldn't quite remember how it was. "She may be relocating here."

"Ken'll like hearing that," the captain said. "He was telling me he stopped her in town a week or so ago. Her taillight was out. Said he wanted to check up this morning and see if she got it fixed." Mackie gave Gilly a look.

She ducked his gaze. She wasn't going to speculate as to the sergeant's interest in Liz. She wished him luck. For different reasons, Liz was no more ready to enter the dating scene than Gilly. It was one of the things they shared in common besides the fact that they were both new to the area. Gilly made change for another customer, and when Sergeant Carter handed her his travel mug, she refilled it.

"Don't guess you could put in a word for me," he said, giving a nod in Liz's direction.

"Sure, for all the good it'll do."

The captain guffawed, and Gilly grinned. She liked the sergeant and Captain Mackie. She didn't have much use for cops—detectives in particular—but these two officers seemed like good guys.

"Be careful out there," she told them.

"Always," the sergeant said.

"Pretty quiet these days," Captain Mackie said, "which is exactly how I like it."

Sergeant Carter rapped the counter with his knuckled fist. "We'll be back around noon for lunch. I'm already thinking double cheeseburger and fries."

"If I ate like you, I'd be as big as a house," the captain said.

Gilly lost the rest of the conversation when the men went out the door, passing Jake on his way back in. There was some manly exchange of greetings, all of it silhouetted there in the doorway, and watching them, Gilly knew Jake hadn't found his wallet.

"You left it at home," she said when he came to the counter.

"Yeah, I must have." He looked chagrined. "At least I hope that's where I left it."

"Daddy loses his head sometimes," Zoe said, rolling her eyes.

Gilly smiled at her, and her mind was taken with how like a tiny adult Zoe was at times. *Precocious* was the word, Gilly guessed, and even as she was thinking this, she heard herself telling Jake where to find his wallet. "You left it in the garage," she said. "On top of the old wooden tool chest. The one with the initials engraved on the lid, in the center—AJH, or maybe it's JHA."

Jake stared at her.

"She's right, Dad. 'Member?" Zoe took his hand, getting his attention. "We got the spark for the lawn mower yesterday, then you fixed it in the garage. You had out your wallet. I saw it."

"Spark *plug*," Jake said absently, his eyes moving to Zoe. "It's called a spark *plug*."

"Whatever." She shrugged her shoulders.

"I don't know where that came from." Gilly said. It was the truth. She felt as astonished as Jake looked.

"Well, wouldn't it be something if you were right," he said, meeting her gaze.

She thought it was gracious of him to treat her prediction as if it were reasonable. *I'm a nutcase.* She wanted to say it. Of course she couldn't know where his wallet was. If she were still drinking, she'd think she was hallucinating. But maybe she was. Maybe hallucinations—like the blank, dark places in her memory—were part of the package of side effects that had followed her out of addiction into sobriety. "You can bring the money by any time. After you find your wallet, that is."

"Sure. Thanks. C'mon, squirt." He lifted Zoe off the stool. "Let's get you to school."

"See you later, alligator," Zoe said, waving at Gilly over her dad's shoulder.

"After a while, crocodile," Gilly said, waving back.

Even then, Zoe was squirming, asking Jake to put her down. "I'm not a baby, Dad." She drew out the word, emphatically derisive, as if being a *baaaby* had potential as a featured occupation on the old TV show *Dirty Jobs*.

It made Gilly smile; it hurt her heart. She didn't let herself think about why. It was part of the deal she'd made with herself after moving out of Houston. What had happened there was staying there. Or what was the point of leaving—of making a new start?

She went into the kitchen, where April Warner was cleaning the grill, and Nick, April's twentysomething son, was washing dishes. April and Cricket did most of the cooking, and they were training Gilly. She was a reluctant cook—no kind of foodie. She'd been hired as a waitress. Zoe's specially shaped pancakes were about the extent of her repertoire. But then most narcotized drunks couldn't care less what they ate, and in her case, her eight months of sobriety hadn't increased her desire for cuisine, haute or otherwise. But as the saying goes, necessity is the mother of invention, or something like that.

She kept waking up mornings to find she was still breathing. Empty inside but alive. Beached on a strange shore but with a heartbeat. Still functional like a faulty circuit. She scratched at the margins, worked a job mainly to keep herself occupied and out of trouble. Her mom was appalled. *You took a job as a waitress?* Her incredulity had been almost funny. But even Gilly had her moments of doubt and confusion. She'd been trained as an architect. Sustainable residential design had been her focus, her passion. But passion had no part in her new life. It was much safer that way.

"Has it slowed down?" April asked, looking over her shoulder.

"Saw the last customer out the door a minute ago. You guys need any help?"

"I think we're good." Nick untied his apron. "I'm taking off, Ma. I've got class." He was finishing his second year at the community college in Greeley and talking about enrolling at Texas A&M. Nick was whip smart, especially in math, but he'd gotten into some trouble in high school with crystal meth. April had confided in Gilly that she'd thought he'd kill himself overdosing before he straightened out.

"Don't do anything I wouldn't do," Gilly said to him.

Nick grinned. "That leaves me wide open."

It was their usual smart-ass exchange. She'd never told him or his mom she was an addict, too—albeit a different drug of choice—but she thought he knew. Addicts gave off a certain vibe, especially the newly recovering ones. There was something raw and careful in their demeanor. They had a way of navigating the world as if it were a small shop filled with priceless art objects, all made of glass. Gilly was scared every moment of backsliding, falling, breaking her fragile hold on sobriety into a million jagged pieces.

Her phone rang, and she pulled it from her apron pocket, studying the ID window.

Carl.

"You going to answer that?" April asked as she passed Gilly. She was carrying a tray stacked with freshly washed coffee mugs, and she paused, her backside to the swinging doors that divided the kitchen from the dining area.

Gilly looked up at her, and without answering, she turned away, swiping her phone's face, holding it to her ear, saying, "Hello," as if she weren't acutely aware of who was calling and the disturbance it caused her.

There were heartbeats of silence. Behind her the swish of the doors, the gust of air April's exit created. And then his voice.

"It's business," Carl said, "or I wouldn't be calling."

She'd asked him—begged him, actually—to stop it, stop the near daily check-ins. She'd said if there was a need to contact her, he should ask his partner, Houston detective Garrett Quinn, to do it. Carl had agreed it was probably best, and yet, here he was.

"Garrett's out today, and I didn't think this should wait."

Gilly paced several steps, making a circle, eyeing the floor, the toes of her sneakers.

"We have a lead, a pretty good one, I think."

She still didn't answer. She wasn't impressed. She'd heard it before—all about the good leads that never led anywhere.

"We got a call from one of the bartenders at Sully's, said he overheard a couple guys talking about the shooting."

"C'mon, Carl, it's been almost three years. What can two guys in a bar have to say about it now?"

"You know our theory, the reason we haven't caught the shooter. He's hiding in plain sight. Still in the neighborhood, still going about his business. Sully's Pub is three doors down from the convenience store—"

"You mean the local stop and shoot," Gilly said bitterly. "Convenience for robbers and killers."

"You know leaving Houston doesn't change what happened, right? The investigation doesn't stop because you left town, and whether you like it or believe it, your life is still in jeopardy. There's still a murderer on the loose, and it's my job to find him and get him off the street. If it takes till my dying day—" Carl broke off.

Gilly imagined him, head down, pinching the bridge of his nose. He had told her once he thought he was too sensitive to be a detective. The brutality, the heartlessness got to him. Worse, he thought, than it did other guys on the force.

"I know you're scared," he said.

Gilly closed her eyes. She was scared. Not so much of the killer but of her memory of that night. She would undergo a lobotomy to forget what had happened, if she could.

"Look, Garrett and I are going to get the bastard who shot Brian and lock him up. I promised you that on December sixteenth, three and a half years ago, when your husband was murdered, and I'm promising you now." Carl's kindness, the intensity of his commitment to do just as he said, almost undid her. "We'll track these guys down and get their story. The way they were talking, one, or both of them, could know the shooter, know where he is."

Gilly tucked her free hand beneath her elbow. Her palm was cold against her ribs.

"Until then I want you looking over your shoulder, you hear me? You can't be too careful—"

"I know, Carl."

"I don't think you do, Gilly. If you did, you'd never have moved two hundred and fifty miles away."

"We shouldn't be talking. I've told you, it's a mistake."

"Our mistake was sleeping together," he said, and she saw it again.

The night of her husband's murder, when she'd clung to Carl, a total stranger, the one solid presence in all the horror. He'd held her, sobbing and shaking, against his chest, until, gradually, she'd become quiet. In the months that followed, he'd been her refuge—her go-to place on nights when she couldn't sleep, days when she couldn't work. He'd taught her to sail and to shoot. But they hadn't been intimate until she'd gotten sober eight months ago, and then it had only been for a few weeks. But it had cost her.

Now he was calling it a mistake.

Good.

"How's Bailey?" he asked, getting back on safer ground.

Bailey was her six-year-old terrier mix. Gilly and Brian had picked him up, a puppy not more than six months old, off the side of the road one rainy night in Houston. "He's fine. He likes having a yard again."

"So you're still happy with your job?" Carl asked as if it weren't possible, and it wasn't, not in terms of who she'd once been. The year before Brian was shot they'd opened their own architecture firm, B&G Architects, in Houston. They'd been full of themselves, launching their mutual dream. They'd had such hopes, made so many plans. Brian had brought flowers to their office every week for her desk. The last time, he'd given her gerbera daisies. Soft red.

Carl said, "I told your mom I wouldn't have believed it—you a waitress—if I hadn't seen it with my own eyes."

The lightness of amazement in Carl's voice matched the look he'd had on his face the one time—that Gilly was aware of—he'd come to visit, a month ago. He'd wanted to spend time with her, to spend the night. She'd sent him back to Houston. "I have to go," she said. "The salt shakers need filling."

He didn't answer right away, and she could tell he didn't want to break their connection, that there were more things he'd like to ask her. Like, *How's the new probation officer? What about Twelve-Step? You find a meeting? A sponsor?*

"Thanks for the heads up," she said, cutting him off before he could speak. "Good luck with the lead." She regretted sounding snarky but not enough to apologize.

"Be careful, Gilly, I mean it. This guy—Brian's killer is dangerous—"

"It's been over three years—"

"Yeah, he's had three years to get even more desperate. He knows you saw him. Don't think for a second that it's not still on his mind, that he can't track you down. Doesn't matter how far you run."

She started to object, but if she were to say she wasn't running, they'd both know she was lying.

"Just promise me you'll be vigilant. Lock your doors. Carry the Mace I gave you. I still wish you'd let me get you a gun. I know the answer is no," he said before she could. "You don't like them. Still . . ." He paused, regret deep in his voice.

He offered her his care with such sincerity, ignoring her rancor, refusing to take it personally. He wanted her to see it—the reflection of her bitterness, the loss of her faith—in the mirror of his gentle complaisance. He thought the contrast would get to her, and it did. Ending the call, some combination of resentment, loneliness, and longing knotted her heart.

"Everything okay?" April asked, coming into the kitchen.

"Fine," Gilly said. She pushed through the swinging doors and crossed the café to the plate-glass window. Outside, the street was quiet at this midmorning hour. She could leave Wyatt and go farther north. She could go clear to Alaska, the North Pole, if she felt like it.

There was nothing and no one to stop her.

There was nothing holding her here.

2

"Does Mommy know where I am?"

Jake looked at Zoe in the rearview, then back at the SUV he was tailing up the U-shaped drive that led to Zoe's preschool, the Little Acorn Academy. "Why are you asking?"

"'Cause I wonder," Zoe said, as if he were dense.

But why now—out of the blue? It had been months since she'd mentioned her mom—since Christmas, he thought. Long enough that he'd begun to hope her heartbreak over Stephanie's absence was finally fading from her mind. He glanced in the rearview again, meeting his daughter's chocolate-brown eyes. They were his eyes, same shape and color. In everything except the dainty uptilt of her freckled nose and her build—Zoe was small-boned and delicate—she favored Jake. She was a brown-eyed blonde, too. She had his dimples and squarish chin. He'd wondered sometimes if the resemblance was why Stephanie had never really bonded with Zoe. Maybe every time Steph had looked at their daughter she'd been reminded of Jake, the bad guy who'd dragged her out of New York City. From day one Steph had acted as if Texas were a third world country and living in Wyatt was punishment.

"Your mom knows where you are," Jake said to Zoe. He could only thank whatever gods there were that she hadn't asked if her mom *cared* about her. He didn't know how he'd answer that one. He wouldn't lie even though it might make life easier. Like when Zoe had watched *Finding Nemo* for the first time and decided that, like Nemo's mom, her mom had been eaten by a shark, too. He'd wanted badly to say yes, that was exactly what had happened. It was a concept Zoe seemed able to grasp, and it was much simpler than the truth. But he'd gently dissuaded her of that notion. While her mom did live elsewhere, she wasn't in the ocean. She wasn't at risk of being eaten, at least not by a shark.

"Can we watch a movie and have pizza tonight?" Zoe asked. "We could ask Miss Gilly to come, and I could paint her fingernails."

Jake met Zoe's gaze. "You like her, huh?"

Zoe nodded. "She's funny, and she tells funny stories."

Jake liked Gilly, too. More than that, he felt drawn to her, and it wasn't a good thing. He didn't have much luck when it came to his relationships with the opposite sex. The only one that had worked so far was with Zoe.

"Can we, Daddy?"

"Friday is movie night," Jake answered. "This is only Wednesday."

"Can we invite her on Friday then?"

"I don't know, ZooRoo. I kind of like having you all to myself."

"Daaaddy . . ."

He pulled to a stop at the school entrance doors, and turning to look at her, he asked, "Do you know how much I love you?" It was a daily ritual, one he'd started around the time he'd accepted that Zoe's mom was gone, possibly for good.

Steph had always been a drinker, but it wasn't until she and Jake were married that he realized it was a problem, one that had only gotten worse. After Zoe was born Steph began leaving home to do her drinking. She might stay away overnight or as long as a couple of days; once she'd left for a week. He started finding pills, random colors and shapes, where she'd leave them in the bathroom or on her night table. If he questioned her, she'd swear she'd gotten them from a doctor, that she was depressed, couldn't sleep. It got bad enough that she'd gone into rehab more than once. The thing was that no matter what provoked her absences, in the end she'd always come back. So when she'd taken off almost two years ago, he had figured it was the same song, different verse. Until she called and told him she was done with it. She wasn't cut out for family life. Being domestic, living in the sticks—it just wasn't in her DNA.

Zoe had cried off and on for weeks, and Jake had comforted her with the only story that held a grain of truth: her mommy was sick and had to go away to get better. He doubted that would happen. Stephanie had no desire to get better, and it almost killed him, the loss of her, the hole it left in his life and Zoe's. He did all he could to fill Zoe up with his love of her, asking her multiple times throughout the day: *Do you know how much I love you?*

"My borned day was the best day of your life." Zoe's answer was the one he'd given her, tossed off now with disheartening nonchalance. Clearly he needed a new question, a new routine.

Kenna Sweet opened the back door of his truck, calling out a cheerful, "Good morning, Halsteads," leaning into the cab, helping Zoe unsnap her car seat restraints.

Jake mumbled, "Good morning," in return, keeping his eyes on his daughter. She was chattering away, something about the garden she and her classmates had helped plant adjacent to the playground earlier in the spring.

"I helped my grammie in her garden yesterday," Zoe said. "We weeded bad plants and squished bad bugs, little green ones with black dots."

"Did you?" Kenna was riveted.

"Yes, like this." Zoe hitched up her backpack and squeezed her thumb and forefinger together to demonstrate. "I deaded ten and weeded all around the merry, the merry—" She broke off, frowning.

"Marigolds?" Kenna offered.

"Yes! Merry-go-rounds!"

Jake was grateful for Zoe's chatter. There'd been a family cookout a few weeks ago with his neighbors, Mandy and Augie Bright, at their house that he and Kenna had both attended. Jake had gone with Zoe; Kenna had gone alone. Wyatt was a small town; it wasn't unusual to run into Kenna at social gatherings. Jake had even gotten the sense that because they were both single it was expected that at some point he and Kenna would hook up. Maybe on a subliminal level even he had harbored an idea of that happening. At the cookout that evening, in a roundabout way, they'd talked about it—the whole living-alone thing, although Jake didn't technically live alone. Kenna had said she didn't either. After all, she had El Jefe, her German shepherd. She'd called Jefe the man of the house, making Jake laugh. It hadn't been flirting, exactly. But something had passed between them, and whatever it was, Jake had felt awkward around Kenna ever since. Maybe it was the thought of kissing his kid's preschool teacher, who was also the school's owner.

She found his gaze. "Are you still available to drive the van for the picnic?"

"Absolutely," he said. "Next Thursday, right?"

The picnic was an end-of-the-school-year event that took place every May. This year it was being held at a local ranch, the xL. There would be supervised hay wagon and horseback rides and a barn tour that would involve a close-up look at sheep and cows. "I need to be here at nine that morning, right?"

Kenna nodded. "It's about a half-hour drive out there."

"Yeah, Zoe's taken a couple of horseback riding lessons from Shea, AJ's wife."

"Daddy said maybe I will get a horse," Zoe said.

"When you're older," Jake qualified. "And I'm rich," he added, half under his breath.

"Don't forget to get your wallet, Daddy," Zoe said. "It's on your grandpa's toolbox in the garage, Miss Gilly said."

"Thanks for reminding me."

"He would forget his head if I didn't," Zoe told Kenna, skipping away. "Bye, Daddy Radish," she said over her shoulder.

"See you later, Zoe Macaroni," he answered.

Kenna's smile might have meant everything and nothing. She closed the truck door a bit hard, he thought.

He checked in at work, telling his office manager, Mary Alice, the situation with his wallet.

"You'd lose your head," she said.

"You've been talking to my daughter," he said.

"Zoe's got your number."

Jake laughed. Mary Alice had worked for his dad for nineteen years, and she'd stayed on when his dad passed away a bit over two years ago—before Stephanie had left. His death had happened without warning. Ben Halstead had walked around the corner of the house to turn on the sprinkler, and Jake's mom had found him there, ten minutes later, when she'd gone to see why he hadn't reappeared. It had been such a shock. Jake had never known his dad to take a sick day. He and his mom, with Mary Alice's help, had managed to keep Halstead Concrete going. Jake hadn't planned to make concrete his life's work. But the business was his dad's legacy, and it was solid. He couldn't see selling it, but he was thinking of expanding into building homes, using concrete forms. The idea appealed to him—that he might construct something that was not only beautiful and serviceable but long-lasting and incredibly strong. He needed design support, someone with the expertise to put down on paper the visions he had in his head. Someone like Gilly O'Connell, who for reasons unknown to him had quit being an architect to become a waitress.

"So do you know where you left it?" Mary Alice's voice broke into his rumination. "Or is this fixing to be an identity theft nightmare?"

"Zoe thinks I left it in the garage yesterday, when we fixed the lawn mower." No way was Jake going to mention Gilly had originally offered the theory.

They talked a few more minutes, confirming that Jake would bring Zoe to the office after school so he could do his five-mile run, something he tried to do every other day. He said after he picked up his wallet, he'd be at the job site, Ferguson Hills, a new subdivision that was going in on the south side of town, if she needed him. "We've got trucks scheduled to pour over there through Friday. At least I hope we'll be done Friday."

"Your lips to God's ear," said Mary Alice.

Pulling into his driveway a bit later, he killed the truck engine and sat for a moment, looking at the garage. The way Gilly had rattled off the information had been so matter-of-fact. She'd recited his great-grandfather's initials as if she'd known the man personally; she'd looked stunned, as if she didn't know where her information had come from. It had been a weird experience. Unsettling.

Jake punched the garage-door opener and got out of the truck. Ducking under the rising door, he paused for a second, allowing his eyes to adjust to the gloom, and he saw it right away. His wallet was sitting on his great-granddad's tool chest, right where Gilly had predicted he'd find it. And he was relieved. Sure. Who wouldn't be? He walked across the concrete floor to the back wall, where the tool chest sat next to his worktable, and he stood there for a second, looking at it.

His wallet was near the center and half concealed the initials.

Gilly's first guess, AJH, was the right order. His great-granddad, Andrew Jake Halstead, had built the chest in 1919. He'd carved his initials into the lid. Jake was named for him.

The chest was solid. Fashioned out of pine, it was hand planed, with mortise and tenon joints, a flip-top lid, and three drawers. All the old tools were inside, worn smooth by his great-granddad's hands. They were cool to the touch, weighted with time. Jake loved them. But

Gillian O'Connell, a waitress and resident of Wyatt, Texas, for a mere six months, with whom he had had only a handful of encounters one-on-one, had never laid eyes on the chest or the tools inside it. She'd never been to his house, and the handful of times he'd dropped in at Cricket's and sat with Gilly over coffee, he had never mentioned the tool chest's existence, much less spoken to her of his great-grandfather. He picked up his wallet and shoved it into his back pocket. The experience confounded him, and he didn't like being confounded.

He hoped someone else—April or Cricket—would be at the cash register when he returned to the café to pay his tab. But when he arrived, Gilly was the only one out front, and the dining area was mostly deserted.

"You found it." Judging from Gilly's reluctant tone, Jake thought she was as disconcerted as he was by the outcome.

He handed her a twenty. "Yeah, right where you said, in the garage, on the tool chest."

She plucked his ticket from her apron pocket and made change.

He waved it away. "Keep it," he said. He tried a smile. It felt stiff. "You have time for coffee?" He hadn't known he was going to ask. He felt his cheeks warm; he felt like a kid, and it half annoyed him.

She nodded. "It's pretty quiet. If you want to sit down, I'll bring it."

"How did you know? Where my wallet was, I mean?" he asked when she set down their mugs of coffee and slid into the booth across from him.

She met his gaze. Her eyes were the gray of dark smoke. Shadowy. Bottomless. Something in them pulled at him. She shrugged. "Fluke?"

"I dunno," he said. "Maybe you can go through walls, too, like Kitty Pryde."

"Kitty Pryde?"

"The X-Men?" Jake said. "Her code name was Sprite. She could go through walls."

"Ah. Never read comic books."

"Really?" Jake remembered she'd never seen *Finding Nemo* either.

"My mother has a thing about them. She's convinced they can permanently damage your brain."

"If you can't go through walls you must be—what's the word? Psychic? Clairvoyant?"

"No." Gilly was emphatic now. "It was a coincidence, that's all."

"A one-shot deal."

"Yeah." She picked up her mug, then set it down without drinking.

A beat became two. There were sounds from the kitchen: a burst of laughter, followed by the clang of pans like cymbals. Jake met Gilly's gaze; the smile they exchanged was awkward.

"So, I've been wondering," Jake began, and even to his own ears he sounded lame, "do you think you'll ever go back to it?"

She raised her brows.

"Being an architect?" God, what a fool, he thought. It was none of his business, was it? "You mentioned once, that you were in the profession."

"I did?"

"Uh-huh. It's just I've been thinking about getting into building houses myself." The jolt of excitement Jake felt, giving it voice, the gist of his dream, eclipsed his misgiving. He'd never talked about it to anyone. Instinct said he should shut up, but he didn't listen. "Not conventional homes. I want to try something more innovative, more environmentally responsible."

"Really?" A sparkle came into her eyes, an animation that, if it was possible, made her even prettier.

Jake bent forward on his elbows. "Have you ever seen a house built out of concrete?"

"No, but I've read about them. We were really into that sort of thing, the trend toward greener housing, making it affordable for less affluent folks. Concrete was one of the materials we wanted to find out about."

"We?" Jake didn't like the sound of it, the way she'd said *we*.

"My—my husband and I. We had a firm, B&G Architects in Houston. He died—suddenly."

"Oh, I'm sorry." Jake was taken aback. He hadn't known she'd been married. Hadn't heard so much as a whisper of it around town. But word was she kept to herself.

She thanked him for his condolence, and Jake waited for her to say more. When she didn't, he went on, babbling like an idiot, filling the silence. "Quite a change for you from designing buildings to waiting tables."

"Some things—you know, drastic times call for drastic measures." Her smile wobbled. "Listen, I need to get back to work."

Except for a woman bent over her laptop in the back corner, the café was empty, but Jake went along, saying he had to get going too. He slid out of the booth and, producing his wallet like a trophy, he asked, "What do I owe you?" He was jittery again, like a kid out of high school. He barely knew Gilly, but she had that effect. It was unnerving.

"Coffee's on me," she said, taking their mugs behind the counter.

Now it was Jake's turn to express thanks, and she nodded, but her glance was shuttered. The glimmer of enthusiasm was gone, as if it had never been there. It had been dumb, telling his plan to her, a virtual stranger, a woman who'd lost her husband. But he'd known there was something, because with a female there was always something.

Back in his truck, he keyed his ignition, and glancing through the windshield, he saw her standing there, watching. Gilly had come to the plate-glass window, and she was looking at him.

The moment lingered, becoming prolonged. A sense of unease drifted through Jake's mind. What did he know about her? Nothing, really.

And it was odd in this town, where everyone talked about everyone else, that no one was talking about her.

3

He's good-looking, isn't he? Jake? That's his name, right?"
With a start, Gilly turned from the café window, feeling her face warm slightly at having been caught watching him drive away. She gave Liz a quick hug. "When did you get into town? I didn't know you were coming. You're working, I guess." Gilly's glance took in Liz's attire, a navy pencil skirt and jacket to match over a tailored blouse. Sensible navy heels on her feet.

Liz made a face. "I have on hose, even. Can you believe it? But listen, coming here was a last-minute order from my boss, and it's kind of exciting, actually. You know that new hospital going in between here and Greeley?" Liz didn't wait for Gilly's confirmation. "The company finally gave me the go-ahead to get familiar with the staff, start establishing a relationship. Schmooze, in other words."

Gilly grinned. "You can take a page out of Sergeant Carter's book. I saw him back there, chatting you up."

"Oh, I know. I sat in the corner, hoping he'd overlook me. I told you I'm trying to keep a low profile, just observe and get a feel for the area."

"On the q.t."

"Exactly."

"The sergeant wants me to put in a word for him."

"Are you serious?" Liz touched her temple, the corner of her mouth. Color suffused her cheeks.

She was flattered, Gilly thought. Maybe the sergeant had a chance after all. "I heard he gave you a ticket. Something about a wonky taillight?"

"It was a warning. He was just asking if I'd had it fixed." She looked off, brought her gaze back. "I can't go there yet. You know what I mean, right?"

Gilly did, and she said so.

"Have you got time for coffee?" Liz changed the subject. She gestured toward the back booth, where she'd left her laptop. "I think I may have found a house. Can you take a break?"

"I just had one." Gilly glanced around at the empty café. "Let me clear it with April." She came back after a few minutes, carrying two mugs of fresh coffee. Setting one in front of Liz, she slid into the booth across from her. "So is it for sure? You're relocating here?"

"I think so. The hospital finally getting under construction is what cinched it. It's going to bring in more doctors and labs to the area, you know, everything medical. Should add a lot in regard to sales. The territory's going to be so much bigger, though, than the route I'm used to driving in the city."

"But just think," Gilly said, "no rush hour traffic. Maybe you'll get behind the occasional hay wagon going two miles an hour, but that's about it for delays around here."

"Hay wagon?"

Liz's wide-eyed look that combined elements of bafflement and consternation made Gilly laugh. "I'm only kidding—sort of."

"Okay, but is it ever, like, too quiet here? You came from Houston. Do you miss city life?"

Gilly toyed with her mug.

"I don't mean to pry."

"You aren't. The short answer is no."

"But it's more complicated." Liz kept Gilly's gaze.

They'd known each other awhile now, ever since they'd met in the dog park where Gilly walked Bailey. One day, a bit over five months ago, Liz had been there, sitting on a bench, laptop open on her knees, looking at houses. She and Gilly had struck up a conversation, laughed at Bailey's antics, commiserated with one another over how unsettling it was to move to a new town, although at the time, Liz had only been contemplating a move to Wyatt. She'd been scoping it out, she'd told Gilly, while working on her boss, trying to convince him to let her set up a central Texas territory. Like Gilly, Liz wanted a new start, although Liz's wish stemmed from a divorce. Gilly sensed it had been an awful experience—not so much from what Liz said, because she'd only mentioned it a handful of times, but she was bone thin in a way Gilly recognized from the days when her grief over losing Brian was fresh. Liz had said once that along with her husband she'd lost her appetite. *It's not a diet method I'd recommend*, she had said, and Gilly had taken her hand. They'd sat together like sisters, or the way Gilly imagined sisters would be. Gilly had felt compelled to confide in Liz about Brian, giving her an abbreviated version of the horrendous circumstances. She hadn't mentioned Sophie, had felt it would be piling too much on Liz too soon. But they'd spent a good deal of time together since then, whenever Liz came into town, and it felt good, having a girlfriend. Liz made it easy.

"Turns out moving away doesn't switch off your brain," Gilly told her. "You still have your memories." Her smile was wry.

"Amen," Liz said fervently, and reaching across the table she patted Gilly's arm. "Want to see the little house I found?" It was as if she could read Gilly's mind, her need for the subject to change. Liz turned her laptop screen toward Gilly. "It's two streets over from your house."

"Oh, it's so cute." Gilly read the description of the small bungalow-style house. "Two bedrooms, one bath." She looked up at Liz. "Sounds perfect."

"Will you go with me to look at it? I made an appointment to see it at five. We could get dinner after."

"I can go see the house for sure, but dinner—I'd really like to, but can we make it another day? What about Friday? Come to my house. I'll cook." Gilly was relieved when Liz said yes without asking questions. Maybe over dinner at her own table Gilly could tell Liz she was in AA and had a meeting tonight. It wasn't something she could talk about here, where she might be overheard. But Gilly wanted Liz to know. It seemed important for their friendship to have it out in the open between them. "I'd better scoot," Gilly said. "We'll be getting slammed with the lunch crowd soon."

Liz closed her laptop. "Can you pick me up later?"

"No problem. At the RV park?" Rental property in Wyatt was almost nonexistent, especially for the short term, but Liz had found an RV in a park on the outskirts of town that allowed her to rent week to week.

"On second thought, why don't I meet you here around four thirty?" Liz gathered her things.

"That'll work," Gilly said.

Liz was almost to the door when she turned back. "That guy? Jake?"

Gilly paused at the swinging door to the kitchen. "What about him?"

Liz was grinning as if she knew a secret. "You've got a thing for him, don't think I haven't noticed."

"No, absolutely not." Heat climbed out of Gilly's shirt collar, and it annoyed her.

"Hey, I'm glad. You deserve a good guy in your life. I've seen how he looks at you, too. For what it's worth, I think the attraction is mutual." Liz was laughing now.

"I'm like you. I can't go there either."

Liz came to her, and giving her a hug, said, "It's okay, you know."

"But it feels all wrong and so confusing. Is it him or his precious little girl I feel drawn to?"

"Who cares? You're allowed to have feelings for someone. From the way you've talked about Brian, I don't think he'd want you to be alone the rest of your life, would he?"

"But I don't know how to do it, how to go forward on my own, much less start over with someone else."

"Me either." Liz smiled. "Once I move down here for good, we'll help each other."

"Yes," Gilly agreed, smiling, too. "That's what I'm hoping for."

• • •

There was something wrong. While the little girl went willingly with the woman to the car, Gilly felt the grip of cold terror in her bones. She wanted to get at the woman, to yank the child's hand from the woman's grasp. She would have, but there was a barrier between them, a wall of thick glass. She paced along it, walking her fingertips over the surface, heart thundering in her ears. Beyond the barrier, some distance away, the woman was chatting with the child, head bent, listening for the little girl's response.

God, her small upturned face was so sweet and trusting.

"Stop!" Gilly shouted the word, but neither the woman nor the little girl looked in her direction. It was as if Gilly were invisible to them. Her throat constricted; her eyes burned. How could it be this easy, taking a child? There were laws, safeguards.

The woman lifted the tiny girl, who held a Nemo backpack, into a child-size safety seat in the back seat of the car. It should have been reassuring, seeing that, but it wasn't.

"No," Gilly whispered. "No, no, no . . ."

She pressed her face to the glass, memorizing details: the woman was tall, slender, wearing a navy hoodie and sunglasses. Gilly had the impression she was dark-haired, but with her head covered, it was only an impression. The woman's car was a light-metallic-blue sedan, medium size. Newish, she thought, but the make and model eluded her. She wasn't good at identifying cars. It was parked in front of a building—small, one story, faced in dark-red brick. The woods that surrounded it on three sides appeared dark and sinister. But there—that scrap of pink just at the edge of the woods behind the building—what was that? Gilly pressed close to the glass, cupping her hands around her eyes. It was a trike, a child's trike flipped on its side. A soft moan escaped her. The scene began to dissolve now—the woman's face, the building, the car, the pink trike—all of it was retreating, fading into a haze. Except for the child. It didn't seem possible, but it was as if the little girl had climbed out of her car seat to peer at Gilly through the car's rear window. Every feature of her small face stood out. She was smiling; she seemed happy. But somehow Gilly knew it wouldn't last, that she was in terrible jeopardy.

She lunged at the glass . . .

. . . and woke, thrashing and disoriented. Hot. So hot. Gone still now. Rigid. Waiting—for her breath to settle and for a semblance of normalcy, the recognition of her surroundings to return. The bedroom walls swam at her. The furniture—a dresser and a linen-upholstered French country chair—floated in her peripheral vision. A stack of moving boxes against one wall was familiar. It and the furniture belonged to her. The walls belonged to the house she was renting. But they were real, as real as the cold weight of her dread.

Turning her head, she looked at the clock on her nightstand. The numbers glowed: 5:47. The alarm would go off at 6:15. Her shift at Cricket's started at seven, thirty minutes before opening. Gilly wanted the last half hour of sleep, but when she closed her eyes she saw it again—the woman taking the little girl. She felt her suffocating helplessness to stop it from happening—what she knew, knew to her core, was an abduction. Gilly didn't care how unconcerned the little girl had seemed. The woman was dangerous, and the girl didn't belong with her.

Damn it.

Flinging the covers aside, she sat up, propping her feet on the bed's metal frame, bracing her head in her hands. It didn't do any good, telling herself it wasn't real. It was like arguing with a rock. The fact of it—whatever it was, vision, prophecy, head-trip—wasn't moving. It wasn't fading into the nether reaches of her mind in the way an ordinary dream would. This was different. In the same way she'd known it was different a handful of other times in her life.

She had dreamed about Brian's death the night before he was killed, and when she'd wakened in much the same kind of panic, he'd soothed her. He had known about her dreams and visions, that they were sometimes prophetic. She'd told him about them while they were still dating, and she'd been relieved when he hadn't laughed or looked at her as if she were strange—or possibly demented or evil. He hadn't asked her to read his palm or the lumps on his head either, all of which had happened in the past. Often enough that she'd taken her mom's advice and gone silent on the subject. Brian had been different, safe; she could talk to him about anything. He listened; he respected what she had to say.

But their final morning together, when she'd wakened in a cold sweat from the nightmare that predicted his death, he'd teased her.

He had put his ear against her belly, burgeoning at twenty-six weeks with the healthy, growing weight of their soon-to-be-born daughter, and whispered, "Mommy's hormones are being silly, aren't they?" And he listened, nodding, saying, "Yeah, that's what I think, too."

Gilly had tangled her hand in his unruly mop of chestnut-brown hair, laughing. "No secrets, Daddy."

"The dream you had?" He brought his face level with Gilly's. "The sprout and I think it's hormones."

"I heard that, and her name is Sophia." Gilly turned awkwardly on her side, putting her forehead against Brian's forehead. "Sophia Marguerite." She whispered the name they'd chosen for their little girl. Sophia was Brian's mother's name, and Marguerite was Gilly's favored paternal grandmother's name. "We'll call her Sophie." Taking Brian's hand, Gilly guided it to a low spot on her belly, where the baby was kicking.

"Turning cartwheels," Brian said. "She's going to be a gymnast."

It had been right before Christmas, December 16, 2013. Gilly had been due in about twelve weeks, and Sophie—her in utero antics, her personality—was well known to them and a source of pure delight. Even unborn, she was no stranger.

Neither was the little girl Gilly had seen in her dream—vision, premonition, whatever it had been. She went into the bathroom, flipped on the light, stared sightlessly at her reflection in the mirror. She had recognized the girl.

It was Zoe—almost-four-year-old Zoe Halstead.

· · ·

Gilly parked in the area for employees, in the alley behind the café, and she entered through the back service door. April was at the big worktable, dicing peppers for breakfast tacos.

"You look awful," she said, glancing up.

"Gee, thanks," Gilly said.

Her first day at work Cricket had told Gilly—in front of April—that, while April was an expert at food preparation, her social skills weren't so great.

Deadpan, April had cracked: "That's why they keep me chained up in the kitchen."

Gilly had laughed, uncertainly, then. But over time, she'd become accustomed to April's sharp tongue, her trenchant humor. April's jokes were like the chemicals she used to bleach her hair, harsh and inevitable. And she was nearly as much of a fraud as her hair color. Or that was Gilly's impression anyway—that April's wisecracking was a shield. She was a relative newcomer to Wyatt, too, having lived there only a year. Talk around town was that she had done prison time, serving two years of a five-year manslaughter sentence at the Murray Unit in Gatesville for shooting to death her husband, Nick's dad, when he'd gone after Nick in a drunken rage with a knife. Some people might have a problem with that, but Gilly thought, if she ever had the chance, she'd kill the monster who shot Brian in a heartbeat—with her bare hands if that was all she had for a weapon—and gladly serve whatever prison time a judge gave her. God knew what she might do if the bastard hurt her child.

• • •

"You sure you feel okay?" April asked.

Gilly opened the dishwasher.

It had been a hectic morning. Cricket was out—a doctor's appointment, April had said. She and Gilly had handled the breakfast service between them, and Gilly had muffed more than her usual number of orders. Now the lunch rush was upon them.

"I'm fine," Gilly said, which wasn't true. She lifted clean coffee mugs, still steaming, from the rack and set them with a clatter on a tray.

"You seem shaky, and you're awfully pale." April was at the work-table shredding pork for barbecue sandwiches, that day's lunch special.

"I had the worst night—" Gilly stopped, biting back the urge to recount it, the whole thing with the dream. The sense that it had been more than a dream, that it was more like a warning, haunted her. It would be a relief to speak of it, to have April laugh and dismiss it. *Dreams can be so crazy*, she'd say. But who knew how she might react? Gilly could as easily imagine the narrowing of April's eyes, the curl of her lip—the expression on her face would be just short of a sneer. Or possibly April would be alarmed, or dismissive, or pitying. She would think Gilly was unhinged, advise her to seek help, the comfort of anti-depressants, sleeping pills, tranquilizers.

But Gilly had already gone that route. She had consumed a vast array of pharmaceuticals, washing them down with quantities of vodka, or whatever liquor was on hand, and Brian and Sophie were still as dead. Besides, as Gilly's mother so often pointed out, dreaming a thing was going to happen was of little use if no one believed in your ability, if no one—most of all the subject of your dream—paid attention.

"Gilly?"

She jumped, startled by April's touch on her arm. "Sorry." Her apology was rote. "Cramps," she added. "That time. You know." It was a cop-out, the female one-size-fits-all excuse, and Gilly deplored using it. But it worked.

April looked sympathetic; she offered aspirin. "Take a few minutes, if you want, in the dayroom before we get going again. There's only a handful of the regulars here, and they'll keep. Cricket'll be back any minute to help with lunch anyway."

"Thanks," Gilly said. "I've got aspirin in my purse. I'll just run get it and be right back."

April was watching her. Gilly felt her gaze following her progress as she left the kitchen. It unnerved her. She wasn't sure why. It made her feel she had to go through with it, the ruse of getting her purse from the dayroom-cum-office. In addition to a desk and a couple of filing cabinets, the dayroom near the café's kitchen was furnished with an antique iron daybed, a small dining table and chairs. A row of lockers against one wall housed personal belongings. Gilly got her purse from the locker assigned to her, making sure to slam the door loud enough for April to hear. She went into the adjacent employee bathroom, locking the door behind her. Setting her purse on the vanity, she turned, leaning against it, bringing her fingertips to her temples. The thud of her heart was loud in her ears. She felt half panicked and had an urge to bolt. Maybe through the window? It was open. The late-morning breeze was sun warmed. The sheer eyelet drape fluttered in her peripheral view. Gilly held it aside, bent her face to the glass, closing her eyes, drifting, thoughtless. She didn't know how much time passed before the image formed in her mind, the one from her nightmare of Zoe Halstead being helped by a woman—the wrong woman—into the back seat of a car. Gilly felt the looming threat more keenly now than before.

Why? If Zoe Halstead was imperiled, why was she—Gilly—being made aware of it? Why not someone close to the little girl—her dad, or her mother, wherever she was? There must be dozens of people better than Gilly for the universe to tip off about the impending danger to a child, assuming the dream was accurate.

Turning to the sink, she ran the water until it was cold, then rinsed her face and blotted it dry with a paper towel. She tossed the paper towel in the trash.

Cricket was back, and she and April were talking when Gilly returned to the kitchen. She quickened her step. "I'll handle the front—"

"There aren't many folks out there yet."

April's voice caught Gilly midway through the door into the dining area. Her stomach clenched.

"I wondered where you'd gone off to," April said, giving her an odd look.

"I was just in the restroom. I couldn't find—" Gilly stopped. What was she doing, defending herself? From what? But she'd heard something in April's voice. Curiosity? Suspicion? Or was it Gilly's own paranoia working overtime?

"Have you got a sec?" Cricket asked. "I want to go over the schedule."

Gilly joined them, grateful to be included, to have a job and a schedule.

She'd been grateful when Cricket had hired her on the spot even though Gilly had not one day's worth of waitressing experience, and her only reference had been provided from her Houston-based probation officer. If the background check Cricket had run had turned up evidence of Gilly's troubled history, her addiction, the subsequent legal woes, Cricket had never spoken of it to anyone so far as Gilly knew. Maybe the news coverage of Brian's murder, and all the rest of it, hadn't been picked up by media outlets this far north. Or maybe Cricket was one of those rare individuals who didn't hold a person's past against them. Maybe she believed in second chances.

• • •

"I still have boxes stacked everywhere," Gilly said.

The café closed at three o'clock, and she and April were cleaning the kitchen. Cricket was in the office.

"I'd lived here almost a year before I got the last box unpacked. It's only in the last few months I've felt Nicky and I are settled," April said. She scraped browned bits of bacon, beef, and chicken from the grill. "I could help you out sometime." She glanced sidelong at Gilly. "Unpacking, I mean."

"Oh, thanks, but it's mostly the nonessential stuff that's left to sort through."

"Well, if you change your mind, the offer stands." April went to the sink, turned on the tap, and rinsed the basin. Her elbows darted, seeming to jab the air.

Gilly opened the refrigerator, running her eye over the contents. They were low on mayo. It was handmade every morning from Cricket's mother's recipe. She felt April's glance. Was she angry? Hurt? Gilly didn't know. She could never decide whether April liked her or resented her. If Liz were to ask about the boxes, Gilly would have explained she wasn't ready to unpack, that to do so would mean she was making a commitment to this job, the town, her "new" life, but she didn't feel comfortable enough with April to say that. She might turn it into a joke the way she did most things.

"Where is the linen delivery?" Cricket came out of her office.

"They're late as usual," April said, shutting off the tap.

"We're low on mayo," Gilly said.

April was saying she'd stay and make up a batch when the police captain came in through the back-alley door.

"Clint? What's happened?" Cricket wiped her hands on a towel.

It was the look on his face that made her ask. Even Gilly could see he was shaken, and when he said it, said, "Zoe Halstead has gone missing," her heart fell against her ribs.

4

That day, of all days, for no real reason, Jake was late picking Zoe up from school. He got to talking with one of the concrete truck drivers, Marco Lopez, about the Texas Rangers' batting statistics, or something stupid like that, and when he checked the time and saw it was after twelve, his heart sank. Zoe hated it when he was late, hated being the last one to leave. She'd chew him out. Probably let him have it the rest of the day and half the night. It would seem outrageous later—even bizarre, given what was ahead of him—that he thought that was the worst that could happen. He figured he might get out of some of it if he took her up to Greeley to the Mickey D's to get a Happy Meal for dinner. He rarely consented to going there. He was a nut on eating right. Except when he was in trouble. Then he used Mickey D's and the occasional pancake for dinner to get himself back in Zoe's good graces.

He never argued with her over what to wear either. If she put on the same outfit three days in a row, he let her. If she wanted to wear red socks with her orange pants, he told her she looked great. When she'd worn her swim goggles every day and to bed at night, he had only questioned why. It hadn't been that long ago that he'd come into her bedroom to read her a bedtime story and found her with the goggles strapped to her head.

Very casually, he'd asked, "What's up with the goggles?"

"I might fall in the ocean like Mommy," she'd answered, "and get eaten by a shark. If I have on my goggles, I'll see it before it can get me."

"Mommy wasn't eaten by a shark, ZooRoo," he'd answered. "She didn't fall in the ocean."

"You don't know, Daddy. You don't know where she is."

Technically speaking, Zoe had been right. Jake hadn't known where Stephanie was, not precisely. "The ocean is hundreds of miles from here," he'd told Zoe.

She'd been unfazed, worn the goggles anyway, nonstop, for weeks.

He parked in the drive, near the front entrance to the Little Acorn, and went inside to the office. A girl he didn't know looked up from where she was sitting behind the tall counter. She was young, twenty-something, with pink-streaked blonde hair.

"I'm here to pick up my daughter, Zoe Halstead," he said. "I'm late."

The girl blinked, looking nonplussed, like he was speaking in a foreign tongue. She put a hand to her hair, and he noticed she had a tiny bee tattooed between the first and second joints of her right ring finger.

"Jake? What's going on?"

He looked around at Kenna. "I'm here to pick up Zoe. I'm late. I'm really sorry. I got stuck at the job site. Is she with you in your office?" Jake knew Kenna often kept the children with her there when their parents were delayed.

But now there was something in the glance Kenna exchanged with the tattooed girl that twisted Jake's gut into a knot. "Where is she?"

"Zoe's gone already." The way the girl's voice rose, it was almost as if she was asking.

"What do you mean *gone*? With who?" Jake was gruff.

"Her mom picked her up," the tattooed girl said.

"No, I'm the only one authorized—" Jake turned back to Kenna. "Is she with you?" He repeated the question as if he might get the response he wanted.

"You know which little girl Zoe Halstead is, don't you?" Approaching the counter, Kenna addressed the young woman behind it. "Marley's new," she explained, glancing at Jake.

"She always has the blue ribbon," Marley answered. "She was wearing the little skirt with butterflies on it that she wore yesterday. She was on the playground when her mom came for her."

"There's a note in her file—" Kenna began.

"There's a goddamn court order, and you know it." Jake locked Kenna's gaze. His heart was pounding furiously in his chest. "Did she say where she was taking Zoe?" he asked Marley, but before she could answer, he was back in Kenna's face. "You know Steph doesn't have so much as visitation, not without supervision. What kind of car was she driving?" He stopped, trying to think. "Her car was repo'd," he said more to himself. He figured it must have been, because when Steph had called the last time, weeks ago now, and asked for money to make the payment, he'd refused. She'd hit him up for money one too many times. She spent every dime he gave her on dope anyway. He struck the counter with his fist. "How did this happen?"

Kenna backed off a step. "Marley was working dismissal today. I thought she had it under control—"

"I got distracted—the gate back there was open—"

Jake barely heard Marley. His focus was on Kenna. "You're in charge. This is your school. You know the routine, the danger Zoe could be in from Steph." He had told Kenna about his former wife, the drinking and drug use—how he'd had no choice but to have his lawyer petition the court to set limits on Stephanie's visits with Zoe. He turned to Marley. "What exactly did Zoe's mom say?"

"She was early. Like I said, I was on the playground when she came up to me and said she was Zoe's mom, she was there to pick her up.

She went right to Zoe. There didn't seem to be any problem, and I was busy, getting the rest of the kids lined up—" Marley looked at Kenna. "That's when I saw the gate was open and went to close it. I told you. Remember?" Marley switched her glance to Jake. "It's not supposed to be open unless we're on a field trip."

"Did you see Zoe get in the car with her mother?" he asked, striving to keep his cool.

"No," Marley answered, and his heart constricted. She went on, describing a scuffle that had broken out among some of the boys. Jake caught about every third word. The upshot was Marley had been distracted, and by the time she looked for Zoe again, she was gone.

"You don't know what happened, do you?" Jake heard himself, how he sounded, loud and menacing. He couldn't help it, couldn't dial it back. He thrust his face at Marley. "You don't know if she got into a car, or walked away, or what the hell happened. For all you know, she and her mother could have walked through the goddamned gate that wasn't supposed to be open." He hammered the counter with his fist.

The momentary silence they shared simmered with distress.

"There was something . . ." Marley offered this bit timidly.

"What?" Jake bent over the counter.

"I thought it was odd, the woman—Zoe's mom—was wearing a hoodie. Dark blue. She had it zipped all the way up, the hood pulled over her head. It's so warm out. It seemed strange—"

Jake hooted. "Yeah, she gets cold when she's stoned out of her mind."

"Maybe one of the other parents waiting out front saw Zoe. At least then we'd know she left with Stephanie." Kenna rounded the reception counter. "Can you pull up the student roster?" she asked Marley. "Who was the first to leave after Zoe? Do you remember?"

"Katie Dunhill," Marley answered.

Kenna dialed the phone number Marley read off the computer screen. "Corinne?" she said, and turning away from Jake, she questioned Katie Dunhill's mom, keeping her tone light and pleasant.

Jake waited. His gaze bored into her back.

Kenna ended the call and turned to face him, white around the mouth, brow furrowed. "She says she's pretty sure she saw Zoe get into a light-blue sedan with a woman in a hoodie."

"Pretty sure," Jake echoed.

"I know it's not a lot of help—"

He pulled out his cell phone.

"Who are you calling?" Kenna asked.

"The police. I need Clint to put out an APB—whatever they call it. If Steph's drunk, on dope, God knows what could happen."

"Maybe she just took Zoe home. To your house, I mean," Kenna suggested.

But when Jake checked there a half hour later, at one o'clock, there was no sign of Zoe or Stephanie, no indication either of them had been there.

He tried Steph's cell number and got a message that it was no longer in service. Surprise, surprise. Undoubtedly, it had been cut off, repo'd like the car.

He reported everything he discovered to Clint when the police captain called him from the school. "She wouldn't stay in town," Jake said. "She'd be afraid of being caught."

"Yeah," Clint said. "That's my feeling, too."

"I'm going to Houston," Jake said. "My gut's telling me that's where Steph is headed with Zoe, but if she thinks she's going to take our daughter, she's got another thing coming." Jake adjusted his Bluetooth, turned left out of his subdivision.

"Jake, no. Let me handle it. I know a couple cops down there. Let me get hold of them. They can go by her place—"

"Sorry, I'm losing you." Jake ended the call, pulled out his earpiece, tossed aside his phone. His head felt on fire. A voice inside his brain exploded, harsh, accusing: *How could you let this happen? Let yourself be late—for no reason? Nothing's more important than being there for Zoe. Nothing!* An image of her in the arms of a stranger filled his mind. Even if that person was a cop in a uniform, she'd be so scared.

He shot up the freeway on-ramp, dropped his foot down hard on the accelerator. He had to get to her. Now.

5

What do you mean, missing?" Cricket addressed Clint Mackie, wanting the police captain to spell it out, what Gilly already knew. Even in the moment, images of her dream were rising from the floor of her mind.

Clint said, "She wasn't at school when Jake went to pick her up at noon. He's pretty sure Stephanie got there before he did and took her."

"Stephanie?" Cricket sounded perplexed.

Zoe's mother, Gilly thought. Her supposedly unstable, alcohol- and drug-addicted mother.

"You haven't heard from her, have you?" Clint was looking intently at his wife.

"No," she said. "I would have told you."

She seemed defensive.

Why? Gilly wondered.

"How did it happen?" Cricket asked. "Everyone at that school, in this town, knows only Jake is authorized to get Zoe from school. There's a court order—"

"Kenna hired a new teaching assistant. Marley Waits. She didn't know the routine. She says no one told her."

"She let Zoe go with her mom." Cricket said what was obvious.

"Marley let Zoe go with a woman *claiming* to be Zoe's mom, but when we showed Marley a photo, she couldn't say positively it was Steph. The woman was wearing a dark-blue hoodie and sunglasses that covered half her face."

"That doesn't sound like anything Stephanie would wear." Cricket glanced at Gilly. "She's a fanatic about clothes. She was a fashion designer in New York before she and Jake married." Cricket looked back at her husband. "Did Zoe go with her willingly?"

Yes. The word blared in Gilly's brain before the police captain confirmed Zoe hadn't made a fuss.

"You've got your answer then," Cricket said. "Zoe knows not to go with a stranger. She knows to yell her head off."

"The mom, she'll hurt Zoe? She's abusive?" April sounded affronted.

"Not on purpose," Cricket said. "It's a sad situation," she added, and Gilly thought she wouldn't say more, but then she sighed as if in resignation. "Steph had a hard time after Zoe was born, really suffered from postpartum depression. I—Clint and I—tried to help her and Jake with the baby. So did Jake's mom. Justine and I traded days, staying with them."

"Stephanie's been drinking and taking drugs for a while, since before Zoe," Captain Mackie said. "She won't stop."

"She tried," Cricket said. "She went to rehab. Once a sixty-day program, then a ninety-day program, but neither one took."

The police captain huffed a derisive breath. He wiped his hand over his face in a way that made Gilly glad she had chosen to attend Twelve-Step meetings in Greeley and not in Wyatt.

"I told you the other day I was worried about her." Cricket addressed her husband. "She hasn't been back to Wyatt in months. When I called last time, I got a recording that her number's not in service—"

"I don't know why you keep trying," he said. "Some people are just hell-bent on destruction. You can't save them."

A phone—what turned out to be April's—jingled, and she pulled it from her apron pocket, walking away a few steps to answer.

Cricket got out her cell phone and tried Stephanie's number, shaking her head when there wasn't an answer. "Still dead," she said.

"That was Nick." April rejoined them. "He got an Amber Alert for Zoe on his phone."

"An Amber Alert? Really, Clint?" Cricket was dismayed. "She's with her mother."

"My gut is telling me otherwise. But even so, if Stephanie does have Zoe, she's in violation of a court order, and her intent may be to take her out of the state, or out of the country. Not that any sort of an alert is going to do much good in this case."

"What do you mean?"

"There's so little to go on—a woman in a dark-colored hoodie and sunglasses, the car she might be driving might be blue—" He broke off with a shrug.

Gilly wanted to clap her hands to her ears; she wanted to run. What the captain described—the woman in her hoodie, the blue car—were straight out of her dream.

"Jake must be frantic," Cricket said. "Justine, too. I should call her."

"No, don't. Jake is on his way to Houston—against my advice. He's hoping he can catch up with Steph and get Zoe back before his mom has to know."

"But the media could get hold of it, couldn't they?" Cricket said.

Gilly said, "Stephanie lives in Houston?"

"Yes. Last we heard. Why?"

Gilly held Cricket's gaze. "Zoe isn't with her."

6

Jake was halfway to Houston when he got hold of his family law and divorce attorney, Andrew Hargrave, and filled him in on the reason for his trip. Ordinarily the most careful of drivers, Jake seldom talked on the phone when he was behind the wheel, and when he did, he used his Bluetooth. But ordinary was out the window, and while he'd managed to locate his phone after tossing it into the passenger seat earlier, he hadn't been able to grab the Bluetooth.

"I've got to say it, Jake." Andrew had waited for Jake to finish recounting the morning's events before speaking. "If you had only gone ahead as I advised last year, when Stephanie wanted to sign away her parental rights . . ." Andrew paused. It was his tendency to be diplomatic, but he and Jake had a history, going back to Jake's divorce from Stephanie, the early days when Jake had been determined to keep Stephanie in Zoe's life, if not his own. Andrew had hammered away, insistent that neither he nor Jake could force Stephanie into a role she had no desire to play. Andrew had seen the reality, not Jake's deluded fantasy, but nothing about cutting Stephanie out of Zoe's life had felt right or good to Jake.

"What difference would it make?" Jake changed lanes, shooting around a slower traveling eighteen-wheeler.

"Zoe missing with her mom, who has parental authority, however restricted, isn't as critical as if she were abducted by a stranger. The FBI would be all over it if that were the case. They may get involved anyway, if Stephanie tries to take Zoe across state lines or out of the country."

"But she wouldn't do that—she can't be planning—" Jake broke off. He'd heard stories about parental kidnappings, but the noncustodial parent—the one who took the kid—was usually frantic about their child's well-being, convinced they were the better parent. That wasn't the case with Steph. Even she knew that as a mom she was a nightmare. "Why now?" Jake asked as if Andrew would know. "It makes no sense, does it, that she would take Zoe now when she's given her up in every way except on paper?" His objection was the reason Steph hadn't been able to go through with it. The whole idea of a mother rejecting her kid sickened him. What would it do to Zoe if she were to find out? He couldn't stand thinking how it would crack her heart in two.

"You're the one who says you can't rationalize what's irrational," Andrew answered. "But I wish you'd let the police handle her. Clint's in touch with the HPD, isn't he? They're sending an officer to her apartment?"

"Yeah."

"So why not wait, see what they find? You should know pretty quick what the situation is."

"Zoe'll be scared out of her mind, seeing cops everywhere."

"Okay, but how can you be so sure that's where Stephanie is taking Zoe? She must know you've contacted law enforcement."

"I've got to do something, Andrew, start somewhere," Jake said. "God knows what shape she's in. She could be hitting the booze, downing pills. Suppose she gets arrested? I don't want CPS taking my daughter." Naming his fears raced Jake's heart.

Talk about children and family—talk of any kind—hadn't been high on the agenda the times he'd gone to New York to visit Steph after meeting her there at the wedding of mutual friends. They'd stayed at her apartment, a funky, five-hundred-square-foot walk-up in Manhattan's Washington Heights, where they'd spent most of their time in bed. Jake's dad had been annoyed. He'd kept calling, wondering when Jake was coming home. There was work to do. Jake had put him off. The relationship with Steph was the first he'd had since his divorce from Courtney. He'd been in lust, sick with desire. Steph was all he could think about, or that's how it seemed when he looked back. There were times when remembering shamed him. His mom had accused him of acting like a hormone-crazed teenager. She'd tried getting him to see it, how his obsession with Stephanie was the same as one he'd had going on with a classmate, Karen Clayton, their senior year. *Except you're thirty-six now*, his mom had said. She had taken his face in her hands. *I don't think you love Stephanie any more than you did Karen*, she had said.

He should have listened.

"You said earlier Clint's got some doubt that it was Steph who got Zoe—"

Andrew's voice cut across Jake's thoughts. "No." He cut the lawyer off. He couldn't look at it, the possibility that someone other than her mom had Zoe. She'd been taught that if a stranger approached her in a way that made her uncomfortable, she was to yell her head off. They had practiced dozens of times until he'd thought her ear-splitting shrieks would crack his skull open. But Steph was no stranger, and the fact that Zoe hadn't yelled proved it. "That's just the way cops are, never satisfied with the simple answer," he told Andrew, and he remembered something now, Zoe's question from this morning: *Does my mommy know where I am?* He repeated it to Andrew and said, "I thought she asked out of the blue, but it's possible Steph called her on the landline."

"Without you knowing? Zoe wouldn't tell you?"

"Not if her mom asked her to keep it a secret, and if Steph timed it right, I could have been in the shower or outside. I don't keep moment-to-moment tabs on Zoe." Jake didn't want to be one of *those* parents—the sort that hung around their kid's neck like a ball and chain. His mom said the trick was to watch without *looking* as if you were watching.

His mom . . . God, unless he found Zoe in Houston, he was going to have to tell her . . .

Andrew said, "You think Stephanie arranged with Zoe to pick her up today?"

"Why not? I'm betting they're at her apartment right now. You know—it's Steph in her 'trying to make it up' mode. It's what she does sometimes when she's high; she goes on a guilt trip, starts feeling sorry for herself. Look"—Jake changed lanes—"when I get back, let's wrap it up—the paperwork, whatever has to be done to get her out of our lives. I've had enough of her bullshit. She can't just show up and be Zoe's mom whenever she gets stoned and feels like it."

"Yeah, all right. But, Jake, when you get to Houston, don't do anything crazy, okay?"

Jake said he wouldn't, but as soon as he ended the call and dropped the cell phone onto the truck's passenger seat, he set his foot down hard on the accelerator, pushing the truck to eighty-five, then ninety, then ninety-five, and he waited to hear a siren.

He prayed to hear one.

Once he'd explained his urgency, he'd get a police escort. He and the cop would go to Stephanie's door together. What could she do then but give Zoe back? If only she would, Jake thought. If she would just give Zoe to him, he wouldn't make a big legal deal out of this. He wouldn't press charges. Wouldn't risk Zoe seeing it: her mother hand-cuffed and stuffed into the back seat of a patrol car.

But no cop appeared. Naturally. The law was never around when you needed it. It might have been funny if he wasn't so pissed and scared. By the time he exited onto I-45, it was nearing five o'clock rush hour, and traffic was heavy even in the southbound lanes that led into the city. The downtown skyline loomed ahead, a jumbled mass of buildings, glass-fronted, sun struck, alien. Stephanie lived in its shadow, on a street in the first ward. Jake didn't know Houston well, but what he'd heard about the wards—there were six, designated as political districts back in the day—was nothing good. His impression was that they were full of thugs and crackheads. No kind of place for a single woman to live. Steph had said he was behind the times; the area was undergoing gentrification. She'd said it was fine. She lived in something she called a garden apartment. A pretty little place, she had said. In a neighborhood as safe as any in Wyatt, she had said.

He'd programmed her address into his phone, and he swiped it now and punched the "Maps" icon. A voice led him through a series of turns, down a rabbit warren of narrow streets. He passed blocks of new construction, high dollar from the look of it, and when, a few hundred yards later, the disembodied phone voice advised him to turn right onto Stephanie's street, he did. He was in the midst of registering the contrast, the decided shift down in accommodations from deluxe to derelict, when he saw the patrol car parked in front of a small shotgun-style clapboard house that had once been painted white. The car was empty. Jake pulled in behind it and got out.

"No one home over there," a woman hollered from the front stoop of the house next door. "I told that cop."

Jake went to the woman's front gate. "Do you know the woman who lives there, Stephanie Halstead? Have you seen her today—with a little girl?"

"Ain't seen her or her man 'round here, not in a week, maybe two. Ain't never seen her with a little girl."

Her man. It wasn't lost on him. Jake glanced next door. The driver of the squad car—it was from the Houston police department—wasn't anywhere in sight. Gone around back, Jake thought. He looked at the woman. She might have been fifty, or thirty, or seventy-five. She looked rough. *Rode hard and put up wet.* The phrase went through his mind. "Do they have a car? Stephanie and her—her man? Would you know the make and model?"

The woman had lit a cigarette and regarded him through a cloud of smoke. "Are you the law, too? A detective, right? What you want with her anyway?"

"She's my ex-wife, and she's got my daughter—"

"Oh, now, I don't want nothin' to do with no custody fight. Child belongs with its mama anyway, you ask me."

"Do you know where she might have gone? That's all I want to know—"

"Mr. Halstead? I'm Sergeant Kevin Kersey, Houston Police Department."

Jake wheeled and the uniformed officer stepped back. Jake thought it must show on his face, how bad he wanted to smash something, someone—the woman on the porch.

"You want to walk over here with me?" Kersey asked. He was older, Jake's dad's age, if he'd still been alive.

Jake followed Sergeant Kersey down the busted sidewalk. "There's no one in the house that I can tell," Kersey said, pausing beside his cruiser. "No one answered when I knocked or when I shouted out."

"We have to get inside. My ex-wife drinks and does drugs. Whatever she can get," he added. "She could be in there, passed out."

"I'd need a warrant—"

"So get one. My little girl could be with her."

"I checked around back, looked in the windows. There's no sign anyone's home. No sign of trouble at all."

"Zoe could be scared, hiding." Jake went up the sidewalk.

"Mr. Halstead." There was a slight warning inflection in the sergeant's tone.

Jake ignored it. "If she knows I'm here, she'll come out. Zoe?" He raised his voice, but not too much. "It's Daddy, ZooRoo. You ready to come home?" He went up on the porch and peered through the window beside the front door. His view was unobstructed, a straight shot from the front room through the kitchen to the back door of the house, and it was grim, no garden apartment. The walls were hole pocked, the carpet shredded. The couch had no cushions. A lamp on the floor beside it was missing a shade. Jake didn't want to accept it, that Stephanie lived here. He thought of his house in Wyatt.

It was an older home in the historic section of town, Mustang Hill, a snug three-bedroom Craftsman bungalow that he'd renovated. The kitchen, with its glass-front cabinets and window-seated breakfast nook, had been Steph's favorite room. He had repainted it for her. The soft shade of yellow she'd chosen was the color of buttercups. *The color of happiness*, she'd said.

But there was nothing happy here in the dark, damaged heart of this house.

His glance fell from a kitchen cabinet door that hung askew to the table and one straight-backed chair, tipped against the wall. But it was the pitcher—the small white milk pitcher with the roses painted on it—that caught his attention. It was sitting beside a paper plate that had a slice of pizza hanging over its edge. The pitcher was Limoges, from France, circa 1825. Jake knew because Stephanie had told him.

The pitcher was one of the few heirlooms she had from her family, all dead now. It was one of the only things she'd brought with her from New York. Once he'd finished painting the kitchen of the house in Wyatt, Stephanie had bought flowers almost weekly at the HEB, where she grocery shopped, and kept them in that little pitcher on the table in the breakfast nook she had loved.

And now the pitcher was here, surrounded by garbage.

Jake thought how Stephanie was like the pitcher, small and delicate. Dark-haired and dark-eyed, she was as fragile as china. She cried easily. He remembered her tears, but he couldn't remember the sound of her laugh.

He thought of the shit that went down in houses like this. Drug houses, crack houses. It scared him to think Steph had brought Zoe here—that his little girl might be inside. On another level, it ripped his heart open, seeing how low Stephanie had sunk He had tried so hard to save her.

"No one's here, trust me."

Jake didn't answer. He went off the porch and around back, Sergeant Kersey following in his wake. Jake had the sense Kersey was letting him do this—trespass on private property—allowing him to satisfy himself that the house was empty. He knew it was; the air of desertion was palpable. Still he went through the motions. He tried the back door; it was locked. He looked in the bedroom window, where the only furnishings were a stained mattress shoved into a corner and a chest of drawers with a busted leg. He looked in the bathroom window at the mildew-spotted shower curtain and blackened tub, the filthy sink and seatless toilet bowl. And then, feeling weak, he turned to lean against the house, letting the heat from the sun-warmed clapboards soak through his T-shirt.

"Mr. Halstead?" The sergeant's voice was kind. "We're doing everything we can to find her. We've got the Amber Alert, photos, a description of what your daughter was wearing. If your ex has her, and they're in the area, we'll find them."

"She doesn't have custody. You know that, right? Stephanie isn't allowed to see Zoe anywhere but in Wyatt in my presence. She can't bring Zoe here. She can't see her unsupervised. There's a court order."

"Yes sir, I understand."

"The woman next door says there's a man living here? Do you know who he is? Maybe they're in his car?"

"We've had some calls in the past to this address. Could be any number of guys. This house—a lot of folks—addicts—" The sergeant broke off, looking away.

"Shit." Jake said it under his breath.

"I'm sorry."

"I have to find Zoe. I have to find my little girl before it gets dark." Jake looked at the sergeant. He felt embarrassingly close to tears.

"You should go home, Mr. Halstead."

"No, you don't understand. I promised her I would never disappear on her the way her mother did."

"Yeah. I get that, but your ex, if she's got your daughter, maybe she'll . . ." Sergeant Kersey paused again, hunting for a word, settling on *wise*. Instead of *sober up*, he said maybe Jake's ex would *wise up*. "She could do the right thing and bring Zoe home on her own, you know? You've got someone at your house in Wyatt, right, in case?"

Jake shook his head. His mom was the logical person, but he wasn't ready to involve her yet anymore than he was ready to leave here without Zoe. He looked at the sergeant. "You're right. I should get back to Wyatt." Jake led the way to the front of the house, walking with the police officer to his squad car, expecting him to get in the vehicle and drive off. But he didn't.

Instead, in a friendly, conversational tone, he said, "If you go inside the house, Mr. Halstead, you'll be breaking the law, and I'll know it, because I'm going to be driving by here, checking on the place." Kersey let his gaze drift. "I know how bad you want your daughter back, but you're damn sure no good to her if you're sitting in jail on a breaking-and-entering charge."

Jake didn't answer. He knew the sergeant was serious, a by-the-book law-and-order man. "You've got my contact information?"

Sergeant Kersey got his phone from his pocket, and finding Jake's cell number, he read it off. He stowed his phone again once Jake had confirmed it was correct, and walked Jake to his truck.

"I don't care what time it is." Jake got into the cab, keyed the ignition, and lowered the window. "I'll never sleep," he told the sergeant. "Not until I get Zoe back."

• • •

Jake was on the outskirts of Houston when he pulled off the interstate to call his mom. He thought he was calm, that he had himself under control, but then the sound of her voice, the valiant effort she made, for his sake, to keep from showing her panic, almost undid him. She already knew what had happened, most of it anyway. Jake didn't have to ask how she'd heard. The Wyatt grapevine was never more efficient than when a catastrophe was brewing.

"I'm at your house," she said. "I figured someone should be here in case Steph decides to bring Zoe home."

Of course, she would already know what to do, how to help. Jake thanked her. He said, "It'll probably be close to eleven before I can get there."

"You sound exhausted," his mom said, and she went on worriedly, asking when he'd last eaten, things like that, but Jake was only half listening. He was thinking about Gilly, remembering how she'd told him where he could find his wallet. Would she know where his kid was if he asked her? But she'd said herself the thing with his wallet had been a fluke. He didn't believe in any of that mumbo jumbo shit anyway. He wasn't that desperate. Yet—

"Jake? Are you there?"

He pulled his gaze back in. "Yeah, Ma, I'm sorry. I'll get a burger somewhere and be home quick as I can."

They exchanged promises to call if either of them heard any news, and he was pulling his phone from his ear when his mom said his name again. "Jake? You're sure Stephanie is who picked Zoe up?"

"Who else could it be?"

"Well, of course it's her. It has to be."

His mom's conviction was a show she was putting on for his sake. *What if it isn't Stephanie, Jake?* That's what she really wanted to ask him. *What then?* But he had no stomach for that discussion right now much less any answer.

7

"Miss O'Connell?" Clint Mackie prompted Gilly. "I asked how it is you know Zoe Halstead wasn't taken by her mom? Do you know Stephanie? Were you at the school? Did you see Zoe with someone other than Stephanie?"

Gilly didn't answer, although she knew from experience not answering when a cop asked you a question wasn't an option. Even Carl, for all that he'd been kind and gentle about it, had pressured her for information in the wake of Brian's murder. Sophie had been barely an hour old and still clinging to life when he and his partner, Garrett, showed up at the hospital. The interview they'd been conducting with her outside the convenience store had been interrupted when a sharp pain low in her belly had doubled her over. As she'd straightened, hand pressed to her side, she'd felt breathless, lightheaded. Something warm was running down her legs, and she'd looked at the bloody discharge leaking into her ballet flats. She would have fallen if Carl hadn't steadied her. At the hospital, after Sophie was born, he had said he was sorry, but they needed her to finish telling them what she'd witnessed while her memory was still fresh.

She'd been given a dose of something postdelivery to dull her anguish, but even so when the detectives came into her room she was trembling. She had no control over that or her tears. She wanted desperately to help the police, and she told them everything she remembered, which wasn't much, and then, before she could stop herself, she told them she'd seen the whole thing happen the night before in a dream. Garrett could barely contain his derision, but Carl asked Gilly to close her eyes and focus on her breathing, and then he directed her to try and recall the dream scenario.

"Do you see what the shooter is wearing?" he asked. "Does he have any distinguishing marks? Tattoos? Is he wearing any jewelry? Is there anything unusual about his clothing?"

As Carl spoke, Gilly unspooled the dream sequence before her mind's eye, but just as Brian's killer had been in reality, in her recall of the dream the man was little more than a shadow dashing across the terrified field of her vision. The grim wash of sodium vapor picked out the white of an eye, the blade of a jaw. He could have been anyone.

If Carl was disappointed—and he must have been—he gave no sign. He handed her his business card. "My cell number's on there. Call me, okay? Anytime. If you remember anything else. No matter how unimportant you think it is."

Garrett was already in the hallway when Carl paused in the doorway, and turning to her, said in a low voice, "You can call me if you just need to talk, too."

She thanked him.

"I hope Sophie is okay," he added after a beat, and Gilly was moved by his kindness, the compassion in his eyes.

But Sophie wasn't okay. Only hours after Gilly gave birth to her in a shambles of shock and grief, her tiny, underdeveloped heart and lungs gave out. If Brian's death took Gilly to her knees, Sophie's death leveled her flat. The world went dark. If it had not been for her mother, Gilly wasn't certain she would have survived those first awful weeks.

She didn't always get along with her mom. There had been hard times between them, weeks when they'd barely spoken, but whatever their grudges were, they'd been erased, washed away in the flood of their mutual grief. Gilly's mother had lost, too—her first grandbaby and her son-in-law, whom she adored. She couldn't have loved Brian more if he'd been her own. But everyone had loved Brian. Unlike Gilly, he'd been outgoing, warmly affectionate, and funny. He'd seek out the person hovering on the fringe of the crowd and set them at ease. It was how he'd found her. Lost in the crowd at a party her University of Houston roommate had dragged her to only to promptly abandon her for the first guy she met. Brian had made a silly joke, something that had made Gilly laugh.

He was like a tonic. *A blessing*, Gilly's mother had called him.

What Gilly knew was that while she and Brian were together, and especially after they created Sophie, life had made sense. But when she had lost them, life was only pain. Her heart beating in her chest hurt. Her lungs filling with her breath hurt. Her brain churned an endless circuit of what ifs and if onlys. What if she'd gone inside the store with him? If only she hadn't mentioned her craving, he wouldn't have stopped there.

He was dead because of her. That was all. The cold fact. The guilt shouldered in alongside her sorrow, and the pain was intolerable, constant, and wearing. At first she limited herself to the drugs the doctor prescribed, and she only allowed herself one or two glasses of wine in the evenings—to take the edge off. But that edge was so sharp and her agony so consuming. She tried to work. There were many projects, calls to return, deadlines to meet. At the time of Brian's death, they had been immersed in the design of a half dozen projects. They blurred in her mind. She made mistakes. She was negligent, not paying the bills, not getting back to clients. Some days she couldn't get out of bed. The landlord, a friend, held out as long as he could, but finally, he gave up on Gilly and her promises to do better, and the day came when B&G Architects was no more.

She drank seriously then. There was no reason not to. It was easy enough to get the booze. Drugs were a little harder to come by after the doctors stopped her prescriptions, but she learned, eventually, how and where and from whom to get pretty much whatever she wanted—oxy, fentanyl, dilaudid.

She prayed to die.

And through all that time, her mother held on to her. When Gilly was sick from the drinking and doping, and retching into the toilet, her mother had held her hair out of her face. She had climbed into bed when Gilly woke screaming from her nightmares. She had cajoled Gilly to eat, take a walk, ride to the store. She had never lost her faith that Gilly would pull through.

In the early days of Gilly's sobriety, her mom had been so hopeful, and the light had come back into her eyes. She had wanted to keep Gilly close, and it had been hard and scary, leaving her. But Gilly knew she couldn't lean on her mother forever. She had to learn to live again on her own. Her mom was concerned she wasn't ready. She had been so grateful for Carl. She'd wanted Gilly to stay in Houston with him, where he could protect her. Going to another part of the state, miles away, wasn't safe. Even if Brian's killer—whom Gilly had witnessed, however briefly, running from the store—wasn't still on the loose, there was Gilly's precarious sobriety at stake. The problem was that neither of them—not Carl or her mother—understood how burdened Gilly was by their constant worry and concern.

She felt the weight of the Wyatt police captain's gaze now and couldn't meet it. The sense of her mother's presence rose as distinctly as if Leeanne Gray were standing beside her. *Not another word.* Her voice clattered into Gilly's mind. *For God's sake, don't say you had a dream. Don't give the man cause to doubt your sanity, to go looking into your background.*

"Miss O'Connell?" The police captain prompted her again. "Who did you see Zoe with? How do you know it wasn't Stephanie? Are you acquainted with her?"

Mackie's look was intent. Gilly could nearly see his nose—his cop nose—twitching in anticipation that he had stumbled on something, a clue, perhaps the very one he needed to resolve the mystery of Zoe's disappearance. *If only* . . .

"They could have met in Houston," Cricket said, but it came across more as if she was asking. Unlike her husband, though, she sounded perplexed rather than suspicious.

"No," Gilly tried to backpedal. "I didn't mean—"

"No, you don't know Zoe's mother? Or no, you don't know the identity of the woman who took Zoe?" Captain Mackie was all business now.

"I—I saw her yesterday. Zoe, I mean. She was here with her dad for breakfast. I made her an elephant pancake." *I told Jake where to find his wallet.* "I haven't seen her at all today." *Except in a dream, a horrible nightmare.* Gilly stopped, clamping her jaw against that bit.

Mackie stared.

She looked away.

"Miss O'Connell, I'm getting the distinct impression you know more than you're saying."

Mackie waited for her to fill in the pause. Gilly didn't.

He went on. "Where were you between eleven thirty this morning and one o'clock, say? Can you account for your whereabouts?"

"She was here," April said. "All morning, from the time we opened."

Gilly shot her a grateful look.

But Mackie wouldn't let it go. "If you were at the school, if you saw who picked Zoe up, you need to tell me."

"Trust me," Gilly said, "if I knew, I would. But I don't. Truly," she added, meeting the captain's eyes now. "I've never been to the school."

He looked back at her, openly disbelieving, wary.

It was something Gilly hated about cops, the way they never took anything at face value. She'd once asked Carl how he could live like that—doubting everyone and everything they said. He hadn't denied it made life, especially relationships, difficult. He'd confessed that his wife of seven years had left him in part because of his inability to trust her—that and his god-awful hours.

"You heard April. I was here all morning. She's a witness." Gilly glanced at April, who looked apprehensive, perhaps even regretful, now.

"Yeah, I heard."

The silence lingered, becoming prolonged, uncomfortable.

Gilly looked past Mackie at the door behind him that led to the alley behind the café. She thought again of leaving Wyatt, driving north or west. She'd always wanted to see California.

Mackie's phone went off and as if a reset button had been pushed, everyone moved. Cricket followed her husband out the back door that led to the alley.

Gilly followed April into the walk-in pantry. "Thanks for speaking up for me in there."

"Sure," April said. She was moving spice bottles around as if the activity absorbed her. Abruptly, she turned, shooting Gilly a probing glance. "You were gone awhile."

"What do you mean?"

"Earlier, when you went to the restroom? You were gone a long time, maybe as long as forty-five minutes, from like eleven forty-five to near twelve thirty."

"No. No," Gilly repeated. "You must be mistaken. I was only in there a few minutes." She remembered patting her face with a damp paper towel. She'd been thinking about Zoe, the dream—

"I don't think so." April was insistent. "I shredded the pork, sliced two or three pounds of chicken, a half dozen onions, the tomatoes, and grated a ton of cheese, plus took orders while you were gone—kept me busy a half hour at least."

Gilly stared at April. She'd had blackouts before, back when she was still drinking. She'd lost time on a couple of occasions since then, too, but early in her sobriety. Was it happening again? She remembered the open window, the heavenly breeze—outside. Had she gone outside?

"Did you go out to the Little Acorn for some reason?" April asked. "I mean, I get it if you don't want the cops to know, but this is a little kid that's missing, so like if you saw something—"

"I couldn't have gone to the school. I wasn't lying when I said I don't know where it is. I didn't see anything that way."

"That *way*?" April was perplexed. "What does that mean?"

"Excuse me, but I have to go. Bailey—my dog—if I don't go home right now and walk him, he'll make a mess on the floor." Gilly went around April to the dayroom, where she retrieved her purse. She didn't look at April again, but she felt April's eyes on her right up until she left the café, closing the alleyway door behind her.

. . .

Tommy Houseman had been Gilly's best friend—the last real, close friend she'd have—until third grade, when she told him she'd dreamed his big brother, Blake, whom Tommy idolized, was going to die in a hunting accident. Gilly had wakened from the dream, disoriented and scared, and she'd gone into her parents' bedroom and wakened them, begging them to warn the Housemans.

Her dad was furious. "It's three o'clock in the damn morning."

Her mom flipped on the bedside light, squinting at Gilly in the doorway. She was clearly unhappy, too. "You have got to stop this, Gillian," she said.

It was what she always said after Gilly had one of her dreams. *Stop this.* As if Gilly could control what she dreamed. "Just call them, please," she begged. "They're going in the morning before it's even light outside. Tommy said—"

"I'm not calling anybody at this hour." Her dad punched his pillow. It might have been her face, Gilly thought. He'd never hit her, but Gilly had always felt the threat of it. She thought he wanted her to feel it. Sometimes he'd stand her between his knees, cup her cheeks in his rough-palmed hands and search her eyes. She didn't know what he was looking for. Some other little girl, one who didn't have dreams and wild imaginings. "Go back to bed," he told her. "Leeanne, turn off the light. Goddammit, I've got to get some sleep."

Gilly's mom switched off the lamp, rendering Gilly blind. She groped her way to her mother's side of the bed. "Mommy, please."

"No, Gillian. Go back to bed now. Your father has to get up in the morning and go to work. He's got no time for your drama. None of us does."

Gilly hesitated, but there wasn't any use pushing. She was in the hallway outside her parents' bedroom when her mom spoke again.

"Don't go calling over there yourself either. Do you hear me?"

Gilly didn't call. Instead she waited in her bedroom until she heard her father's snores, and then, walking quietly through the house, she let herself out the back door. Tommy's house was on her right, and she went from her backyard into his the way she always did: on her hands and knees, crawling through the hole in the hedge of scraggly Ligustrums that defined the property line. It was fall, the beginning of deer hunting season, and cold out. There was no moon. Even the stars were gone. She was scared, and her heart was beating hard and fast. But she couldn't let it go the way her parents wanted. Even if she had been wrong before when she'd dreamed stuff, she'd been right, too. Like last month, when in the split second after she'd seen it happen in her mind, a limb as big around as her mother's leg fell some thirty feet from the pine tree in their backyard. Her mom, who had been weeding the groundcover beneath it, had just gotten to her feet when Gilly jerked her to safety. What if this was the same kind of thing? What if she could save Blake's life?

She went to Tommy's bedroom window, scooping a handful of dirt and small stones on her way. He was there immediately after she tossed the rubble at his window, as if he'd been awake and waiting for her.

"What are you doing?" he asked her through the screen. He used his normal speaking voice, and she shushed him, looking over her shoulder in the direction of her house, half expecting to see the back porch light come on, her father emerge, hands on his hips. If he found her, he'd jerk her up, maybe whip her all the way home.

"Can't come out now. We're going hunting," Tommy said. "I told you."

"I know," Gilly said. "That's why I came over. You can't go, Tommy. Blake's going to get hurt if you do, maybe killed."

"What are you talking about?"

"Tommy? You dressed yet?"

Gilly recognized his dad's voice and ducked down below the window just as he opened Tommy's bedroom door. "Who are you talking to?"

"Gilly," Tommy said. "She says Blake's going to get hurt if we go hunting."

"Gilly?"

She looked up at Mr. Houseman, framed in the window. She couldn't see Tommy.

"Your parents know you're here?" he asked, not unkindly, but the edge of annoyance in his voice was unmistakable, like a pinch.

She shook her head.

"You have one of those dreams?"

She nodded. She could tell from the way he spoke that he thought as little of her dreams as her parents did.

"We talked about this, right? Dreams don't tell the future. No one can do that."

"I saw Blake, though. I saw him fall in the woods; blood was on him. He screamed—"

"What the hell is she talking about?"

Gilly heard Blake's voice. He was twelve, four years older than Gilly and Tommy, and he thought he was superior, smarter and tougher than they'd ever be. But once when her foot had gotten tangled in her bike chain, Blake had loosened it and then carried her home six blocks, because it hurt too much to walk on it.

"Language," his dad admonished over his shoulder. He turned back to Gilly. "You get on back home, okay?"

"You won't call my parents?"

"You need to quit making up all this dream crap, okay? You scare people."

Gilly wanted to tell him it wasn't crap. She wanted to say she was scared of herself, too, that she did everything she could to keep from sleeping, even splashing cold water on her face to stay awake. But all she said was, "Yes sir," and when he asked her to promise, she agreed it was the last time his family—Tommy or any of them—would hear "any bogus dream prediction about their future" out of her.

"I think she's just starved for attention." Gilly heard Mrs. Houseman say as Mr. Houseman was closing Tommy's window.

She'd heard her mom say a similar thing to her dad during arguments they had about her, about what to do with her.

She only makes up this terrible stuff to get your attention, her mom would say.

You let her get away with it, her dad would say. *And don't give me that horseshit about her having a vivid imagination. We both know she flat-out lies. She invents shit on purpose just to rattle folks and scare them. She gets some kind of rush from it.*

The kid's mental.

She needs a shrink.

Gilly had overheard her dad say it a dozen, a hundred times. If he was fed up with her and the dreams before Blake, he was off the deep end after.

Because Blake didn't die that day, but after that, everything else did.

Gilly and Tommy were never friends again. His folks had forbidden it, and the following month, Gilly's dad packed up and left, and her parents divorced. Her mom said it had nothing to do with Gilly, but Gilly knew better. She knew her dad had left because she was a freak, and he couldn't handle it. Her mom couldn't handle it either, but she'd made the best of it, out of obligation. She was that sort of person. She wouldn't abandon her child. She overlooked a lot. She had a gesture—a habit of fluttering her fingers in front of her face if something disturbed her, and Gilly's dreams, the prophetic ones, did disturb her. They set Gilly apart. Made her too different. She would never have friends, or not the sort she would want, meaning not the sort her mom wanted for her. It had turned out to be true—the friends part. Gilly was never really close to anyone after Tommy Houseman.

Until Brian came along.

But now Brian was gone, and Gilly's brain was weird again.

April had said Gilly had been gone a half hour or more this morning. At least thirty minutes of her life had passed, unaccounted for. Minutes Gilly couldn't recollect.

Bailey greeted her as soon as she opened the door, all doggy smiles and rump-wriggling joy, and Gilly went to her knees right there on her kitchen floor, gathering him into her embrace, burying her nose in his wiry fur, fighting tears. Moments later, when she'd gotten control of herself, she snapped on his leash and walked with him through the neighborhood to the small park six blocks from her house. He was well behaved, trotting along beside her, matching her brisk pace. Brian had undertaken his training. Watching Brian with Bailey, Gilly had known then, if she hadn't before, that Brian would be a fantastic dad.

· · ·

"Gilly? What's wrong?" her mother asked, reading the emotion in Gilly's voice.

Gilly had fought calling her. She had intended to go to the grocery store to buy the makings for tomorrow night's dinner with Liz. But instead, after walking Bailey, she'd changed the sheets on her bed and done a load of wash. She'd brought chicken salad home from the café, and she'd made herself a sandwich for dinner, but she'd been unable to eat more than a bite. She'd left it sitting on a plate in the breakfast nook and gone outside into the backyard with Bailey and her phone. It was after eight, and the last of the daylight was gone, but she could see him, sniffing intently at something only he could smell along the fence line.

She'd been lucky, finding a house with a nice yard to rent in a town as small as Wyatt. Especially one where she was allowed to have Bailey. Ruth Rendell, the realtor Gilly had worked with, was her landlord. Ruth had inherited the house, she'd said, from her aunt Tildy, who had died not long ago. Gilly had felt odd about taking possession of it, saddened in a way, but Ruth had assured her that her aunt had lived a long and satisfying life. Ruth had hinted that she'd be open to the idea if Gilly wanted to buy the house, but Gilly wasn't sure of her plans long-term. She'd been here six months and had yet to unpack the boxes except for the most essential items. She couldn't seem to deal with it—the future.

If Brian were here, he'd snap it up, the house and the small-town life. He and Gilly had talked about it. Before his death they'd been working on a drawing of a white clapboard farmhouse with four bedrooms to accommodate the three children they'd planned. They'd pictured it on acreage somewhere in central or south Texas.

"Two story," Brian had said, quickly penciling a basic outline.

"With dormers and a wraparound porch," Gilly had said, and she'd added those details when he'd passed the drawing to her. "We'll have a swing." She'd looked at him.

"Absolutely," he'd said, grinning. He took back the drawing and outlined a bench swing. "It'll be big enough for all five of us. Our land should have water, a small lake or a pond, where we can fish."

"And have picnics," Gilly had said, and the vision of their shared dream had seemed to float from the page and shimmer in the air between them.

Tildy's house wasn't exactly in the style or the rural location they'd dreamed of, but Gilly thought Brian would encourage her to buy it. The yellow clapboard bungalow was on an oversize lot in a pretty, tree-studded subdivision called Lacey Oaks. It was as much property as Gilly felt she could adequately handle on her own. The morbid irony was that because of the benefit paid to her through the life insurance policy Brian had taken out shortly after they married, not only could she afford it, she could pay the full asking price and own it outright with a generous amount left over. The amount on the check she'd received embarrassed her. She wondered how anyone could put a dollar amount on someone's life. She wondered why it wasn't called death insurance.

"A little girl is missing," she said to her mom now.

"Where?" her mother asked. "There in Wyatt?"

"Yes."

"You know her?"

"Yes. Not well. I make her pancakes when she comes to the café with her dad on Wednesdays."

"Oh, Gilly." Disappointment and a harsher note of alarm threaded her mother's voice. "How long has she been gone?"

"Since around noon today. I had a dream about her last night, and I saw who took her. Not clearly. Just enough that I know it was a woman driving a blue car."

"Gilly, your car is blue."

"Yes, but it's an SUV. The car in my dream was a sedan, and the color was lighter than mine, more a silvery blue. Metallic."

"Your dream could be wrong."

Of course her mom would think that, Gilly thought.

"It wasn't—"

You. The word hovered between them, not quite an accusation.

"No," Gilly said. "No, of course not."

"You're sure you didn't—?"

"No! Mom, why would you even think such a thing?"

"You know why, honey."

She meant there was a history. Gilly had done it before.

8

Jake was only doors away from his house when he spotted the Wyatt patrol car parked in his driveway behind his mother's MINI Cooper, and he floored it, reaching his house in seconds, mindless when the truck jumped the curb. "Zoe?" he shouted, bailing out of the cab. "Zoe?" He screamed her name, running across the yard.

The front door flew open, and his mother appeared. Clint Mackie was silhouetted in the light behind her.

"Zoe?" he said from the bottom of the porch steps, and he knew before she shook her head that his daughter wasn't here. "You found her, though. You know where she is." Jake persisted even though he knew from his mom's expression, the slump of her shoulders, there was nothing new.

"I'm sorry, honey." She opened the screen, and he came up the steps.

He shook hands with Clint, who clapped him on the shoulder, squeezing it.

They went into the kitchen.

"We were just having coffee," his mom said. "I can pour you a cup. It's still fresh."

He shook his head.

His mother and Clint sat down, but Jake remained standing. He pulled his phone out of his pocket, thumbing it on. Panic kept trying to stand up in his belly. He kept shoving it down. "Maybe the sergeant—Sergeant Kersey in Houston—has heard something."

"I talked to him a few minutes ago," Clint said. "He's been by Steph's house. There's no sign of her. House is dark, he said. No sign of anyone."

"God! Where is she? Where has she taken Zoe?" Wheeling, Jake slammed his hands down on the countertop, shutting his eyes against the bite of tears.

"Oh, honey—" His mom came to him. He felt her hand, rubbing circles on his back.

"She'll turn up—" Clint began.

"You should see how she's living." Jake got a glass from the cabinet, filled it with water, and drank it down, collecting himself, settling his breath. "Everything she told us about her cute little garden apartment in the Ward, how the neighborhood has turned around—her place is a dump. Kersey might as well have called it a crack house."

Neither Clint nor his mom spoke. What could they say?

He blinked at the ceiling. "Now she's got my kid. She's got Zoe and taken her God knows where."

"But I'm like Clint, Jake. I can't see her doing this." His mom sounded genuinely perplexed. "The whole point of leaving here, leaving you—she didn't want to be a mother. Clint? Isn't that what she told you and Cricket, too?"

"Yeah." He moved his coffee mug between his hands, studying them.

"So what are you thinking?" Jake asked him.

He glanced up. "I don't know. Call it cop brain, but I can't see Stephanie having it together enough to plan something like this. Skulking around in a hoodie, taking Zoe on the sly."

"But if it was random, the sickos who take kids—they don't operate this way, do they? Picking out a kid, posing as a parent. A stranger—it's more like a grab and go, isn't it? Or they try to lure the kid with candy or something. Zoe knows all about that. She would have yelled her head off if a stranger had offered her candy to get in the car." Jake looked from Clint to his mom.

She said, "Maybe Steph has changed her mind about being a mother."

"Or maybe the boyfriend changed it." Jake stopped, sickened at the idea of some other guy trying to be Zoe's dad.

"She's got a boyfriend?" his mom asked.

"According to her neighbor, she does."

"Houston PD is trying to find out who he is and where he is," Clint said.

"What if he's with Steph?" Jake said. "He's probably like her, some doper, and they have my kid."

"If there's a boyfriend involved, if he's participating, there's no telling—" His mother paused.

"Mom? What?"

"What if they try to take Zoe out of the country? We've all heard the stories about other parents who've done it. Given what she's already done, how far she's already gone . . ."

Jake turned to Clint, blood like ice in his veins. "Are you guys checking the airports?"

"Yes, and the bus stations south from here to Houston and north to Dallas, and so far there's no trace of them. They'd need passports for international travel," Clint said. "It takes time to get one."

"She might have planned ahead," Jake said, "she and her dickhead boyfriend—sorry, Mom." He paced a line in front of the kitchen sink.

"If only she'd call." His mom sounded hoarse.

From worry, Jake thought. And exhaustion. She liked to say she went to bed and rose with the chickens. "You should go home, Ma. Get some sleep."

"No, I couldn't," she told him firmly.

Couldn't leave him to handle the situation alone, she meant. Not when he was in such dire straits. No matter what, she was always there for him. He had almost choked on his shame, confessing to her and his dad that Stephanie was pregnant. It wasn't his first experience, getting a woman in trouble that way. His folks could have rightfully asked him how he could let it happen again, and the second time he was no kid. But they hadn't even brought up the first time. Other than to say that a baby on the way wasn't a good reason to plan a wedding, his mom had never told him or Steph what to do.

But the day came, and at the last minute Stephanie couldn't terminate the pregnancy despite how little she wanted it, and Jake had felt honor bound to stand by her, to marry her and make it right. Women didn't get pregnant alone. He'd been eighteen when his mom pointed that out the first time, barely out of high school.

Clint stood up now. "Y'all should both try and get some rest. I hear anything from Houston, or anywhere, you'll be the first to know."

"What do you know about Gilly, the waitress at the café?" Jake asked him.

"Gilly O'Connell? Not a lot. Why?"

There was a leap of something more than curiosity in Clint's eyes. He seemed intent now. Jake felt his mother's questioning glance, too, but he wasn't sure he wanted to talk about it—the business with his wallet. It was too crazy, the way his brain kept trying to make the leap from Gilly knowing where he could find that to her knowing where he could find his daughter. Zoe wasn't some object he'd mislaid. She was his flesh and blood, his kid.

"Jake?" his mother prompted.

"No, it's . . . This is going to sound nuts, but when I couldn't find my wallet yesterday"—was he really going to get into this?—"she told me where I'd left it in the garage, on Great-Granddad's tool chest." Jake looked at Clint. "You ever heard of anything like it? I mean has she made other predictions that you know of?"

Clint's glance did an odd shift.

Jake's mom said, "Are you saying Gilly's clairvoyant?"

"It's nuts," Jake said, although he had asked Gilly the same thing, and she'd denied it.

"Maybe not," Clint said.

Both Jake and his mother looked at him.

"I don't know much about psychics, but talking to her today, I got the impression Gilly O'Connell knows something more than she's telling."

Jake's heart began to pound. Now he understood Clint's look a moment ago. "What, man? Does she know where Zoe is?"

"No." Clint said it emphatically. He locked Jake's gaze and held it, making sure Jake got the message.

"What then?" Jake asked.

"She claims to know Stephanie isn't the woman who picked Zoe up at school. But she also said she doesn't know Stephanie, which could be a lie—" Clint broke off again, frowning.

"You're thinking there's a connection?" Jake was guessing.

"Gilly's from Houston," Clint said.

"The two might have met," Jake's mother said.

"It's a pretty big city," Jake said. "Gilly wouldn't have to run in the same circles. She doesn't strike me as the doper type."

"I dunno," Clint said. "We're looking into her background."

"You're kidding." Jake was incredulous.

"She's relatively new in town." Clint's gesture was vague, and his eyes kept shifting in a way that bothered Jake. "If nothing else, we need to rule out the possibility she's involved."

"I can't see it," Jake said. "She's great with Zoe." He was thinking of the silly pancakes Gilly made for Zoe, and the way Gilly would just pick up telling Zoe a story. The way she'd admire Zoe's nail polish, and Jake's, as if it were the most natural thing in the world for a man to go around with painted nails. Yesterday when he'd gone on about his idea for building houses out of concrete, the light in her eyes, her interest, had been genuine and real. Like her interest in Zoe. Was it too much? The other times they'd had coffee together, had she been working him to get to Zoe?

"You never know about people," Jake's mother said.

"You can get fooled for sure," Clint said. He pushed his chair under the table. "Thanks for the coffee, Justine."

Jake went with him to the front door. "About Gilly O'Connell. What if she does know where Zoe is? What if she saw who took her and where they are in her mind the way she saw my wallet?" Jake thought Clint would laugh or dismiss the idea, but he didn't.

"Her husband was murdered in Houston a few years back in a convenience-store robbery down there."

"Are you serious?" Jake was stunned. "She told me yesterday that he'd died suddenly, but I had no idea—"

"Yeah," Clint said. "It was a wrong place, wrong time kind of deal, a total fluke."

"How did you find out?"

"Background check. Cricket does one on all her employees prior to hiring. The case is still unsolved."

Jake didn't know what to say.

"One other thing Cricket found out in the news reports about Gilly's husband—there was some reference to her being—what's that word Justine used?"

"Clairvoyant?" Jake said. "I asked her if she was when she 'found' my wallet. She was pretty adamant that wasn't the case."

"Huh. Well, supposedly, according to what the media reported, Gilly knew her husband was going to be shot beforehand. It's probably a lot of hype."

"Yeah, probably," Jake said. But he was thinking, *What if it isn't?* It was a fact that she'd located his wallet. Maybe she had also predicted her husband would be killed, as horrible as it would have been for her. And if she could do those things, wasn't there a chance she could know Zoe's whereabouts?

Clint said, "What bothers me is that Gilly can't, or won't, say how she's so sure it's not Zoe's mom who took her."

"Maybe it's just a gut thing," Jake said.

"Yeah, maybe." The police captain pondered it a moment, then clicked his tongue. "I never know what to think when I hear stuff like this, do you?"

"No," Jake answered. "I don't either."

• • •

After Clint left, Jake argued his mom into lying down on his bed. He bedded down on the sofa, but sleep was impossible, and after a while he left the house. He drove his truck out of his neighborhood, Mustang Hill, over to Lacey Oaks, the subdivision on the other side of Wyatt where Gilly was living. He knew the location because the house she was leasing belonged to Ruth Rendell, a local realtor he worked with sometimes. He'd run into her at the grocery store a while back, and she'd told him. Jake turned down Little Sandy Lane, where the house was, and hoped Gilly wasn't a night owl. The street was deserted, awash in the murky glow of the streetlight. Overhead, a misshapen moon wobbled in a high corner of a midnight sky. He went slowly, feeling like an intruder, possibly a stalker, hunting the house that he knew was yellow clapboard. When he spotted it, he pulled to the curb. The porch light was the only light that was on, and a flight of moths shadowed it, dipping, fluttering. Doomed, he thought.

Now that he was here, he didn't know why he'd come. It was well after midnight. Gilly was probably asleep. It would only scare the shit out of her if he were to bang on her door. He wiped his hands down his face. Maybe it was crazy, the whole idea that she could be in there dreaming, having some vision that would lead him to Zoe. But maybe it was for real. Maybe Gilly's mind was some kind of conduit tuned into a cosmic channel only she had access to.

The big screen of the universe.

What a joke.

Or not. He didn't know. That was the hell of it.

Not knowing where Zoe was right now—that was a worse hell. His brain wanted to explore possibilities, feed him scenarios, all of them terrifying. He shut his eyes, clenching the steering wheel as if squeezing it might choke them out. It didn't. It was hard now getting his breath. His heart pounded. He felt its hammer blows against his ribs. A sound broke from his chest. He bit down on it, bent his head to his knuckled fists, and told himself to get a grip.

After several minutes, he wiped his eyes, shifted into drive, and pulled away from the curb. He was going to find her, if it was the last thing he did, if it killed him. Like Nemo's dad, Marlin. He remembered telling Zoe one of the gazillion times they'd watched it that if they ever got lost from each other, the way Marlin and Nemo had, he would be just like Marlin. He would never give up searching for her. But he couldn't think about it—timid Marlin who when it came to his missing son had the heart of a shark. This was no movie, and he and Zoe weren't clownfish.

"Daddy's coming, ZooRoo." He said it aloud. He needed to hear himself say it. "Don't be scared, okay? Just hold on. I'm coming."

He left Lacey Oaks and drove to the Little Acorn Academy. He couldn't have said why, except it was the last place Zoe had been seen before she was taken by a woman driving a sedan, exact make and model unknown. Not any woman. Stephanie. His mind clung to the hope despite the growing evidence that it might not have been her. He didn't know where he'd be if he opened that particular door. As long as he believed Zoe was with Steph, he could believe she was safe. But even in this, he was snowing himself, and he knew it. He pulled up to the school entrance and cut the truck engine.

The front of the small, one-story building was illuminated, bathed in a pool of greenish light—security light. There wasn't a security camera. Kenna had said her budget didn't allow for outside cameras, and while it did allow for lights, they were only across the building's front. The sides and back were dark except for an eerie glow through a window that he decided must be coming from a computer or some other electronic equipment. Or even the aquarium. Maybe that light was left on all night.

The school sat in a three-quarter-acre clearing eight miles west of Wyatt on a meandering county road named Shady Oaks Lane. The rural setting suggested a wholesome and safe atmosphere. But what Jake saw now was the school's vulnerability, its isolation from town or any populated area. He doubted that the Madrone County sheriff or the Wyatt police patrolled out here on a regular basis outside school hours. The nearest subdivision was a good five miles away, and houses there were on acreage. Ranch land, and land that belonged to a state park— Monarch Lake State Park—surrounded the school on three sides. A high game fence separated the properties, but it wasn't well maintained, and even in daylight, sections of it were obscured by a heavy growth of underbrush and woods.

The same woods Zoe and the other children were warned to stay out of unless they were accompanied by an adult. The very woods where— according to waitress and so-called clairvoyant Gilly O'Connell—the fairies had charmed the monsters out of eating eyeballs.

If you could believe her fairy tale.

Jake wasn't sure what to think about her. He couldn't wrap his mind around the idea that she might be involved in Zoe's disappearance, and yet he couldn't entirely dismiss Clint's suspicion of Gilly either. She'd been through some shit for sure. Lost her husband to violence. Knowing that did explain some things. Like why she'd left Houston, even why she wasn't an architect anymore. But why had she chosen Wyatt to run to, if running away was what she was doing? He might think of the town and its location as some of the most beautiful country on earth, but most big city hotshots would call it the ass end of nowhere.

Feeling the need to move, to get away from his thoughts, Jake got out of the truck and instantly felt a jolt of foreboding. He looked alongside the building toward the back, where the playground was located, the last place Zoe had been seen for sure. Beyond the fenced boundary the woods loomed. The moon had sunk behind the thick wall of trees, and the shadows that layered the ground shifted with a restless wind. The air seemed alive, bursting with the sound of children laughing, but reason said it was his imagination. He remembered a nature walk he'd taken in these woods earlier in the spring. The school regularly sponsored the walks for children and their parents. The kids gathered bits of moss and twigs, whatever caught their fancy, and made collages out of the stuff. Zoe had made a heart and printed on it in alternating shades of red and green crayon: FOR DADY. Jake could see it in his mind's eye, the crooked red and green letters, her misspelling: *Dady*. His throat closed.

She would be so afraid if she were in those woods now when it was so dark. God—

Clamping his teeth, he got a flashlight out of his glove box, and switching it on, he followed the beam, playing it over the area, illuminating in flashes a colorful collection of molded plastic playground equipment, the seat of a swing, the glint of a metal chain. He passed the white four-foot picket fence that surrounded the vegetable garden Zoe was so crazy about. The tomato plants, already towering out of their cages, were covered in blooms. They'd be choking on the harvest by summer's end.

He was some twenty feet past the garden when he found the fence line. Raising the flashlight, sweeping a path to his right, he spotted the gate almost immediately, and his heart dropped. It was open.

Wasn't it? Hadn't the assistant said she'd closed it?

He paused, focusing his gaze in an attempt to discern exactly what he was looking at. Panic wrecked his mind. Fatigue sanded his eyes. He couldn't trust either. Pulse hammering in his ears, he walked closer to the gap that the gate was designed to fill, keeping the beam from his flashlight trained on the location, trying to make the gate be there, closed and locked the way the assistant had claimed she'd left it.

But it was ajar.

It was no lie, no trick played on him by senses overloaded with fear or a body dragged down by exhaustion. He paced short lines, walked a few tight circles, toeing the ground with his boot, using his flashlight to search the greening grass, the coarse tangle of shrubbery. He didn't know what he was looking for, but the notion that this was the last place Zoe was seen pounded in his brain. Looking up, he panned his light over the area beyond the juniper-choked fence line until the bright beam found the narrow trail. Jake knew it led to a small pond about a half a mile away. He'd been there with Zoe and her classmates a handful of times.

He went through the gate now, drawn by a mix of anticipation and dread, following the path made by his flashlight. The wind sighed; the chirr of crickets rose and fell. He stopped once, certain he heard the fall of other footsteps, and he waited, hardly daring to breathe. The hair on his scalp, the warning voice in his brain—every sense was on alert. But no one appeared. No one stepped onto the path. He was almost a quarter of a mile beyond the gate before he spotted it. The pink tricycle was turned on its side at the edge of the path, as if someone intent on concealing it under the trees had been interrupted. That was Jake's initial impression before a rush of fear-fueled adrenaline kicked his emotions into gear, got his feet moving toward it. Kneeling beside it, he ran his hand over the front fender, following the movement with the beam of his flashlight. The trike was painted two shades of pink, colors that were repeated in the tassels hanging from the handlebars. He stood the trike upright, and set his hand on the tiny seat. Zoe had a tricycle like this one. She'd gone with his mom to pick it out for her birthday last year.

But it was at home, wasn't it? Hadn't he seen it there yesterday, in the garage? This one couldn't be hers. There had to be dozens of little girls who had this same trike. Heidi Buchanan, who lived two doors down, had one. She was a year older, and Zoe copied everything Heidi did. Jake was almost certain that was why Zoe had insisted on having this exact—

His phone sounded, and he pulled it from his pocket, eyeing the screen. Seeing Clint's name amped his alarm. His heart was a jackhammer. He stabbed the phone's face, opening the connection, but then he couldn't utter a word, not a sound.

"Jake?" the police captain said. "You there? Did I wake you?"

"Hell no. I'm out here at the school. The gate's open. That new girl—Mary, Misty, whatever—she said she closed it, remember? But it's open, Clint. It's open, and there's no sign of the padlock anywhere. It's the last place Zoe was seen—"

"Jake! Slow down. Are you talking about the gate behind the school? Because we looked around back there yesterday—"

"Yes. There's a trike—a pink trike here down the trail a ways—" Jake interrupted himself. "Did you—are you calling because you found them?"

"No. No, I'm sorry. But I did get information on the boyfriend." Clint sounded grim. "His name's Andy Duchene. He's twenty-eight, ex-army. Did his basic at Fort Hood. Served in Afghanistan. Lifelong resident of Houston."

Jake snorted. "A younger guy, a party boy." Jake had never been a party boy.

"Yeah, well, I imagine he does like to party if his track record of drug arrests and DUIs is any indication. But there's something else on his record that's a bit more concerning—other than his less than honorable discharge for dealing drugs, that is."

Jake waited.

"He was married when he enlisted, and by the time he was discharged, he had two kids by the ex-wife. She got custody when they were divorced." Clint stopped.

"Yeah, okay. So?" Jake prompted.

"So he took them, the kids. This was around a year and a half ago. He was supposed to have them for a regularly scheduled weekend, but he didn't bring them back. The ex reported them missing. A BOLO was issued and an Amber Alert."

Jake knew where this was going, and his chest squeezed.

"When law enforcement caught up with him, he was boarding a flight out of Oklahoma City for New York. He had fake passports for him and the kids and had booked tickets for a flight to Amsterdam. Turns out, he had a buddy there, someone he knew from his army days, who was going to help them get lost, so to speak."

"Duchene's got connections then, a way to do this. He and Steph . . . they could have been planning to take Zoe for weeks." Jake sat back on his heels.

"Like I said earlier, we've got eyes on the airports. We're doing our best to find them, Jake."

"Yeah." *What if your best isn't good enough? What if they get out of the country with my kid?*

"Tell me about the gate," Clint said. "It was shut, and the padlock was on it when we were back there."

Jake got to his feet. "It's not now, and this—the playground back here—it's the last place Zoe was seen, Clint."

"I talked to Mrs. Dunhill, Katie's mom. She's pretty sure she saw Zoe get into a blue sedan out front—"

"Yeah, well, what's her name—tattoo girl, the assistant—was dead certain Zoe was on the playground when Steph came to the school. And it's for damn sure from her own mouth she never saw where, or how, or in what direction Zoe and Steph left."

"Okay, but when I spoke to her, *Marley* was pretty clear she had locked the gate *before* speaking to Stephanie, which would indicate—"

"After the way she screwed up, how can we trust anything she says, Clint? Maybe the airhead was on her way to lock the gate when the boys got into a fight and distracted her. Steph could have gotten Zoe through the gate then, and Zoe would have gone right with her. She would have been thrilled, showing her mom the trail."

"You say you found a trike back there. How does that fit—"

"I don't know." Jake rubbed his eyes, fighting an urge to lie down. Clint asked for a description of the tricycle, and Jake gave it to him. "Zoe has one like it," he said.

"It doesn't make sense," Clint said. "Why would her trike be there? How would it get there?"

"No idea," Jake said. "Maybe it's not Zoe's. Maybe none of this has anything to do with her or Steph. You've got to admit, it's pretty damn strange, though."

"Well, leave it as it is, will you? The gate and the trike—like you found them. I'd like to have a look at the area again, talk to Marley and Kenna about it."

Jake said he would and started to end the call when Clint's voice caught him, dishing out some final advice. "We need to keep an open mind as to what went down here," the police captain said.

"I know what went down, Clint." Jake retraced his steps to the school. "Steph and her boy toy have got Zoe. They could be out of the country by now, way to hell and gone." He got into his truck, slamming the door. "You find Steph and Duchene, you'll find Zoe. I'm telling you that's a fact," he added, because he was that convinced now that it was the truth. And part of him was relieved.

Relieved!

What a joke.

Clint said, "I've touched base with Madrone County, the sheriff's department there in Greeley, asked them for support. We just don't have the resources they have."

"Good," Jake said. "I'm glad for whatever help we can get."

"Yeah, well, here's the thing—they want you to take a lie detector test."

"What? Why?"

"It's standard in cases like this. They look at family members—"

"C'mon, Clint. It's bullshit, and you know it."

"It's out of my hands at this point, son. Your best bet is to cooperate. Go in, get it over. They want to conduct a search of your property, too. The house, garage, and so forth."

"You're kidding."

"Wish I was. I did manage to talk them into letting me do it."

"You've got to have a warrant, right?"

"Yeah. They're working on it. Probably have it later today. You might want to let your mama know."

"Are they going to give her the third degree, too?"

Clint didn't answer, which was answer enough.

9

Gilly was in the car but parked in her driveway on Friday morning when her cell rang, making her heart race. She was supposed to be on her way to work; it was still early. The sun was lingering a few feet above the horizon, shooting brilliant rays of light between houses, sending gleaming daggers through the tree canopy. She was only marginally reassured to see Liz's name flash on the caller ID.

"You heard, I guess," Gilly said instead of hello. She couldn't think of any other reason Liz would call at this hour other than to talk about Zoe Halstead's disappearance.

"No, what?" Liz was immediately concerned.

"I thought everyone in this town would know by now. Zoe Halstead is missing."

"Zoe Halstead, Jake Halstead's daughter? That adorable little girl? Are you kidding? I haven't heard anything—has it been on the news?"

"I don't know."

"How did you find out? When did it happen?"

"We were closing up at the café yesterday when the captain—you know the Wyatt police captain is Cricket's husband, right?"

Liz said she did.

"He came to tell Cricket." Gilly explained all that she knew of the details. "Evidently the Mackies looked out for Jake's ex before the divorce. They seem to think she's the one who took Zoe."

"Wow. That's awful. Parents taking their own kids—I've heard sometimes they take them out of the country, and it's years before they're reunited with their mom or dad. Sometimes never—poor Jake."

Gilly ran a fingertip along the lower arc of the steering wheel. She couldn't decide whether to say it, that she didn't think Jake's ex had a thing to do with it, that the whole situation was much more dire than anyone imagined—if anyone could, or would, believe Gilly's dream. It sounded so stupid, too ridiculous to even talk about—at least on the phone. "Are we still on for dinner tonight?" she asked.

"Yep. That's why I'm calling so early. I'm going to be on the road all day, visiting with area doctors. I wanted to check and see what time and what I could bring. Wine? Dessert?"

"Either," said Gilly after a troubled moment's hesitation. But wasn't it a good thing if Liz brought wine? It would provide the opening Gilly had been waiting for to explain. Liz would either be bothered by Gilly's sobriety or not. It was a chance Gilly had to take, if she was going to be true to herself, the person she was now.

"I'm so glad for you," Liz said. "For your friendship, do you know that?"

There was an odd quaver in her voice, one Gilly picked up on even as she agreed, saying, "Me too." She waited a moment. "Are you okay? Did something happen?"

"No. Oh, I'm not sure. I think someone was outside my RV last night, that it might have been my ex. I heard noises, like someone was walking around on the little deck in back, and when I looked out, I swear someone was there just beyond the porch light in the shadows. Scared the shit out of me."

"Did you call the police?"

"No. A couple minutes later when I worked up the guts to look again, they were gone—if they were ever there."

"You think it was your ex?"

"He's done it before, followed me. It's part of the reason why I want to move. Listen, we can talk more tonight, okay? I need to get going."

"Me too," Gilly said. "We'll eat around seven, if that's good for you."

"It's perfect," Liz said. "Bad things happen in this world, don't they?" she asked after a pause.

Gilly straightened. "Liz, are you worried about your ex? That he might try something? Maybe you should call the police now, this morning."

"No, it's fine. I'll see you soon."

"I'm looking forward to it," Gilly said, and Liz agreed she was, too, but on ending the call, Gilly's worry lingered. Sharing an evening with Liz . . . who knew what might get said? Maybe they wouldn't even be friends tomorrow.

Bad things happen in this world. Liz's caution followed Gilly into the café.

April and Nick were already there. Cricket came in soon after Gilly. No one said much. It wasn't long before people began to gather on the sidewalk. Cricket opened the door earlier than usual, and soon every seat was filled. Maybe Liz hadn't heard about Zoe, but the rest of the town certainly had, and they were up in arms. Waiting on them, hearing their talk, Gilly knew if the worst happened—if it was discovered she was involved, and she needed to make a run for it—California wouldn't be far enough. The moon might not be far enough away if she was somehow implicated. It could happen. Folks were subdued, but that only made their talk seem more intense, more adamant, and the gist was the same, regardless whose coffee and eggs Gilly was serving. They were ready to lynch the monster who had taken Zoe, and from what Gilly was picking up, not many of them believed it was Stephanie.

"She abandoned that child not two years ago," Izzy Belle said when Gilly set her plate of french toast in front of her. "She couldn't handle the responsibility. So what now? She's changed her mind? Had some kind of epiphany? A come-to-Jesus moment?"

"She's a drug addict," said Charlotte, Izzy's breakfast companion. "She's desperate for money."

"What are you saying?" Izzy asked, appalled. "She took Zoe for ransom? Her own child?"

"That's exactly what I'm saying. Stephanie knows better than all of us Jake Halstead will do anything, pay any amount, to get his daughter back. Look at everything he's done for that woman already—the way he's supported her even though they're divorced. But I heard a while back she asked for money to make her car payment, and he said, no, finally."

"So she took that poor little girl," Izzy murmured.

"I never thought of it, Charlotte, but it makes sense." Pete Waltrip, sitting in the adjacent booth, spoke over his shoulder.

Gilly set the coffee carafe on the burner behind the counter.

Augie Bright tossed aside his napkin. "I don't know that I can buy it. Last time I saw Steph, she was pretty strung out."

"But if it wasn't her, where does that leave us?" Hamp Echols spoke from his perch on a stool at the counter.

"It's got to be a stranger," Augie said and paused.

"Or someone right here in town," Hamp said. "Someone we know, who's new, an outsider—"

Gilly froze. Did he mean her? If she were to turn, would she find him, find everyone, looking at her? The silence pooled around her, prescient, waiting. She had to face them, to see what was on their faces, and when she did, she found they were looking at each other, exchanging alarmed, half-panicked glances. She shifted her gaze from Hamp and the others seated at the counter to Augie and the rest of the folks, who occupied the tables and the row of booths along the windowed wall.

Morning sunshine slanted across their plates of mostly untouched food. It was almost nine. On any other morning, the majority of these people would have left by now to go to work, run errands, get on with their day. But this was not any other morning.

The bell rang above the café door when it opened, making everyone jump. It was as if a spell had been broken. All eyes turned to the person on the threshold, who hovered there as if arrested in midstep. The light made identification impossible, but when she spoke, calling her husband's name, "Augie?" Gilly recognized Mandy Bright's voice.

Cricket came through the swinging door from the kitchen, and Gilly heard the clatter of dishes, the slosh of water. Cricket didn't, or wouldn't, meet Gilly's glance. April would have had time by now to have told her about Gilly's absence yesterday—the thirty or forty minutes when her whereabouts were, allegedly, unaccounted for. The very window of time in which Zoe Halstead was snatched from school by a woman wearing a hoodie and dark glasses.

It wasn't me. Gilly wanted to say it to Cricket, but she knew how it would sound if she were to defend herself. How would she word it anyway? *April is mistaken? I wasn't in the restroom that long?* Blaming April wouldn't win Cricket's confidence. The truth was, even Gilly didn't know what she'd been doing all that time. Trying to hold herself together? That was her main focus these days.

"I just ran down here for a minute." Mandy was addressing the room even as she slid into the booth where Augie was sitting. "Janie was just at the school."

Like Mandy, Janie was a hair stylist at A Cut Above.

"She was going to drop Tina off, but she brought her to work instead."

Tina must be Janie's daughter, Gilly guessed.

"They found something—a trike." Mandy sounded breathless.

"A trike?" Augie asked.

"A little girl's pink trike. Evidently Jake went to the school last night, and the gate at the back of the playground where Zoe was playing—the one that goes into the woods—was open, and he found the trike pushed over on the path. He said it was Zoe's trike, or that's what Janie heard—"

Voices erupted, a frightened chorus of denial, protest.

Augie's voice rose above the others. "How does he know it's Zoe's?"

"It's pink," Mandy said, and Gilly's heart slammed the wall of her chest. She saw it, the dream image took shape in her mind, the pink tricycle turned on its side.

"C'mon, folks, let's not go off the deep end here." Augie spoke firmly. "A lot of little girls have that same pink trike. Our Amy had one before she outgrew it. Anybody—a mom or dad—could have left it there by accident—"

"The thing is, Augie," Mandy interrupted him, "Jake keeps Zoe's trike in the garage, but Janie heard when he looked, it wasn't there."

"Did she hear that from Jake?" Augie asked.

"No," Mandy admitted. "But you know—everyone must know Stephanie isn't the one who took Zoe. It's someone else."

"You're still losing me on the significance of finding that trike," Augie said.

"I can't put it together." Mandy spoke sharply to her husband. "If Zoe was kidnapped by a stranger, though, maybe he lured her with it. Maybe he came out of the woods with it, and that's how he got her to go with him."

"But I thought she was seen getting into a car with a woman at the school entrance." Someone, Gilly didn't see who it was, spoke up.

"Corinne Dunhill thinks she saw Zoe get into the car, but she's not sure," Mandy answered. "And the new teaching assistant was distracted by some boys who got into a scuffle. She can't say one way or another what happened. She didn't actually *see* Zoe leave. She just assumed she got into a car out front. But what if Zoe didn't?"

"You can hear anything in this town," Augie said.

"I know," Mandy said. "But if there is any truth to it—that a stranger might have taken Zoe—the police—" She cut her eyes to Cricket. "I'm sorry, but Clint should be getting a search effort together. He should be looking for the real kidnapper, not wasting time taking the easy way—"

"Mandy." Augie was warning her.

She said no. She wasn't having it. "Whoever took Zoe, they're getting away."

"What if they come back?" a woman said.

"What if they take another of our children?" another female voice chimed in.

"We can organize a search." Hamp Echols's voice sliced across the rest. "We don't need the police for that."

"Hamp's right," Augie said. "We can set up at the school. Whether the trike has anything to do with what happened to Zoe or not, the playground is the last place anyone saw her."

Folks were getting up, asking for checks. Gilly went to the cash register. They were like a herd of cattle, she thought. Half-spooked as if by lightning. She saw Cricket slip her phone from her pocket. Calling to warn Clint, no doubt.

A half hour later, the café was empty, and Cricket turned from locking the door.

"Are we closing?" Gilly asked.

"Yes, for the time being. Maybe until Zoe is found." Cricket brought her hands together. "I can't believe this is happening. Clint and I couldn't love that little girl more if she were our own granddaughter."

"They'll find her," Gilly said, and then wished the words back. They sounded so empty and glib.

"It seems odd that you knew it wasn't her mother who took her." Cricket locked Gilly's gaze.

Apprehension heated her temples, tightened her jaw. She didn't respond.

"Clint's never believed it, either, but you know as a policeman he has a sense, a kind of intuition—but you—how would *you* know? Unless you were there?"

"It's just a feeling . . ." Gilly began, but then she broke off, struck by a thought: What if it was more than that? Her dream about Zoe, what if she'd acted it out? Somehow found her way to the school during that half to three-quarters of an hour April said Gilly had disappeared? She kept looking at it, that missing time, and there was no memory other than the one of splashing water on her face. Ten minutes. She couldn't account for more than ten minutes. She pressed her fingertips to her temples.

April came out of the kitchen, holding her cell phone. "Nick says a lot of the kids on campus are going out to the school to help with the search."

Cricket untied her apron. "When I called Clint, he said dispatch is flooded, people phoning in with tips or wanting to help some way."

"I'd like to go out there," April said. "Since we're closed anyway."

"All right," Cricket agreed. "But could you and Gilly stay and help me put together some food? People will need to eat."

Gilly was surprised to be asked, but maybe Cricket was keeping tabs on Gilly. Maybe she'd been assigned by Clint to watch Gilly's every move.

They made sandwiches, working side by side, assembly-line style, until they had enough to fill the two large Coleman coolers Cricket had hauled out of the storage room. They didn't talk much, but Gilly felt under scrutiny. It bothered her, yet she could hardly blame Cricket or April. She'd wonder, too, if one of them had claimed to know not who had taken Zoe but who had not. What had possessed her? The dream had shown her almost nothing of the woman's face.

She followed April out the restaurant door, wheeling one of the coolers. Together they lifted it and the second cooler into the bed of Cricket's truck. Cricket locked the door and joined them.

"I truly don't know anything." Gilly felt pressured to defend herself, and it irked her. She didn't owe these women, or anyone in this town, an explanation.

Cricket fastened the tailgate and turned, searching Gilly's face.

"It's just weird, what you said—that it isn't Zoe's mom who has her." April shouldered her purse.

"Are you accusing me of something?"

April's eyes rounded; her "noooo" was drawn out; her expression, like Cricket's, was wary, as if Gilly was overreacting.

Was she? Gilly didn't know. She was uncomfortable; she wanted to go. She said, "I would have told you if I knew, if I had evidence—concrete evidence of where Zoe is, or who took her."

"I hope so." Cricket slid on her sunglasses.

After a round of uneasy goodbyes, they got into their cars. Driving away, Gilly's mind churned. That missing time she couldn't account for—what if it led to her being investigated? But there was more to it than missing time, wasn't there? Much more for them to find out about her—unless they already knew.

It was called tunnel vision when law enforcement honed in on a suspect, when they made up a story to fit the crime.

A horn honked, and Gilly jerked her glance to the rearview, where a driver, a man, had his arms thrown up in question. She lowered her gaze, looking now through the windshield. It was a moment before the scene assimilated itself into recognizable form. The intersection where she sat was familiar. A right turn would take her to her house, but she had no idea how she'd gotten here, no recollection of the drive from the café, nor any idea how long she might have been sitting here. The man behind her, giving up, roared around her. She kept her head down, bent to her knuckled grip on the steering wheel.

Come home. Her mother's plea drifted through Gilly's mind. She didn't even know where home was anymore.

She wanted a drink. The longing was visceral, biting. There was a liquor store in the strip center back about a half mile. She passed it every day. It seemed sensible to go there. The idea was a finger, pointing. A remedy within reach . . .

Where was Zoe?

What if Gilly had taken her? What if she had hidden Zoe? But where? Where would she hide a little girl?

Her house? Was that possible? Could she have put Zoe in a closet? The extra bedroom?

Oh my God!

She made the right turn too fast, and the tires squealed, the rear end of the SUV fishtailed. Still she kept her foot on the accelerator, hard, only backing off when she saw the truck, the light gray F-250, in her driveway. She recognized it. It was Jake Halstead's truck. She recognized him, the man himself, sitting on her front steps. She stopped in the road, looking at him through the windshield, heart slamming her chest wall. She could keep going, but he would come after her. If she had taken Zoe, the entire town of Wyatt would chase her down.

Jake was standing by the time she pulled to the curb and got out. She came around the front of her car, stepped onto the sidewalk.

"I've been waiting for you. I hope you don't mind," he said.

She stared at him, thrown by his demeanor. It was as if he'd come to her hat in hand. As if he were making an appeal. He looked awful. It wasn't only his physical appearance—the scruff of his beard, or the clothes he wore that looked slept in and reeked faintly of body odor and despair. No. The change in him was deeper than that. She sensed his panic, of course, but there was something else working in his eyes, something equally, or perhaps even more, horrific—guilt. She recognized it. She knew it well. Her hand rose almost of its own volition. If he had been close enough, she would have clasped his arm, used her touch as a means to say she understood. But neither of them moved to close the distance, and she lowered her hand to her side. She heard a car in the street behind her.

Jake waited until it had passed to speak. "You've heard about Zoe. You know she's missing, right? I thought you could help."

Gilly eyed him, still confused.

"You did hear about what happened?" he prompted.

"Are you here because you think I have her?" Gilly found her voice.

His eyes narrowed.

Gilly could almost see the wheels turning in his brain.

"Do you?" he asked, and the edge in his voice might have drawn blood.

"I don't know," she said.

10

Mind reeling, Jake followed Gilly into her house. It was all he could do not to shove her aside, not to call out for Zoe. Instinct warned him not to yell, not to get rough. It made no sense that his daughter was here, but if by some bizarre chance he was wrong and Zoe *was* here, the easiest way to get her back was to let Gilly lead him to her. So he went with her from the front room through an arched doorway into an adjacent smaller front room, an office area if the desk and single chair were any indication. One wall was stacked with cardboard boxes. Books were piled along another wall. A second door led into a bedroom that was empty.

Gilly yanked open the closet door.

From behind her Jake saw it was empty, too.

Gilly whispered something that sounded like, "She isn't here," but his pulse was so loud in his ears, he couldn't be sure.

They left the room, heels ringing as they crossed the hardwood floor. He followed her into a hallway.

"I didn't know when I moved here how long I'd stay," she said, and he thought she sounded panicked, as panicked as he felt.

He caught her by her shoulder, spinning her around. "What is going on? Do you have my daughter or not?"

They were standing in front of another door, one that was closed. She gestured toward it. "My room." And she reached to open it.

But Jake was faster, almost violent when he thrust open the door ahead of her, making it hit the wall. From the sound, he figured the knob had done some damage. He crossed the threshold, sweeping the room with his glance, taking in the furnishings: an antique vanity, one of those French-looking upholstered chairs, a four-poster bed. More unopened cardboard cartons.

But no Zoe. She wasn't there, not in the room itself or in the closet. Not in the master bath or the tiny powder room across from the kitchen.

"What the hell?" Jake pushed his hands over his head. They were in the kitchen now, having searched the laundry room and the walk-in pantry.

"I didn't take her, thank God. Thank God." Gilly repeated herself, sagging against the countertop. Jake had the sense if it hadn't been there she would have crumpled to the floor. He realized she was fighting tears.

Jake eyed her, wary, suspicious. "What made you think you did?"

She met his glance. "It's a long story. I doubt you'd care to hear it."

"Try me," he said, because he needed her, needed the ability she had—or might have—to help him find Zoe.

"Why are you here? How did you find out where I live?"

From the lift of her chin and the note of challenge in her voice, he thought she'd guessed his reason for seeking her out and had decided to shut him down.

"Your landlord, Ruth Rendell, is a friend. We work together sometimes. She and Augie Bright and I have done some construction projects together." Jake looked out the breakfast nook window. House finches shopped a feeder hanging from an old maple tree. A garden, or the remains of one, ran the length of the back fence line. "Up until this morning I was positive my ex-wife and her boyfriend had Zoe." He turned his gaze back to Gilly.

She didn't try to fill the silence, and he had the impression she was waiting for him to lay it out: Why he'd come. What he wanted.

"You told Clint—Captain Mackie—that it wasn't Stephanie, Zoe's mom, but some other woman who took Zoe. I want to know who she is. You can tell me."

"I wish I could."

"You can," he insisted over his own doubt. "On Wednesday when Zoe and I were at the café, and I couldn't find my wallet, you knew where it was."

"Yes, but that was some kind of fluke. I don't know how I knew."

"But you did. So you must know where Zoe is, who she's with."

"It doesn't work like that," she said.

"I don't care how this bullshit works—"

She interrupted him. "By *bullshit* I'm assuming you mean my 'knowing.'" She quirked air quotes. "If you don't believe in it, why are you here? Why are you asking me where Zoe is? And just for the record, if I did 'know' such a thing, I'd have told you or the cops—"

"Jesus Christ! Don't you get it?" Desperation made him shout. "My little girl's safety—her life—is at stake here! Do you understand what it's like—to lose your child?"

"Yes. Better than you know."

Gilly's reply was barely audible above the heated sound of his breath, but it caught his attention. Jake looked sharply at her.

"When I told you Wednesday that my husband died suddenly? He was murdered in Houston three years ago in an armed robbery."

"I'm sorry." Jake wasn't going to say that he knew, that Clint Mackie had told him. As private as he sensed Gilly was, he knew she wouldn't

Barbara Taylor Sissel

appreciate hearing that her personal history had been a topic of conversation between men who were virtual strangers to her. Nor could he bring himself to mention the media coverage—that it had been reported she'd known it would happen in advance. What if Clint was right, and it was only a lot of media hype?

"I was six and a half months pregnant," Gilly went on in a low voice, "and the shock, they think it was the shock, caused me to—I went into labor. Too soon. I lost our baby, Sophie, our little girl. She would be near Zoe's age, a little over three years old now."

Jake was so much taken aback that his head reeled. "I'm so sorry." He repeated his apology, and he was thinking Clint must not know Gilly had lost her baby, too. The fact must not have surfaced when Cricket was checking her out. But Jake had sensed it, hadn't he? That there was something about Gilly—a poignancy, some tender vulnerability. He didn't know how to characterize it. Only that he'd felt attracted to her, to her warmth, to the quiet light in her eyes that was belied by an underscore of grief and an anxiousness that seemed entrenched. He'd resisted an urge to draw her out. His mother often said—and his history with women proved it—that he had a mostly unfortunate penchant for those who were lost, a wish to reach out to them, to give them his hand. But he had no time for that now. "I'm really sorry." He offered a third apology.

"Thank you. But my point in telling you is to show you that I do know what it's like."

"Yeah, okay, but you told Mackie it wasn't Steph—my ex—who has Zoe, which would suggest you know who does."

"What I saw was in a dream, as weird as that sounds, and somehow—it's like I have an impression of something in here." She touched her temples. "Maybe it's intuition that tells me it's not Zoe's mother who has taken her. For whatever that's worth. I did see a woman, but not clearly enough to give you a description."

"How can you have this—do this? You really don't know how it works?" Jake wanted to call bullshit on her. He bit back a renewed urge to tell her he'd heard how she'd seen her husband's murder before it happened, too. He wanted to say that if she was in the habit of dreaming events before they happened, she must have some clue how it worked. But he was afraid of scaring her or pissing her off. He could lose her, lose all hope of her help entirely if he did that. Still, he said, "It's your own brain, your own mind, for God's sake."

"I know. It's the worst—I'm never shown anything useful." She seemed crushed, making the admission. "Some people think it's cool, a gift. To me it's a curse."

"Is that how you knew about my wallet? You saw it in a dream?"

"No. The information was just there in my mind. I wasn't even aware of it until it came out of my mouth. It happens that way sometimes."

"Were you in a trance?" Jake pulled a chair away from the kitchen table and spun it toward her, an invitation. "Couldn't you do the same thing now? Sit down here, close your eyes, and it would come to you. Right? You'd see—"

"I told you—"

"It doesn't work that way—yeah." Jake picked up the chair again and set it down. "They want me to take a polygraph." He didn't know why he was telling her. He was just so goddamned panicked on so many levels.

"Who?"

"The Madrone County sheriff's office."

"How did they get involved?"

"Mackie called them in."

"You aren't happy for their assistance."

"I'm glad for whatever help I can get to find Zoe." He paused.

"But?"

"They're getting a warrant to search my house."

"Are you serious? I thought you and Captain Mackie were friends."

Jake hooted. "Yeah, he said I shouldn't take it personally. It's routine, ruling out family, blah, blah, blah. Like I'd kidnap my own kid. Or, hey, maybe my mom, Zoe's grandma, is the one."

Gilly averted her face, but not before Jake saw her expression harden.

"What?" he said.

"Nothing, really," she answered. "I just don't have a lot of faith in cops."

Jake gave her time to explain, and when she didn't he said, "Well, maybe they're right to polygraph me."

Gilly glanced at him, brows raised.

"Ah!" He pushed his hands in front of him, a gesture of disgust. "It doesn't make sense. It's just that after Zoe's mom left, Zoe was really scared. She cried a lot, had nightmares. She was afraid I'd go away, too. I promised her it wouldn't ever happen. I should have been there, protected her—" Jake swiped his face, under his nose. He shifted his glance to the window.

There'd been nights—although not so many in recent weeks—when Zoe had wakened, sobbing, and he'd gone to her, pulled her snugly against him, and paced with her through the darkened house, letting her cry it out against his shoulder. Some nights, she came to him, crawling into his bed. She'd pat his cheek, whispering, *Monsters, Daddy.* And he'd pull her close, barely waking, mumbling nonsense. He could feel her now, the shape of her small warm bulk in his arms, the silky top of her head nestled underneath his chin. He smelled her powdery sweetness. But the memory was shot through with the cold reality of her absence, and his anguish—that he hadn't been there, hadn't kept her safe—seared his chest.

"I wasn't there." Jake looked back at Gilly. "I broke my promise."

"You can't possibly be with her every moment, Jake. It's not your fault. You can't take this on."

Gilly's defense of him was pained, as if she took it personally that he would blame himself. But she didn't know the history, and to fully explain it would entail entering a labyrinthine cave full of his missteps, dating back to the moment of Zoe's conception, the initial days when he'd first learned he was going to be a father. If he were to relate the details, he could only imagine Gilly's disgust. It hadn't been his finest hour.

He said, "Zoe asked me about her mom on Wednesday, when I dropped her at school." It was a simpler explanation and valid as evidence that he lacked fatherly skills. His inattention was inexcusable. "It was almost the last thing she said to me. She wanted to know if her mom knew where she was. I should have followed up, made her tell me why she was asking."

"It was unusual, Zoe bringing up her mom?"

"The way it came out of the blue was weird. But I let it go. If I'd pushed, she might have told me she'd talked to her mom, given me a clue of their plans."

"Unless her mom asked her to keep them secret."

"Yeah," Jake said. That was a possibility. As young as she was, Zoe was good at keeping secrets. Especially her mother's secrets. After Stephanie had moved out, they'd been eating Froot Loops one morning when Zoe said suddenly that she knew where her mommy hid her "med'cine." That was how Steph had explained it to Zoe. The bottle of vodka she'd been caught stowing in the linen closet was "Mommy's medicine." *Don't tell Daddy*, Steph had said. She had made Zoe promise, and promises were serious business. Telling Jake had made Zoe cry. She might be young, but she understood about betrayal. It had nearly killed him. He'd wanted to smash the half-finished bottle of Smirnoff when he'd found it. Or drink it. But he wasn't much of a drinker, near zero now since Steph. He could be kind of militantly antidrinking, actually, a real teetotaler, the way an ex-smoker could become a zealot about not smoking.

He glanced at Gilly. "It's hard to believe after everything Steph has done, that Zoe still wants her mom. She wants Steph's attention, her approval. You've seen the satin ribbon she carries?"

Gilly nodded.

"It's from one of Steph's nightgowns. After she left, Zoe got scissors and cut it off herself. She wasn't even two. I couldn't believe it—when I think what could have happened! She's never let it out of her sight since. Then there's the front of the refrigerator at home. It's covered up with pictures Zoe's done for her mother. She draws them faster than I can mail them."

"That sounds—" Gilly broke off.

"Sad," Jake supplied.

"Do *you* think Zoe's with Stephanie?"

"I don't know," Jake answered. "Of all the possibilities—"

"Yes," Gilly said, understanding his meaning at once: that from a veritable menu of horrors, the one possibility Jake—or anyone—would choose was that Zoe had been taken by her mother.

He kept Gilly's gaze. Her eyes, their expression, were commiserative. He had noticed them before. They were an unusual color, all shades of gray like a sky before a sudden summer storm.

He said, "Did you know Clint is looking into your background?" He thought maybe it was her eyes that made him want to clue her in, or the air of vulnerability about her that seemed somehow braced with a kind of tensile strength. He didn't miss it either. The flash of panic that leaped through her gaze was as sharp and silvery as a minnow and gone as fast. He thought of what Clint had said, that Gilly knew more than she was telling. Jake felt it, too, but she'd been through so much—maybe what she was withholding had nothing to do with his ex, or his missing daughter, and everything to do with maintaining control, some degree of privacy.

Gilly said, "I guess I expected it. Would you like some coffee? Wouldn't take a minute to brew. Or iced tea—"

"You're from Houston, right? That's where Steph lives. Maybe you know her, crossed paths with her." Jake repeated the theory Clint had floated.

"No. I don't—"

"I think it's the connection, both of you living there—that's what's got Clint's interest. But like I said to Clint, Stephanie's into booze and drugs. I told him I didn't think you ran in those circles."

Gilly looked at the floor.

"You don't, do you?"

It was a moment before she looked back up at him, and when she did there was something in her eyes, the set of her jaw—a kind of defiance. "I've been sober eight months and six days," she said. "It's still a battle. Some days I don't know that it's worth it. I don't know your ex, though. I didn't have anything to do with taking your daughter."

A silence gathered while Jake fought a muddy river of conflicting emotions. Part of him felt bad for Gilly. The handful of words she'd given him were freighted with new hope and old misery, but he wasn't sure he trusted her, or maybe he just didn't want to. It pissed him off, hearing she'd been on the same path as Steph. So now she was reformed. How long would that last? Stephanie had never stayed sober longer than a year.

Jake studied Gilly, her straight spine, the stiff angle of her shoulders. Steph had never held herself so upright while speaking of her failings. She had never looked him so directly in the eye. Gilly wasn't apologizing; she wasn't making promises. It was as if whatever strength she had, she'd found it in her weakness. He remembered something his mom had said, that the other side of a person's greatest character flaw was often what turned out to be their saving grace. Something like that. But he didn't want it, this war in his head.

"Clint doesn't think Zoe's mom is involved either," he said. "He's got local law enforcement helping folks from town set up a search center at Zoe's school, where she was last seen."

"I heard about it," Gilly said. "Look, you should know, Captain Mackie has a reason, or he thinks he does, to be suspicious of me— more than just the fact that I'm from Houston."

Jake waited.

"Back when I was really out of it, after Brian was murdered, and I had lost Sophie, I suffered from blackouts. I lost time, lost track of where I was. I did things and later I couldn't clearly remember doing them. I was in therapy for a while, and the psychiatrist I saw said it was to be expected—not only because of the drinking and drugs but also just the trauma of Brian being murdered and losing Sophie the way I did. He said the blackouts were also symptomatic of posttraumatic stress."

"It makes sense," Jake said. "I have a buddy who fought in Afghanistan. Maybe you've met him? AJ Isley? He's struggled with it, too—PTSD. He's doing great now, but it's taken a while."

"Yeah, I thought I was past it. But maybe not."

"What makes you say that?"

Gilly tucked her hair behind her ears. "On Thursday, evidently around the time Zoe was picked up from school, I was—I can't really account for my whereabouts for about thirty or forty minutes."

"What do you mean?"

"I was upset. I'd had the dream about Zoe, and the day before, I'd gotten an unsettling call from the detective who's working my husband's case. I went to the restroom and splashed water on my face. I thought I was gone a matter of minutes, but according to April I was gone a lot longer."

"What? Is she your keeper or something? She knows how long you're on a break? Even if she does, let's say you were MIA, what makes you think you went off and took Zoe?" As he questioned Gilly, though, the thought was there in his mind—how easily Zoe would have gone with Gilly. There was no doubt the two had formed a bond.

"But I didn't, right? She isn't here. We both looked and didn't find her."

Gilly looked uncertain, even frightened. Jake didn't know what to make of her answer, her demeanor. It unsettled him, caught at his heart. Somehow he found himself wanting to pull her into his arms and comfort her. He said, "I think April must be jerking your chain. Anyway, a half hour, even forty minutes, is only enough time to drive from Cricket's to the school and back. You wouldn't have been able to make it here, or much of anyplace else, and then back in time to work your shift."

Gilly traced a line across her forehead, ran her fingertips around the shell of her ear.

"You did work your shift?" Jake held Gilly's gaze.

"Yes. But there's still the missing time."

He could see it was working on her, that she honestly didn't remember what she'd been doing. Either that, or she was a damn fine actress.

"I honestly couldn't account for my whereabouts when Captain Mackie asked, so naturally, he's suspicious. If he knows about the drinking and drug use—that's bound to make his impression of me even worse. But I swear to you, I've never met your ex-wife, and I would never—" Gilly broke off, jerking her glance away.

"You'd never . . ." Jake prompted.

Instead of answering, Gilly said, "April covered for me with Captain Mackie."

Jake sensed her sidestep was deliberate, and it gave him pause, but it was true, what he'd told her. She'd have needed more than thirty minutes to take his daughter. Clint must have come to the same conclusion. He'd indicated he had some concern in regard to Gilly, but it couldn't be too serious, otherwise he'd have taken Gilly in for questioning. It was possible he'd have arrested her. In Jake's experience, Clint wasn't the kind of cop to mess around or take chances.

Gilly said, "I don't know why April spoke up for me. I don't think it's because she trusts me."

What about a motive? The question rose and fell in Jake's mind, subliminal, fleeting. "Did you know—the statistics on kidnapped children, the ones who are taken by strangers—the longer it goes past the first twenty-four hours—" His voice cracked, and he paused, working to keep his cool. "If you know anything, I don't give a shit how woo-woo it is, you have to tell me."

"I wish I did."

"I found a trike, a pink trike, in the woods behind the school. The same woods in the story you made up for Zoe about the eyeball-eating monsters."

Gilly hugged herself, rubbed her upper arms.

Something in the gesture, her expression, brought Jake upright. "That mean something to you?"

"No," she said, and then, "Yes."

She was flustered, and Jake made himself wait, giving her space to sort it out, whatever was in her mind.

"I saw a pink tricycle in my dream. It was turned on its side. There were trees—"

"That's it! That's exactly how I found it—" Jake's phone went off, and putting up his finger—a plea that Gilly hold on—he pulled it from his jeans pocket, intent on silencing it. But on seeing it was the Wyatt PD, he swiped the phone's face, head empty, heart paused.

"Jake? It's Sergeant Carter, Ken Carter, with the Wyatt police."

"Yes?" Jake knew Ken but not well.

"Listen, we're up here north of Greeley, on FM 1097, at a Texaco station in Nickel Bend. You know where I'm talking about?"

"My grandparents had a farm there." They were dead now, but when Jake was a kid he had often spent summers with them, getting up before first light to help his granddad milk the cows and gather the eggs before they headed out to do other chores that centered around the crops he grew, mostly corn for silage and cotton. The farm had been sold years ago, but Jake still drove that way whenever he had business in Waco, or the Dallas–Fort Worth metroplex. Nickel Bend was a speed trap, a one-light, wide space in the road. Blink and you'd miss it.

"Well, we found something here, in a dumpster behind the station. Clothes. A sack with some clothes in it."

Jake couldn't speak. His gut squeezed into a hard knot.

"Mr. Halstead? Jake? You there?"

"Yeah." He managed to work the word out of his mouth. He caught movement from the corner of his eye, became aware of Gilly, that she'd pushed a chair close behind him.

"Sit down," she said, and he did.

"Zoe. Are they Zoe's clothes?" he asked.

"Might be. They definitely belong to a little girl—"

Jake jerked to his feet. "The Texaco is at the corner of 1097 and CR 231, right? I'm on my way."

"Yes sir, but hold up a second—"

Jake didn't. He hung up on Sergeant Carter and left Gilly's kitchen, aware of her half running to keep up as he strode through her house.

"What's happened? Did they find Zoe?" She grabbed his arm at the front door. "Maybe you shouldn't drive. You look ready to pass out."

Jake shook free of her grasp. "I'm fine," he said. He started down the front steps, then paused, turning back to her. "What you saw in your dream—the trike, the woman in her blue car—it's no coincidence, you dreaming those things. I bet you saw more—more than you think. Please, please—whatever you can do to see where Zoe is, please try. Please." He held her gaze.

"Yes. All right," she said.

He pulled his wallet from his pocket, handed her his business card. "My cell number's on there. Call me if you—" *What?* What did he expect her to do? Pull Zoe out of a hat?

"I know what it's like to be frightened for your child," she said. "If I can help, if something comes—"

He nodded, started to go, turned back a second time. "The call I got—Sergeant Carter found Zoe's clothes in a dumpster in Nickel Bend."

"He knows for sure they belong to Zoe?"

"That's what I'm going to find out."

11

After Jake left, Gilly went back to the kitchen where she gripped the lip of the sink, working to steady herself, her breathing, the rate of her heartbeat. God, she wanted a drink.

You going to blow eight months of sobriety? a voice in her brain, the one she'd named Miss Goody Two-shoes, asked.

Gilly hated that voice.

Call your sponsor, it said.

Shut up, she told it. Hearing the click of Bailey's nails on the tile, the jingle of his tags, she knelt beside him, scooping him into her embrace, burying her nose in his furry neck, glad for his doggy smell, his warmth, his happy wriggle. "That's what Brian and I should have named you," she whispered to him. "Wriggle. Mr. Wriggle Bottom." A half hour later, she was snapping on his leash, and the doorbell rang. She went still. *Did you know Clint is looking into your background?* Jake's earlier question jumped up in her mind. Was it the police captain out there? Some other cop?

Bailey accompanied her as she crept to the door as furtively as if she were a burglar. He kept giving her glances. She could almost read his mind: *Is this a game? Are we playing? Are you crazy?*

Most probably the latter. She answered him in her head.

Looking through the peephole, instead of the police she saw April Warner, a distorted image of her coworker in the flesh, and Gilly's heart dropped. What was April doing here so soon after Jake? Did everyone in town suddenly know where Gilly lived? She turned her back to the door.

April rang the bell again. She called Gilly's name. "I know you're in there," she said. "Your car's in the drive."

Gilly opened the door. "Actually, I was getting ready to leave." She brought Bailey forward on his leash. "We're walking to the park."

"I'll walk with you," April said.

"I'd rather you didn't." Gilly brought Bailey out onto the porch, and as if he sensed her wariness, her barely stifled offense, he only eyed the hand April held out to him. "Not if you're here to harass me some more about the time I spent in the restroom at work."

"If I've pissed you off, I'm sorry." April followed Gilly down the sidewalk.

Gilly didn't say anything.

"I covered for you."

"You think that entitles you to question me?"

"Look, you've got to admit it's damned strange you being gone so long at the same time Zoe was supposedly taken. And what gives with the bit you told Captain Mackie—that you know it wasn't her mom who picked her up?"

Gilly stopped, turning to look at April. "*Supposedly* taken?"

"Let me rephrase. That Zoe is gone is the one and only verifiable fact. Somebody's got her."

Gilly resumed walking.

"You know I was in prison for killing my husband," April said.

Gilly's step, along with her mind, faltered at the baldness of April's confession, but not noticeably. The sidewalk wasn't quite wide enough for two, and April walked a little behind Gilly, speaking to Gilly's shoulder.

"I'm by myself, too," she said. "It gets lonely, doesn't it?"

"Did you do it?" Gilly glanced sidelong at April.

"Kill my husband? Yep. I did." April answered as if she was glad to be asked. "I'd do it again, too, a thousand times. Guys like him, abusers, woman haters—they can mess with me but not my kid. We were divorced when he came over one day, just barged in and went after Nicky in a blind rage for no reason. Nicky was his own son, for God's sake. I had to stop him. No one else was going to do it. Not the law. I had a restraining order. I did everything the court said, everything the cops and my attorney said. That son of a bitch still came after me, and that was okay. I'm an adult. I could give it back as good as that bastard. I broke his fucking kneecap with a baseball bat once."

She sounded grimly proud.

Gilly turned into the park entrance, heading for the path that meandered for nearly a mile around the perimeter. Bailey pranced ahead, nose to the turf, or in the air, mapping his surroundings, every so often raising his leg. She thought if they were to become separated, Bailey would find his way back to her by way of the trail he was marking. Humans—especially children—didn't have the same ability. Birds had eaten the crumbs Hansel and Gretel left. Gilly thought of Sophie, of how precious she had been, and anger at Nick's father jammed her throat. How dare he abuse Nick?

"I know what it's like to have folks judge you when they've got no clue what you've been through, or what you're up against. Walk a mile in my shoes, I say." April's tone, her demeanor, invited commiseration, an exchange of confidences, but Gilly didn't trust April. She didn't think of April as a friend.

"People usually prefer their own shoes," she said, and she sensed April's disappointment.

They walked several moments in silence, shoulder to shoulder now because the path through the park was wider than the neighborhood sidewalk they'd left behind.

"Why are you here, April?" Gilly asked finally. "Did Captain Mackie send you?" It seemed farfetched, but who knew? "Did he think I'd talk to you, tell you all my secrets?"

"No!" April's affront sounded genuine. "I can't believe you said that." She halted her steps.

Gilly stopped, too, and turning, locked April's gaze. "I don't know anything about Zoe Halstead's disappearance." Bailey sat at her feet, leaning into her, looking anxious. He didn't like controversy.

"You think I'm going to help a cop?" April asked. "Are you kidding? After the shit that's gone down in my life? I've got no use for law enforcement, the legal system, none of that."

Gilly didn't respond.

"Okay, so maybe I did come here because I think you know something about where Zoe is. I'm not saying you had anything to do with it, and, trust me, Captain Mackie didn't send me. But I feel like there's more going on with you and that little girl than you're saying. When she comes into Cricket's with her dad, you get this look. You, like, light up or something, practically trip all over yourself waiting on them, and those pancakes—you told me from the start you weren't much for cooking, then the next thing I know, you're showing off, showing me up. I thought you were after my job."

"No! Oh God, I'm really sorry if I gave you that impression." Gilly meant it.

"Listen, we've all got history, crap we have to deal with. I think you've got your own issues with the cops for whatever reason, that like me, you've had trouble in your life. So I thought maybe we had that in common and maybe you could use a friend."

April's offer caught Gilly by surprise. She bit down on the urge to point out they had nothing in common beyond their employment, and even that connection wouldn't have been established if Brian were still alive, and they were living the life they'd planned, the one where they'd been partners, lovers, and best friends. The one where they'd planned to grow old together.

Don't you dare die before me. Don't you go off and leave me here . . .

Remembering their foolish promises to each other made her heart ache. Why was she here? The one left? That was the question that dogged her, inexplicable, unanswerable.

Now the threat of tears came, searing the undersides of her lids, and she pressed the thumb and index finger of her free hand to her eyes.

April said her name. "Gilly?" She found a tissue and handed it over.

Gilly blew her nose. Bailey was distressed, and she bent to soothe him. "I had a dream about Zoe." She regretted it, but she felt pressured to say something, and she'd sooner have cut out her tongue than share a word with April about her husband and daughter, and their loss, which was unspeakable.

"You had a dream," April repeated, tipping her head to one side, waiting for the rest.

"Yes," Gilly said. "I saw a woman taking a child from what might have been the Little Acorn Academy. I saw very clearly that the little girl was Zoe, but I've never seen the school, so I can't be sure of the location."

"The woman you saw, you know for sure it wasn't Zoe's mom?"

"Not on any level I can explain. Honestly, if I saw the woman's face, I don't remember it. It was mostly covered by dark glasses anyway. You know how dreams are—" Gilly broke off, distracted when the image of the woman from her dream came together abruptly in her mind. She was walking around the back of the metallic-blue sedan, and as if Gilly's eye were the zoom lens of a camera, she captured the motion when the woman lifted her hand to poke tendrils of dark hair beneath the hood of her sweatshirt. Now the sunlit glint of an earring was revealed. A hoop—Gilly saw it clearly—with a heart dangling from its lower arc.

"What?"

Gilly was aware of April's gaze, intrusive and sharp.

"Nothing," Gilly answered, although it wasn't. The dark hair, the earring—had her brain added those details to her vision of the woman, or had they been in Gilly's mind all along? "I didn't recognize her." Was she asking?

April was exasperated. "Then how do you know it wasn't Zoe's mother?"

"It's more like a gut feeling. It's weird. Even to me." *You really don't know how it works?* Jake's query, his disbelief, surfaced in her mind, feeling like an accusation.

"You just said, though, that you don't remember the woman's face, what she looked like." April studied Gilly. "Maybe you do, but for some reason you don't want to."

"Of course I want to." *Did she?* "Why wouldn't I?"

"You'd have to do something about it. If you knew the woman's identity you'd have to tell the cops, right? Something you want to avoid as much as me."

What if I was wrong? That was Gilly's biggest fear. That if she were to see the woman's image vividly enough to describe it, the police would find a woman to match the description, and not necessarily the right woman. It had happened before. Crimes were committed, and the wrong people were arrested for them. She couldn't live with it if that were to happen.

April shrugged. "I didn't mean anything. It was just a thought."

They shared a beat of silence, one long enough that Gilly had time to regret it again, confiding in April of all people. Gilly hadn't even told Liz, and it felt wrong somehow that April knew and Liz, with whom she actually felt a kinship, didn't.

"I'm going out to the Little Acorn." April broke into Gilly's thoughts. "I could take you there. Maybe you should check it out. See if it's the same building as the one you dreamed about. Who knows, it might shake something loose."

"I don't know . . ." Gilly looked into the middle distance, conscious of her pulse beating in her temples, a less prominent drumroll of alarm.

"Maybe nothing will come of it, but you should at least check it out. What if something clicks that helps the cops find Zoe?"

Gilly didn't answer.

"I thought you wanted to help."

"I've got plans for dinner." Gilly debated. If she went out to the school and joined the search, who knew how long she'd be? She doubted she'd have time to cook. But she could call Liz. Maybe she'd want to help hunt for Zoe, too. "Okay," she said to April. "I'll come." Gilly brought Bailey around, retracing their steps toward the park entrance. It was the idea that Zoe could be in the hands of a stranger, frightened and bewildered, that weighed on her. That, and her memory of Jake, the panic and grief in his eyes that was so like Gilly's own.

"So you can really see the future in your dreams?" April asked. "You're psychic? I've never known anyone who could do that. It's so cool."

"Not really."

"Maybe you could see my future? Not now but sometime? We could sit down—"

"You realize I'm probably a suspect," Gilly said. Anything to divert April's attention.

April laughed. "Yeah, me too. Half the town is. I heard even Jake and his mom are suspects."

"That's ridiculous." Gilly left it there, keeping it to herself that she already knew.

"Yeah. But you know how people talk, the way they spread rumors, especially in a town as small as Wyatt. Have you had other dreams like this one about Zoe? I mean where something terrible happens?"

They were all terrible. Every precognitive dream Gilly had ever had involved a tragedy of some sort. "You think it's cool, having the dreams," she said. "But it's not."

"How often do they come?"

"Sometimes I go a long time, months, as much as a year, between them." Long enough that, at a few times in her life, Gilly had felt she was rid of them. She'd been relieved, as if a curse had been lifted. "They always come back, though, and they're always about something bad."

"But if you have a dream far enough in advance, you can stop whatever it is from happening, right?"

Gilly thought of Brian, the robbery and his murder—how he had dismissed her dream about it, how she had gone along, both of them ignoring the rightful warning they'd been sent. And she thought of Tommy, how she'd been rebuked for relaying what turned out to be a false alarm about his brother. She thought if she were to tally the score, her dreams and visions had been wrong more often than right.

But Jake believed in them.

Funny what desperation could do, the way it could cause you to toss aside your usual skepticism. She felt that about Jake, that in his ordinary life he was a cautious man, a good man, steady and reliable. Grounded. She doubted that in handling his current crisis, should it continue, he would do what Gilly had done and drink, or take drugs, to escape it. She had noted his surprise and the accompanying flash of his distaste when he realized she was the same as his ex-wife, only sober. For now anyway.

Could she speak to the future? Could she alter it? No. Gilly glanced at April, and gave her the same answer she'd given Jake. "The dreams don't work that way."

She took Bailey into the house and unsnapped his leash, then tried to reach Liz. When she was instructed by her voice mail to leave a message, she said, "Hey, it's me, Gilly. Change of plans. They've set up a search headquarters for Zoe at the Little Acorn. I'm going out there now. I'm hoping you'll want to come out, that we can meet there instead of the house. I doubt I'll have time to cook. Maybe we could go out to dinner? Call me, okay?" Clicking off, she stowed her phone. At her feet, Bailey wagged his tail, looking at her with soulful eyes, already missing her. "I'll be back," she told him.

He trotted with her to the front door. She closed it behind her, shutting him from view. Didn't matter how many times she left him, she always felt vaguely guilty.

She waved her car keys at April, who was parked and waiting at the curb. "I'll follow you," she called.

"Oh." The syllable popped out of April's mouth, a little puff of disappointed air. "I thought we'd ride together."

Gilly shook her head. Telling April about the dream had been enough of a mistake. She wasn't about to trap herself inside April's car, too. She was curious now, fascinated. The eager light of belief shone from her eyes. She had questions. She would go on and on, picking at Gilly, wanting to know all about her "cool" so-called "psychic" power. For different reasons, the believers were as bad as the skeptics. Throughout her life, at a party or with a group of people, when Gilly had slipped and let on that she sometimes knew the future, she'd been hounded for the lottery numbers, or next week's stock pick, and her refusal to provide such tips had been met with disgust. She was screwing with them, people would say. She was messed up, a weirdo. A fake, a fraud.

Why can't you be normal?

Her mother's worn-out, oft-repeated query ran through Gilly's mind. *Dreams are just dreams . . . They aren't real . . . I don't want to hear it . . . You're too sensitive . . . You let your imagination run away with you.*

Gilly's mom had said it all.

"I'll follow you," Gilly repeated now.

It wasn't until they left the Wyatt city limits, where Main turned into FM 1620, heading west, that Gilly began to wonder, actually to worry a bit, where April was taking her. She had expected the Little Acorn Academy to be in town. It crossed her mind that if she were to drop back, turn around, April might not notice. What could she do about it anyway?

April's turn signal blinked on, and Gilly followed her onto a meandering road named Shady Oaks. The tarred, two-lane ribbon of asphalt rose gently and then more sharply where it had been cut through the bleached bone of a limestone cliff. Spiny ears of prickly pear cactus and sharp-leaved clumps of yucca clung to the dry, rocky sides, fiercely green, tenacious, defiant in their hold on life.

Gilly was back to telling herself she was on a fool's errand when, cresting yet another hill, she caught sight of it, the building from her dream, and her foot backed off the accelerator. Her blood cooled in her veins. The Little Acorn Academy was isolated and small and eerily familiar. Gilly knew it as well as if she had seen it for real dozens of times. She knew the half-circle drive in front, the rectangle of black asphalt parking lot to the right. She recognized the picnic grounds, an area some distance away from the school, beyond the parking lot. Sturdy tables and a couple of barbecue grills were scattered over the wide apron of shade cast by a grouping of massive live oaks. The scene that had been quiet—except for Zoe and the woman—in Gilly's dream was now teeming with activity.

Cars, many of them belonging to law enforcement, were parked everywhere. Dozens of people were gathered in the picnic area, a majority wearing orange vests. There were several dogs, and a helicopter waited in a nearby field. Gilly pulled over behind April across the road from the school, nosing her RAV4 onto the graveled shoulder.

"Were you listening to the news?" April asked, meeting Gilly at the back of her car. She went on before Gilly could answer. "The tricycle Jake found in the woods? They're saying it's Zoe's, that he confirmed hers is missing."

"Really?" Gilly's composure was pretense. It frightened her having the images from her dream become confirmed fact—first by Jake and now the media. She thought of the call he'd gotten, the one advising him that Zoe's clothing had been discovered north of here in a dumpster near Greeley. It was horrifying—all of it. Gilly didn't know what to hope for. That the trike and the clothing proved to belong to Zoe? That they didn't? She crossed the street with April, and paused with her at the edge of the parking lot.

"Look, KTKY News is here, and that's Suki Daniels." April nodded at a nearby news van, where a strikingly beautiful Asian woman was interviewing a man in a uniform. "She is so gorgeous, isn't she?" April sounded in awe. "I watch her on the news all the time."

KTKY broadcast out of Greeley. Like April, Gilly watched the station's newscasts. Suki Daniels was an investigative reporter for the channel. There were other reporter types scattered throughout the crowd, poised and waiting. Like vultures, Gilly thought. And necessary at the same time. They performed a service, getting the word out. But the media's presence lent a kind of surreal and terrible urgency to the atmosphere. It was a feeling Gilly remembered from when Brian was murdered, and she felt the same sick sinking in her stomach. The same icy fear seized her heart.

Across the parking lot, from behind one of the picnic tables, someone—Gilly recognized it was Sergeant Ken Carter—hollered for the crowd's attention. There were other folks who looked familiar from when she'd served them at Cricket's. Gilly saw Mandy and Augie

Bright, sitting at a table with Shea and AJ from the xL Ranch east of Wyatt. *What was their last name?* Jake had mentioned it earlier, but she couldn't remember. She did know Shea's mom, Dru Gallagher. A local and well-loved baker and caterer, Dru supplied Cricket's with a variety of breads and pastries.

But it was catching sight of Kenna Sweet, the owner of the Little Acorn Academy, that jolted Gilly's heart. Kenna was by herself, part of the crowd but not. And although Gilly was several feet from her, Kenna's grief, her exhaustion and shock, was palpable. She would have to live with the consequences of this, a child having been abducted from her school—and the possible legal ramifications—for the rest of her life.

"First, thank you to all of you for coming out here today to help us hunt for Zoe. I know most of you know her and her dad, Jake." Sergeant Carter's voice lifted over the crowd. "We all want to find her, but for the search to be effective, we need to be organized. Make sure to sign in before you head out. I know most of you are familiar with the terrain. You know how difficult it is getting through a heavy growth of cedar. You're not careful, it'll poke your eye out, scratch up your skin right through your clothes, so go slow. Keep each other in view. I see some of you have got loppers and such and can cut a path. Maybe those of you who don't could join up with the ones who do. Remember you're not only looking for Zoe but also for clues. You see anything the least bit suspicious, or questionable, anything looks out of place, you give a shout, okay?"

A general mutter of assent rose.

"Above all, folks, be careful and stay safe." Clint Mackie stepped forward to address the volunteers. "We appreciate—Jake here does, too—we appreciate y'all coming out."

Gilly caught sight of Jake now, standing in the police captain's shadow. His gaze, meeting hers briefly, was hard and lightless, his jaw rigid, back and shoulders stiff. But Gilly knew his terror and anguish. She saw the raw vulnerability fishing through his eyes. She'd seen the same look in her own eyes every time she'd looked in the mirror in the days after Brian's murder. And like Jake, she had tried holding on to what little control she'd had left through sheer grit. She'd been where Jake was now. She still went there on nights when she couldn't sleep, when the memory would seize her in its monstrous fist, forcing her to relive it—Brian's loss and then Sophie's. She wouldn't wish the nightmare on anyone.

Her throat tightened in commiseration. What had been found in Nickel Bend? What had he been forced to look at and identify?

Something awful, she thought.

"Do you know who took Zoe, Captain?" A man Gilly couldn't see called out the question. Around her the crowd, which had been on the verge of breaking apart, shifted uneasily back together, becoming still.

"Is it true it's not her mom who has her?" Another man raised his voice.

"Is there some maniac on the loose? Should we be worried about our kids?" A woman spoke up, and from the sound of her, she was already worried.

"We haven't ruled out any possibility, so by all means, exercise caution with your kids, with yourselves. Watch out for each other."

Jake stepped forward, interrupting Mackie. He began by thanking everyone for coming out. Gilly noticed he made eye contact with several folks. He said, "I wonder if any of you would be willing to go up to Nickel Bend and help law enforcement up there search the area around the Texaco station at the corner of 1097 and County Road 231? Do you know the location?"

"Sure," several people answered at once.

"Why?" someone—a woman Gilly couldn't see—asked. "Did you find something there?"

Before Jake could answer, another person, a man holding a notepad, interrupted Jake to ask the question. A reporter, Gilly thought.

"Can you confirm the rumor that the trike you found in the woods here behind the school last night belongs to your daughter?"

"No. Not yet," Jake said. "I know the media is reporting that I confirmed it was hers, but I didn't. I did believe it was Zoe's when I first found it, but when I got it into good light, it looked older than hers, as if it had been outside in the weather for a while. I try to keep Zoe's trike in the garage, but when I looked, it wasn't there. My mother thinks we could have left it at her house. She's checking that out now. It's possible Zoe left it at a neighbor's house. If any of you see it, please let me or the police know."

An assenting murmur rose from the crowd.

"So where's the trike you found now?" the reporter asked.

"The police sent it to the lab—"

"Okay." Captain Mackie moved to Jake's side, making it clear he wanted an end to the questions.

The reporter ignored him. "Can you tell us more about what was found up at Nickel Bend?"

"We've got volunteers at that location working with the Madrone County sheriff's department." Mackie spoke before Jake could. "If you want to go there to help out, go right on. Sheriff Wiley, John Wiley, is handling that operation. Those of you staying here, if you'd gather round a minute, we've gridded out and color coded a search area from the woods here through the back gate, extending east and west of a line on either side of the trail back there. We're assigning a team to each grid so we don't miss anything."

"I'm staying here." April caught Gilly's eye. "I know these woods a bit. I've done some hiking around Monarch Lake. You?"

Gilly answered she was staying put, too. "I just need to make a call."

April nodded and headed for the picnic table where Sergeant Carter was dividing folks into teams.

Gilly dialed Liz's number, and, getting her voice mail again, she left a second message, telling Liz where she was. "It's really scary," she said. "There are a lot of people here, but they can use all the help they can get. Come if you can, okay? Or maybe you're here?" The possibility flashed through Gilly's mind, and she looked around as if she might spot Liz. "I'm canceling dinner," she said. "I feel like I've got to stay and help." Gilly paused. "Call me back. If you're here maybe we can get something to eat later."

Stowing her phone, she saw Jake and the police captain, and she started to go in the opposite direction, but then she stopped. She wasn't doing herself any favors avoiding the inevitable.

"I'd like to clear the air, Captain, if I may." Gilly addressed the man in uniform as she approached him, but she was aware of Jake. She had an impression of his surprise. Maybe he had imagined she would confine herself to the shadows in the hope of escaping notice.

"How can I help?" Captain Mackie asked.

"You have some concerns about my whereabouts at the time Zoe was taken, you think I was involved—"

"We can't rule out anyone—" the captain began.

Jake interrupted. "The sack with Zoe's clothes in the dumpster—"

Mackie said, "That isn't something we're ready to make public."

"He's worried folks will panic." Jake ran a hand over his head.

"I'd appreciate it if you'd keep the news to yourself," Captain Mackie said.

"Yes, of course," Gilly answered.

He went on. "What interests me about you in regard to Zoe's disappearance is your claim that it isn't her mother who took her. I understand now your certainty stems from a dream you had? Is that right?"

"You told him?" Gilly addressed Jake, disbelieving, appalled.

"I'm sorry," he said, but it barely registered with Gilly.

She was furious, mortified, some combination of the two.

He said, "It's my daughter's life that's at stake. If you can help—"

"I can't," she said. She turned to the police captain. "As I explained to Jake, I didn't see anything clearly enough to be of any help, which is why I wasn't as forthcoming as I might have been when you asked me about my statement before. I'm uncomfortable talking about the experience. Obviously, from your tone of voice, you don't believe it's valid anyway," she finished drily.

"Well, to be honest," Mackie said, "I don't know what I believe. Are you psychic? Do you call yourself that?"

"I don't call myself anything, Captain, and if the dream had shown me in any detail how Zoe was taken, or by whom, or where, I would have told you immediately." A flash in her mind illuminated a dark tendril of hair, a heart dangling from the gold loop of an earring. Gilly slammed the door on the images.

"If only you'd give it a chance," Jake said.

Gilly looked away into the middle distance, wishing she'd remembered her sunglasses. Light in the Hill Country could be harsh, more brilliant than in Houston. It was all the rock, she thought. Beneath the sun's unforgiving glare, the wind-scoured limestone ridges and cliffs shone as blinding white as glacial snow.

Captain Mackie said, "I've run into a few officers who've worked cases with psychics. One I heard about recently, a woman—a psychic in Florida—told police where to find the weapon in a pretty high-profile murder case down there. She saw the location in a dream. It led to the killer's arrest. I can't argue with results like that."

"So you know it can work." Jake was animated.

"It's not reliable." Gilly was almost pleading with him.

The captain's phone rang. He stepped away a few paces to answer it.

A whirring noise cut the air as the helicopter's rotor blades began slowly turning.

"The first forty-eight hours are critical." Jake's gaze was intense, full of his urgency.

Carl had looked at her the same way; he'd said the exact same thing after Brian's murder. He'd warned that every hour that passed without an arrest diminished the possibility that Gilly would ever see Brian's killer brought to justice. He'd reminded her that not only had she dreamed about the man, she'd been at the actual scene, watched him run across her field of vision as she sat waiting in the car. Carl was convinced that if Gilly tried she would remember something more definitive than the general idea of the killer's height and weight. There had been no more distance separating them than the length of the hood of Brian's car. The fluorescent light had been glaringly bright. Carl insisted she must have seen his face, what he'd been wearing. Possibly she'd seen identifying marks unique to him—a scar, a tattoo. Carl didn't buy it when she argued, when she said her memory of that night was a blank.

You don't want to remember, he had said. Not in disgust or impatience. But in sadness. He had said forgetting, like drinking, was a defense. It was avoidance. Maybe fear induced.

A cop-out. He hadn't said that, but Gilly had, to herself.

"You don't want to be involved. Is that it?" Jake said now.

Her chin came up. She was tired of people—Carl, April, and now Jake—telling her what she did and didn't want to do. "I'm here, aren't I? I came because I want to help."

"There are a lot of people here." He chopped his arm in the direction of the crowd.

Again his implication was clear. He didn't need another volunteer searcher. He needed a direction to go in. Like Carl, he needed concrete information. Where was his daughter? Who had her? In her dream, who had Gilly *seen* taking Zoe? She looked toward the spot on the road where she'd parked her car and saw April, talking to the KTKY News reporter.

Suki Daniels was holding a microphone in front of April's face. April was animated, full of herself. Her fifteen minutes, Gilly thought.

The sound of the helicopter's blades thundered, churning the air. Folks retreated to a safer distance, hands clamped to their heads. Even April and Suki moved some feet away, the cameraman, juggling his rig, tracking them.

Gilly turned back to Jake. "You don't know everything about me."

He kept her gaze, waiting for her to explain.

But she couldn't. It was one thing to profess her sobriety, but it would be something else to talk about the behavior that had put her there. If Jake had seen her, the stumbling drunk she'd become in the wake of Brian and Sophie's deaths, if he'd seen what she'd done, he'd realize her mind was a train wreck, a house with no lights. She was always a whisker away—even less—from falling down the rabbit hole again. He would know he was asking the wrong person for help.

The details that kept trying to push their way into her brain—the dark hair spilling from the hood of the sweatshirt, the gold earring—who could trust that those details were real? It was just as possible, wasn't it, that they were products of her so-called vivid imagination? Or, even more believably, she might be recalling them from some other dream.

"Jake?" Captain Mackie shouted as he shoved his phone in his pocket. "A word?"

Jake shot Gilly a searching glance before he walked away, half-accusing, half-pleading, altogether vulnerable, and dark with panic. The look got into her; it went to her core. But there was nothing she could do for him other than what she'd come here to do. Walking past him and the police captain, she approached Sergeant Carter. "Can you put me on a team?" she asked.

• • •

They found things, a child's faded red sock hung up in a desiccated witch's fist of cedar sticks, a tube of lipstick crusted in dirt, a half-empty packet of yellowing tissues. Bones, which according to a man on Gilly's team—Charlie Phipps, a local hunter who said he knew—belonged to an animal, a fox maybe. Hope flared and died throughout the afternoon and evening hours a dozen times and still no one spoke of it—the very real and brutal possibility that Zoe Halstead was gone forever.

Like Sophie.

Gilly's mind kept dragging her there. It didn't matter how she pushed away the nightmare, her body remembered the onset of Sophie's birth—the short-lived, debilitating pain low in her abdomen that struck her in the same hour as Brian's death, the warm rush of amniotic fluid down her bare legs, splattering the gritty pavement. The utter silence while she—and everyone present—stared at the widening pool around her feet. Her body remembered trembling so hard her teeth had clacked together. She had wanted to push right there, standing on the side-walk in front of that awful store, where, inside, boxes of Minute Rice, Kraft macaroni and cheese, and Hamburger Helper, stained with Brian's blood, littered the aisles. She had fought the sensation, pressing her legs together, cradling her belly in her arms. But her effort, her will, was nothing—a wisp in the wind, pitched against a force of nature she was powerless to stop.

The hours searching for Zoe brought it all back. She couldn't stop remembering.

Sophie's loss and Zoe's disappearance—the possibility that Zoe had been kidnapped by a stranger—which, as time wore on, was becoming more probable—weren't the same. But Gilly's heart ached for Zoe's absence in the very same way. Every moment she spent look-ing for Zoe, Sophie was there. In her mind there were two little girls, the image of who Sophie would have been had she lived floated over Zoe's image.

Gilly fought it as best she could, the comparison, the terrible tide of her thoughts, and by the time the search effort was halted near dark, she was aching with the effort. Around her there was talk of returning tomorrow. But she couldn't do this again. As much as she wanted to help, she couldn't come back here. She was afraid for herself, the ground she would lose. She needed a meeting. She told herself that, but what her body said, what it craved, was a drink. *Here we go again.* The voice in her head, Miss Goody Two-shoes, spoke up. *Pay attention*, it said.

Gilly couldn't find April on her return to the school grounds, nor did she see Jake or Captain Mackie, and Liz didn't pick up when Gilly called. She disconnected without leaving a third message. Stowing her phone, she overheard the helicopter pilot telling Sergeant Carter that he'd take his machine up again at daybreak.

A woman standing near Gilly—Mandy Bright, Gilly recognized her—said she wouldn't get a wink of sleep for worrying about "that poor little girl."

"We could keep going if we had flashlights, or those portable sodium vapor lights they use over at the high school football field." A man's shout cut through the deepening shadows. Other's joined in his demand that they continue the search.

"Emergency responders are already stretched to the max as it is." Sergeant Carter's voice rose above the general mutter, aggravated, strident. "We don't need people getting hurt, getting themselves into trouble some way. We'll reconvene here at first light. We'll broaden the search area. Unless something changes," he added. "Keep it tuned to the local news, folks."

The sergeant meant if Zoe was found, Gilly thought. Whether dead or alive. But Sergeant Carter wasn't going to put that into words. Folks knew, though. They were discouraged, frightened of the outcome—that it had been too long now to be good. As they broke apart, heading for their individual cars, their faces were grim with ongoing worry and exhaustion. A woman walking next to Gilly said nothing so awful had ever happened in Wyatt before. She said she doubted there was anything on earth worse than losing a child. Turning to Gilly, she said, "I'm going home and hug my kids extra hard tonight. Do you have children?" she asked.

Gilly stumbled.

"You all right, dear?" The woman caught her elbow.

Gilly said she was fine, but she was far from it. At her car, frantic to be gone, she dropped her keys and had to scrabble for several seconds in the dirt before she found them. Inside, she gripped the steering wheel, shaky with the need for a drink, almost sick with the desire. It dried her mouth, pounded her brain. It was a monkey jumping around in her mind, yapping at her, drowning out Miss Goody Two-shoes, reminding Gilly how easy it would be to drive to a liquor store.

You could get a bottle of something, take it home, said the monkey. Gilly imagined it, taking the glass out of the cabinet there, adding ice and two or three fingers of booze—scotch, or bourbon, maybe Seagram's. *Old number seven*, whispered the monkey. Or Jack Daniel's.

Sipping whiskey, they called it.

You remember. The monkey grinned.

She could do that, right? Just sip it while she fed Bailey and walked him. The monkey hammered her ribs in anticipation, some kind of crazy elation. He turned cartwheels inside her head. Gilly waited and, when her turn came, joined the traffic headed back to town. She pictured the liquor store in her neighborhood. They would have what she needed. It would be all right. She could handle it. She'd only have one and then stop like a normal person, a normal drinker.

You can do it, said the monkey.

• • •

She was late. The meeting had already started by the time Gilly arrived at the Knights of Columbus hall. A man she didn't recognize was at the podium. From his demeanor, she could tell he had some time in. He didn't have the deer-in-the-headlights look of a newly and precariously sober drunk.

She glanced around the room, searching for her sponsor, and when she spotted Julia Benton sitting in a row of metal folding chairs near the back, Gilly made her way there. She looked at no one else, saw nothing else. It was as if she were drowning, and Julia was a life raft.

"Honey, are you all right?" Julia looked Gilly over.

"No," Gilly said.

Julia's grasp when she took Gilly's hand was warm and comforting, a mother's grasp. She was old enough to be Gilly's mother, with two grown children of her own. Gilly looked at their hands, intent on the contrast between her own very pale skin and Julia's, which was the color of rich mocha chocolate. She felt Julia's gaze, her concern, but Gilly knew if she were to look at Julia, if she were to see the compassion that was most certainly there in Julia's expression, she would lose it.

"Can we go for coffee when we're done here?" Gilly asked in a rough whisper. "Do you have time?"

"Yes," Julia answered, and she squeezed Gilly's hand.

12

The coffee at Bo Dean's was awful and the food was worse, but the truck stop across the street from the Knights of Columbus hall in Greeley was convenient, and the waitresses were nice. Gilly sat across from Julia in a booth at the back. And the silence sat between them, measured in minutes. Julia was waiting. Gilly didn't know where to begin.

"It would have been easier, stopping at the liquor store," Gilly finally said, and the monkey in her mind winked.

"Yes, maybe. Until you sobered up and had to face yourself all over again." Julia spoke from experience.

She and Gilly had talked one-on-one many times since Julia had agreed to become Gilly's sponsor at her second meeting six months ago. Julia knew about Brian's murder and Sophie's loss, and Gilly knew Julia's story, who she'd been and what she'd done while under the influence. She knew Julia had lingering issues with members of her family, but the family was still together. Julia's husband, Bonner, had stayed by her, and her children—daughter, Tanika, and son, Duron, both in their thirties now, and married with their own children—still spoke to her even though she'd robbed them of a thousand intangibles—trust, confidence, the right to a childhood free of heartache and drama—and quite literally, of their college funds, cleaning out their savings accounts to buy drugs and booze. That had come at the end, when the family's intervention had forced Julia into a ninety-day rehab program.

Gilly knew Julia's story was true. Still it was hard to see the drunk Julia had been—who she'd described as worse than foolish, often combative, and militantly defensive of her right to drink—in the calm, intelligent, and elegant woman sitting across from her. But Julia had been sober a long time now, nearly ten years. Gilly couldn't imagine that either. Ten years of one day at a time. It seemed impossible, a mountain she'd never summit.

"What happened today?" Julia asked gently.

Gilly started to answer, but her phone chimed, signaling a text. She made a face. "I'm sorry, but I'd better check it out." She pulled her phone from her purse, telling Julia, "A friend and I were supposed to have dinner. We've been missing each other."

"Go right ahead," Julia said. "I'll run to the restroom."

Gilly switched on her screen. The text was from Liz. Gilly read it quickly. So sorry about Zoe. Wish I could help. Back in Dallas. Trouble with the ex. Dad helping me get a restraining order. The good news? Made an offer on that cute house we saw. Cross ur fingers we'll b neighbors soon.

Gilly looked into the middle distance, worrying over it—the business about Liz's ex, and happy at the same time that Liz might make living here permanent. Looking back at her phone, she typed: Sending u a hug. Stay safe. Call me!!! Soon as u can!

"Is your friend okay?"

Gilly looked up as Julia sat down across from her. "I think so." She took a moment to stow her phone, collect herself, not wanting to say more. It was Liz's personal business. Gilly wouldn't feel right talking about Liz and her need for a restraining order. But there was the happier possibility she would move to Wyatt, too—buy a house, begin a new life—like Gilly. Maybe it was the answer for both of them, Gilly thought.

The waitress came, and Gilly and Julia ordered the same thing they always did when they came to Bo's after a meeting. Coffee with extra cream.

"You heard about the little girl who's missing," Gilly said when the waitress had gone.

"Zoe Halstead. Yes. It's been on the news. It's awful. They said earlier her mother took her, but someone at the meeting said they heard the police have found evidence that indicates it was someone else."

Gilly thought about the clothing, Zoe's clothing, that had been found in the sack in the dumpster. It wasn't information she could share with Julia. "It's not her mom," she said instead, and then she paused. While she was free to talk about the dream she'd had, she'd never done so with her sponsor. She'd never told Julia she was on probation. Gilly hadn't wanted to test Julia that way, to burden her with so much.

"I hear Zoe's mother is a drinker, bad enough she's been in rehab a couple of times."

Gilly said she'd heard that, too. She said, "I was at the school earlier, where they set up the search operation. I helped look for her. That's when—when things started to unravel."

The waitress brought their coffee in thick-walled mugs, setting them down, along with two small pitchers of cream. Real cream, not the fake nondairy stuff. It was the only thing that saved the coffee.

Julia added cream to her mug and picked up her spoon, keeping a questioning eye on Gilly.

"I saw it happen in a dream." She spoke in a rush. "Wednesday night I saw a woman take Zoe, and I knew when I woke up on Thursday—and I'm just as certain now—it wasn't her mother."

"You're psychic?"

Gilly's heart sank. She dropped her glance. The way Julia asked—the high, flippy lilt of amazement and eagerness in her voice, her wide-eyed look—was the same reaction Gilly had gotten from April. Gilly braced herself, waiting for it—the inevitable request that Gilly look into Julia's future. "I don't think of myself that way," she said.

"It must be difficult, seeing a terrible thing in a dream and then having it happen in real life."

Gilly shifted her spoon.

"Do you want to talk about it?"

After a bit, she said, "The last time I saw Zoe and her dad, Jake, was on Wednesday. They came in for breakfast. It's a ritual with them. Zoe was born on a Wednesday, and her dad—I think it must have been Jake who declared her Wednesday's princess. It's also Pancakes for Breakfast Day."

Julia smiled.

"She's so adorable," Gilly said. "Just a little ray of sunshine."

"You've become attached to her."

"Yes. I wasn't aware—I really got into the whole pancakes-for-breakfast thing. I look forward to it. Somehow I got started telling her stories, fairy tales. Her favorite is 'The Twelve Dancing *Princesses.*'"

"Who danced their shoes to pieces." Julia smiled.

"Yes. Sometimes I make up a story. I catch myself thinking I would do this for Sophie. I would tell her stories, make her special pancakes. I shouldn't compare the girls, but it's hard. Zoe is only a few months older than Sophie would have been. She has the personality I imagined Sophie would have." Tears pressured Gilly's throat, and she stopped. In the few short months she'd carried Sophie, Gilly had imagined so much more: first steps, kindergarten, the feel of Sophie's hand in hers when they crossed the street. Fleetingly, her wedding gown . . .

"It's transference. I know that," Gilly said. "I don't need a psychiatrist to tell me."

"I didn't know you were under psychiatric care."

"It was court-ordered, part of my probation agreement."

The flare of surprise was there in Julia's expression, but she didn't immediately respond. She would give Gilly a chance to explain. That was Julia's way.

Gilly looked out the window. She couldn't see much—occasional headlights from the frontage road that gave access to the truck stop, running lights from a couple of eighteen-wheelers, idling in the parking lot adjacent to the gas pumps, her own pale reflection. She turned back to Julia. "I took a child, another woman's baby girl, from the hospital. I thought—I wanted her to be mine—to be Sophie."

13

Gone. More than thirty-six hours now since Jake had last seen her. It was night, Friday night, 9:12. The numerals glowed green from the clock on the truck's dash. Was she scared? Injured? Crying for him? Mad? Jake hoped Zoe was mad, just pissed as hell. She'd read him the riot act when she saw him. He could see her in his mind's eye, hands on her hips, little elbows jutting, the very image of righteous female indignation. *"Daaaddddyyy, where were you? I waited and waited . . ."*

A sound came, clawing out of Jake's chest, choking him. He bent forward over the steering wheel, coughing, dragging in air, eyes forward, trained on the dirty path of his headlights. The highway straightened; solid yellow lines were replaced by a broken white line. The land fell away from the road into crevasses and boulder-strewn canyons. It crossed creek beds and led through towering cliffs. In the distance, rows of moonlit hills were packed solid against the horizon, older than time, immutable, uncaring.

She could be anywhere by now. Anywhere . . .

His phone rang, jarring him. Jake grabbed it, not bothering to check the ID. "What?" The greeting a bark, truncated, hurt.

"Honey?"

His mom, worn out, shaken, working not to show how badly. He was instantly contrite, apologetic. "I'm sorry."

"It's all right."

In a corner of his mind he registered that neither one was asking the other whether there was any news, the way they had in those first raw hours when they had believed they would find Zoe with Stephanie. Looking back, those initial hours seemed like a walk in the park. Had he given up now? Had his mom? Had they recognized and accepted they were in for a longer haul? Who would break first? He wished to God his dad were here, that his parents were together. He'd been so self-absorbed as a kid, taken them and their deep, quiet love for him and each other for granted. He had assumed he'd have a marriage like theirs, first with Courtney, then with Stephanie. He'd never valued the gift he'd been given—a relatively drama-free, stable childhood.

"I wish Dad was here," he said.

"Yes." A beat. "Where are you?" she asked. "Still at the school? Is the search still going on?"

"No. Folks wanted to keep on, but Clint called it. It's too dangerous, people in the woods after dark. They'll be back in the morning. You wouldn't believe how many volunteers there were, Mom, all the places they came from. I met a guy and his wife from Wichita Falls, another woman was from Houma, Louisiana—"

"I didn't find her trike, Jake."

"Yeah, Clint said you'd called. It's not at your place."

"It's not anywhere. I've checked with the neighbors, yours and mine." Her voice rose precipitously. The silence fell like a warning that worked both ways: *Don't lose it.* They might have said it out loud to each other.

She said, "I haven't gotten hold of the Hendersons yet." She named a family that lived two streets over from Jake. Tulia Henderson was Zoe's best friend, her BFF. Whenever Jake heard the two refer to each other that way he wondered at it. How did the concept of *forever* appear to almost-four-year-olds? "I left a note on their door to call as soon as they could."

Jake didn't answer. He dreaded going home. How would they get through another night? Walk the floor, he guessed. Lie down and pretend to sleep.

"I'm at your house," his mom said as if he'd asked. "Making chicken soup."

Jake had a sudden memory from when he was a kid, six or seven, in the first grade maybe. He'd been getting over a bout of tonsillitis, and his mom had come into his bedroom, carrying a bowl of chicken soup on a tray. Homemade. It had smelled delicious, made his stomach rumble. "This will be easy to get down," she had said, sitting beside him on the edge of the bed. "I promise," she had added, dipping the spoon into the bowl. She'd blown on it before she'd offered it to him, and then held her free hand underneath in case of spills. He had thrust his head forward, opening his mouth to receive it as if he were a tiny bird. He remembered how their eyes had held; he remembered feeling safe.

"How long will you be?" she asked.

"Twenty minutes." His phone beeped, and he checked the caller ID. "Mom, Clint's calling me."

"Go," she said.

"Yeah?" He greeted Clint, steeling himself, his voice, his spine.

"No news about Zoe," the police captain said right away.

Jake sagged, falling in on himself. He felt sweat break out along his hairline, under his arms. He didn't know if it was from relief or terror. His foot backed off the accelerator. He couldn't help it, but checking the rearview, there was no one behind him.

"Jake? We found Stephanie."

14

Gilly held Julia's gaze, but there was no judgment of her there, only compassion.

"You were drunk?" Julia asked.

"Out of my mind. I'd taken Oxy, too. To this day I can't tell you how I managed it. Even hospital security can't say for sure."

"This was right after you lost Brian and Sophie?"

"It would have made more sense, but it was actually eight months ago, almost two years after their deaths. I went back to the hospital where Brian and Sophie died, and I went up to the maternity floor, went into the nursery—no one was around—and I picked up a baby, a tiny girl only hours old—" Gilly bent forward, clutching her elbows.

Julia patted her arm. "It's all right. You don't have to tell me."

"No," Gilly said. "I want to." She took a breath. "Her name was Anne Clementine Riley. She was wrapped in a pink blanket. I made sure it was tucked around her so she was snug, and I carried her to the elevator. A couple of nurses passed me, but they were talking, laughing. They never even looked. After I was caught, a woman who rode down in the elevator with me said I sang to the baby all the way down, a lullaby I remember my mom singing to me. 'Baby's Boat.' Do you know it?"

Julia shook her head.

"*Sail, baby, sail, upon the silver sea*"—Gilly's voice wavered over the notes—"*only don't forget to sail back again to me . . .*"

A silence filled with the clatter of cutlery, the dissonance of chatter, a barked laugh.

Gilly made herself go on. "The woman thought it was odd, me holding a newborn, leaving the hospital with her, but not so odd she felt the need to notify anyone. She only realized the baby was stolen when she turned on her television and heard about it on the news. By then I'd been identified on hospital security footage and someone from the HPD had called my mom."

"Where did you take the baby?"

"Home," Gilly said. "I brought her into Sophie's room, her nursery. The walls were the palest shade of pink, and the ceiling was silvery blue like the sky. I'd painted billowy white clouds there, and a weeping willow tree in one corner. There were tiny rabbits in the grass and flowers along the baseboard." Gilly's gaze turned inward.

She saw herself bent over the crib. She was watching little Anne Clementine sleep when she heard her mother speak her name softly—so softly—from the doorway.

"Gilly?"

"It's all right now, Mama. See? I found her. I found Sophie. She's not dead; she's only sleeping."

Her mother joined her.

"Isn't she beautiful?"

Her mother didn't answer.

"Brian and I don't even care who took her from us. You don't either, do you?"

A sound, awful in its torment, something between a sob and a groan, had caused Gilly to look at her mom, and in that instant, seeing her mother's grief, the spell—or whatever it was that had Gilly in its grip—broke. She had looked back at the baby in the crib in horrified astonishment.

"My mom found me before the police did," Gilly said to Julia now. "One minute I was telling her how beautiful my baby was and the next I was shocked out of my mind at what I'd done. Shocked sober. I haven't had a drink since."

"Well, something good came out of it then. Right?"

Gilly grimaced. "What I did was unforgiveable. The baby's parents were so scared. I felt—still feel—so awful for what I put them through."

"Oh, Gilly, you weren't yourself. You went through hell, lost so much. What you did was wrong, I'm not saying it wasn't, but—"

"There was a lot of talk about the extenuating circumstances. It's what kept me out of prison, that and I had a good lawyer, a friend of the detective who's working Brian's murder case. Mark Riley, Anne Clementine's dad, was not happy, but her mom, Jessica—" Gilly stopped to clear her throat. She didn't want to cry. "Jessica wrote a letter to the judge, asking him for leniency on my behalf."

"How long is your probation?" Julia asked.

"Five years. I'm banned from ever going near the parents, or the hospital, and I was fined, too. Ten thousand dollars. I was lucky I had it."

"I'm surprised you were allowed to move from Houston."

Gilly pressed her fingertips to her eyes, swiped under her nose, gathering her composure. "You can transfer your probation if you have a good reason. The judge agreed when I explained it would help if I could get away from the city, the neighborhood. The store where Brian was murdered—it's only three blocks from our house, what used to be Brian's and my house. And then I wanted to get away from the crowd I was drinking and doing drugs with, too."

"You were smart to move. I'm glad it worked out. But, honey, what a rough time you've had."

"I feel as if I got off too easy."

"That's a matter of perspective. What I see is you're still punishing yourself when it seems everyone else who's concerned has forgiven you."

"Everyone except Mark Riley. He'd like to see me behind bars, or possibly dead."

"Are you serious? Has he threatened you?"

"He said if he ever caught me near his family . . ." *I'll put a bullet in your brain.* Gilly couldn't say it aloud, that he had wished her dead. She understood his rancor, but it unnerved her. "I don't blame him," Gilly said. "You might feel the same way if someone took your child."

"I would hope to be more like the man's wife and show mercy." Julia drank her coffee.

Gilly folded her napkin, addressing it. "Jake thinks I can find Zoe." She looked up when Julia didn't respond. "I ended up telling him I'd had the dream, but it's what happened before that—" She broke off, and when she spoke again, she explained how she'd located Jake's wallet through a vision that had come into her head. "I saw it as clearly as I see you. I could smell the oil and sawdust in the garage. It was unreal."

"You've not had visions like that before?"

Gilly started to answer no, but then she was caught by a fragment of memory. When she was around twelve, the Jameses' neighbors who lived down the block, had lost their dog, a collie named Timmy. "I saw the poster," she said, more to herself than to Julia. "In the window at King's." She named the corner grocery, where she'd ridden her bike on summer afternoons to buy comic books, bubble gum, her beloved ice cream sandwiches. The image on the sign floated behind Gilly's eyes, a fuzzy black-and-white photo of a happy dog, sitting on his haunches, looking eagerly into the camera, topped a small placard with the details laid out in three lines: LOST BROWN AND WHITE COLLIE. ANSWERS TO THE NAME OF TIMMY. LAST SEEN TUESDAY. There was a final fourth line with the Jameses' phone number. Gilly looked up at Julia. "I found a neighbor's dog. I saw him in here"—Gilly tapped her temples—"where he was. Some kids had penned him up in their fort, four streets over. I'd almost forgotten."

"So dreams aren't the only way you—"

"My mother has always discouraged me from seeing anything, whether it's dreams or visions. She acts as if it annoys her, but really, I think it scares her. She thinks it's why I never had any friends. You know how kids are—if you're odd in the least way you're ignored, or worse, bullied. I really tried not to do it, not dream, not see things. A lot of the time I was wrong anyhow."

"Are you sure of that? Maybe your mom's influence has undermined your confidence. Maybe you've had more visions—more correct visions—than you'll allow yourself to remember."

Gilly lifted her shoulders slightly. "I don't know." It was a jumble in her head, and she was tired now. She thought if she were to lay her head down on the table she would fall asleep.

"You did accurately see the location of Jake's wallet," Julia said.

"I wish I hadn't. I think without that he'd never have thought twice about the dream, but with the two together—"

"He's desperate."

"The dream isn't like the vision of his wallet, though, and he doesn't understand that I don't—I can't control what comes, or how it comes—" Gilly brought her fist to her mouth, fighting tears, her misgivings. "I don't usually talk about this. I don't like people knowing. They get ideas, and usually what I know—it's just useless."

"Oh, honey." Julia patted her arm.

"Jake thinks I should be able to give him—give the police—something, a lead that would take them somewhere. I wish I could. I wish it worked like that. I'm as desperate to find Zoe as anyone."

"I can only imagine how difficult this is."

Gilly cradled her mug in her hands, looking into it. The coffee had grown cold, and the cream she'd added had congealed into a milky scab. "I dreamed Brian would be murdered before it happened. We didn't pay attention." Her throat narrowed, and she swallowed, and when she could, she went on, wanting Julia to hear it all. "After Brian was shot, when I told Carl Bowen, the detective who's working the case—when I said I'd dreamed the whole thing the night before, he was like Jake. Even like you." Gilly flashed a glance at Julia. "Carl thinks if I would let it come, my memory of that night, if I would really focus on it, I would see Brian's murderer in enough detail to give a description."

"I'm surprised a detective would give a dream so much credence."

"It isn't only that I dreamed it. I was there, and I saw the guy who murdered Brian when he ran out of the store. He went directly in front of our car. The light was nearly as good as if it had been eleven in the morning instead of eleven at night, but when I try and see him, the image is all blurry, the same as the dream image of him. Carl thinks I'm being stubborn. He doesn't understand—" Gilly stopped.

"Understand?"

Gilly didn't answer. The truth was that sometimes she did catch glimpses of the man, Brian's murderer, hulking in the dark behind her eyes. She would feel him there, wanting her attention, the power of her gaze, her acknowledgment. She looked at Julia now. "Carl says they have a new lead on the guy. They could find him, arrest him."

"Well, that's good, right?"

"They'll put him a lineup, and ask me to identify him. What if I'm wrong? Brian wasn't the only one shot and killed that night. The clerk was murdered, too. He was only eighteen, a high school basketball star, valedictorian of his graduating class. Everyone loved him. The neighborhood where it happened—people were—they're still shocked and angry and scared. They want him caught."

"Yes, I would, too. Don't you?"

"If it's the right man." Gilly said the only thing she was sure of.

"You're afraid if you push it, if you let yourself remember, your memory won't be accurate."

"What if the person I see in here"—Gilly pointed to her temple—"is just someone I've conjured from imagination? Or what if he's a guy I passed on the street, or someone from my childhood? I couldn't live with it, if an innocent person were arrested and went to prison based on some vision I've had."

"But suppose it's your fear that's cutting off—"

"It probably is, but as my mom likes to point out, I've been wrong more times than I've been right." Gilly pushed her mug away.

"You said you saw him. Did he see you?"

"He could have. I used to worry about it, but it's been so long now." Carl was still uneasy. *Stay vigilant. Don't let your guard down.* He, and other law enforcement types connected to the case, had issued the warnings from the early days of the investigation, but Gilly couldn't live like that, always looking over her shoulder. When she was drinking and on dope, she felt brave. After downing a couple of shots, or a handful of Oxy or fentanyl or what have you, it was easier to pretend she hadn't lost the loves of her life and her future to a killer who might be gunning for her. A fellow reformed addict in her Twelve-Step group in Houston, a war vet who'd lost an arm and a leg in Afghanistan, had told her when he drank enough, he could fool himself into believing he still had all his limbs—until he fell on his ass. Dark humor. Addicts thrived on it.

Gilly drew in a lungful of air and let it out. "I'm sorry to load you up with this."

"No, I'm here to listen. I wish I could do more."

"I'm so tired of myself, you know? So tired of fighting to stay sober. I came pretty close to blowing it today." She pointed to her head. "The monkey almost won against Miss Goody Two-shoes."

"I don't have to tell you Miss Two-shoes has got the right answer, hands down, every time."

Gilly shifted her glance. "I'm sick about Zoe. It's terrifying, and I'm scared for her, but I don't want to be involved. I wish Jake could understand I can't help him."

Julia didn't offer a response.

Gilly said, "I've been thinking I could leave Wyatt, find someplace else to start over. Maybe even move out of state."

"You could, but the trouble is that you can't leave yourself." Julie might have said more, but she was distracted—she and Gilly both were—by a young woman passing their booth, who paused abruptly.

Doing a double take, her eyes locked on Gilly. "You work at Cricket's in Wyatt, right? I'm Marybeth Cargill, Joni's daughter? We come in every Thursday. Mother-daughter lunch date. We order the same thing every time."

Half a chicken salad sandwich on wheat with fruit and a cup of tortilla soup.

"You were on TV. Did you see? The six o'clock news, KTKY. Suki Daniels was doing a story about that little girl, Zoe Halstead, who's gone missing in Wyatt. She showed your picture. I didn't know you were psychic!"

Gilly stared at the girl.

"You heard, didn't you? They found Zoe's mom."

15

Y ou found Stephanie?" Jake jerked the wheel of the truck, getting it off the road. "Where?"

"Dallas. She's in jail up there. She says she's got no idea where Zoe is."

"What about the boyfriend? Duchene? Andy Duchene. Where is he?"

"I don't know. I'm trying to get information on his whereabouts now. But, Jake, you know what this means." The words were a warning, a caution.

Jake had the impression Clint was trying to prepare him. If Jake had thought the situation was bad before, it was about to get a whole lot worse. He stared through the windshield. He didn't know if he could handle worse.

"The investigation's got to go to a whole nother level now we know Zoe's not with her mom. You realize that, don't you? I'm in contact with the FBI. Wyatt, even Madrone County—we just don't have the resources." Clint paused, and then he said that with Jake's permission, law enforcement would run a tap on Jake's cell phone and his landline. "In case there's contact from whoever has Zoe. We'd want to try and trace the call—"

"Call?" Jake repeated the word faintly.

"They might want money, a ransom. It doesn't happen that often, but you never know."

"What? Like I'm Warren Buffet? Jeff Bezos? I don't have that kind of money. Not even close." He'd get it, though, lay hands on it somehow.

Clint said, "Money's just one possible motive."

Jake sat back, unable—unwilling—to sort it out.

"Madrone County—Sheriff Wiley—he's still looking for you to come in and take a lie detector."

"It's bullshit, Clint."

"Yeah, I know, but the quicker they can rule you out, the better, you understand?"

"I'll go in the morning. They aren't after Mom to take one, are they?"

"Not so far as I know, but you might warn her."

Jake said he already had, that she was prepared.

Clint said, "Do you know of anyone who's got a grudge against you? Maybe an ax to grind? A customer? A vendor? Someone more personal than that?"

"No. What are you saying? That this is revenge? Some bastard took my little girl out of revenge? It doesn't make sense—"

"What about your dad? That lawsuit—"

"That was five years ago, before Zoe was even born." A former employee had brought the suit the year before Jake's dad died. After showing up drunk on the job on numerous occasions, Carlos Hernandez had claimed discrimination was the cause for his termination. No one had believed Hernandez. Jake's dad hadn't had a biased bone in his body. The suit had been tossed by the judge. As far as Jake knew, his dad had never heard from Hernandez again.

"What about Stephanie?" It was more a suggestion on Clint's part than a question. "Do you know of anyone who might be angry enough with her to take Zoe?"

"The life she's been living the past couple of years, who knows?" Jake checked the rearview for traffic, and pulled back onto the highway.

"I'm going to Dallas. I'm pretty sure Zoe talked to her mom recently. I want to find out what that was about, what Steph was planning. Maybe there's a connection." He was thinking of Duchene. What if Steph had left Zoe with him, and he was waiting somewhere for Steph to get back? What if he got fed up when she didn't show? Ditched Zoe? *Jesus.*

Clint was talking caution. "Let the Dallas police question her. You should get some rest. See Sheriff Wiley in the morning, like you said."

Jake could have laughed. "Steph won't talk to the cops up there, Clint. You know that. I need to see her, see for myself the shape she's in." Hearing himself say it, he was surprised he cared. "She's Zoe's mom, for God's sake."

Clint didn't argue.

"If she's not involved, the shock has got to be—" Jake stopped again, feeling the ragged edges of his terror, his anguish and denial. It saved him, being out here, being able to act, do something, anything to find his daughter. He didn't know what in the hell he would do if he were locked up. Squat in a corner and howl. Bash in his brain.

Take himself out.

Would he?

Would Steph?

"What jail is she in, do you know? What's she charged with?" Jake was thinking drunk and disorderly, something like that.

"She got into it with a dealer, pulled a knife on him, cut him up pretty good."

"Are you kidding me?"

"I'm thinking Duchene was there. He may have been the 911 caller, but he took off as soon as he saw the cops. Drove down some back alley and left Steph there like the rat he is."

Jake had no words, no insight, nothing of value to offer. Only disgust, a sense of futility bitter enough to burn his throat.

"I don't know how she took the news about Zoe," Clint said. "I didn't talk to her directly."

Clint sounded fed up, irked. He would have given up on Steph long ago, but Cricket wouldn't let him. Jake wondered what Cricket thought now, if she would still welcome Stephanie into her home, her heart. He didn't ask.

• • •

Jake took Clint's advice when he said that if Jake was determined to go to Dallas, he should wait until morning. He went home and ate a little of the chicken soup his mom had made. He told her about Steph.

"She's going to kill herself, or someone else will do it for her one day." His mom took their bowls to the sink. "I know you don't want to hear it, but you didn't need to marry Stephanie to keep Zoe. That relationship—it was so like the obsession you and Karen had for each other, and we both know how that ended up."

With police involvement and heartbreak. She didn't need to say it for Jake to get her meaning. "You're right, Mom. It's not a subject we need to discuss."

"I know. I'm just scared."

"Me too," Jake said. "What if Steph and Duchene had Zoe, and she saw it, her mother knifing a drug dealer? What if Duchene's got Zoe now?"

"But Clint would know that, wouldn't he?" His mom shut off the water. She picked up a towel. "The police in Dallas would have told him if they had a little girl with them."

"Not if Duchene took off with Zoe before the cops got there." Jake kept his mother's gaze.

Anyone might have Zoe. Some creep. A monster. A pedophile. A murderer. The possible horrors shimmered in the air between them.

Jake got up after a moment and helped his mom with the dishes. She washed, and he dried.

Letting the water out of the sink, she said, "I saw you on TV when you talked to Suki Daniels earlier. You did a good job. I recorded it, if you want to watch."

"Thanks," Jake said. He didn't. He stowed the soup bowls in the cabinet. They were printed with a variety of insects—honeybees, mantids, and butterflies. Zoe had chosen them. She loved bugs. She was his bug. He called her that sometimes. *Bug.* Jake cleared his throat.

"I should have been there," his mom said, shaky-voiced. "People—whatever horrible person has Zoe, they should know how badly I want her back, too."

Jake glanced at her, but she kept her eyes on the dishcloth, wringing the water from it, white-knuckled.

Her mouth trembled.

"You can't be everywhere at once, Mom." Jake flattened his palm between her shoulder blades. "If you hadn't gone door-to-door and talked to the neighbors, we'd never have found Zoe's trike." It had turned up at Tulia Henderson's. Tulia's mother had finally called back to say it was at their house. Zoe had gone off home, leaving it behind, when the girls had played together on Tuesday, two days before Zoe went missing.

"But it's hardly reassuring, is it? That trike you found, it belongs to some little girl, but no one has come forward to claim it. What was it doing there?"

Jake didn't have an answer, not one he wanted to look at anyway.

His mom's persistence had uncovered another bit of unsettling information, a possible lead. In the course of hunting for Zoe's trike, a few of Jake's neighbors had mentioned seeing an unfamiliar, metallic-blue sedan with a woman inside it parked at the curb near Jake's house in the days before Zoe vanished. Helen Vanderslice, who lived three doors down, said she'd seen the woman outside the car, taking photographs of several houses, Jake's included. Helen, who was eighty-one and sharp as a tack, had said she thought the woman was a real estate agent, maybe gathering information for a prospective buyer or seller.

Helen had described her as slender, five foot six or seven, wearing jeans, western boots, and a blue work shirt pulled over a white tee or tank top. She'd had her hair—dark blonde or maybe light brown, Helen wasn't sure—tucked under a plain black ball cap, and her sunglasses had been dark and big. *Jackie-O big* was how Helen had characterized them. It had seemed a little odd, but Helen hadn't really thought much of it.

Jake's mom might have dismissed Helen's sighting of the woman, too, but on hearing Helen's description of the car, knowing it was a match to the car Zoe had last been seen climbing into at the school, she had alerted the Wyatt police before Jake got home. Dispatch had indicated an officer would be sent to Helen's house to take her statement. Helen hadn't been the least bit upset to hear the police were coming to talk to her. *Anything I can do*, she had said. *Anything at all.*

How many times had Jake heard that in the last thirty-six hours? He'd lost count.

He doubted Helen's information would come to anything. Who knew how many metallic-blue sedans passed through town on any given day? There were a lot of real estate agents coming into the area, too. Wyatt was growing. There was a lot of activity in real estate these days. *It's the lead that won't lead anywhere.* That's what he'd said when his mom told him about it.

"I always wonder if it does any good," she said now. "I mean when a family member goes on television asking for their child, or wife, or whomever, to be given back. You've seen them, other families—"

"I never thought we'd be one of them." It had been surreal, standing with Suki Daniels, in the white-hot media light, addressing an audience he couldn't see, pleading with them. *If you've seen my little girl, if you know anything, if you're the one who took her, please, just give her back. We—her family loves her. We need her to come home . . .* He'd choked out the words. He'd never know how. Afterward, people had come up to him. They'd shaken his hand, or hugged him. Even some of the men had hugged him, tears in their eyes. *I've got a kid Zoe's age*, they'd said. *A niece. A granddaughter.* If everything folks said was true, the entire county was praying for him and for Zoe, her safe return. *We'll find her. We'll bring her home.*

Jake picked up the dish towel and folded it over the oven door handle, and then as quickly, he ripped it off. "Goddammit, where is she? Where?" His voice broke. He stared at his mother, and when she came to him, when she put her arms around him as best she could, he bent his head to her shoulder, and the sound that came, something between a sob and a groan, raked his ribs.

· · ·

He was flat on his back on the sofa in the living room, staring, sleepless, at the ceiling, when his cell phone vibrated. Jerking upright, he grabbed it from the side table, righting the lamp before it tipped off the table's edge. It was dark in the room, but he could read the number glowing on the phone's face. It wasn't one he recognized.

His "Hello?" was cautious, and when no one answered right away, he said, "Gilly?" His mind was leaping on the possibility that she'd had a dream, one of her middle-of-the-night visions, or whatever the hell they were, and had called to tell him where he could find Zoe. Desperation did that. It left no space for rationality.

The silence deepened. His pulse slowed. His head felt full of the demand for the caller to speak, but he couldn't work his tongue off the floor of his mouth to put a voice to it. And then he heard her, Zoe, and he realized he'd known—in some deep recess of his mind he'd known it would be her.

"Daddy?" She sounded woolly, the way she did in the morning when she first wakened.

"ZooRoo?" Jake's chest swelled with soaring elation, and for a single moment he had her back, safe in his arms. He could smell her, her sleepy morning smell, fading notes of laundry softener and baby shampoo. He could feel her warm bulk in his arms. But he knew better, knew she was not here, not safe, and his heart burned with his fear for her even as his brain scrambled for sense, an answer, the way to get her back. "Are you all right? Do you know where you are? Is anyone with you?" He knew even as the questions shot from his mouth that he was too intense, talking too fast, and he made himself stop, clenching his jaw.

"I want to come home, Daddy." She sounded on the edge of a meltdown.

"I'm coming to get you right now, snickerdoodle. Where are you? Do you know? Can you tell me?"

But she was gone, and the voice that replaced hers was singsong, whispery. "She's mine, my little girl now," it said. "You never deserved her. After what you did to me, you never deserved anything good in your life. You didn't want her anyway."

You didn't want her anyway. The words cut through his heart.

Jake shot to his feet. "Who is this? Where is Zoe? Tell me. Tell me where she is!"

No reply.

"Do you want money?"

Nothing.

"I'll give you whatever you want. Please just give Zoe back to me. Please . . ."

The silence was as deep as the ocean, as fathomless as the sky. He took his phone from his ear and realized the connection was broken. The caller had hung up. He couldn't have said precisely when.

"Jake?"

He held up a finger to his mom, hitting the redial on his phone, but whoever had called him didn't answer. They'd said all they cared to say, scared the hell out of him. But what was the point?

"Jake! What is happening?"

He looked at his mom, framed in the doorway of the den. She looked rumpled and frail—old, suddenly. What if he lost her, too? His knees weakened, and his mind went loose, but it was only a moment before reality kicked him in the head. *Get a grip on yourself.* A cold voice spoke in his brain. "Someone has Zoe," he said, and he was scrolling through his directory. "They let her talk to me."

"Who? Where is she?"

"I don't know. They took the phone away before she could tell me. They said—" But he didn't want to repeat what the caller had said. *You didn't want her anyway.* It shook him—the awful reminder of his ambivalence when he'd learned Zoe was on the way. His brain wanted him to look at it, how when he'd learned of her existence, he'd wished she'd never been made. But other than Stephanie and his parents, no one knew he'd had doubts, however momentary and stinging. And no one but Steph knew how badly it had pissed him off when she'd ended up pregnant.

How? he had demanded. *You said you were on the pill.*

The discussion had ended with Stephanie's decision to abort. Jake had felt relieved. He'd be done with it. He and Steph would be done with each other. Just as his parents had known, the relationship had been a mistake from the start. But then Steph couldn't go through with it. Jake had driven her to the clinic, a nurse had prepped her for the procedure, but at some point, lying on the table waiting for the doctor, she'd changed her mind. Jake had driven her back to her apartment, and a few weeks later, they'd gotten married. Six months after that, it was only Steph who had seen Jake tear up at his first sight of their daughter cradled in her arms. He'd touched Zoe's cheek, put his fingertip into the fragile pink cup of her hand, feeling it close, a tiny clamshell over a pearl. *Mine*, it said. And he was hers. Zoe had owned him from that moment on, body and soul.

"Did Zoe say who she's with?" His mom took a few steps, coming closer, peering at him in the half light of a new morning.

"No." Jake punched Clint's number into his phone. "If she knows, she couldn't—Clint?"

"Jake, what's up?" If the police captain had been sleeping, it didn't show in his voice. He sounded wide-awake.

Jake met his mother's glance. He took her hand to reassure her and himself. They would help each other stay sane, stay in control. He repeated for Clint's benefit and his mother's the little Zoe had been allowed to say, and he registered the sharp intake of his mother's breath when he replied in answer to Clint's question that someone—he couldn't say if it was a man or a woman—had taken the phone from Zoe, and speaking to Jake, had said he didn't deserve her. It ripped him up, repeating it now, hearing in his own voice a truth he'd carried inside himself for almost five years. But the caller had it right. He didn't deserve his daughter, the joy she had brought him, which grew daily. If he'd been any kind of dad—any kind of man—he would never have let this happen to her.

But there was nothing to be gained from dwelling on regret. He was all Zoe had, her only hope, and he swore to himself he would get her back or die trying.

Clint asked for the caller's number, and Jake, putting Clint on speaker, checked his screen and rattled it off. "I don't recognize it."

"It's probably a burner anyway. But maybe we'll get lucky." Clint went on, talking about plans to widen the search area. He mentioned the taps on Jake's phones again and said he was meeting later with a couple of agents—child abduction experts—from the FBI. "They'll get on this now they know it's not a custodial issue."

"Holy Christ," Jake muttered.

"Yeah. Look, try to hang in there, okay? Hey, while I've got you, we could use a few more photos. The more we can get Zoe's face out there, the better. Think you could arrange it?"

Jake looked at his mom.

"I've got pictures of Zoe on my phone," she said. "I'll get it."

She came back in a few minutes, as Jake was lacing up his shoes.

"I printed out three." She showed him the top one. It was the photo of Zoe she'd taken over the weekend when they'd weeded the garden. In it Zoe was holding up for display a fistful of green, dirt-caked roots dangling. Her grin was pure sunshine. She couldn't have been more triumphant if she had vanquished a dragon.

Jake couldn't look at the image longer than an instant. He grabbed his keys and his phone.

"Where are you going?" His mom followed him from the den to the front door.

"Dallas," he said. "I have to see Steph. Can you run those over to Clint? He's at the police station. He said he'd wait."

"Yes, of course. But, honey, is it necessary for you to go? Wouldn't Steph have told the police there if she knew anything? It's not even light out yet. You should eat something first—"

"I need to talk to her myself. She's Zoe's mom, no matter what she's done." That was only part of it. The rest of it was what *he'd* done, his own source of shame. *You don't deserve her*, the caller had said. *You didn't want her anyway.* The words—that ugly truth—uttered in a breathy, high whisper, hung in his mind, mocking him, accusing him.

"Jake? What is it? What's wrong?"

Beyond the obvious, his mother meant. Jake didn't want to talk about it. He didn't want to add to her worry, and bending his head, he kissed her cheek in the hope of distracting her, of shielding her from his turmoil.

It startled her.

When he straightened, she was looking at him, nonplussed. They weren't kissers, barely huggers. Even the handholding they'd done a while ago wasn't usual. A simple touch, an encouraging look, a joke shared—that was their way.

He waited, willing her not to press him, and she didn't. Instead she asked when he'd be back, and he told her he wasn't sure. "It's possible they might not let me in to see her. Clint said there are all kinds of rules about jail visits. He's calling in some favors, trying to get it arranged."

"Be safe," she said, and she let him go.

16

*P*sychic.

    It was so wrong, calling her that. A total lie.

Now it was out there. Again. Her picture and her name associated with that label. The one thing Gilly dreaded most.

She brushed her teeth, fuming, elbow jerking, wondering if she had grounds for a lawsuit. Didn't what was reported in the news have to be accurate? If you were going to be labeled in some way, shouldn't you be consulted first? Didn't the media have to get permission before they paraded your photo across the television screen? That girl at Bo Dean's the night before—the one who had recognized Gilly—she was just the start. Everywhere Gilly went now, she'd have to be prepared. People would comment, give her looks. *That's her—the psychic. The weirdo. The fake, the fraud.* And on and on it would go, and no matter how she responded, she would be an object of interest, or pity, or revilement. She would lose her privacy. Her very life would be up for discussion, debate, and judgment.

But that wasn't the worst that could happen. Gilly met her glance in the mirror. The worst would be if the media dug into her past and discovered she had taken someone else's child before. Then, digging further, they would find out why. They would dig Brian and Sophie right out of their graves and talk about them, Gilly's family, and what had happened to them as if they knew. Gilly would be forced to relive it again. And again. The demons would come, and this time she wouldn't have the will to fight them. She just wouldn't . . .

Come home. Her mother's plea surfaced in Gilly's mind. She imagined it, sleeping down the hall from her mom in her girlhood bedroom, the two of them having dinner at the table in the kitchen. They would do the dishes after. It would be fine as long as their talk never dipped below the surface. Gilly remembered her mother's happiness the day Gilly had been awarded her degree in architecture. Finally she had done something normal: she'd managed to graduate from college. Even Gilly's dad had come to the ceremony. After years of Gilly's weird dreams and dire predictions, her *drama drama drama*, as her dad characterized it, here was something to be proud of. Something her parents could talk about related to their daughter that didn't elicit advice to get Gilly to a shrink.

The day of her wedding had been another occasion for joy. Her mom and dad had loved Brian.

Now you have someone in your life strong enough to keep your feet on the floor.

Her mother had bent toward Gilly's ear and whispered that to her as she'd fastened the row of tiny buttons on the back of Gilly's wedding gown. No doubt she and Gilly's dad had felt gleeful, handing Gilly off, relieved of the responsibility for her, the constant concern. They had never known what to do with her. The only difference between them was that her dad had left, pretty much washing his hands of her, while her mom had stayed. Out of duty. Because one of them had to. That was Gilly's guess. Her father's retreat had scared her. She'd been afraid her mom would desert her, too, or put her out on the street and change the locks. She'd tried very hard not to dream once her dad was gone, and if she did wake terrified in the night, she'd slapped her hands over her mouth to keep from calling out. Sometimes her mom had heard her anyway, or she'd known somehow.

You could control your mind, if you'd try, she would say the next morning at the breakfast table. Once she had taken Gilly's chin in her hand, and locking her gaze, she had said, *What you see in your head, what you dream, it isn't real. Tell that to yourself enough times, let it be your mantra, and I promise this nonsense will stop.*

Gilly had done as her mother advised, repeating the phrase *it isn't real, it isn't real,* when a dream showed her some alarming event. She'd tried not to remember, not to speak of the experiences, and while the frequency of the dreams and visions lessened, they never left her entirely. She was aware of them, of her brain's capacity to see the future, but it was like looking at a shadow sidelong, there but not there.

She intended to tell Brian early in their relationship, but then she fell headlong in love with him. It frightened her that, like her father, Brian would leave her, too, once he knew. She might never have confessed if fate hadn't forced her. While they were still dating but serious enough they were talking about marriage, her thrashing and whimpering had wakened him. He'd held her, and once she grew quiet, she'd turned, spooning against him, and told him, whispering in the dark. That time she had dreamed about her mom.

"She's going to fall and break her wrist. If I tell her to be careful she'll be annoyed. She hates that I have this—do this. She thinks it makes me seem crazy."

"It is kind of crazy," Brian said, "but in a good way."

Three days later they were doing the dinner dishes when Gilly's mom called to say she'd had an accident.

"She's in a cast up to her elbow and mad as a wet cat." Gilly set down her phone. "Mad that I dreamed it, that I told her."

Brian tucked the dish towel over the oven door handle. "Well, I don't pretend to know how it works." He came to Gilly, cupped her face then pulled her into his embrace. "But I love your mind, every firing neuron and cell."

That had been the difference between him and Gilly's folks. His approval hadn't been conditional; she was herself with him. "Some people have migraines," he'd said. "You have visions and dreams, which is way more interesting."

But then he was murdered, and the media heard from somewhere—the police? The hospital? A so-called friend?—that Gilly had dreamed it would happen, and along with her, Gilly's parents were dragged into the ensuing backlash of media hype.

Now she was back in the news. From what she could tell, the coverage so far was local, limited to KTKY's audience. But how long would it be until other, bigger news outlets picked up the story? How long before her mom—or worse, Carl—heard?

Gilly rinsed her mouth and spit forcefully into the sink. She dressed and snapped on Bailey's leash, giving his ears a distracted scratch, barely registering his tail-wagging happiness, which on an ordinary day gave her such joy. Outside, the street was quiet, the light dim. Shadows as thick as sheep's wool huddled under the trees. The air was cool, and she walked quickly. Bailey kept pace, keeping his forays to either side of their path to a minimum, as if he sensed his mistress's anxiety. Because underneath her fury and the indignation she had so little right to feel, she was scared. It had always scared her—this so-called gift. Her parents had never understood that Gilly was as confused by her mind as they were. She didn't want the ability any more than they had wanted it for her.

Maybe you should be more open to it.

Julia had offered Gilly that advice last night as they were leaving Bo Dean's. *Just go with it,* she'd said. Instead of fighting, let the dream, the vision of Zoe's whereabouts become clear.

Suppose what you see could find her? Julia had said. *Suppose for whatever reason the universe has tapped into your mind and given you the knowledge of where she is? I don't mean to make you feel responsible*, she had said. *But . . .*

But nothing.

Whether Gilly did or did not "see" Zoe and her circumstances, she would feel responsible. It was what she hated most about being labeled psychic. Damned if you do, damned if you don't. There were no winners. Ever. Last night, Gilly had told Julia and Marybeth Cargill the same thing she had told Jake. She couldn't go into a trance, and *poof*, behind her eyes have Zoe appear along with the kidnapper, as if by magic. But it had been as if she hadn't spoken. Marybeth had quoted the news report as if it were the gospel, and Julia had reiterated her suggestion that Gilly had only to allow the vision to take form for Zoe to be rescued.

Gilly had called Jake after she left Bo Dean's, and she'd done her best to keep from sounding angry. She'd left him a message when he hadn't picked up. *I know you're desperate*, she had said, *but you've got no idea the trouble you've caused me, telling the media you've hired me to find Zoe.* He had returned her call a while later, but by then she'd seen him on the ten o'clock news, pleading for his daughter's safe return. She had heard him say he would do anything to have her back. He'd looked directly into the camera as he spoke, seemingly straight into Gilly's eyes, and he'd said, "Zoe, if you can hear me, Daddy loves you, sweetheart. I'm coming to get you, I promise."

His anguish had reached into Gilly and taken her heart in its cold, panicked grasp. It had jerked open the door to her own ghosts, letting them out of the cellar in her mind where she kept them. What would she do to have Sophie back for one day, one hour, one minute? Like Jake, she would beg. She would go to her knees, promise anything. It shook Gilly, seeing Jake's vulnerability that was the mirror of her own. And when her phone had rung a short while later, and she'd seen it was him, she hadn't been able to answer.

He had left a voice mail in return: *I don't know what you're talking about.*

She left the bathroom for her bedroom now, where she pulled on linen crop pants, a loose shirt, slipped her feet into her sandals. She wished she could help him, but her compassion for him was bound by a perimeter of rage at his nerve in dragging her into his drama, making her part of it, as if she didn't have her own panic and grief to shoulder. There were days when she could barely hold herself together, keep herself from sinking—drinking. Days when the monkey danced, grinning, asking: *What's the point?*

Gilly prayed Jake wouldn't learn what it was like. She prayed Zoe would be found safe and wasn't gone forever like Sophie. But he needed to understand—people needed to realize—that Gilly wasn't the key. What she had seen in her dream, or what she might see should she have another one, was useless.

Carl called as she was leaving the house. "Your mom says there's a little girl missing up there. I checked, and sure enough there's an Amber Alert."

"Yes, they thought it was her mother who'd taken her."

"But not anymore, according to the information here. Your mom's worried."

"I didn't have anything to do with it."

"I don't think that's the cause for her concern so much as she says you dreamed about it."

"Well, it's no secret my dreams upset her. I shouldn't have told her."

"My concern is that the media will get hold of it."

Gilly made no comment.

"This guy we have the lead on, Brian's killer—if the story blows up, and he sees you on television, finds out where you are, it's not safe for you up there."

She started to argue.

"What about Mark Riley?" Carl cut her off. "You think he can't find you, you're wrong. I told you that when you left here."

"I know, Carl, but I can take care of myself."

He was quiet, and for a moment there was only the sound of their breath.

"I can't protect you when you're so far away, Gilly." Carl's voice was low and gruff.

It was the voice she'd heard mornings when, newly sober, she'd wakened next to him. As soon as he felt her stir, he'd pulled her into his arms, and she'd burrowed against him. The sound of his heartbeat beneath her ear, strong and sure, had soon lulled her anxiety, and calmed her yearning for a drink, or for Brian and her old life. She remembered Carl's lovemaking, the way he had touched her, entered her with such reverence, as if she were a precious gift. *I can't believe I'm so lucky.* How many times had he told her?

"I'm off in a couple of days. I'm thinking of driving up."

Gilly's heart surged with longing. But no, she told him, no, and when he asked why, she said she'd made plans with Liz. It was easier than the truth, which was that there was nothing she could give him, or any man, without betraying Brian.

They hung up, and Carl texted her almost immediately. I'm coming anyway.

• • •

Gilly had a flat tire on her way to the police station and wondered, as she stood looking at it, if it was a sign. She didn't have long to think about it before a white van pulled in behind her. Shading her eyes, Gilly watched the driver—a man wearing a red ball cap—get out. It crossed her mind that if this were Houston and not Wyatt, she might be concerned. That was the difference between a small town and a big city.

"Howdy," he said, joining her to look at her right side rear tire. "Looks like you've got a flat there."

"I was considering whether I could drive on it. I have to get gas anyway. I thought maybe I could ask someone at the station to change it. I've never done it," she added, feeling dumb.

"I can do it. Won't take two shakes."

"I hate to impose."

"It's nothing. I'm familiar with the RAV4. Guy that lives next door to me, his daughter owns one. What year is this?"

"Sixteen," she answered. She'd bought it new after she got sober, paying cash for it. One more thing the payout from Brian's life insurance policy had made possible. A woman, overhearing her tell the salesman it would be a cash deal, had said how she envied Gilly.

"No car payment. Wow!" she had said. "What I wouldn't give."

Would you give your husband? That's what Gilly had wanted to ask her.

"Katy's RAV—that's the neighbor next door—hers is a twenty-ten," the man said. "She bought it used. It's been a good car. I help her with it. Her dad don't know squat about cars. Can you open the back?"

"Oh, yes." She popped the hatch, using her key fob. "Sorry."

"No worries." He took out the spare, and setting it down, introduced himself. "I'm Warren," he said. "Warren Jester."

She hesitated for a moment, worried he'd have seen last night's news, and if she gave him her name, he'd put it together with her photo. "Gillian O'Connell," she said. "Most folks call me Gilly." She watched, but if he recognized her, he gave no sign.

He put out his hand, and she took it, losing hers in his larger grasp. His palm felt dry and rough, and his knuckles were large, reddened knobs. They were a workman's hands. Gilly had the impression he'd struggled, that if she were to ask him, he would say nothing in life had come easy to him, and he had no expectation it would ever be different.

He seemed old to her. His face was deeply creased on either side of his nose, and his eyes were kind but looked weary. He might have been fifty or seventy. She wasn't good at guessing ages.

He squatted down, and setting his lug wrench to one side, he maneuvered the jack in front of the tire until he was satisfied with its position.

"I knew something wasn't right," Gilly said. "It was steering funny."

"Yeah? Well, it's a good thing you stopped. You drive on a flat, you bend the wheel rim. Cost you a lot more, replacing that."

She looked out at the highway. They were east of town on FM 1620, the major route through Wyatt. Traffic was steady, and the air was laden with gas fumes, the more acrid smell of warm tar. The wind buffeted her legs, rippled the fabric of her shirt. Although it was barely midmorning, it was already hot, and where she'd pulled over there wasn't a shred of protection from the sun's glare. She felt bad for Warren, having to do this chore in the heat. She thought of retrieving the umbrella she kept in the car for rainy days, but she didn't want to embarrass him, holding it open over his head. At least he had the cap.

"Are you a Rockets fan?" she asked, spotting the logo.

"Not so much since Olajuwon left the team. Never been a player since like him."

"That's what my dad says."

"Y'all live here in town?"

"I do. I moved here not long ago. My parents are in Houston, though." She bit her lip, afraid he'd put it together now for sure, turn to her and say she looked familiar, that he thought he'd seen her on the news. *Aren't you that psychic?*

But he went on with his task, and his movements were calm, practiced, methodical. He didn't seem in the least perturbed. She was sweating, but he didn't appear to be. "What about you?" she asked. "Are you from Wyatt?"

"Victoria," he said, naming a town close to the gulf coast. He had popped off the hubcap, and he was dropping the bolts into it as he unscrewed them. "I heard about the little girl who's missing in the area. I work with search teams sometimes. I like to help out when I can." He sat back on his heels, pushed his cap back on his head, stirred the bolts in the hubcap with the tip of his index finger.

Counting them, Gilly thought. Making sure he hadn't dropped one. He was careful with the details.

He was a journeyman carpenter between jobs, he said, pulling off the flat. Within minutes, he'd settled the spare into place, tightened the bolts, and lowered the RAV off the jack. "You want me to set this back there in the hatch?" he asked, indicating the flat tire. He wiped his brow and his hands on a handkerchief he pulled from his pants pocket. It looked freshly washed and ironed.

Old-fashioned.

Gilly couldn't recall seeing a man with a handkerchief in years, if ever. She glanced up at Warren, half smiling. It was endearing somehow. She said, "If you don't mind."

"There's a nail in it." He showed her the nail head where it had pierced the tread. "You can get it fixed. Don't let them boys at the tire store talk you into buying a new one." He rolled the tire to the rear of the car and lifted it inside.

Gilly closed it remotely. She offered to pay him for his help, but he refused. "Then let me buy you lunch, or at least a cup of coffee," she said. "I work at Cricket's. It's the café on the town square?"

He picked up the tools. He was familiar with the place, he said. "I've seen it driving through town. I'm staying at the Motel 6, and I'll be there as long as there's a need for search and rescue." He stowed the jack and the lug wrench.

Gilly thanked him.

Warren lifted his cap, resettled it. "I'll stop by Cricket's sometime, take you up on that cup of coffee."

"Yes," she said. "Please do." She'd make sure to offer Warren a slice of pie, something sweet to go with it, she decided, as she slid behind the wheel.

. . .

Gilly drove on her spare tire to the police station, and she was at first relieved to run into Sergeant Carter and not Captain Mackie on her way inside. The sergeant held open the door for her, and she asked about the search effort.

"Tip line's generating a lot of calls," he answered.

A woman in uniform was on the phone behind the lobby counter, and looking up at the sergeant, she shook her head, a gesture Gilly understood to mean the call she was taking was nothing that required the sergeant's attention.

He turned to Gilly. "So what can I do for you?"

"I need your help," she said, and it almost killed her having to ask a cop for assistance.

"All right. You want to come this way?" He led her through a battered metal door and across a large room that was broken into cubicles, framed by shoulder-high partitions. Phones rang in discordant harmony. There was a jumble of voices.

"Volunteers." The sergeant explained the source for all the chatter. "We don't have enough staff to handle the calls that are coming in."

"I could help with that," Gilly said, but if he heard her offer, he didn't acknowledge it.

"There's coffee." He paused beside a table set with a huge, ancient-looking commercial machine.

Two hard water–stained glass carafes sat on two warmers. The smell was stale, burned, with an underscore of something sweet. Gilly noticed the crushed shape of a pastry box in the overflowing waste can.

"I can't vouch for it." The sergeant poured some of the brew into a foam cup, handing it to her.

Gilly didn't want it. She only accepted out of courtesy and the need to do something with her hands. She followed him into a nearby cubicle, sat in the chair he indicated, and while she fumbled with the cup and her purse, he sat behind a battered desk, regarding her without expression. Waiting for her to speak first.

Because that's how cops operated. Gilly knew that. "I guess you know Cricket has closed the café for the time being. To everyday traffic," she said, and it irked her that she'd done what he wanted, filled in the silence, as if she were here to pass the time of day.

"She brought the sandwiches y'all made out to the search teams yesterday."

"We're doing it again—every day the search goes on." Gilly repeated what April had told her earlier.

"There were at least a hundred folks out there," Carter said. "I expect there'll be more today with the word getting out through the news and all." His look seemed intent, pointed.

Gilly crossed her knees.

"We've never had anything like this go on around here before." He nudged the desk blotter. "A couple of folks have gone missing from Wyatt in years past but never a child."

"The trike Jake found in the woods at the school—on the news last night they said it didn't belong to Zoe. Hers was found at a neighbor's house?"

"Yeah, well, we never figured it had anything to do with Zoe. I know folks thought it was some kind of bait, but it belonged to Megan Phillips. Her dad, Ben—you know him?"

Gilly nodded. *Red hair, freckles, English muffin, coffee black, 8:00 a.m. sharp, Monday through Friday, regular as moonrise.* He sold insurance and always had a joke to tell.

"Kids like to ride the trail back there, behind the school." Ken's tone suggested he couldn't imagine why. "Ben said he got a phone call, some kind of semi-urgent thing, and somehow Megan's trike got left there."

Gilly didn't say anything. She'd gone along with the idea everyone in town seemed to have, that the trike had significance. She'd seen it in her dream. But the dream had been wrong. Again. She tucked her hair behind her ear.

The sergeant drummed his fingers on the desk edge.

"The news story last night," Gilly began, and she noted the slight lift to his chin, a look in his eyes that seemed to say, *Here we go*. "It was inaccurate."

"In what way?"

"I'm not a psychic, and I'm not employed by, nor have I been consulted by, the Halstead family about Zoe's disappearance."

"All right. But I'm not sure what your purpose is, telling me this."

"I'd like you—the Wyatt police—to correct what was reported, or make KTKY and Suki Daniels issue a correction." Gilly didn't want to name Jake, to cause him more trouble by accusing him of giving a false impression of her to the reporter. "Ms. Daniels should have checked with me before airing such nonsense."

"Well, that's not—the media isn't under our jurisdiction. Freedom of speech and all that—"

Gilly set her coffee, untouched, on the desk. "They made it seem as if it's going to be me and not the police who finds Zoe. They practically came out and said the Halstead family has no faith in local law enforcement. I wouldn't think you or your department would like it any more than I do."

"We don't."

"Then I don't understand why you can't make them retract the story."

"As I just said, here in the USA there's such a thing as free speech."

"So they can deliberately mislead the public—" Gilly stopped. Of course they could and did. All the time. She looked into her lap, irked—at the sergeant, at herself.

"You could try a lawyer."

Her gaze came up.

"It's possible an attorney might be able to advise you if there's a way to make KTKY set the record straight."

Gilly didn't answer.

"Look." The sergeant bent, his weight on his elbows. "I've got to tell you, I'm a skeptic. I don't believe people can see the future, or anything else other than what's as solid as their hand in front of their face. But even if I did, what good is it? Of what possible use is it to me as a cop to know you dreamed Zoe Halstead was abducted the night before she actually was? I'm not trying to be an asshole here, okay? I really want to know."

"Yeah, me too. When I have the dreams—it makes me sick and angry. They're like a terrible joke because there's nothing I can do. I'm never shown what to do."

"We've had a couple of calls come into the tip line since the KTKY story about you. Two other women, claiming they're psychic. One of them saying Zoe's body is somewhere near water—"

"Are you kidding? You mean as if Zoe's—"

"Dead. Yeah. The other so-called psychic says Zoe's alive but being held captive. She claims the kidnapper is a man, and he's holding Zoe in an apartment in Waco with a name that has something to do with cowboy boots or cactus. She doesn't know which."

"Is there any evidence to support either theory?"

"Not so far, but that's the thing, see? We've got to run down every call, every lead. We're looking at apartment complexes in Waco, and blue sedans—that lead's per your dream. We're looking at lakes and rivers, even stock ponds, statewide. It takes time. And if there's one thing that little girl doesn't have, Ms. O'Connell, it's time."

"You're not looking for blue sedans because of me and what I dreamed. You have a witness, don't you? One who actually saw Zoe get into a blue car."

"Yes, but my point is, real or bogus, we have to follow every lead."

Gilly stared at him.

"The potential is always there that someone like you, calling in with this type of information—"

"I didn't call in—"

"Maybe you're just looking for attention, your fifteen minutes, so to speak. Or maybe you're involved somehow, and you're trying to manipulate the investigation. Or maybe you think it's funny, misleading law enforcement."

"I don't think a single thing about this is funny, Sergeant."

The short silence was heated.

Gilly broke it. "I hope you aren't suggesting *I* took Zoe." Could he be? Hadn't Captain Mackie said she was clear of suspicion? She wished now she could have spoken to him and not the sergeant. "I would never do that—"

"Uh, wait a minute." The sergeant raised his hands a bit above the desktop. "Before you say more—we know you're on probation for abducting a baby from a Houston hospital. So it wouldn't be exactly true, would it—to say you'd *never* take a child?"

Gilly shifted her glance. The urge to defend herself, to ask the sergeant if he knew the circumstances, jammed the space behind her teeth. But she wouldn't play the pity card. She wouldn't say that under ordinary circumstances, when she wasn't insane with grief and doping herself to forget, she would never have committed such a horrible act. "I don't know what your intention is, Sergeant, in reminding me of what I did and the fact that I'm on probation for it."

"You aren't a suspect in this case if that's what's got you worried."

"That's good to know, but maybe, unlike Captain Mackie, you continue to have doubts about me. Would I have come here if I'd had anything to do with Zoe's disappearance? Would I be asking for your help in getting the truth out through the media?"

"Well, like I said, a lawyer's your best bet there."

He didn't trust her. That was obvious. But wasn't it the nature of law enforcement personnel to be suspicious? It was probably a job requirement. She knew Ken Carter was well liked and well respected around town. She had liked him, too, the times she'd served him at Cricket's. She stood up, shouldering her purse.

"It's nothing personal, Ms. O'Connell. Something like this—when it involves a child—everyone's a suspect, you know? Friends, family members. Everybody in this town is looking at everybody else."

"I understand," Gilly said, and she did to a degree. April had said the same thing. But as far as she knew, April hadn't been questioned by the police. She hadn't come under suspicion or been featured on the news, and April had served time in prison for murder. "Thanks for talking to me," Gilly said.

"No problem." The sergeant followed her from the cubicle. He held the door to the lobby open for her.

There was a man at the duty desk, talking to the uniformed officer behind it. Gilly had a moment to observe him, long enough to feel he was familiar, even to feel a kind of dread, and when he turned to her and she saw who he was, her heart stalled.

"You!" The word was a bullet. It was hate coming from his mouth, and Gilly stiffened.

She felt Sergeant Carter come to attention behind her.

The man, addressing the uniformed desk officer, asked if Gilly was under arrest. "Are you cops finally doing your damn job?"

"You know him?" Sergeant Carter asked quietly.

"It's Mark Riley," Gilly said. "The father of the baby I took in Houston."

Sergeant Carter stepped around her, drawing Mark Riley's attention, saying his name, introducing himself, hand extended. "I'm Sergeant Carter. How can I help you today?"

Mark ignored the sergeant's hand. "You putting her in jail? That's all the help I need."

"Why don't you come with me? We can talk about it."

"There's nothing to talk about, goddammit. How many kids are you assholes going to let her take before you do the right thing and lock her up? Or am I going to have to take care of it? Huh?"

"Mr. Riley—"

"Just answer the damn question. It's simple enough, isn't it?" Mark took a step toward the sergeant, where he stood in front of Gilly.

She caught Sergeant Carter's glance. He nodded toward the police station entrance. "Why don't you go on?"

Gilly started across the lobby, and when Mark lunged at her, when he shouted, "You're a monster, a sick bitch, and I will see you in jail, do you hear me? Or dead!" she ran for the double glass doors, flinging one open, hurling herself through it.

"No! You can't let her go!" Mark's shout followed her.

Gilly didn't look back.

● ● ●

She was shaking and pulled into a strip center down the street from the police station. Parking in front of a dry cleaner's, she sat staring, sightless, hands gripping the steering wheel.

Carl had said it would happen, but how had Mark Riley found her?

She bent her head to her knuckled fists. The Rileys knew she'd moved. She had written a letter, telling them. Gilly had wanted them to know. She had thought it would help, bring them some kind of relief, knowing she was no longer in Houston, nowhere near their daughter. But she hadn't given her destination. Carl had warned her even before she'd left Houston. He'd said Mark was a danger to her. He'd seen guys like him before, chip on their shoulder, wild in their eyes, take no shit off anybody. Carl had said Mark Riley wasn't the kind to let some woman get one over on him.

Mark had threatened her once, outside on the courthouse steps after the judge sentenced Gilly to probation.

He'd come out of the crowd quickly, and before she could react, he'd put his lips near her ear and said, "You ever come near my family again, I'll put a bullet in your brain."

Carl had been with her, and he'd been a witness. The two had scuffled. Other cops had jumped on Mark, too. He'd had no chance. But she understood the motive for his attack. She knew how fear for someone you loved—your little child, who relied on you for protection—could morph into rage, how you might want to kill the person who had created the danger. Sometimes she wished Mark had done what he wanted—taken her down, ended it for her. Then she wouldn't have to live with the shame of the harm she'd caused. She wouldn't have to fight so hard to be normal.

Gilly got out her phone now, but Carl didn't pick up. His voice mail came on.

"Hey," she said. "It's nothing. Just—I'd like to talk to you when you get a chance."

She severed the connection, sorry she'd made the call. She didn't want to add to Carl's worry or encourage him in the idea they had a future. She didn't want him to come here, where she would be tempted to lean on him. It wasn't fair to him. He could do better than her, better than somebody who wasn't sure she cared whether she had a future.

You can't outrun your past.

Someone had warned her about that recently, Gilly thought. Who? Her mom? Julia?

Barbara Taylor Sissel

What was Mark Riley telling Sergeant Carter about her right now? She guessed it wouldn't have been all that difficult, finding her, not with the internet. It could be done, if you were determined. Obsessed. A control freak. That was how Carl had described Mark. After he threatened her at the courthouse, Carl had looked into Mark's background and learned he'd been arrested for punching his wife. Not his current wife, the mother of Anne Clementine, but his first wife. It was years ago. He'd been ordered to attend anger management classes as part of his sentence. He'd been in a couple of bar fights since, but the charges had been dropped. Carl said Mark's history showed an affinity for violence—specifically, violence against women. *You watch out for that guy. If you see him, don't engage with him. You call me immediately.*

Gilly hadn't followed Carl's instructions. She had written to the Rileys, possibly reigniting Mark's hostility, his need to see Gilly punished, and now not only had he found her, but he knew about Zoe, that Gilly had been implicated in yet another child abduction.

If only Brian were here. *But he's not*, said Miss Goody Two-shoes. *Pull up your big-girl panties.* Gilly blinked away the burn of tears. She got a tissue from her purse, blew her nose, wiped her eyes. Of all the places and all the times she could have chosen to start over, why here? Why now? Sergeant Carter had said nothing like this had ever happened in Wyatt. The town had never lost one of its children. He had seemed to soften toward her by the end of their interview. But he would likely change his mind once Mark Riley went through it step-by-step—how Gilly had taken his child, an infant barely one day old, and had gotten off with little more than a slap on the wrist.

She would be under suspicion again. Her probation could be revoked. She'd be sent to prison. It was what Mark wanted. Maybe that was the whole idea. He wouldn't stop with the local police. He'd tell his story to Suki Daniels. Then everyone in Wyatt—Jake—Jake Halstead would know. Gilly hated that as much as anything. But she was angry at him, too. He'd been wrong to go behind her back and speak about her to the media, telling them lies about a dream—a damn dream she'd had that meant nothing.

Less than nothing.

Why couldn't he see it? How useless it was?

Maybe she should refer him to Sergeant Carter for an interpretation. Ken Carter would happily share his impression of Gilly's so-called psychic skill. She picked up her phone again, punching in Jake's number.

The call was answered, and she straightened, but it was only Jake's voice mail. She groped for words, having nothing prepared for a message. "We need to talk." She paused. "You can't pretend you don't know what this is about." Pause. She let her stare drift. Then, not caring how he took it, "If you don't call me back, I will find you."

17

It was no ordinary jail visit—Jake had needed special permission to see Stephanie—but then the circumstances weren't ordinary. It occurred to him that reality TV had nothing in its programming that compared to his life now. He shifted uneasily in the plastic chair.

Habit had him reaching into his jeans pocket for his cell phone, something to do, but then he remembered he'd had to surrender it, along with his wallet and keys, before they'd let him come back here. He leaned forward, setting his elbows on the table. According to the guard who had escorted him, the room itself was an exception, not one ordinarily used for jailhouse visits. He wondered if it was bugged, whether he was being watched. He couldn't see how. It was windowless and empty except for the table and two chairs. There wasn't a camera, not that was visible to him anyway.

Jake sat back, shifted his feet. Waited. Dry mouthed. Panic kept trying to stand up in his gut, and he kept shoving it down. He was worried about his phone—that he'd had to leave it. The guard had said if he heard any news about Zoe he'd let Jake know immediately. But it wasn't the same, wasn't good enough. He stood up, sat back down.

You didn't want her anyway.

The caller's words circled in his brain in an ever-tightening loop, agitating, shameful. He didn't know how he could have felt that way. It nearly killed him, remembering. Who had he been then? He didn't know. But he did know Stephanie was one of only three other people besides himself who had known his state of mind. She'd shared his fear of becoming a parent, possibly feeling the weight of looming responsibility even more deeply. What was he going to say to her? *Where the hell is our kid?* Jesus God, if the woman—if that bastard Duchene—if they'd done something to Zoe—

The door opened, and she was there. A small-framed woman lost inside an overlarge suit of clothes, a boxy shirt and pants, striped in faded black and white. DALLAS COUNTY INMATE was stamped across a pocket. The woman was wild-haired, wild-eyed. Twitchy. She picked at her arms, reached for her earlobe, touched her temple, pulled at her lip. She looked scared. But maybe she was still high. Jake couldn't tell. She was barely recognizable to him. It was hard to believe she'd once been the object if not of his love then of his obsession.

The guard pushed her forward. She said his name. "Jake?"

It was the sound of her voice that did it, snapped into place his acceptance that it was indeed Stephanie, his ex-wife. He thought about standing up, but he didn't feel capable. In all their history, he'd never seen her in jail garb; he'd never had to. The times she was picked up in Wyatt, Clint had been there to bring her home. Folks in town had looked out for her, covered for her on Jake's account, for his and Zoe's sakes. But Stephanie wasn't known here. She'd landed someplace now where no one gave a shit about her.

Pulling out the opposite chair, she sat down. Her fingertips danced across the tabletop, then plucked at her shirt. She was as pale as an egg and sweating. She swiped the wet from her hairline, from beneath her eyes, below her chin. She was suffering, coming down off whatever she'd been on.

Jake looked away, fighting disgust, pity, an angrier, half-panicked urge to run.

"You got thirty minutes," the guard said, and he left the room, closing the door. But he didn't go far. Jake could see him. A part of his uniformed shoulder was visible through the window in the door behind Stephanie.

"I never expected to see you here."

It was the belligerence in her voice that got to Jake. He rapped the table with his knuckles, making her jump. "Where is Zoe?"

She straightened, blinking at him. "What are you talking about?"

"A woman picked Zoe up from school Thursday afternoon," Jake said. "She told the assistant she was Zoe's mother. That's you. Zoe hasn't been home since. Where is she?" Jake kept his tone civil, but there was no absence of menace. He watched Stephanie's expression, watched her grow paler than she had been, if it was possible.

She said, "I didn't—"

"It had to be you, Steph. You and I both know she would have hollered her head off if it was a stranger who got her."

"Look, I swear to you, it wasn't me. Jake! My God! She didn't come home?"

"You called her, right? Sometime recently, you called Zoe at my house—the landline—and you told her you were going to see her soon."

"Yes, and I—I meant to, you know, but I—"

"I'm not interested in your excuses, Steph. Where is our daughter?"

"I don't know. The cops asked me, too. I thought it was a joke, a mean joke they were playing—" She broke off, frowning deeply now, and a dawning urgency in her eyes was like a shaft of light through a fog.

Jake saw it, an inkling of comprehension, along with the nascent thread of alarm, which once she grasped the sense of the danger Zoe was in—assuming she was telling the truth and didn't know Zoe's whereabouts any better than he did—would balloon into a bright and all-consuming terror. But he refused to consider the possibility that

Stephanie was ignorant of the circumstances. He didn't care what she had said to the police earlier, or what she claimed now. She was a liar. She'd proven it again and again. She had even told him before that she would lie when the truth would serve her better.

"Look, it's no joke. I got a phone call last night—Someone said— You're the only one who—" He faltered to a stop. He was the uncertain one now. He shot her a glance. "Was it Duchene? Did he call me last night? Did you give him that line to say?"

Stephanie's face was creased with strain, the effort to find some solid mental ground. "I don't know what you're talking about. Zoe lives with you. You're the one who has custody. How would I know where she is?"

"What about Duchene? Where is he?"

"What does he have to do with it?"

"He's your boyfriend, your drug buddy. He ran off, didn't he? While you were stabbing the dealer. What a damn fool thing—"

"I was defending myself, and so what if Andy took off? He was smarter than me, landing in this hellhole."

"Where is he, Steph? Where did he take Zoe?"

"I don't know what—"

"Don't tell me he doesn't have her. I got that call last night, and this morning Clint told me a half dozen folks have called the tip line in the past few hours to say they saw a little girl matching Zoe's description with a man—"

"Tip line? My God!" Stephanie stared at Jake, and he could see it, that she was putting the pieces together now—his visit to her and the reason for it. "You're really serious," she said. "Zoe's gone, and you don't know where. What the hell, Jake?"

Her shock and the suddenness of her panic, the lash of her damnation of him, cut through to his backbone. Shame rose anew, an oily tide that gagged him. He couldn't look at her, couldn't stomach seeing in her eyes the reflection of his failure to protect their daughter. Yet some part of him clung to the idea that she was acting, creating a show to throw him off. But the sense of it—that she truly had no idea where Zoe was—shook him. "Duchene has her, doesn't he?" Jake insisted over his doubt. "You planned this together."

"What kind of a monster do you think I am?" Her offense was instant, clarifying, the rising sun burning through the haze of his suspicion, and it infuriated him.

"You didn't want her!" The accusation was gone from Jake's mouth before he could think.

"Neither did you!" she retorted.

He looked away. They were squabbling like children, pushing each other's buttons the way they always had. He couldn't back off, though. Couldn't dial it down. "Duchene's taken his own kids." He brought his gaze around. "Did you know? He tried to get them out of the country. He was arrested—"

"Yes, yes." She was equally impatient. "I know all about that, but Andy doesn't have Zoe. I swear."

They stared at each other.

"Unless . . ." Stephanie's gaze drifted.

"Unless what?" Jake half stood, bristling, agitated.

She shifted her glance.

"Unless what, Stephanie?" He was bent over the table, shouting now. He wanted to shake her. It took everything he had not to grab her.

The guard's broad face lowered to fill the window. Jake waved him off. He took a moment, getting a grip on himself, then looked back at his ex. "Tell me where Duchene is, Steph."

"We talked about it, you know, having our children together. His and mine. Making a family with them. But we were high."

Jake groaned. "Jesus God."

Stephanie folded her arms, cupped her elbows in her hands. "I never wanted children. I thought—you always said it was fine. You could be fine without them, too."

"Do you remember the day Zoe was born?"

"You cried."

He didn't answer.

"I hated you for it, you know."

Jake looked up.

"That you could love her so spontaneously, without reservation, unconditionally. We had the same doubts. You were all for the abortion."

"Yeah, and I took you home after you changed your mind."

Steph took her gaze away.

"Why didn't you go through with it? You've never told me."

"I was scared. I thought maybe I'd be better off, having the kid, try-ing to make some kind of life with you." She looked back at him. "God knows there was nothing for me in New York. The fashion designer gig was over, worse than over. I had a dream, but they cut it up and crammed it down my throat. How many times can you take it? Getting told your designs are boring, or irrelevant, or unflattering, basically that you suck, every day of your life?"

Jake waited, not responding. He'd used to try and comfort her, to get her to see the possibilities. Maybe New York wasn't the place for her designs. Maybe it was Dallas, or LA, or even the internet. Who knew? But he'd learned she didn't want to be encouraged, to move on. She was in love with her story, her role as the victim. It gave her an excuse to quit trying, and finally, it had given her an excuse to take her drinking to the next level.

"No one cared," she said.

"I cared," Jake said.

"Out of obligation. It's the kind of guy you are. You can't help yourself." After a moment, she laughed, and the sound was one syllable, a harsh bark. "I thought you'd rub off on me."

He kept her gaze.

"Something happened with you, inside you, the day Zoe was born. The minute you saw her something in your face changed. Your tears . . . I don't know . . ."

Jake knew what she meant. He could still remember his feeling of awe.

"Me? I was just scared shitless. I knew I'd fuck it up, and guess what, I was right. Give me a gold star." She kept his gaze. "I wanted to feel like you did about Zoe," she said, speaking so quietly, Jake had to strain to hear. "I wanted to feel that bond that all the new-mother books talk about. But I never—felt—anything. Except tired. Burdened. Pissed off and sick inside." She looked up, ineffable sadness shadowing her eyes. "She wouldn't take my milk. Wouldn't have my breast in her mouth. Do you remember? The nurse gave her a bottle, and that was the end of it. She was on a bottle from then on. She was her daddy's girl, too. Nothing left over for Mama."

"She asks about you, waits for you. The day before she disappeared she wanted to know if her *mama*"—Jake's emphasis was deliberate, heated—"knew where she was."

Steph's mouth flattened.

Jake planted his elbows on the table. "Do you? Was Zoe with you when you were making your drug deal? Was she there when the cops came? When Duchene ran off? Where would he take her?"

Stephanie said, "Zoe wasn't with us."

"Stop lying! Duchene wore a hoodie and big sunglasses, trying to look like a woman when you picked Zoe up. Was that your idea? Did you think you could outsmart the cops?"

"No, I—"

"They found them—Zoe's clothes—where you tossed them in the dumpster. You and Duchene—you won't get away with it." Jake waited, giving her time to answer, to tell him the truth. She didn't.

"Kidnapping's a felony, Steph. It's big time. Clint's called in the FBI. You could spend the rest of your life locked up. Is that what you want?"

"I don't know what you're talking about. Andy and I didn't take Zoe. I swear to God we didn't."

"Swear to somebody you know." Jake stood up fast enough that the chair shot back, hitting the wall behind it. Rounding the table, he banged on the door. "Guard!" He had to get out of here, get to his phone.

"Take it easy," the guard said.

Jake turned to Stephanie. "What kind of car does Duchene drive?"

"He doesn't have her, Jake."

"What kind of car?"

Her mouth flattened, but she answered him. She seemed resigned. "Nissan. Old. Gray or maybe it's blue. The trunk won't close. He has to tie it shut."

"What's the model? Sentra? Altima?"

"I don't know."

He started out the door.

Stephanie called him back. "Jake?"

He turned to her.

"Whoever the woman is who got Zoe, it must have been someone she knew, or she wouldn't have gone. Not without a fight. Not without screaming bloody murder, the way you taught her."

"Yeah, Clint—the cops, everyone—knows she would have made some noise," he said, but now another alternative occurred to him for the first time. He couldn't believe he hadn't thought of it before. He kept Stephanie's gaze. "What if the woman told Zoe she was taking her to you? She could have said she was your friend."

"But Zoe knows better than to believe anything a stranger might say to her about us, that we're sick or injured—you warned her—"

"Yes, but here's what you're not getting, Steph. Zoe was ready to believe anything if it meant she would see you. That's what I'm saying. That's how much she misses you."

Stephanie didn't answer. She looked breathless, shattered. Her glance fell from his, and he turned away. But he heard it. The soft sound of her weeping followed him and his escort to the farthest end of the corridor.

• • •

Jake waited until he was outside the jail before checking his messages. There were two. The first was from Clint, asking Jake to call, advising him there was nothing new. He was only looking for a recount of Jake's visit with Stephanie.

The next was from Gilly O'Connell. "We need to talk," she said, and her voice was tight, her agitation more obvious than before. She'd find him, she said, if he didn't call her back. Jake pulled the phone from his ear and looked at it. Was she threatening him?

Really?

So he was a liar then? Because clearly Gilly didn't buy it, the message he'd left her last night denying he was the source for that garbage Suki Daniels had spouted on the news. Fine, he thought. Come on with it. Let Gilly confront him, accuse him. He'd give her an earful.

He got into his truck and keyed the ignition. He returned Clint's call first, and when the police captain answered, Jake gave him the gist of his conversation with Stephanie, sticking to the facts about Duchene. It was difficult, keeping a lid on his emotions.

"I want to kill him," Jake said. "He's got my little girl. Duchene has got Zoe, Clint."

"I know you want to believe it's him, but there's nothing to support that."

"Can you find out the make on his car and get an APB, a BOLO—whatever it is—can you get that out on him? I know it's not much to go on, but we need to find him. Guy's a doper. God knows what he'll do."

"Already done. The car's a ninety-nine Sentra. The color's listed as gray not blue. We've put the information out there, but so far there's no sign of him or the car."

"You're checking airports, bus stations, the trains?"

"Yes, all that. Trust me, we may be a small-time, small-town police force, but we know what we're doing."

Jake said he was sorry. He said, "I'm just so fucking scared, Clint. Every hour that goes by that she isn't found, it's—it's like she's disappeared off the face of the earth. How does it happen? How—" His voice cracked. He swallowed, cleared his throat. He saw the traffic ahead through a prism of tears, and he blinked to clear them. He'd be in the breakdown lane if he kept this up, and not the one for vehicles. *Suck it up, buttercup*, he told himself.

"The phones are still ringing, son." Clint got Jake's attention. "We're running down every lead. You never know when one of them will pan out."

"Duchene tried to look like a woman—" Jake couldn't let go of it.

Clint cut him off. "Think about it, man. A guy doing that—the teaching assistant, Marley, would have noticed."

"Maybe it was Steph then. I don't know. They changed Zoe's clothes; they're obviously trying to disguise her. That's what's got me freaked out. She won't be recognizable from the photos we're putting out." It had torn a hole in his heart—seeing her clothes, Zoe's tiny clothes. They had been laid out on the hood of Ken Carter's police cruiser by the time Jake had pulled up to the dumpster in Nickel Bend. He'd known they belonged to Zoe before he'd cleared the front bumper of his truck. The little skirt, printed with butterflies that Zoe had insisted on wearing two days in a row, had been fanned out, smoothed into a careful semicircle as if to be admired, coveted. Jake had gritted his teeth to keep from howling.

"Maybe. It's a possibility." Clint was placating him. "The thing is, folks have called the tip line saying they've seen a little girl Zoe's age with a woman, thirty-five to forty. One came in a half hour ago. Someone down at Monarch Lake said they saw a woman and a little girl down at the south end yesterday, early evening, sixish, wading in the water near one of the picnic areas. He said they were driving a truck with a camper top. They stayed there last night. If that's true, there could be footage on the security camera at the park entrance."

"There wasn't a man with them?" Jake switched on his signal and changed lanes.

"I don't know. Ken's checking it out. Maybe we'll get lucky. The thing is, we can't focus on Stephanie, or Duchene, or any one person at this point. We've got to keep an open mind."

"It's been almost forty-eight hours since Zoe disappeared, Clint."

"I know that, Jake. Don't you think I know?"

He didn't answer. He didn't trust himself, the words that might come out of his mouth, and he needed Clint—his expertise, his resources and connections—everything law enforcement could do.

"Gilly O'Connell was here at the station this morning. Ken talked to her."

"I heard from her, too. She left me a message, says she's looking for me." Jake slowed almost to a stop. Highway construction had traffic down to a single lane now; they were only creeping along. It was no use getting worked up about it. It went on for miles. He knew that from the drive north earlier.

"Did she say why?" Clint asked.

"You heard Suki Daniels, KTKY News, last night—"

"The bit about Gilly being the psychic you hired to find Zoe?"

"Yeah. Gilly thinks I'm Suki's source. Ha! Like I'd feed the press bullshit when my daughter's life is on the line."

"According to Ken, Gilly's not any happier than you about the report. She wanted to know what law enforcement could do to get the station to retract the story. Ken advised her to get an attorney."

"So who's behind it? You have any ideas?"

"No, and there's basically no way to find out. Not easily anyway. Somebody who wants to cause Gilly trouble, maybe . . . I dunno." Clint was quiet.

Jake stared at the car bumper ahead of him, but the image in his mind was of Gilly and the look of defiance in her eyes when she'd declared she'd been sober for more than eight months. It had come off like a dare, as if on seeing the taint of his disgust—which he knew had been visible on his face—she'd waited for his challenge. The way she'd looked straight at him, she wouldn't have taken anything off him. She might be holding back like he and Clint thought. There could very well be more to her story than she was telling, but he was pretty sure now it had nothing to do with him or Zoe. "Your investigation of Gilly," he said to Clint, "did it turn up anything? You find any connection to Steph?"

"No, but Gilly's record isn't clean. She's had some issues," Clint said.

"She told me she lost her baby after her husband was shot—"

"Yeah. Carl Bowen, the detective in Houston who's working the husband's case, called me. He's concerned about her. The guy who shot her husband is still out there."

"Really." Gilly hadn't mentioned that. "That's got to be scary."

"Bowen said they're working a new lead, but she's their main witness—not to the actual shooting, but she got a look at the guy as he fled the scene. It's likely he saw her, too. Bowen said he'd warned her to stay on her guard. He asked me to keep an eye on her, watch out for strangers around town, let him know about anyone I'm not familiar with." Clint's laugh was dry. "I said that'd be kind of hard given our current situation, the number of volunteers coming from all over."

"She's still in danger then." This must be it, Jake thought. What was behind the flash of her panic, her anxiousness. This was the rest of the story, the part she wasn't telling. He thought how he'd wanted to dismiss it, dismiss her, when she'd said she knew what he was going through. He remembered his disgust when she'd told him she was in recovery, and yet he'd felt the pull of his heart toward her, and he felt it again now. Yeah, so she'd turned to booze, but look at her. Look at how she'd fought, and continued to fight, to stand on ground that kept crumbling under her feet.

"Look," Clint said, "like I said before, she's had some issues, and one of them, something she did in Houston—hold on a sec—" He returned seconds later. "Let me call you back."

Jake's grip on the steering wheel tightened. "Is it Zoe? You hear something?"

"I'm not sure. I'll call—"

"No. Tell me now. What is it?"

But there wasn't an answer. Either the call had dropped, or Clint had hung up.

18

Gilly's speech, the one she had planned, died in her mouth at the sight of Jake, rumpled and grave, haggard with worry. The screen door was between them, but his distress was palpable.

"I hope I'm not interrupting lunch," Gilly said, although it was after two o'clock, and the lunch hour was long over.

Jake didn't answer. He seemed to be considering his options, and when, after a moment, he opened the screen, she stepped inside.

"I left you a message," she said.

"Yeah, well, when I talked to Suki Daniels, I never told her anything about you, so if last night's news story is why you're here—"

"If it wasn't you, then who?"

"I thought it was you."

"Me? But I told you I'm not psychic. I said I couldn't help you. Why would I talk to a reporter?"

He shrugged. How should he know? Maybe she was crazy. His rejoinder couldn't have been more clear if he had spoken out loud.

"Look, I really wish I could help you." She spoke with a fervency that, while genuine, was regrettable.

"Yeah. It would be fantastic."

He might have intended sarcasm, but what Gilly heard was the crumbling edge of Jake's hope. "I'm so sorry," she said. She wanted to touch him, to cup his cheek, unshaven and furrowed with exhaustion, in her palm. She wanted to trace the creased plane of his brow with the tip of her finger. She wanted to tell him it would be all right, but that might be a lie.

He ran his hands over his head. His look considered her. "You're sure?"

"Of?"

"You're certain that if you were to sit down right now, and close your eyes—I mean who's to say you wouldn't see something?"

"Jake?"

He turned to the older woman who had spoken his name.

His mother. Gilly saw the resemblance as the woman came down the hall toward them. It wasn't only the look of exhaustion they shared. They were alike physically. She was tall like Jake and carried herself with the same easy grace. And while her mostly white hair was pinned at the back of her head in a loose chignon, Gilly could tell she'd once been blonde, a brown-eyed blonde like Jake, like Zoe.

He said, "Mom, meet Gilly. She's a waitress at Cricket's."

"I've seen you there, but we've not been formally introduced."

"I'm Gillian O'Connell—but everyone calls me Gilly."

"Justine Halstead." She kept Gilly's gaze. "Jake told me you located his wallet the other day."

"Yes." Gilly crossed her arms, looked at the floor, feeling her face warm with regret, annoyance, embarrassment—some combination of the three.

"I saw the news last night, too, your photo. You're the psychic."

"No," Gilly began.

Justine looked at Jake. "You didn't tell me you'd hired her to find Zoe."

"I didn't," Jake said.

"The news story," Gilly said, "I don't know where they got their information, but it's wrong. Worse than wrong, it's a lie. When I find out who's responsible, I'm going to make them go back on TV and say so."

"So you aren't psychic." Justine was at sea.

"Sometimes I have dreams," Gilly admitted reluctantly. "Or I see things."

"Like Jake's wallet," Justine said.

"Yeah, and Zoe," Jake answered before Gilly could. "She saw Zoe and the woman who took her in a dream, before it happened."

"Really?"

"Yes," Gilly said, "but not in enough detail to be helpful."

"My college roommate had a precognitive dream once. That is the right term, isn't it? Precognitive? The night our dorm caught on fire, she dreamed it was happening. It broke out in the furnace room, but she felt the heat so strongly in our room on the fourth floor it woke her. She was scared enough she woke me. We banged on doors, got all these people up even though nobody saw flames anywhere, or smelled any smoke. We gathered outside, and I am not lying—not five minutes later, the basement windows shattered and flames shot out. It was surreal."

"You never told me about that," Jake said.

"Haven't thought about it in years. As far as I know, that was the only dream like that she ever had. A fluke, I guess. And lucky, so lucky for all of us who lived there."

"A fluke." Jake said it under his breath, but Gilly heard him.

It was more sarcasm, or that's how Gilly perceived it. She'd called finding his wallet a fluke, meaning the act wasn't repeatable and shared no correlation with finding a child. She didn't blame him for the dig. "I understand how you feel, truly. If it were my daughter who was missing, and I thought you knew where she was, I wouldn't leave you alone either, but—"

"But what?" Jake found her gaze.

"April," she said.

"April?" Jake repeated.

"April Warner, the cook at Cricket's—*she's* the one who gave the story about me—about you hiring me—to KTKY."

"You think she talked to Suki Daniels?"

"I *saw* her talking to Suki. Yesterday at the school, before we were assigned to search teams. April was being interviewed."

"So you told April about the dream?" Jake was nonplussed. "I had the impression you liked to keep this stuff private."

"I do, but she came to my house, and she was—" Gilly looked away and looked back at Jake. "I don't quite know how it happened, but I told her. It's on me, and now it's all over the news." Gilly pressed her fingertips to her eyes, biting back a groan.

Jake's phone rang.

Justine offered iced tea, and Gilly was in the process of declining, of saying, "I should go. I have a dog at home who needs walking," when Jake said he was sorry to interrupt.

"That was Clint. He's got the film footage of the woman and little girl who were seen wading at Monarch Lake yesterday."

"They think it's Zoe?" Gilly asked.

"They aren't sure. I'm meeting Clint at the sheriff's office in Greeley to have a look. I guess I'll take the polygraph, too."

"Yes," Justine said. "Let them get it over with so they can focus on the monster who's taken our little girl." Her voice wavered, and she took a steadying breath, waving away Gilly and Jake when they both extended their hands to her. "I'm fine. I'm going to lie down for a bit, then go on back to the school to help Cricket with the food out there. You'll call me?" She was asking Jake.

"You know I will," he said.

"It was nice meeting you, Gilly." Justine took Gilly's hand in her warm grasp.

"Thank you. I wish the circumstances were better."

"Next time," she said, giving Gilly's hand a little shake before releasing it. "Once we get Zoe back. I'll buy you a cup of coffee on your break."

"I'll look forward to that," Gilly said.

Jake pulled his keys from his pocket. "I'll walk out with you." He held the door open for Gilly. "Ma, if you don't feel like going out to the school later, don't," he called over his shoulder.

"I'm fine," she called back.

"I worry about her, going through this," he said, shutting the door.

"She's a lovely person," Gilly said.

"Yeah. She's pretty tough, too. I'm lucky to have her."

They paused in the shade at the foot of the porch steps. His truck was in the driveway; her car was at the curb.

The small silence seemed prescient, and they broke it together. Gilly said, "I need to explain something—" And Jake's words were nearly identical, "Before you go, there's something—"

"You first," he said.

"You'll hear it sooner or later, if you haven't already. I'm on probation for kidnapping." Gilly said it quickly, thinking it was best that way, like ripping off a Band-Aid.

Jake's eyes widened, but he made no comment, giving her time and the space she needed.

"Eight months ago I took a baby from the hospital in Houston where Sophie was born and where she later died. I brought the baby to my house, and for a little while I believed with every cell in my body that she was mine. When I came back to myself and realized what I had done, my mom and the cops had already found me."

"You told me before that you blacked out. Was this one of those times? Were you on something?"

"Does it matter? There is no defense for what I did. But I want you to know from me"—Gilly locked Jake's gaze—"that I didn't take Zoe."

He started to speak.

Gilly put her hand on his arm. "I'm going to try. To *see* Zoe, I mean. Dream her, if it's possible. I will do everything in my power to see where she is and who has her."

Jake bowed his head, pinching the bridge of his nose, and when he'd regained his composure, he thanked her. "Thank you—"

"I'm not making any promises. I've never done this—asked for it—a dream or a vision." Gilly took back her hand. "I'm not doing it so you'll trust me. You have every right not to." She wasn't sure why she said this. Maybe to keep him from having illusions about her ability.

Jake's expression, the dismissal in his eyes, suggested trusting her was the furthest thing from his mind. His desperateness had driven him far beyond such concerns. He said, "Clint told me the detective down in Houston who's working your husband's murder case called him. I thought you'd want to know."

"Carl called Captain Mackie?" Gilly felt a stab of annoyance.

"From what Clint said it sounds as if he's concerned the shooter is still walking around somewhere. Clint said you saw him the night your husband was killed?"

"I did, but it was only a brief glimpse. Anyway it's been three years. If he hasn't come after me by now—He's probably dead or in prison."

"Don't you want to know? Don't you want him caught?" Jake sounded incredulous. He punched his open palm with the fist of his other hand. "When I get Zoe back—I swear to God whoever has her—I could kill them myself. I'm scared about it—what I might do."

Gilly shifted her glance. How could she explain it? That no amount of revenge, no amount of justice dished out to the man who'd taken their lives would ever bring Brian or Sophie back to her. She could beat him bloody with her bare hands. She could cut out his heart and hold it up before his dying eyes, but for what? There would still be a hole inside her, a place that would never be filled, an ache that would go on forever.

She met Jake's glance. "You'll think it's crazy, but I don't think about that night and what happened. I did at first. I drove myself insane. I was obsessed, playing it over and over in my mind, all the what ifs—if I hadn't had a craving for an ice cream sandwich, if Brian and I hadn't stopped at that particular store, or if the guy had chosen some other location to rob, or if we'd gone there five minutes earlier or later—you know. I started to drink more and more. I took drugs. The detectives—Carl wants me to remember, and all I want to do is forget." Gilly heard herself, the emotion that threaded her voice and clamped her jaw, hugging herself to still her trembling.

"I'm sorry for everything you've been through, but you're right, I don't get it—the guy gunned down your husband. How can you not want him brought to justice? What if he's still doing it? Robbing stores, killing people? Don't you think you have an obligation—?" Jake stopped. "God, I'm sorry."

Gilly felt the tears blinding her eyes. He must have seen them. She swiped roughly at them.

He caught her hand, thumbing her cheeks, holding her gaze, his eyes intent. She felt his remorse, his compassion and kindness, the rougher scrim of his panic. She took the smallest step toward him. He touched her hair, lifting the strands that had fallen across her face, drawing them behind her ear. The moment held them. Gilly didn't know the amount of time that passed. A handful of seconds? An eternity? But it was wrong on so many levels, and as if they both agreed to it, they stepped back from one another.

Jake shifted his feet, rubbed a hand over his head.

Gilly hoisted her purse higher on her shoulder. "I should get going. Bailey—"

Jake said, "Yeah. I've got to get to Nickel Bend."

"The film—the woman and little girl—is there a chance the woman is your ex-wife? Yesterday when we talked you were thinking she might have Zoe—"

"No, it can't be." He rubbed a line beside his nose, looked off. He seemed ill at ease, agitated in some way.

"I'll just go now," Gilly said. "I'll call—"

"She's in jail—Zoe's mom. She was arrested sometime last night in Dallas."

"Oh, no. What happened?" As soon as she asked, Gilly put her hand to her mouth. "I'm sorry. It's none of my business."

"No, it's okay. It'll be all over the news soon enough anyway. She and her boyfriend got into it with a dealer. Steph pulled a knife on the guy. Her boyfriend took off. I thought he might have Zoe, but that's looking less likely."

"I'm sorry." Gilly couldn't think of anything else to say.

"Thanks. As much as I want it to be her, I'm pretty sure what I'm looking at is a lot worse. That's why I'm pressuring you, do you know what I'm saying?"

"I said I'd try."

"I appreciate that."

"You'll let me know if there's anything new?"

"Yeah. You do the same, okay? If you—" He didn't finish.

Gilly nodded. There were words to say, things like, *Good luck* or *It'll all work out* or *My prayers are with you*, but she and Jake were past the stage where platitudes would suffice. She closed her hand over his forearm, gripping it briefly, then she left him, got into her car without a glance back, and drove away.

19

Kenna texted him as he was leaving the sheriff's office in Greeley:
I'm at my office at school. Can u meet me?

Heart leaping, he tapped out his response: I'm headed that way.
Word about Zoe?

No. I'm sorry. Just need to see u.

K. B there in thirty.

His pulse settled. Doubt sat in his mind, a dog scooting on its
haunches ever closer to the raw vein of his hope. If something had happened to Zoe, if she was hurt, or worse, he would know it, wouldn't he?
He would feel it, and he did not. He. Did. Not.

On the highway back to Wyatt and the school, random memories
sifted through his mind of other times he'd met with Kenna—when
the subject was Zoe and her progress, or at some social occasion, where
they'd flirted with the prospect of making something more of their
acquaintanceship. A sense of unreality swamped him. It was as if he

were entertaining flashbacks of some other man's past. He thought how quickly a mind could veer off normal into insanity, like putting his truck into a ditch. One good jerk of the wheel. That's all it would take.

The police had looped the school building in yellow crime-scene tape and ordered the press to stay behind it. Still they went after Jake, wanting a word, a statement, his heart on a stick. They were like vultures after roadkill, a necessary evil. He needed them. At the front door, he turned and said, "I don't have anything new to say. I want my little girl back. I love her more than my life, and I want whoever has her to know I will do anything, give anything. Just bring her back safe to me. Please. That's all."

He turned from the flurry of questions. They pelted his back and rattled his ears until the door closed behind him, muffling the clangor of voices.

Kenna stepped into the hall from her office, and Jake sensed that what kept her there was an act of will. She was white-faced except for her eyes, which were rimmed in red. They darted over him. He wondered what she was looking for. Forgiveness? Reassurance? Maybe she thought he would sue her. Maybe she was scared what this ordeal would cost her. She had a degree in early childhood education. He'd been impressed by her credentials, even more by her commitment. He thought how little any of that mattered to him now, how little feeling he had to spare for her troubles.

She said, "I was hoping we could have a word alone," and without waiting for him to respond, she went into her office.

He followed her, but seeing Marley seated in one of the two club chairs that faced Kenna's desk, he paused in the doorway.

"Come in, sit down." Kenna gestured at the chair next to Marley.

"I'm fine," he said.

Disappointment flashed across Kenna's face. She and Marley exchanged a glance. "I'm sorry—" They spoke at once.

As if by mutual agreement, Kenna continued, launching into a rambling speech that revolved around steps she would take to prevent "events of this nature" from happening in the future.

She faltered to a stop when Jake held up his hand, indicating he'd heard enough. "This is all well and good, but my daughter is still gone, and I need to keep looking for her, so you'll have to excuse me." He didn't say the measures Kenna would take were too little and too late. It would be so easy to get sidetracked by anger, but Zoe needed every ounce of his focus now.

"I could lose my license, Jake." Kenna followed him into the corridor. "This school is everything I worked for. You know how much— how hard—"

He wheeled, feeling the slap of incredulity on his face. "Do you think I give a fuck about this school right now? My daughter is gone because of your incompetence, because your teaching assistant let a stranger take her—"

"Marley doesn't work here anymore. She's only here today—"

"Without proper identification. Without even checking the procedure when it's a matter of goddamn record and has been since I enrolled Zoe here, that I'm the one"—Jake punched his chest with his thumb—"the *only* one authorized to get Zoe from school. Do I look like a woman?"

"It was a mistake—"

"A mistake? How do you make a mistake like that, Kenna? Your assistant can't even say whether Zoe got into the car. Why was she out there, working dismissal alone, or doing anything by herself when she was too new to know the procedure?"

Eyes locked, the moment hung, Kenna's in chin-trembling silence, Jake's in heart-knocking fury. Finally he said, "I don't have time for this. I have to find my little girl."

Kenna broke then. Jake heard it happen, the crack of her sobs followed him out the door.

The reporters stood back; they parted like the Red Sea when he walked out. It was the look on his face, he guessed. Mad enough to kill, he thought. And they could see that he was. What would they make of it? What would he hear about himself later? Read in their newspapers? That he'd hired a hit man?

He drove over to the picnic area, jaw tight, mind in a heated knot, and he parked there because he didn't know where else to go, what else to do with himself. His glance fell on a group of people, gathered around the nearest table. He recognized some of them from town. Augie Bright, Tim Jeffers, Frodo Tate, several others. They'd all gone through the Wyatt school system together, and while they'd been different ages and graduated at different times, Wyatt schools were small. Everyone knew everyone else.

But when he got out of the truck, and the group approached him, he realized there were other faces—a handful of women and other guys who had been classmates, too. People he hadn't seen in a while. Years in some cases. Cody Blake and Evan Hardy came up to him first. They'd been baseball teammates back in the day. Cody had played shortstop, Evan had been at third base, and Jake had played in center field. They came up to him now, grave-faced, and embraced him, thumped him on the back. No words were spoken, but their kindness and commiseration showed through their eyes and gestures.

"What are you guys doing here?" Jake asked. The last he'd heard Cody lived somewhere up near Dallas, and Evan had moved to San Jose to work for some up-and-coming tech firm.

"We heard about your little girl, man. We had to come," Evan said.

A woman said, "We want to help."

Jake met her glance. It was Janet Westerbrook. They'd dated a few times when they were sophomores. Jake thought she lived in Atlanta now.

She embraced him warmly. "I have a little girl, too, not much older than Zoe."

"You came from Atlanta?"

"Yes," she said. She backed out of his embrace, keeping her hands on his forearms, holding his gaze. "As soon as Augie called and told me, I got on a plane. I'll stay until we find her. We all will." Her gesture encompassed the small crowd gathered behind her.

"What I hear, there's a lot more of our classmates coming, bro. Word is getting out." Augie spoke at his elbow.

"You did this?" Jake asked.

"Mandy started it," Augie said.

"Oh yeah?" Jake wasn't surprised. He loved Mandy. She was possibly the sweetest person in town, would do anything in the world for anyone, but the woman hadn't an ounce of discretion. Telephone, telegram, teleMandy. That was the joke. Mandy told it on herself. *I know, y'all,* she'd say. *I'm such a blabbermouth. I just can't help it.*

"She only made a couple of calls," Augie said now. "But it grew."

Jake felt tears score his eyelids. He pinched the bridge of his nose.

Mandy and Janet showed him the fliers that had been printed. Above a centered column listing Zoe's physical description, there were two photos, her class picture and the one Jake's mom had taken of Zoe holding up a fistful of weeds.

Janet said, "We'll put these up everywhere we can. Wyatt, Nickel Bend, Greeley, along I-35 toward the metroplex, too. Carly Jo Whitcomb—you remember her?"

Jake nodded.

"She's living in Georgetown now. She's taking a pile over there and then going into Austin. We're going to plaster the state of Texas with them, and we'll keep on until we find Zoe. People—little kids—don't just vanish. Somebody has got to have seen her."

Jake wiped his face. "I don't believe you guys. Thank you—"

"We've scheduled a candlelight vigil tonight at the pavilion in the courthouse square."

Jake searched and found the woman who had addressed him. She stepped around Janet.

"Karen Clayton?" A heartbeat's width of space passed before he made the connection and said her name. The sense of his surprise broke over him, fizzing along his veins like the first cold sip of champagne.

"You remember." She seemed gratified.

"It's been—"

"A long time." She finished his thought.

Twenty-two years. Jake did the math in his head.

"It's Karen *Ames* now, though. I'm married."

"Married." He repeated the word, thinking, Wow.

"No children. You?"

"Divorced," he said.

"I'm sorry—divorce is hard, but it's Zoe, it's your little girl—what's happened is so awful. When I heard, I had to come. We all did."

"Thank you," he said.

Their shared silence was small and misshapen, clouded with awkward memories of the intimacies they'd once shared.

Karen broke it, angling her gaze to Jake's. "Is it too late to tell you how sorry I am I didn't answer the door that night?"

He huffed a sound, not quite a laugh, rubbing his hand across his head. He was stuck somewhere between irony at the timing of her apology and give-a-shit indifference. Forget the years that had passed. How could she imagine he could care under the current circumstances?

"I forgot you stood him up for prom." Janet was grinning, but Jake sensed she was remembering the rest, too—the weeks that followed prom night, when it got really crazy.

He'd had a feeling that night it might go wrong, but he'd made the date; he'd felt obligated. He'd felt he was doing the right thing when he'd knocked on Karen's door, dressed to kill in a rented tux, corsage box in hand. A close friend of his dad's had lent him the Thunderbird—a 1957 flame-red convertible—idling in her driveway, waiting to take her to their senior prom. He'd made a mixtape of their favorite songs. He remembered his heart knocking against his ribs. He remembered the rosebush twining a nearby porch post had been smothered in blooms. Even today, smelling a rose could overcome him with bittersweet feelings of regret and heated desire, the paler shades of old anger and shock.

"It was a difficult time for me," Karen said. She looked from Jake to Janet. "You all haven't changed."

"You either," Janet said.

It wasn't exactly true. They had all aged. Karen was much thinner, almost gaunt, and her hair was shorter and darker than it had been in the past. In high school she'd worn it shoulder length, and it had been a color she'd called honey blonde. The first head of hair Jake had ever run his fingers through. He'd numbered the constellation of freckles that bridged her upturned nose. He'd measured the weight of her breasts in the palms of his hands, tasted her nipples, and nearly every other part of her, with his tongue. Entering her the first time had been ecstasy. After that, he had not been able—they had not been able to get enough of each other. They'd had sex in his truck in the high school parking lot, in her bedroom or his, when their folks weren't home. They'd stopped an elevator after quitting time in the old bank building on the square, and done it in the alley behind the row of shops that flanked Cricket's. They'd had sex half-submerged in the water at Monarch Lake, her legs locked around him, while he gripped a ladder at the end of a deserted boat dock.

One Thanksgiving, with her whole family over for dinner, she'd taken him out behind her dad's workshop, and he'd held her, impaled on him, against the wall, both of them fully clothed. He'd called her his kryptonite. Somehow he'd known it wasn't love but obsession that drove them. Still, when they'd talked about marriage, he had wanted it, wanted her in his bed. They had dreamed of days spent building a life together.

"We were so young then," she said now. Her gaze on his intent as if she could see the memories rising like vapor in his mind.

"Yeah," he said. Then, "I should go—" But he didn't know where. He glanced at his watch. Just past four. More than fifty hours since Zoe had disappeared. Two revolutions of the earth, and he was no closer to finding her. He felt like he was approaching the edge of an abyss. He felt like running, full tilt, headlong. He locked his knees.

"You'll be at the vigil?" Karen asked.

"I guess, yeah, if I can. If nothing—if Zoe isn't—" He looked over Karen's head and spotted his mom talking to Augie and Mandy. "I should go," he repeated.

Karen caught his hand.

Her touch jolted him. Their eyes locked. Her shift toward him was almost imperceptible, but he felt it, the moment shimmered with the heat of old desire. He might have cupped her cheek, bent to brush her lips with his, and he knew she would welcome him. It was all he could do not to act on the impulse. He could lose himself in her, lose his mind, the god-awful panic.

"Zoe will be all right," she said. "I just know it."

He nodded and left her, wishing he had her faith.

"Hey, bud, how you holding up?" Augie asked when Jake joined him.

"All right," he said.

"You passed the lie detector, did they tell you?" his mom asked.

"Yeah, but how did you find out?"

"The Madrone County sheriff—deputy—whatever he is—John something—called Clint and he was kind enough to tell me. As if you wouldn't—"

"It's okay, Ma. At least now the cops are focused where they need to be—on other suspects."

"But the film of the woman and little girl, wading in the lake, it wasn't of any use?"

"Nah. Too grayed out. It showed the woman driving, her profile. You could tell there was a car seat with a child in it—" He broke off, seeing the image again in his mind. The tech had run the film in slo-mo, and he'd bent close to the monitor, hardly daring to breathe. The figures were the right size and appeared to be the right ages to be his ex and his daughter. But that was his desperation talking.

He wasn't an idiot. He knew none of the timing worked. Even if the little girl in the film was Zoe, the woman with her wasn't her mom. Stephanie had been in Dallas, in an altercation with a dope dealer, one that had landed her in jail. Alibis didn't get better than that.

Jake said, "I don't get why the park installed security cameras in the first place when the film quality is crap. Why even have them?"

"They only got them last year," Mandy said. "Remember? After AJ Isley's truck was found burned up there."

"The truck—Clint said it was a Ford."

Jake met Augie's glance. "F-250 with a camper top. Not so new. Early two thousands, I'm guessing. Light colored, maybe white or tan. Texas plate, but it was smeared with dirt. Maybe on purpose. They're still looking at footage, trying to find where the two left the park."

"Maybe it's time to offer a reward."

Jake looked at his mom.

"I've got fifteen thousand cash we can put up right now. We can borrow money on our houses, the business, whatever it takes." She kept his gaze. "I think we have to face facts here, honey. Zoe wasn't taken by anyone we know. She's not with Stephanie, or even Stephanie's boyfriend."

"We don't know that for sure, though, until we find Duchene."

"But he's no less a stranger than someone else would be, is he? A reward might entice him to come forward, give Zoe back."

"And risk getting caught?" Jake asked.

"Someone could have seen him with her," Augie said. "The reward might work to get a witness to come forward."

"I can probably lay hands on thirty, thirty-five thousand," Jake said, and somehow he felt as if he were signing off on some kind of death warrant. He felt this was it, the end of the road.

"What about a GoFundMe campaign?" Mandy asked. "I know folks would contribute, and the money could go toward a bigger reward for information, or it could go for more resources—you know, more personnel and equipment, what local law enforcement can't afford. Another helicopter."

The county had pulled the one that had gone up initially when, after hours in the air, it had detected nothing. Eventually it would all go, every resource—the search-and-rescue teams, the dozens of volunteers, Jake's old friends. They wouldn't stick around forever. They had lives, other obligations. There would be other crimes, other missing children, God forbid. Jake knew this; he knew every hour that passed lessened the chances that Zoe would be found safe and unharmed. But he couldn't stay with the knowing. He couldn't look directly at it. He said, "I don't want to take people's money."

His mom said, "Sometimes you have to accept help when it's given, honey."

"We want to help," Mandy said, and her voice trembled. "You have to let us."

Janet joined them, and if she was aware of the tension in the air, she gave no sign. "We're headed into town with the fliers. Y'all want to take a stack?"

"You bet," Augie answered. "Anybody need a ride?"

Janet said she was riding with Karen and Cody.

Mandy hugged Jake and then his mom. "We'll see you at the vigil? You heard about it, right?"

"From Karen," Jake said. He looked toward the edge of the parking lot, where she was getting into a car.

Mandy squeezed his hand and left with Augie.

"I saw you talking to her." Jake's mom was watching Karen, too.

"Yeah," he said. "It was weird. She apologized."

"For?"

"Prom, I guess. Not answering the door, she said."

His mom made a face.

The list of Karen's offenses had gone way past that. But Jake knew he wasn't blameless. The head games they'd played, certainly the sex, had been mutual. The night of their senior prom, when she'd left his knock unanswered, had been it for him, though, the final seconds of the final game in the series.

He had known she was there, standing on the other side of the door. He'd left the box with her wrist corsage, a circlet of tiny pale-pink rosebuds accented with white blooming stephanotis, on the seat of the porch swing. His parting gift. Then, for reasons unknown even to him, he'd parked the Thunderbird out of sight, and concealed himself in the neighbor's shrubbery. She'd come onto the porch, as he had known she would. She'd looked up and down the street as if she knew he was there, a witness, and it thrilled her that he was watching. He was dead certain of her excitement when she took the corsage from the box and shredded it, taking her time, making sure every petal and leaf was destroyed. His stomach had twisted, seeing that.

His reaction just now when Karen had touched him—the heat between them, the specter of old desire he had felt—confused him. It was as if his body had a separate agenda from his brain, and it rattled him; it burned him up. There was no room for that sort of distraction.

"She lives in Lubbock with her husband." His mom added special emphasis to it—the word *husband*. "No children," she added.

"Yeah, she told me," Jake said.

"You're okay?"

"Mom, it was years ago."

"I know, it's just you were so—" She paused, changed direction. "I'm glad to see your old friends, so grateful for their support. But the reason for it—" Her voice broke. "Where is she, Jake? Where is Zoe? What if we never find her?" Now, as if horrified at having put it into words, their darkest fear, she clapped her hand to her mouth.

Jake slipped his arm around her shoulders, tucking her against him, taking comfort from comforting her.

20

Gilly didn't ordinarily take naps, but that afternoon, after she walked Bailey, after she forced herself to eat half a slice of buttered toast, she went into her bedroom and lay down. Not with the idea of dreaming, although it was in her mind, and at first, when the dream began, it didn't seem to have a thing to do with Zoe. The initial imagery was of a house in the country. It sat down from the road, low enough that when passing it, you would see only the peak of the roof, part of a chimney. It was two-story, native limestone with faded green shutters, one of which hung askew. The porch sagged. Boards covered all but one of the six front windows. A thick-trunked live oak towered over one corner of the rusted metal roof, wind-twisted and bent. Sequins of light glimmered through the dense canopy.

Gilly saw the house, the tree, all of it, as if she were looking down into a snow globe, a tiny world under glass. She picked it up, held it at eye level, and that's when she saw the white pickup truck with the camper top. It was parked around back. Something was hanging from the rearview mirror, looped around it, making a bow. Gilly put her eye against the glass, bringing the image closer, and then she was inside the snow globe, inside the cab of the truck, in the driver's seat, reaching for it, the length of faded ribbon tied onto the mirror's metal bracket. It was satin, a blue so faded it was nearly white. Gilly had seen the ribbon before. It was the one Zoe Halstead carried, the one Jake had told Gilly had once belonged to Zoe's mother.

Gilly's breath went down hard. She stared through the truck's windshield at the house, the back door that was only steps away. Zoe was in there; Gilly could feel it. She lifted the truck's door handle, and it wouldn't budge. She scooted across the bench seat to the passenger side, and when that door wouldn't budge either, she grasped the handle, lifted it, and rammed the door with her shoulder, shouting when pain jolted down her arm.

But now she was outside the globe, holding it in her hands, and the shift was so sudden, she dropped it. Bits of glass and liquid spattered her legs, and that quickly it was night. She was in Houston, on the street outside the convenience store where Brian had been shot, staring down at her legs, knowing he was dead, and her water had broken. Soon, she would give birth to Sophie, only to lose her, too, all over again.

Behind her, someone called her name. She wheeled and saw a man, coming quickly toward her. She ran from him, through a maze of streets, breathing hard, lost, flailing. It was the sound of whimpering that woke her. She thought it was Bailey. When she'd come to lie down, he'd jumped onto the foot of the bed, turned in circles, making his usual nest. He was there now, but quiet, head cocked to one side, watching her, eyes worried, and she knew she had been the one to cry out.

"Sorry, buddy," she said. "Bad dream."

Maybe not. A voice—not Miss Two-shoes, not the monkey, *her intuition*—spoke in her brain.

Gilly sat up. Closing her eyes, she saw the house again, the faded green shutters, the boarded windows, the live oak. Now the white pickup. It had been dirty, the windshield bug specked. That ribbon—Gilly felt its satin smoothness. Was the sense of it valid? A real and true clue to Zoe's whereabouts? Gilly's stomach knotted. She swung her bare feet to the floor, ran her fingers through her sleep-matted hair, tucking it behind her ears.

She picked up her cell phone from the night table but then sat with it cradled loosely in her hands. If she called Jake, Captain Mackie, whomever—what would she say? Even if the dream was accurate, and the length of blue ribbon hanging from the dream truck's rearview mirror belonged to Zoe, Gilly couldn't place the location. There must be any number of native limestone houses around the countryside. Any number of dirty white pickups. She'd seen nothing significant. No landmark, or road sign, nothing definitive—as usual. The dream was as useless as all the rest. She dropped the phone onto the bed, dropped her head into her hands.

Why?

Why did her brain do this?

Bailey wormed his nose under her elbow, and she pulled him into her lap, rubbing his ears. "Where would I be without you, buddy?"

He wriggled, turning into her. He had a nose for when she needed comfort, and he used it now, snuffling a trail up under her chin, resting his paws and then his snout on her shoulder, a doggy hug. She buried her face in his fur, leaking tears that irked her. But Bailey was impervious. *Let them be*, he seemed to say.

Gilly lifted her head when the monkey started in, chattering something about fixing a stiff one. *Shut up*, she told him, sniffing, wiping under her nose. *Atta girl*, said Miss Goody. "You shut up, too," Gilly told her.

Bailey jumped off the bed and shook himself. Tail wagging, he looked eagerly up at her.

"You need to go out, buddy?"

A half hour later, when she'd seen to Bailey's needs, she was still fighting with herself about the dream. The image of the blue ribbon looped around the metal arm of the truck's rearview floated in her mental vision. It worried her. She kept eyeing it, sidelong. Other details from the scene, the truck itself, the green-shuttered house, the live oak, flitted through her mind like thieves. What use were they, though, when she recognized none of them?

It was Julia who made Gilly see it. "Just checking up on you, girl," she said when she called.

Gilly sat at her kitchen table, Bailey curled at her feet, and caught Julia up, describing her visit with Jake, explaining that he wasn't the one who had misled the media. It relieved her, she realized. She hadn't wanted it to be him. Nor did she want it to matter. But her heart didn't seem to care what she wanted. When she spoke, when she said to Julia, "I had another dream," it was an attempt to distract herself.

"Oh?" Julia's interest was piqued. "Last night?"

"Just now. I was only going to lie down for a bit, but I fell sound asleep." Gilly didn't say she'd asked for it, to be given a sign. That against her will, her desire to help Jake and Zoe had needled its way under her skin, pricked her heart, and now lodged there at her core. She gave Julia the gist of it, expecting her to agree the dream was like all the rest, totally worthless. But Julia didn't.

"You may not know the house, but what if someone else does?" she said. "You're new in the area, but someone who's more familiar with property outside Wyatt might recognize it from your description."

Gilly straightened. That hadn't occurred to her, and she said so. She slid her feet into her sandals, got her keys, and her purse. She said goodbye to Bailey, who followed her to the door, eyeing her mournfully as she closed it behind her. "What do you think?" she asked Julia. "Should I find Jake, or go to the police? Not Jake," she answered her own question.

"Why not?" Julia asked.

Gilly got into her car. "I don't want to get his hopes up if it's nothing."

"Ah, good thought," Julia said.

"Maybe I could talk to Cricket or try and find Captain Mackie," Gilly said. "He actually seemed open to the idea of working with a psychic. Not that I am one," she added quickly.

"Wouldn't it be some kind of miracle if your dream led to finding Zoe," Julia said.

"Big *if*," Gilly said.

21

Jake talked his mom into leaving the school grounds and going home to rest. He told her he'd pick her up in time for the vigil. "I don't see the point of lighting candles and praying," he said, walking her to her car. "But I'll go."

"People want to do it," she said, shutting her car door, lowering the window. "Prayers—turning your fear over to God—it can't hurt."

Jake didn't answer. He wouldn't say he'd pretty much given up on God.

He was back in the picnic area, talking to a few of the volunteers, when Clint found him and beckoned him to a table out of earshot. He was keyed up, tense.

"We found a car behind Burley's, the bait shop near the lake," he said. "A metallic-blue Toyota Corolla. This was in the back seat." He flipped through photos on his phone, and finding the one he wanted, held up the screen.

Jake looked. Nemo's orange face, the big eyes and friendly smile, looked back. His breath went down hard. "Zoe's?"

"Yeah. It's got her name inside. We're sending it, along with the car, to the lab in Austin. Get the techs to go over it. We already know from the tags that the car's a rental. We should have more information, maybe in a few hours. They know the situation, that time is critical."

Jake didn't answer. He felt stunned. He couldn't find wits to speak.

"You need to sit down?" He gave Jake a nudge, forcing him to sit. "You need water?"

Not waiting for an answer, he got a couple of bottles of water from a nearby cooler, and handing Jake one, settled on the bench across from him.

Jake downed half the contents of the bottle in one gulp. He pressed the cool plastic to his forehead. "This is just surreal," he said after a moment.

"Yeah."

They shared a beat.

"You got any idea—" Clint began.

"Duchene? Have you found him?"

"Not yet. He's still a possibility, but with the film footage and all showing a woman—"

"It isn't likely. So if it's not Duchene—some deal he cooked up with Steph—who else in the goddamn hell could it be?"

Clint started to answer, but at the sound of Jake's phone, he went still. Jake pulled his cell from his pocket, heart tapping, and studied the caller ID. He didn't recognize the number. He locked Clint's gaze. *Maybe this is it, the break we've been waiting for.* The hope—the anticipation crackled in the air.

It wasn't. The caller was Suki Daniels. She and her KTKY crew would be at the vigil, she said to Jake, and she wanted to do another interview. "You can't turn down this opportunity," she said, sensing his objection before he could give it voice.

Her insistence only deepened his reluctance.

She went on quickly, "I'm hoping to get the segment picked up by other major affiliates. Somebody has to have seen something. I'd like to include your mother, too. The more we get Zoe's face, the faces of her family, out there, the greater the chance something will click, someone will remember something."

Jake found Clint's gaze again. "*KTKY.*" He mouthed the letters at the police captain, who nodded, looking weary, deflated.

"I heard you're ready to offer a reward," Suki said. "We can get the word out about that. Trust me, the interview, our coverage of the vigil, letting our viewers know there's a reward—it could make all the difference."

"Okay," Jake said. She was right; he had to do it. "But there's one condition."

"Oh?"

"You correct the misinformation you aired last night about Gilly O'Connell being a psychic and the bit about my hiring her. That's total bullshit."

"Yeah, I heard from Ms. O'Connell," Suki said. "Ordinarily I do a fact check before I run with a story, but we were pressed for time, and April Warner seemed so sure of herself. She said she'd spent time with Ms. O'Connell, that they work together, but are also friends."

"I don't know about that," Jake said. "But I do know Gilly doesn't consider herself a psychic, and you need to make that clear. Don't show her photo again either," he said. "I don't want to talk about why, but it could cause trouble for her unrelated to Zoe."

Suki's interest was piqued. Jake could almost see her reporter's nose twitching, but he cut off her questions, ended the call, and set his phone on the table.

Clint said, "You know who gave Suki Gilly's name?"

"Yeah, it was April Warner," Jake answered, and when Clint asked, he described Gilly's visit to his house—how she'd arrived ready to blame him, until she'd remembered seeing April at the search site talking with Suki while the cameras were rolling. He told Clint how Gilly had come to confide in April about the dream. "She regrets it now." A pause. "She told me about taking the baby. That's what you meant when you said she had issues, right?"

"Yeah. Makes her look good for taking Zoe, too, but it's like you heard me tell her, the timing's off."

"I never really thought it was her, not seriously." Jake bent his weight on his elbows, thinking about Gilly, the way she looked at Zoe with such delight. That was the word, the only word for it. He had waited to see that look dance through her eyes. He'd looked forward to seeing it every Wednesday morning, the odd weekend, whenever he'd brought Zoe to Cricket's when Gilly was working. More times in the last six months, he realized, since Gilly had been hired. She liked his kid—that was why. *It's more than that.* The thought whispered across his brain. He found Clint's gaze. "You think she's in jeopardy from her husband's killer? She doesn't seem concerned. She told me it's been three years. The guy could be dead—"

"She didn't tell you what happened this morning at the station?"

Jake shook his head.

"The father of the kid she took came in as she was leaving. Started shooting off his mouth. According to Bowen, he's hot tempered. Claims he got no justice in the case. Judge slapped her on the wrist and let her go."

"Did he threaten Gilly?"

"Yeah. It could be a lot of nothing, but I damn sure don't want the guy going all vigilante on me."

"He's still in town?"

"As of a half hour ago he was holed up at the café. Cricket says he's mostly on his phone."

"I thought the café was closed."

"Aw, you know how she is. She'd feed the world if you gave her half a chance." Clint drained the last of his water. His phone sounded, and he pulled it from his pocket.

Jake swung his legs over the bench, got up, and walked away a few feet, crushing his empty water bottle, tossing it in the trash can. He wanted to kick it; he wanted to jerk it up and hurl it as far as he could. The urge was hard inside him.

"Just got the word—we got a boat coming." Clint walked up behind him.

Jake turned. "Boat?"

"We're putting a boat equipped with sonar on Monarch Lake tomorrow morning to have a look around the area where witnesses saw the woman yesterday with the little girl."

Jake stared, not comprehending.

"The car with Zoe's backpack inside it that we found at Burley's—that's so near the lake. We've got to consider . . ."

Jake stared at Clint, waiting for him to go on, daring him to say it, but the man couldn't. He looked away. But it was there all the same, the awful thing that had to be done. They were going to drag the lake, look for Zoe there. An image of her floating, bloated, white, seared the backs of Jake's eyes.

He tipped his head back, staring up. Facets of light through the live oak canopy made him blink. He leveled his gaze at Clint. "You heard me say we're putting up a reward? Fifty thousand."

"Yeah."

"Maybe it'll generate some leads."

"Maybe, but it'll bring out the kooks, too, so get ready. You should go home, get some rest." Clint went on when Jake didn't answer. "You look like hell."

Jake made a sound, not quite a laugh. How else should he look? He was in hell.

22

The lights were on inside Cricket's when Gilly passed the café on her way to the police station, or she wouldn't have stopped. She needed gas; she was on fumes. She needed to find Captain Mackie. But it seemed somehow ominous that the café was open, especially given the time. It was after five. Cricket's was never open so late. Why had no one had told her? Pulse jumping, she parked in the alleyway and went in through the back door to the kitchen. April was tending two hamburger patties and a rasher of bacon on the grill. Nick glanced up from the big sink, up to his elbows in dishwater. He grinned. "Hey there, Miss Gilly."

"Hey yourself, Nick."

April looked over her shoulder, turned back to the grill, flipping the patties.

Gilly walked up beside her. "What is everyone doing here so late? I didn't even know Cricket had reopened."

"Just happened," April said.

"Is Cricket here?"

"She just left with a cooler full of sandwiches. There are so many people coming from out of town to help with the search for Zoe. It's incredible. Cricket said we should give them a place here in town, too, to eat, cool off, and relax. I think it's the media, you know, the word's getting out."

"About that," Gilly said. "Did you tell Suki Daniels I was a psychic, that Jake Halstead had hired me?"

"I knew you'd be mad." April toasted a pair of hamburger buns, set them on plates, and added the patties. "She took it too far. She twisted everything I said."

"You shouldn't have mentioned me to her at all, April. I know I didn't ask you to keep what I told you in confidence, but I wish you had."

April had been dressing the plates with fresh lettuce leaves, and thin slices of a fresh tomato and Vidalia onion, but now she paused, locking Gilly's gaze. "I'm sorry, I guess—except what if you could *see* Zoe where she is now? You should at least try, even if it never worked before. I would if I were you."

April didn't sound sorry; she sounded irked. Gilly looked past her. She wanted to defend herself, to tell April about her dream of the stone house with faded green shutters, and her conviction that Zoe was there. But suppose she wasn't? Suppose no such house existed?

"There's a guy out front wearing a Rockets cap who asked for you when he came in."

"Oh." An image of Mark Riley from the police station earlier tried to form in Gilly's head, and she fought it, fought to keep her alarm from showing. "Did he say what he wanted?"

"Yeah." April picked up the plates, handing them to Gilly. "Since you're here will you take these out for me? The couple at table three. The guy said he changed your tire earlier? You promised him coffee."

Gilly took the plates, smiling in her relief. "Warren Jester."

"He's with search and rescue. Listen, can you stay? We're pretty busy."

"I have to run an errand. Thirty minutes tops, then I'll come back."

April nodded, looking unhappy.

Gilly went through the swinging doors into the dining area and paused, running her glance around the room, reassuring herself Mark wasn't there. She caught sight of Warren, and after serving the burgers and fries, she stopped at the booth where he was sitting. "I didn't expect to see you so soon," she said.

"Yeah. I was with a search team at the lake most of the day, got plum wore out. Needed some caffeine. You know." He smiled. "I hope it's okay."

"Absolutely. I want to treat you to a piece of pie, too. I'm not sure what kind we have. We just reopened."

"Coffee's fine, if you got some fresh."

"Let me see what I can do." Gilly went behind the counter and pulled the carafe that looked freshest from its burner. She got a clean mug and returned to the table. "Did you find anything at the lake?" Gilly asked, although she felt she knew the answer.

"Nah. Heard a lot of rumors, though." Warren spoke of the woman and little girl spotted at Monarch Lake, the subject of the film footage Jake had been called to Greeley to view.

Gilly listened, but part of her mind was hovering over the image of herself with Jake, the sense of his touch on her damp cheek when he'd thumbed away her tears, the gravity of his gaze. She had felt he was looking into her bones, her soul. She had felt a connection, something visceral—she had wanted it to be there, a link between them. And it was wrong of her, as wrong as whatever had been between her and Carl. Her desire for either man—any man—made her feel as if she were cheating, a cheating wife.

"From everything I heard," Warren began, "no one's sure if the little girl was Zoe Halstead. They don't find her pretty quick, though, this operation'll change."

"What do you mean?" Gilly asked.

"I've seen it plenty of times. Usually about the forty-eight-hour mark, or a little after, folks start giving up. Law enforcement—they begin to feel the odds are against it—finding the person alive. You know, instead of a search and rescue, the mission becomes a search and recover."

They would be looking for Zoe's body, he meant. Gilly shifted the carafe to her other hand.

Warren said, "I was out with a team in East Texas a while back, a case sort of similar to this one. It was in some rough country outside Marshall, a dad reported his daughter missing. She was older, seventeen, eighteen. She'd gone for a jog and didn't come back. A couple days went by. Long enough, we figured the worst. Most everyone did."

"You found her alive?"

"One of the cadaver dogs did. They're trained to home in on folks who've passed, but it was like this dog had some kind of sixth sense, you know?"

Gilly said, "That's amazing." The words were rote, an automatic response. Her head was full of images from her dream: the stone house, its sagging porch, the white pickup behind it with the bit of faded blue ribbon looping the bracket that held the rearview.

Zoe was in that house.

Gilly knew it.

She'd stake her life on it. Her certainty was suddenly strong in a way she had never experienced before.

She needed to go.

Right now.

There had to be someone she could call—the police captain, Cricket, Jake, his mom—she could ask about the house, a long-timer in the area who'd recognize it from her description. It was simply a matter of finding the right person. She needn't mention the dream. She could invent another story to get the information, then check out the location herself. "If there's nothing else I can get you—"

"I was a fireman down in Victoria," Warren said, turning the thick-walled mug in his hands.

Gilly looked at them, his broad, red-knuckled workman's hands. Age spots dotted the backs like tiny islands. "I thought you were a carpenter."

"Yeah, I am now, when I can get work. But I *was* a fireman. That's how I got hooked up with search and rescue. It was like a natural segue, you know?"

He looked up at her, and she flinched slightly at the pain that lanced his expression. It was old, she thought, and badly healed, like hers.

"I saved my share of folks," he said. "Adults, kids, their pets, sometimes kept their property from becoming a total loss. I wanted to be a fireman all my life so it was a dream come true. I was good at it. I had a good life. I slept good. At nights, my conscience was easy." Head down, Warren rotated the mug another circle.

Something had happened to him. Something had broken his peace of mind. Gilly sensed if she were to ask, he would tell her. He would pour out his soul to her. But she had no time for that now. She hadn't the will to take on his pain anyway.

He picked up his mug, swallowed the last of the contents. He asked for a rain check on the pie, and slapping his hat on his head, said maybe he'd see her later.

Gilly cleared his mug. She returned the carafe to its burner. She got her purse from the office and pulled out her phone, but she had no reception. When she asked, April didn't know where Cricket had been headed when she left with the cooler full of sandwiches. Gilly didn't tell April why she wanted to talk to Cricket. She thought possibly April was like Mandy—telephone, telegraph, teleApril.

Captain Mackie, Justine, Jake, Cricket, even the sergeant—one of them was bound to be at the school, and any one of them might recognize Gilly's description of the house.

She was right outside town, traveling west on FM 1620 on her way to the Little Acorn Academy, and she'd nearly passed it—the Quick-Serv was partly screened from view by a thick growth of oaks and grass-choked underbrush—when she remembered she needed gas, that without it, she'd never make it to the school. She pulled up to the second pump, the one farthest from the store, thankful for whatever intuition had prodded her memory in time.

But going through the routine, swiping her debit card, setting the nozzle in the tank, her faith in her dream, that it was accurate and real, began to waver: What if the house she'd dreamed about didn't exist? What if this was just another dumbass figment of her imagination? But even as the pump clicked, measuring out gallons of gas, even as her gaze traversed the empty L-shaped apron of concrete that banded the front and one side of the store, a voice in her brain—not the monkey or Miss Two-shoes—warned there was no time to lose. That little girl—Zoe—was in trouble, and she needed help now. Gilly's pride and privacy be damned.

Call the cops, ordered the voice.

And say what? she argued.

But she got her phone, and, switching it on, she saw she had reception now and a voice message from Carl. Ignoring it, Gilly found the number for the Wyatt PD and dialed.

A man answered. "Captain Mackie."

Gilly was too surprised to speak, and when she repeated it, "Captain Mackie?" it was with a question mark.

"Yes. Who's this?"

"Gilly O'Connell."

"Ms. O'Connell—"

"Please call me Gilly."

"All right. Gilly. If you're calling about Warren Jester, I want to assure you we're actively looking for him. But you need to keep an eye out, too, let us know if you see anything suspicious or that you don't like."

"What?" Gilly was at sea. "You're looking for Warren Jester, the man who changed my tire?"

"He changed your tire?"

"Yes. What is this about?"

"You haven't talked to Detective Bowen?"

"He left a message—what's happened?"

"A guy named Warren Jester confessed a while ago to his sister that he killed your husband."

Gilly went still. Even her breath paused. "But—How—? He changed my tire this morning. Just now, to repay him, I gave him a free cup of coffee."

"Where?"

"At Cricket's."

"Are you still there? Is he?"

"No. I'm getting gas. I'm pretty sure he left."

"Can you hold on a second? I want to get someone over to the café."

Gilly waited, pacing a short path beside her car.

The captain came back on the line. "Sergeant Carter's on his way over there," he said, "but stay alert, okay?"

"Okay, but what's going on? You're scaring me."

"I'm sorry, but not if it keeps you on your toes. Look, what I heard from Detective Bowen, Jester saw a news story on a local Houston station about you being psychic. Not only that, they talked about your ability to dream events, see things—you know."

"But it's lies." Gilly flung up her arm as if the police captain could see her. "Where did they get their information? How can they continue to broadcast this sort of thing about me? They don't even know me."

"You know the media—they probably picked up KTKY's story. Bowen said they made a big deal out of it before, that you dreamed about it when your husband was killed. I hear you were also a witness. You saw the shooter. Is that right? Bowen said you blanked out the memory."

"Yes, I was a witness, and it's true I don't remember. But the dream—they blew that out of proportion. It was stupid—just totally useless."

"Well, all this time, I guess Jester's felt pretty confident he was safe, until he heard on the news you were hired to find Jake's daughter—find Zoe's kidnapper. That's when he freaked, according to his sister. He told her everything, then took off yesterday."

"He's scared I'll remember, identify him." Gilly wasn't asking.

"But you didn't."

"No, it's been more than three years. He knows *me*, though. He knows where I am."

"Yeah, according to his sister, the sight of your photo on TV really spooked him. She's pretty much in shock. She told Detective Bowen she had no idea what her brother was up to. Evidently that store was one in a series he robbed."

"I don't believe this. He's a fireman—or he was. That's how he got into search and rescue." She paused again. "He seemed so kind."

"Yeah, well, Ms.—Gilly, he could be armed and dangerous, certainly to you. We're looking for him, and we'll get him, but you should go home now and stay put. We'll get someone to drive by your house as often as possible until we've got Jester in custody. If I had a man to spare, I'd park him out front, but Detective Bowen is on his way up. He's going to cover—"

"No, that's not—Can you tell him, please, that isn't necessary?"

"Uh, no. I'm glad for the assist. We're spread pretty thin right now with every officer on the force out looking for the little Halstead girl."

"Maybe I can help." Gilly seized on the possibility. "That's why I called. I think I know where Zoe is. I fell asleep earlier, and I—I dreamed about a house. I think she's being held there—"

"Do you know where it is? Can you describe it?"

"It's outside town, somewhere isolated." Gilly went into detail, describing the house, the truck parked behind it. She mentioned the faded blue ribbon hanging from the rearview.

"Zoe's never without that ribbon," the captain said. "But you know that. You've seen it before, right?"

Gilly took his point, the fact that the ribbon was familiar to her made the detail in the dream less impressive. "Zoe doesn't have it in my dream, though. It's hanging from the mirror."

The captain's silence was considering, and Gilly used the moment to scan the area around the gas station. Late-afternoon sunlight glinted off the pavement, but otherwise the parking lot was empty. There wasn't another vehicle in sight. No sign of the white van she had seen Warren Jester driving. But now that she thought about it, had it been a pickup truck instead, with a camper top? She'd only glanced at it. It was hard to believe—how could a man go from saving lives to taking them? She saw Warren's eyes, the weathered kindness in them. She saw his hands, worn and calloused from work, from tending those in life-threatening circumstances.

Those hands had loaded the weapon that had killed Brian; they had pulled the trigger.

Now the man—her beloved husband's killer—was here. He'd had the nerve to approach her, speak to her. What a stroke of luck for him, coming upon her with her flat tire. How he must have relished her offer of coffee in thanks. The idea that she'd served—

But no. *No.*

She could feel it, the reddened tide of her emotions—anger, panic, some colder wish to do Warren Jester bodily harm—pulsing against the walls of her brain. She would lose it right here if she allowed herself to think about him.

I could kill them myself. Jake had said that about Zoe's kidnapper, and Gilly hadn't understood it, really. But she did now, and like Jake, she found the sudden onset of her rage frightening. Were they all murderers, then? Given the right situation, the perfect storm of circumstances, was everyone capable of taking another's life?

"Would you be willing to come here and describe the house for a sketch artist? It would be really helpful, I think."

Captain Mackie's query drew Gilly back, calming her.

"It would make me feel better, having you here anyway."

"Yes, I guess I could do that—"

"Where are you now?"

"Getting gas at the Quick-Serv on 1620. I was going out to the Little Acorn—"

"Gilly?"

She looked around. "Liz?" Her name was a question. The woman had Liz's coloring and her features, but her demeanor—her expression that was somehow sneering and yet triumphant—was all wrong. But it was the way she was dressed, in a dark hoodie and huge sunglasses—the very clothing as that worn by the woman in her dream—that raised the fine hair on Gilly's neck. "I thought you were in Dallas," she said, and her voice was faint with her bewilderment, a deepening sense of apprehension.

"Well, I'm back."

The gas pump clicked off. Gilly kept Liz's gaze, trying to reconcile it; Liz here in the flesh, clothed in the same garb as the woman in her dream who had taken Zoe.

The captain asked if everything was all right.

"A friend of mine, Liz Ames, is here," Gilly said.

"A friend, you say?" The police captain seemed to have picked up on Gilly's uncertainty.

"Yes." Of course Liz was her friend, wasn't she? Gilly allowed a small laugh. "It's Warren I need to look out for, right?"

"Yeah. Do you have my cell number?"

Gilly said she didn't and recorded it in her phone when he gave it to her.

"Keep your eyes peeled and call me if you see Jester—or even if something doesn't feel right. Okay?"

Gilly said she would, and it was silly, but her throat closed. It was Captain Mackie's concern—so unexpected, so fatherly—that was her undoing. "I shouldn't be long," she said and ended the call. "Are you okay?" she asked Liz. "Did you and your dad get the restraining order?"

Liz didn't answer. She took a step toward Gilly, crowding her. A jolt of alarm loosened from the floor of her brain. "What's wrong? Are you hurt?" It was the only thing Gilly could think of—that Liz had suffered some kind of injury, and it was causing her to act strangely.

"Let's you and me go somewhere where we can talk."

"No. What is wrong with you?" Even as she asked, Gilly made a move to open the RAV's driver-side door, thinking to make it a barricade. But Liz, moving quickly, positioned herself in a way that made it impossible. Gilly spotted the reflection of another car in the lenses of Liz's sunglasses, a black Lincoln Navigator entered the Quick-Serv parking lot. Bypassing the pumps, it pulled into her actual view beyond Liz's shoulder, parking in a slot in front of the store. The driver, a man, got out. Gilly didn't expect he would look her way. She thought he would go into the store.

But he didn't.

He locked her gaze, staring at her as if she were all there was to see, as if he had come here for the sole purpose of observing her. His image shimmered in the light that glared from the roof of his car. It was a moment before Gilly recognized him. She was staring down Mark Riley. Her breath shallowed. Was this some scheme to frighten her? Was Liz part of it? What was happening?

"I have to go." Even as she spoke, Gilly grabbed for the RAV's door handle.

Mark skirted the SUV's tailgate.

Liz's fingers closed, viselike, around Gilly's wrist. "No," she said.

23

Clint had gone inside the school building to question Marley and Kenna again, but Jake had no plan or direction, nothing concrete that might help find his daughter. He got into his truck. Gripping the steering wheel, he caught sight of his fingernails. The glittery blue polish Zoe had painted on them was damaged, only flecks of it remained. He closed his hands into fists. It was too hard to think about it, that it would be gone soon, every trace of it worn away. He reached for his phone. Anything to distract himself. Two messages. The first one was from Mary Alice.

"I'm worried about you. I talked to your mom. I think I woke her. Call me when you get this. Otherwise, I'll see you at the vigil." Pause. "Well, okay, then." Pause. "The job—Ferguson Hills—we finished it Friday on schedule. Maybe that's a good—no, never mind. I'm just—I'm holding down the fort, though, businesswise." Pause. "God, I don't know what to say." Her voice cracked, and she cleared her throat. "Okay, I'm hanging up now. Thinking of you."

Jake hit "Delete." He couldn't bring himself to return her call. If he talked to her for real, he wouldn't be able to keep it together.

The second message was from his ex-wife. Not Stephanie. Courtney. She lived in Virginia with her new husband, Phillip, an attorney, highly successful, descended from one of the wealthy plantation families. One of the bluebloods, he'd heard. They had probably owned slaves back in the day. The mostly unflattering image he had of the guy was put together from stuff Courtney had told him the handful of times they'd spoken over the years since their divorce. She was pleased with herself, landing such a fat fish, leading her cushy life. The last time she'd called, it had been to tell Jake how sorry she was that his marriage to Stephanie hadn't worked out. The fact that Courtney's second marriage was a spectacular, eye-popping success by contrast wasn't deeper than the surface of her voice. She might as well have said it—how she pitied him, raising a kid alone, an over-forty, two-time loser.

"Hey, I heard about Zoe. God, Jake, I'm so sorry." Courtney's voice needled his ear. "I—I want you to know Phillip and I are praying for you. Call me if there is anything we can do." Jake hit "Delete" again, cutting her off. He wondered what she meant by "anything."

He didn't plan to go back to the gas station in Nickel Bend, but that's where he found himself some thirty minutes after he left the school. He parked behind the station, next to the dumpster where Zoe's clothing had been found. There were a couple of Madrone County sheriff's cars in the parking lot, along with a handful of other civilian cars and trucks, belonging to the group of searchers Jake knew were in the area. But they'd moved farther afield into the surrounding woods. He stayed close to the station, circling the building once, walking the broken edge of the asphalt parking lot slowly, swishing his booted foot through clumps of wind-toughened grass, searching for something, a clue, that might have been missed. He walked the route again and again, mindless yet frantic, and he found nothing. His fifth time around, or his tenth—he'd lost count—he stopped at the back of the building, in its shadow, and it was as if he'd hit a wall. The despair was consuming, world-darkening. It bent him over. He lost his breath and sat down in the dirt.

Please God . . .

He prayed as he had not before. He begged as if there were someone somewhere to hear, to help. *Find her*, he said. *Findherfindherfindher . . .*

He didn't know how long he stayed there, uselessly begging, and he had no reason for it when he stood up and headed back to his truck. He didn't see the paper, what turned out to be a folded sheet of notepaper, stuck under his windshield wiper—at least not immediately, not until the wind lifted a corner. Thinking it was advertising, he pulled it out, intending to crumple it, but then he realized it was a message of some kind, written by hand in black ink. The angular letters were printed rather than cursive, and as he read the lines—there were three—his blood cooled.

HOW DOES IT FEEL, JAKE, LOSING YOUR DAUGHTER?
WE BOTH KNOW SHE SHOULD HAVE BEEN MINE.
LIKE I SAID BEFORE, YOU DIDN'T WANT HER,
DIDN'T DESERVE HER ANYWAY.

We both know . . . we who? Jake turned the notepaper over like he might find the answer on the back, but it was blank.

Heart slamming his chest wall, he whipped his gaze in every direction. He would have heard if someone had come. Even as zoned out as he'd been, he would have registered the sound of an engine if someone had pulled off the highway.

His phone rang, making him flinch. Checking the ID, he saw Clint's name. Answering, he launched into a panicked description of the note, how and where he'd found it. "It's what the caller said, same wording."

"You got any idea who would have a reason to think you aren't doing your job as Zoe's dad?"

"Other than Stephanie? No."

"Well, we know *she* didn't leave the note."

"Maybe she had somebody else do it—like Duchene."

"You recognize the writing?"

Jake looked at the note. "No."

"You didn't see anyone around your truck?"

"No, but I wasn't in sight of it all the time I've been here—forty, forty-five minutes, maybe. An hour max. Maybe whoever it was stuck it under the windshield wiper earlier, and I didn't see it. My mind's gone, you know?"

"Yeah. That's a pretty good possibility."

Jake registered the rough note of Clint's sympathy, and it bugged him, that he was an object of pity now, the cause of so much distress. He said, "Maybe it's just some wacko."

"Try not to handle it more than you have to, okay? We'll get it dusted for prints, maybe we'll get lucky. Listen, the reason I called—I just heard from Gilly O'Connell. She called me here at the station."

"Yeah?"

"It was weird, because I was trying to call her. The detective who's working her husband's murder case? They got an ID on the killer. The guy confessed."

"Well, that's good news. They arrest him?"

"Not yet. Turns out he's here in Wyatt, hunting for Gilly. Bowen, the detective, thinks the guy heard about her being psychic, and he's scared she's going to remember and ID him."

"Wow. You got any idea where he is?"

"No, but we're on it. It's just—we're spread so damn thin. Now we've got this Jester guy—But listen, here's the thing. Gilly thinks she knows where Zoe is."

Jake's heartbeat lagged. "She had a dream." He wasn't asking.

"Said she took a nap and saw a house, a two-story native limestone with faded green shutters. Abandoned, she thought. But it's around here. Somewhere near Wyatt. I'm having her come into the station. I've got the art teacher from the high school coming in, too. See if we can get a sketch. Why don't you bring the note in? We can get it to the lab."

"Yeah, okay." But it wasn't okay. It was taking too much time. He looked at the note in his hand, the words: *you didn't want her, didn't deserve her anyway.* And above it: *she should have been mine.* But it wasn't only what it said. There was something about the printing, too, every *e* was written in small uppercase, the *f*s were facing backward—something about the style pulled at him. He just couldn't put his finger on it. "Did Gilly give you any idea of where the house is in relation to Wyatt? East of town, west?"

"She didn't get a chance. Some friend of hers came along—Liz Ames?"

Jake's head came up. "Liz Ames is a friend of Gilly's? Are you sure?"

"I think so. Yeah. Why?"

It's Karen Ames *now, though. I'm married.* Her voice . . . the handwriting . . . He looked at the note. He hadn't heard her voice or seen her handwriting in years, not since high school—

"Jake? Are you with me?"

"The house Gilly dreamed about—she said the shutters were green? You're sure of that?"

"Yeah, I think so. Why?"

The image rose in Jake's mind of himself on a ladder, taking the shutters down from the house to be painted. A radio on the table under the live oaks was playing a Billy Joel song, "We Didn't Start the Fire." She was standing below him, taking the shutters from him, laughing up at him, at something he said. It was a memory from before they graduated, before prom. Before it all fell apart.

"Jake? What's going on, man?" Clint prompted him again.

"Liz Clayton is Elizabeth Clayton is Karen—Karen Clayton. Do you remember her? She was local. We went through school together, graduated in 1995."

"I know the name, but I was in Kuwait then, my last deployment. Wait a minute—is she the one who got so crazy when y'all broke up?"

"That's the one. Gilly's *friend*." The word was bitter in Jake's mouth. "Karen Elizabeth Clayton—Ames." He added her married name. "Those shutters? I helped her and her dad paint them green. Christmas break, our senior year. There was a warm spell. Her dad wanted to get it done before spring. The house Gilly dreamed about—it's the Claytonses' old house. Karen wrote this note." Jake brandished it as if Clint could see. "She's not here to find Zoe; she's here to take her away from me." *We both know she should have been mine. . . .* That line—he should have known. It scared the shit out of him now, putting it together.

"That's pretty bizarre, Jake. Why would she do it? What's her motive?"

"Revenge," he said. "I was going out with Courtney even before prom—I told Karen it was over, but I felt bad ditching her. I knew it would be too late for her to get another date." Jake was remembering out loud. "She was pissed; she started following me. Even her folks were pissed at me. They met a few times with my parents, trying to convince me to go back with Karen. When it didn't work, she started breaking into our house. Once, she slit her wrists in the tub in my bathroom with the blade from my razor."

"Are you kidding me?"

"No." Jake pushed a shaky hand through his hair. "Jesus, I haven't thought about any of this in years. We were out when she did it, but it was like she knew we'd get back in time. The cuts weren't deep." It had been a call for attention. That was how his mom had characterized it.

"I didn't know about the suicide attempt," Clint said. "I did hear she tried to set your bed on fire."

"Yeah. That was another time."

"It's hard to believe she went that far off the deep end over a breakup."

"It wasn't only that. She was pregnant. She was going to have our kid. Karen's got Zoe. I'm going over there and get her back."

"That's not a good idea—"

"Karen came up to me at the school, Clint. She told me about the vigil that's planned. She talked about how awful it was—Zoe missing— and all the time—all the time—God, I don't believe this." Jake was remembering her touch, his jolt of desire, some distant echo from his past. Still, it sickened him. "She's insane. She must be. Who knows what she's capable of? I've got to stop her."

"No." Clint's order barked in Jake's ear. He heard a scrape, move-ment, as if Clint was standing up. "If what you're telling me is right"— the captain's voice was needle sharp—"you do not want to go storming in there. She could be armed. You already know she might be unstable. Let me—let law enforcement handle it."

"I can talk to her, get her to give Zoe back—then you guys can come in—"

"No, Jake, I'm warning you. Stay away from there—"

He didn't hear the rest. He cut Clint off, and hopping into his truck, he tossed his phone onto the passenger seat and keyed the ignition. He didn't have a plan or a thought in his mind, other than he wanted his daughter. He wanted Zoe back, and he was going to get her. Now.

24

Liz's hands on her body. Phone clattering to the concrete, lost in the scuffle, her fruitless attempt to break away. Now something stung her on the upper part of her thigh.

Gilly brushed wildly at it. "What is that? What are you doing? What is wrong with you?"

Her questions went unanswered. Very quickly, the liquid warmth from what she recognized was the beginning of a drug-induced high radiated from the injection site. Her body began to loosen. In one final coherent moment her eyes found Liz's and clung there, shocked and disbelieving. Now with a strength that belied her small stature, Liz pushed Gilly against the side of her SUV. Her arms were jerked behind her with enough force to almost pull them from her shoulder sockets, and she was handcuffed.

Handcuffed!

She felt the bite of metal bracelets tighten around her wrists.

Was she being arrested? Was Liz—this woman whom Gilly had begun to consider her friend—was she a cop? But that couldn't be right. She'd just been talking to Captain Mackie . . .

Gilly was losing focus. The cool blue flame of deep lassitude lighting her veins was familiar and welcome in the way an old and much-loved enemy might be welcome. The monkey turned cartwheels. Miss Goody clapped her hands to her head in dismay. *Not again.*

But it wasn't only the drug rush that was recognizable. This scenario, too, had a familiar vibe. The store in Houston, where Brian had been shot—by Warren Jester, she now knew—had been set back from the road, on a quiet corner. Brian had been the only customer, and theirs had been the only car until moments after Brian had entered the store. Gilly had watched another car pull in, only to leave as quickly as it had come, as if the driver knew a robbery had been in progress. The difference was that crime had happened under cover of night, and this was happening while they could still be easily seen—by a witness, a passerby, the store clerk.

Was he looking?

Gilly squinted in the direction of the small building. The man, the driver who had pulled in moments ago, who she could have sworn had come around the back of his SUV toward her, was now looking at her over the roof of his car. He seemed to be smirking at her as if he was enjoying himself. Was it Mark Riley, or had she been mistaken?

Gilly saw another face pressed against the store window from the inside. Was it the clerk?

Or was she imagining that, too?

Liz's grip on Gilly's elbow kept her upright. Something hard was jammed into the small of her back. *Gun?* Gilly didn't know. Liz pressed against her, using her body to keep Gilly moving forward, strong-arming her. She couldn't manage her steps; her legs felt rubbery; her feet wouldn't mind. She had an urge to laugh.

Was this a joke?

"You'll pay for this," Gilly told Liz, sniggering. "Miss Two-shoes doesn't like it."

There was no response. Maybe she hadn't spoken aloud? She tried again. "Hey!"

Nothing. A grunt. The two of them kept moving around the building's corner, passing from sun to shade. Now Gilly was slammed face-first against the side of a different vehicle. Truck? Van? She flipped her head, one cheek to the other, trying to get a look. It was white, dirty white. She'd seen it . . . Warren Jester . . . had a white van . . .

"You move again, I'll kill you." Liz's voice was low.

"Why're you doing this? I thought we were friends." Gilly worked her tongue, trying to form into words the mush of thoughts passing through her brain.

Something made of cloth—a pillowcase, maybe—dropped over Gilly's head, sweet smelling, suffocating. It pissed her off, and she thrashed, side to side. An open palm struck her ear. She was stung a second time, her other thigh.

More drugs.

Again, she felt the warmth spread out from the injection site. Some kind of opiate, she thought. Vicodin? Oxy?

Yippee! crowed the monkey. He'd always wanted to try it. Shooting the dope. Muscling. Skin-popping.

She'd had offers, like at a party somebody was always willing to share their works, needles and such, but there was too much risk. She'd known a couple of people who'd died from abscesses they'd gotten at injection sites. Anyway, she hated needles. It had been easier, snorting or swallowing the stuff. But booze was her thing. She really loved to drink.

A door opened, a vehicle door, and Gilly was forced into what felt like a back seat, bench style, made to lie on her side. She drew up her knees, tried to mind the details. She had seen enough episodes of *Dateline*, watched enough Investigation Discovery TV, to know those victims who paid attention were the survivors, the ones who lived to tell. But her mind was full of fog as thick as curdled milk. She urged her eyes to stay open, but they kept drifting closed. *Why fight it?* asked the monkey. *It's not like you can see anything.* When he laughed, he sounded like a hyena.

A high hyena, Gilly thought, like a fool. Her lips were numb, but she felt them curve into a smile. *Don't you know? You are in real trouble here, dumbass.* The voice drifted.

Miss Two-shoes?

The monkey?

Did she care?

The vehicle—whatever it was, truck or van—took off, leaving the store parking lot, turning right, or at least that's what Gilly thought. Within minutes, the driver accelerated, going even faster, and Gilly imagined they were at the point on the highway where the speed limit rose from fifty-five to sixty. Her eyes grew heavier, her mind drifted, humming with the sound of the tires, and she floated in a nether world, not quite sleeping, but not awake either.

She had no idea how much later it was when she felt the vehicle slow and then stop. The driver-side door slammed. The back door opened, and Gilly was hauled out. What did turn out to be a pillowcase was plucked from her head.

She blinked. In the clear, silvery light of early evening, it took several moments for her eyes to adjust, for her to make sense of her location, but when she did, her heart did a hop into her throat. They were standing behind a house built of limestone, the very one from her dream. There were no shutters on the windows back here, but the wood trim was the same faded green. The yard was overgrown. Junipers shouldered above a dark and seemingly impenetrable wall of vegetation. It encroached from every side as if to consume all in its path. Had Gilly had the will to make a run for it, even had she not been drugged, she doubted she would have gotten far.

"Home sweet home," Liz said.

Gilly turned to look at her, and even in her altered state, she realized that Liz was different, changed in some way as if something inside her had come unhinged. Gilly was alarmed, but it was as if she were observing the scene from a distance, as if the fear belonged to someone else.

Keeping a grip on Gilly, Liz opened the passenger door of the truck, the same dirty white truck with the camper top from her dream, and brought out a gun, but it was the bit of blue ribbon—Zoe's ribbon, looping the bracket that held the rearview mirror—that riveted Gilly's attention. She stared at it.

Zoe was inside this house.

The dream had been right.

Her glance jerked to the back door. The urge to get inside, get to Zoe, was visceral, burning through her haze, but like her fear of Liz, Gilly felt separate from the sensation, as if she were viewing herself through glass.

Even that was the same as her dream experience, though. During Wednesday night's dream, Gilly had felt as if she were trapped behind a thick glass wall, and earlier today, while napping, she had watched this scene play out inside a snow globe, which had shattered to bits when it had slipped from her hands.

But suppose she was dreaming now?

The possibility that this wasn't real bolted through her brain.

Gah!

Could she have set this up during lost time? Doped herself? Shot herself up with something, and now she was hallucinating? She swung her head to clear it, making her stomach roll. Bile rose in her throat, and she clenched her teeth, willing the sensation to pass, fighting to stay on her feet.

Liz's grip on Gilly's elbow tightened. The gun—it looked like Carl's duty weapon that Gilly knew was a Glock—rose level with her face, muzzle glimmering in the fading sunlight. She looked down the tunnel of the dark bore and saw an image of herself from the past.

She is sitting in the car outside the corner market, waiting for Brian. Her palms are splayed over her belly, heavy with their baby girl. Gilly is singing softly, an old and silly children's song her mother sang to her— Mairzy doats and dozey doats and liddle lamzy-divey—*when she catches the movement from the corner of her eye. She looks out her window, the passenger side window, expectant, half smiling, but it isn't Brian hovering outside the store's doorway. The man is older and too tall, thin and rangy in a way Brian is not, and even though he is wearing a red ball cap, she is somehow aware that he's terrified. She sees his hesitation, the wild swing of his gaze. Now their eyes lock, and they share an awful moment of desperation. His knowledge goes into her—that he has done something unspeakable, a thing that can't now, or ever, be undone. Then he is coming toward her. She sees his face as plain as day, and it is Warren Jester's face. Her eyes track his progress through the glass of the windshield as he dashes across her field of vision. It is when he has passed her that she sees the butt of the gun—a revolver of some kind—jutting from the waistband of his jeans.*

Where had the memory been all this time? Gilly saw it so clearly in her mind's eye now. The December night when Brian had been killed had been freezing, but the man had been coatless. She saw the hem of his red shirt, rucked up over the gun butt. It was a T-shirt. Short sleeved, red like his hat. The back was printed in white with the name Olajuwon and the number thirty-four. Hakeem Olajuwon, the Houston Rockets basketball player. She had known that. Brian had been a fan. But she had not remembered the hat, the shirt, or the gun on the night he was murdered. *I don't remember. It's all a blur.* That was how she'd answered Carl's questions.

But here, now, was the memory—the image of Warren Jester's face—as pristine as if it were new, dredged from some black hole in her mind. He was still wearing the cap, the same red ball cap.

"I know how to use this." Liz waved the gun in front of Gilly's face. "In case you were thinking of taking off."

Looking past Liz's shoulder, Gilly imagined it: running. What would it be like to be shot in the back? You wouldn't know; you wouldn't see it coming. She imagined staggering, falling, her life oozing from her.

She'd be gone in a matter of minutes, less even, maybe seconds. She'd see Brian and Sophie. They'd be waiting for her. She was overcome with longing, an ache so deep it drew her forward. The jab of the gun muzzle against her chest stayed her.

"Trust me, you don't want to try it." The humor in Liz's voice was bitter. "Woods out here go on forever, and they're full of stuff you don't want to tangle with. Rattlesnakes, for a start, wild hogs, coyotes. I heard even running across a bear or a mountain lion's not an impossibility."

"Zoe's here, isn't she, Liz. Why did you take her? Why have you brought me here? Are you working for someone?" Gilly saw again the black Navigator, parked at the Quick-Serv. The man, who might have been Mark Riley, staring at her. She caught Liz's gaze. "You know him, don't you? Mark Riley. He put you up to this." But even as Gilly spoke, something told her it didn't make sense. Why would he take Zoe?

Liz didn't answer. She pushed Gilly up the back porch steps and cautioned her when she stumbled. "Careful. Wood's rotten. Daddy was always promising Mama he'd pour her a set of concrete steps. But he never did."

"You could let me have Zoe, and we'll go. I promise we won't tell anyone."

Liz laughed at Gilly's offer. "Get inside." She ushered Gilly through a screen door and across a screened porch. Against the wall, in the shadows, an old, narrow iron bedstead was topped with a stained, ticking-striped mattress. A length of faded pink cane on the wicker rocker next to the bed was coming unspooled along one arm. The seat was broken clean through. Powdery layers of dust rose in swirls as they crossed the kitchen.

"Where is Zoe? Can I see her?"

No answer.

Gilly was prodded, gun muzzle jammed against the small of her back, across a living room, where sheet-draped furniture hulked like ghosts. An underscore of mildew mixed with the smell of ruination and abandonment. The silence was thick, the heat stifling. No wonder. All but one of the windows was boarded just as they had been in her dream. They entered a narrow hallway. Doors. Four in all. One at the end, two on Gilly's left and another on the right. A couple of camp lanterns, sitting on the floor, gave off a murky glow.

"I need to lie down," she said, and she wasn't kidding. Her legs were trembling. Her mouth was dry, and her ears rang. She was sweat drenched. All side effects of whatever narcotic she'd been shot up with.

Liz paused outside one of the closed doors, and flinging it open, said, "Here you go. Ask and ye shall receive."

Gilly balked, flinching from the heat, dank smell, and near impenetrable dark beyond the threshold. It was a moment before she saw that the single window in the room was boarded, too, from the inside. She made out the shape of a bed pushed against the opposite wall. Like the one on the screened porch, it was topped with a stained, ticking-striped mattress. The only other furniture was a straight-back chair.

"Go on." Liz prodded her with the gun.

"No." Gilly balked on the threshold. "You tell me what is going on. Why're you doing this? Where is Zoe?"

Liz gave Gilly a shove and retreated, shutting the door.

Gilly heard her key the lock. "Can you at least take off these handcuffs?"

No answer.

"Water," Gilly said. "Could I have some water?"

But if Liz heard her, she didn't respond. Maybe Gilly hadn't spoken aloud. It was hard to distinguish her real voice from the one in her head. Groping her way to the bed, she sat down, but the smell her weight displaced—a history of unwashed bodies and old urine, something danker, mold, mouse droppings, who knew—brought her upright, got her back on her feet. She crossed to the window, where the fast-fading light broke along one edge of the plywood covering. Putting her eye to the crack only blinded her further. She sat on the floor, brain floating in her skull. Her thoughts, barely formed, drifted.

Her physical awareness skittered from the hard surface under her butt to the metal chafing her wrists to her thirst. She needed a bathroom.

She didn't know what amount of time passed. She might have dozed.

Eventually, she made herself get up and walk the room's perimeter, feeling long the wall with her shoulder for the light switch, jubilant when she located one, but when she managed to flip it up, nothing happened.

She found the door and kicking it, yelled, "Let me out!" She shouted it again, "Let me out!" And she kept it up, kicking and shouting until she was footsore and hoarse. The door barely moved. It felt sturdy, as if it was solid rather than hollow. But the racket she'd made was enough to raise the dead, literally.

She heard it when she stopped. The sound of crying was more an exhausted whimper. It was the sound overly tired children made when they had long forgotten the reason for their unhappiness.

It raised the hair on Gilly's neck; it jolted her with fresh energy.

"Zoe!" Gilly shouted her name, paused to listen.

Silence.

"Zoe?" She tried again. "It's Gilly from Cricket's. Can you hear me?"

"Gilly?"

"Yes, honey." Relief closed Gilly's throat. "Are you okay?"

"Is my daddy here? I want to go home."

"Oh, I wish he could—" Gilly paused. She didn't know how to go on, what she could offer as reassurance. Zoe didn't sound right. Her voice was thick, her words slurred. It might be exhaustion, her tears. But Gilly didn't think it was only that. She had a bad feeling, a sick feeling. She could no longer believe this had anything to do with Mark Riley. This was all about Zoe. Had to be. Oh, if Liz had doped that little child—

A sound of footsteps approached, stopped some way down the hall. A lock was keyed, a door opened. Voices. Liz's low, soothing. Zoe's higher, rising now into a shriek that turned Gilly's blood to ice. Moments passed before Zoe's cries subsided, resuming a monotonous, heartbroken rhythm. Shortly after, Gilly's own door was unlocked.

Liz's silhouette hovered on the doorsill.

Gilly thought of rushing her. She imagined head butting Liz dead center, a move that could very well knock her down. But then what? Gilly's hands, cuffed behind her back, were useless, and even if they were free, Liz had the gun.

She waved it vaguely in Gilly's direction. "Sit down."

"What did you give Zoe?"

"A little something to help her rest. We can all use that about now, I think," Liz answered serenely. She crossed the room. In addition to the gun, Gilly saw she was carrying two camp lanterns like the ones she'd seen in the hall. Kneeling, she switched them on, and Gilly blinked at the sudden brightness.

"I need to go to the bathroom," she said.

Liz looked up at her, lips pursed, considering.

"Please."

"All right, but no funny stuff." She brandished the revolver, and there was something too relaxed in the gesture, as if she didn't mean it seriously. But maybe it was an act, some kind of head game to keep Gilly off balance.

"Trust me." She spoke over the hammer of her pulse. "I'm not into funny stuff when someone's got a gun on me."

Liz's grin was snarky, which seemed out of place. Was she high? On the same dope she'd given Gilly and probably Zoe, too?

They crossed the hall, and at the bathroom doorway, Gilly turned, looking deliberately into Liz's eyes. Although the light wasn't good, she could make out that her pupils were contracted, not more than pinpoints. Her face and neck were flushed, too, all signs she was on something. It didn't surprise Gilly. She raised her arms. "Can you take the cuffs off? Either that, or you'll have to—"

Liz huffed in disgust, annoyance.

"This wasn't my idea," Gilly said. "I'm ready to leave anytime."

"There's no way out of the bathroom, so don't even think about it." Liz pocketed the gun, unlocked the cuffs, and slipped them from Gilly's wrists. "Get on with it." Stepping back, Glock in hand, she pulled the door, not closing it all the way, giving Gilly some privacy.

Not that it mattered. The only window above the tub was boarded with plywood from the inside, the same as the one in the bedroom. Gilly couldn't have left had it been wide open, though. Not without Zoe. She did her business, and Liz pulled her across the hall, entering the bedroom behind her. She stood inside the doorway, dangling the cuffs. "I'll leave these off s'long as you don't try anything." Her speech was slurred, her posture careless.

Gilly smiled. "Not going to try anything," she said. "Scouts honor." She put three fingers above her brow in salute. "Or is it two?" She fumbled, giggling. It wasn't difficult. She was stoned, too. But some sharper urgency was alive in all the haze, and she knew it was there, fighting to be alert. If not for herself, then for Zoe.

Keeping the gun in one hand, Liz set the handcuffs on the floor and withdrew a syringe from the pocket of her hoodie. "You want to party?"

Gilly retreated. "I'm good."

"Hard or easy." Liz wasn't taking no for an answer.

Gilly snickered, playing it off, pretending coyness.

"Sit down." Liz set the gun on the seat of the single chair, and staring at it, Gilly imagined knocking her aside, running down the hall, retrieving Zoe, and getting the hell out. But for that plan to work, she'd need to scoop the Glock from the chair, wrangle the key to Zoe's room from wherever Liz had stashed it, and get the key to the getaway truck outside. *Fat chance.*

Liz sat beside her.

Gilly felt the mattress sag. She held her breath when Liz injected her—in her upper arm this time—as if not breathing would stop the drug from entering her bloodstream. "What is it, anyway?" she asked, and she was friendly, all sugar-wouldn't-melt-in-her-mouth chummy.

"Morphine. Pharmaceutical grade. Pure as the holy house of healing where I got it. I figured you of all people would appreciate it."

Gilly stared at Liz.

"You're an addict, right? Girl, I know everything about you."

Faintly, Gilly said, "All this time, I was worried what you'd think. Who are you?"

"Not your friend. Not a pharmaceutical rep, or an abused wife, or any of the crap you thought. When we met it was no accident, trust me."

"You set it up, when I saw you in the park?"

"Getting next to you was the best way to stop you before you wrecked everything."

"Wrecked . . . ?" The word died in Gilly's mouth almost before it was uttered.

Liz picked up the revolver and sat in the chair, balancing her ankle on her knee, keeping the weapon in a loose grip in her lap. "I like you. That's the hell of it. We might have been friends in another time and place, but watching you around Jake and Zoe—the way you look at him all goo-goo eyed, those cutesy little pancakes you make for Zoe, hanging over her, talking a blue streak—like you're her mom—"

"What are you talking about?"

"Jake comes into the café, there you are, hanging over him, like you belong together. He doesn't even see me. He—everyone in that fucking town looks through me like I don't exist."

"You said you were divorced, that you were getting a restraining order. You said your ex was on your porch—"

"I said a lot of things."

"You never said you knew Jake."

"You're no different. You kept secrets from me. Like I had to read online how when Brian was killed you lost your baby. I kept waiting for you to tell me. I actually thought, *If Gilly tells me that then maybe I'll have to rethink the rest.*"

"The rest? I don't know what you mean."

"I lost my baby, too."

"Is anything you told me about yourself true? Are you from Dallas? Are you divorced? What about the house in Wyatt? You put earnest money down—"

"Sounds nice, doesn't it. Like a nice life. It almost makes me wish it was true."

Gilly stared, trying to work it out, but this Liz, the one holding the gun, talking in her flat voice, didn't mesh at all with Gilly's recollection of her friend Liz, the woman she'd looked forward to knowing better.

"My little girl was stillborn. I named her Cassandra Marie after my mama. Cassie for short. It's what Mama's friends called her. So adorable. I had all her clothes, diapers, crib, rocking chair, toys, everything. Had her prom dress picked out, her wedding gown. Ha ha! Not really, but you know. I'd dreamed her whole life. Then she was—she never even took one breath. It killed me. I lost a part of myself. You know what I mean, though, don't you?"

Liz locked Gilly's eyes. The moment felt breathless.

"Don't you?" Liz insisted.

"Yes." Gilly was mesmerized. It was probably the dope, but she felt drawn to Liz in the way you might feel drawn to a cliff's edge to see what sort of wreckage had been flung over the side. Maybe they would go over together, hand in hand, Thelma and Louise–style.

"No one else gets it, do they? The terrible pain it is, losing a child before you even have her." Liz kept Gilly's gaze. "I'm so sorry for you, for everything you've been through."

Gilly cupped her elbows, rocking herself a bit.

"After I lost Cassie—if it hadn't been for Roger—he's my husband—if it hadn't been for him—You okay? You don't look so good. You want more?" Liz grappled in her hoodie pocket, producing another syringe.

"No," Gilly said. "I'm good." *Too damn good.* She touched her face, which felt numb. Her body hummed as if it were inhabited by bees.

"You try to kill yourself? I did—"

"I guess, yes—you could say—" Gilly cut herself off before it could spill out of her—the sordid history of her addictions, her run-in with the law over the kidnapping charge. Liz was holding a gun on her, for God's sake. *It's okay. You're stoned out of your mind*, the monkey said. *Get a grip*, Miss Goody said. *Zoe, think about Zoe*, said some other voice, the one that was most rational. "Are you giving morphine to Zoe? I don't think you should—"

"I'm an RN. Eighteen years. Worked mostly in the OR and the ER. If there's one thing I know about, it's dope." Liz pocketed the needle. "I've got plenty, too."

"Zoe's so small—"

"I know what I'm doing, okay?"

Gilly nodded. The last thing she wanted was to rile Liz further. "Did you get the morphine from the hospital where you work? Is it in Dallas?"

"Lubbock. I live in Lubbock. Don't work at the hospital there anymore, though. Got fired last December right before Christmas. They caught me stealing medication. Har har. Job dragged me down anyway. Most of the patients're nothing but a bunch of crackheads looking for a legal way to get high. I felt like I was just doing what they wanted. Shooting them up. It made me sick."

But you're no better than them. Neither one of us is. The thoughts wandered through Gilly's mind. *Focus!* the voice—the rational one—shouted in her brain. She straightened, dug her nails into her palms. "So you lied about Dallas. What about being divorced—"

"People don't understand, do they—when you lose a baby?" Liz went on as if Gilly hadn't spoken. "They say terrible things, like *You can have another kid*, and *Maybe this one wasn't meant to live*. Or worse, they say God wanted her, and now she's a star in his crown, or she's singing in his angel choir. Give me a fucking break."

Gilly had heard those things, too, from well-meaning folks. Before she could stop herself, she said, "Once I told one of my mom's friends that Sophie wasn't a puppy that could be replaced."

"Exactly!" Liz crowed. "God! It kills me how much we have in common."

"We can still be friends," Gilly began.

"No!" Liz sliced the air with the gun. "That's why I finally did it, took Zoe now, before—"

"Before?" Gilly tried to catch Liz's gaze, which had fallen. She looked disoriented now, as if she were lost. And she was, Gilly guessed, in the drugged haze of her own mind.

"I'm not letting you get inside my head." Liz's chin came up. "Not letting you screw this up. Been planning too long. I'm not having you come in, swooping down like some superhero to the rescue. I know your game. I heard it on the news, how you're supposedly psychic—" Gun in hand, Liz made air quotes. "What a load of shit. I can't believe Jake fell for that garbage. He used to be a smart guy."

"He didn't hire me—"

"If you can see the damned future, how come you didn't see what I was planning that day in the park when we met, or any time since? Huh? How come you've never known why I came to Wyatt? That it was to take Zoe? We've spent time together, but you never saw shit, did you? 'Cause you can't, that's why. 'Cause it's all a lie. Even your damned dream about some woman taking Zoe. Yeah, I heard about it. What the hell use was it? You didn't even know it was me."

"You're right—"

"Shut up. I'm talking now. I've got you, got you here. I can blow your head off or shoot you up. Whatever I want, 'cause you are not taking Zoe out of here and handing her back to Jake like some prize and y'all walk off into the sunset like you're in a romance novel. I didn't come this far for that to happen. I'd as soon see us all dead." Liz rocked forward, planting her feet flat on the floor, eyes blazing. Her posturing was a come-on, a dare.

She looked lit up from the inside as if by some unholy light, and that's when it hit Gilly for real—that she might not get out of here alive. Might not live to get Zoe out. A scream loosened from the well of Gilly's gut, traveling like a rocket toward her throat, but somehow she managed to contain it in the cage of her ribs. She made herself breathe. *Think.* The voice in her brain barked the order. "Are you from Wyatt? Is that how you know Jake?" Gilly was playing a hunch, buying time.

"You want the story? The whole pathetic soap opera of a drama? Yeah, I'm from here, born and raised. Jake and I went through school together."

"You've been driving back and forth between here and Lubbock all this time—two months? That's a lot of miles."

"A lot of time to think. I've been doing it six months. First time was last December. I come whenever Roger's on the road. He's a long-haul trucker. Leaves me on my own. Probably more than he should." Liz's grin was brief.

"Six months? Really? In all this time no one's recognized you? No one has figured out who you are?"

"I'm smart, that's why. Rented that little RV in the park on the outskirts of town. Drove in and out any damn time I pleased. A lot of times, if I was going to spend time in town, I wore this hoodie." She pinched up a bit of fabric. "A cap, my big sunglasses."

"But whenever we got together, when you came into Cricket's— you wore suits."

"Ha! Yeah, I was the pharmaceutical rep, a professional drug pusher. Sweet, huh? They say when you lie, keep it as close to the truth as you can, right?" Liz waited, expectantly, as if for praise, and when Gilly failed to offer it, she said, "Gotcha, didn't I?"

Gilly didn't rise to the bait, if that's what it was.

"Anyway, it's been more than twenty years since I've been gone from this crap town. My hair's a different color now, and I'm wearing it shorter. I've lost weight, too. Anyway, I told you I was keeping a low profile, remember? That police sergeant—Ken Carter—he was freaking me out. He was a year ahead of me in school, but it was only a matter of time till he—or somebody—figured it out. Another reason to make a move."

"You and Jake—did you date?"

Liz threw back her head, hooting like it was the funniest joke she'd ever heard.

Gilly saw herself rushing Liz, pushing her over, chair and all.

Liz's glance fell on her hard as if she'd read Gilly's thought. "Did we date? I gave that guy everything, body and soul. So did my mama and daddy; they loved him. Looked on him like their son. Mama was always going on about our babies, when was she going to get a grandbaby." Liz let go a gust of air. "She was over the moon about Cassie."

"What happened?" Gilly asked, although by now she could guess that it had ended badly.

"The week before our senior prom, he broke up with me and started dating this bitch Courtney behind my back."

"You were pregnant." Gilly wasn't asking. The direction of Liz's story was obvious.

"I'd just found out for sure. Then Mama and I did the test with the pendulum. I know some folks think it's an old wives' tale, but we knew I was having a girl. I didn't tell Jake right then, though. I was so pissed at him, and sick, just sick to my stomach."

"Why?"

"He was breaking up with me!" Liz was shrill. "Saying all this shit about how he didn't love me anymore. Oh, but he'd keep our prom date. Like I'd go along with that. Be his fucking pity date. But I let him think I would. He showed up, too, all dressed like an ad out of *GQ*, driving a candy-apple-red Thunderbird. I saw him, listened to him knock on the door. He left my corsage on the porch, and I tore it up. He was there, watching me. I didn't see him, but I could feel him, you know?"

"Did he ever know about the baby?"

"Not from me. Mama and Daddy went to his parents and told them. They tried to get Jake and his folks to do right by me, but they thought we were too young. They didn't want Jake saddled with the responsibility. They said they'd pay for an abortion if I chose that, or help with adoption, as if either of those alternatives was acceptable." Liz set her free hand on her belly. "I'd felt her kick. How do you consider abortion after that? How could Jake's folks consider it? Their own granddaughter? How could they think I could give her away to another couple when she was mine? Mine and Jake's. I just knew he'd see it, and tell them to fuck off."

But he didn't. Gilly didn't need the words to know the outcome.

"They convinced him Cassie would ruin our lives, and when she died, they were glad. It's their fault I lost my baby. They caused her to die; they took Cassie, took my life from me, and Jake let them."

"You told me when Zoe was kidnapped that bad things happen in this world, but that isn't what you meant, is it."

"No."

Gilly kept Liz's gaze.

"Don't stare at me like I'm crazy." Her voice shook. "It's the same as what that robber, the one who murdered your husband—wouldn't you say he took your life from you? Huh? Wouldn't you? Answer me!"

"Okay. Yes. He took my life." It was true, in all but the physical sense, and God knew Gilly had wished for that to end. She had prayed to be gone from this earth, and it disconcerted her that there could be any truth to the words spoken by someone who was so obviously troubled and unstable.

"Don't you want to take something from him? Something of equal value? Something that would cause him an equal amount of pain if he were to lose it?" Liz sat back. "Like his life. Don't you want to kill him?"

Did she? An image of Warren Jester formed from the haze in Gilly's brain, and along with it, she felt a renewal of doubt that Warren was the one. That kind man. He had appeared ordinary, normal. Like Liz. She'd seemed normal, too, outgoing and friendly—all of it faked.

Gilly watched her now as she drew something from inside the collar of her hoodie—a gold heart-shaped locket on a chain. It glimmered in the uncertain light.

"See this?" Liz didn't wait for Gilly's answer. "It's engraved with Cassie's initials, CMH, Cassandra Marie Halstead. Mama and I settled on her name and bought it the very day we knew she'd be a girl. I was going to show it to Jake—my way of telling him—" Liz's voice broke. She cleared her throat. "Last winter, Roger was gone, he's always gone, I'd lost my job, had nothing to do. It was the week after Christmas—"

Liz's speech hurried, rushing her words that were barely above a whisper. Gilly bent forward to catch them.

"The wind in West Texas—you ever heard it? It makes an awful racket. Dust everywhere. I started cleaning things, and I found the locket. It brought it back, all the awful memories." She looked up at Gilly, stricken. "I saw Jake everywhere; I dreamed about him at night. I remembered how he and his folks treated me like gum stuck to their shoe. It wasn't right, what they did to me. I have to make it right, you understand? I'm the only one who can do it, make it right. He doesn't deserve Zoe. He didn't even want her."

"Oh," Gilly said, "I don't think that's true."

"Ask him, if you don't believe me." Liz picked up the Glock.

Watching her, Gilly waited to feel the bullet tear into her skull. But it did not.

Liz ran a fingertip along the gun barrel, speaking to it. "I knew I had to come to Wyatt. I had to see Jake. It was when I was driving here that first time that I thought of it, how if I were to take his little girl, he'd know how it felt when I lost our little girl. You see?" Liz looked at Gilly through eyes glossed with tears, eyes that begged for understanding.

And as convoluted as Liz's longing was, Gilly did understand it. She wondered if that made her as crazy, as mentally off the charts, as Liz. "You kept up with him all these years, is that right? That's how you knew he had a daughter?"

"Our class has a Facebook page. You know Mandy Bright? She runs it, and you know her reputation. Telephone, telegraph, tele—"

"Mandy," Gilly finished.

"I saw her at the school today. She fell on me like I was her long-lost BFF. She hated me back in the day. She and Augie took Jake's side."

"You went to the Little Acorn today?" Disbelief hollowed Gilly's tone. "Did Jake see you?"

"We talked. He took my hand, and it was like sparks went off. I know he felt something. If we'd been alone, he would have kissed me. It was all over him. I know he still loves me. When he sees me with Zoe, sees how good I am with her, he'll realize we could—we were meant to be together. We can still do it, be the family we dreamed about."

Liz's belief, her will that her vision was true, was fierce in her eyes. Maybe she was right, Gilly thought. Maybe Jake did still love her. The making of a child formed such a powerful bond between a man and woman.

"What about your husband?" Gilly named the obvious obstacle, the one Liz seemed to have forgotten, the man whom she'd claimed had saved her.

"Roger? He'll understand. All he wants is for me to be happy. He tells me all the time." Liz held Gilly's gaze, seeming unfazed.

"The police—"

"You think they scare me?" Liz barked a laugh. "I've had the cops sicced on me before. After prom, that summer, Jake's folks got a judge to issue a restraining order. They accused me of harassing them and Jake. They said I followed him. Because I went in their house a few times. I was only trying to get Jake to do the right thing, to stand up and act like a man—a father. He was going to *be* a father. I didn't get pregnant by myself, you know."

A pause fell. Gilly looked beyond Liz's bowed head at the door.

"I tried killing myself that summer, but I couldn't even get that right." Liz turned over her forearms, offering them for Gilly's examination. The scars led toward the crooks of her elbows. Thin and deadly, they were white now after so many years. "I used Jake's razor. I got into his bathtub when no one was home. I wanted him to find me. I thought it would wake him up."

"You didn't think about what it would do to your baby, to Cassie?"

Liz picked up the gun, aiming it at Gilly, sighting down the barrel. "The last time I went in his house"—she lowered the Glock and went on talking as if Gilly hadn't spoken—"I was just going to wait for him in his bedroom. I went in through the window like I had before. I could hear the TV on in the den. He and his mom and dad were watching the Astros. I was going to sit on his bed until he came, and we could talk. But something happened. I don't know. I kind of flipped out. I set his bed on fire. They made it out like their whole house burned down. They pressed charges against me for arson and attempted manslaughter, some shit like that. They had a shrink talk to me, and he told the court I was nuts, manic, schizo—whatever. So instead of prison, they locked me up in the psych ward at Austin State Hospital. A month later my baby—Jake's baby—was born. In a nuthouse! They let her be born there, and she died there. Mama took me to see her. She was so tiny and blue, but she was perfect. I wanted to hold her, but no one would let me. I don't even know where she's buried."

"Your folks—"

"They left town, moved to Illinois, where my aunt lives. It was hard on them—what happened to me. The way everyone in the fucking town shunned them after—like their daughter was the devil's spawn or something. Ha!" Her laugh was brittle. "I got it all over on them, though. I got a guy who drove the laundry truck to get me out. He dropped me at the highway, and Roger picked me up. I rode with him in his semi for almost a year. He made me sane, got me studying to be a nurse. It was after he saw me do CPR on a guy at this diner up in Cedar Rapids, Iowa—another trucker who had a heart attack. I learned CPR at this Red Cross thing my dad made me sign up for in high school. I guess I saved that trucker's life."

She smiled slightly. "It made an impression on Roger. On me, too. It was cool, knowing that man didn't die because I was there and knew how to take care of him. I thought then maybe I'd be okay. I would help people, make a difference."

"The law didn't come after you?"

"I was using my middle name, Elizabeth, and anyway Roger and I were always on the move. Then, when we finally settled down, we were married, and I'd become Elizabeth Ames. Everyone was calling me Liz by then. We bought a little country place outside Lubbock, half the state away from here. Roger fancies himself a rancher. He's got a few head."

"Does Roger know you're here?"

"I never leave unless he's on the road." Liz picked up the Glock, aiming it at Gilly.

She darted a glance at the door, still ajar, light in the hallway beckoning. Could she, in her condition, get out of here alive, get Zoe, and get away from this lunatic woman? "I'm really thirsty. I could use a drink of water. Would you get it for me? Please?"

The moment held, silent, unyielding, as visceral and taut as a hanging rope.

Gilly was amazed when Liz stood up, and pocketing the syringe and the Glock in her hoodie, said, "Don't move." She was equally amazed when she disobeyed the order, launching herself at Liz as soon as her back was turned.

The collision brought Liz to her knees, grunting in surprised pain. Another shove knocked her flat. Gilly heard the cracking sound when Liz's skull struck the floor. She scooted out of reach, but even as she pulled herself frantically toward the door, and got to her feet, she was waiting for retaliation, a gunshot, the slightest protest.

But Liz lay still.

Winded, Gilly thought. She wondered if she should try to get the gun, but Liz was prone. Her arms and the Glock were pinned underneath her, along with the key to the room Zoe was in, and the key to the truck. Gilly couldn't risk it—turning Liz over, clearing out her pockets. Best to just get Zoe and go.

Gilly backed out of the bedroom, adrenaline fueling her heartbeat and her steps, pushing back the numbing effects of the morphine. Out in the dimly lit hall, she looked at the other doors, and in the moment it took to wonder *which one?* she heard whimpering. The sound was hurt, enfeebled, and Gilly followed it to the door at the hallway's end. She registered it only subliminally when the knob turned easily in her hand. Flinging the door open, the stifling heat and the smell hit her first, a sour, gagging stench of vomit and urine overlay the danker odors of mold and abandonment. But even that was of little consequence when Gilly's gaze, adjusting to the gloom, found Zoe. She lay curled in a fetal position, a small hump atop a narrow iron bed against the wall.

Crossing the room, Gilly knelt beside the mattress, hands fluttering, touching Zoe's damp, matted hair, and her face that was crusted with mucous and tears. Her shirt and shorts looked new, but they were stained and reeked of illness and suffering. She felt warm to Gilly's touch, and her eyes were open, but they were vacant and glassy. She didn't seem to know Gilly was there. "Zoe, honey? It's Gilly. Can you hear me?" Gilly sat back on her heels, staring into those empty eyes, and fury at Liz struck her behind her eyes followed by a prayer: *Oh God, please help me.* Her pulse tapped her temples.

Gilly ran her glance to the end of the bed, and when she saw that Zoe was tethered to the footboard, tied by a length of clothesline to one of the iron rods, her anger nearly brought her to her feet. She had visions of the Glock in her hand, holding the muzzle against Liz's temple, and pulling the trigger.

"I'll be right back," she said, but if Zoe heard her, she gave no sign.

Retracing her route along the hallway, Gilly peered into the room where she had left Liz. She hadn't moved but lay as she'd fallen, on her belly. Was she dead? Gilly stepped over the threshold and froze when Liz's leg twitched, when she groaned, leaving no doubt she was very much alive. If Gilly was going to get Zoe out of here, they had to go now, on foot.

She returned to Zoe's bedside, untied the clothesline, and lifted the child into her arms, trying not to mind the wealth of foul odors that moving her unleashed.

Zoe cried, a series of soft bleats.

"It's okay, baby girl. We're getting out of here."

She paused on her way down the hall to check on Liz, and she was alarmed to see she was up on her hands and knees. She had her head down and didn't seem aware of Gilly passing only feet away.

Gilly picked up her pace. Her heart pounded. Her breath came in weighted gusts. She felt as if she wore a target on her back and kept waiting for the strike of the bullet between her shoulder blades. Would it lodge there, or go clean through her, burying itself in Zoe? They were crossing the kitchen with only the width of the back porch separating them from the outdoors and possible freedom when Zoe came to enough that she found Gilly's gaze.

"Sick," she whispered and retched, a dry, horrible sound.

"Almost there, ZooRoo." She used Jake's pet name.

Shifting Zoe upright into a one-armed embrace, she reached for the back door with her free hand. The shot rang out just as she twisted the knob. The sound deafened her. It seemed to go on for hours, centuries, an eon. Now Gilly was the one falling to her knees. She bent over Zoe, shielding her with her body.

"Don't make a sound," she whispered.

25

"W here are you?" Clint was gruff, angry at Jake for hanging up on him.

"Near the turnoff to Karen's house. If I remember, the road isn't marked. It's that dogleg just past CR 321, isn't it?"

"Pull over. We've got a whole new ballgame here."

It was the urgency in Clint's voice that caused Jake to obey. He bumped onto the weedy verge. "What's happened?"

"The clerk out at the Quick-Serv called about a car abandoned at a gas pump there. I'm out here now. It's Gilly's RAV4. I ran the plate."

"Karen's got her."

"Yeah, maybe, as far out as that sounds to me. Clerk says he saw a woman come up to her, saw them talking, but he got distracted. Next time he looked, he saw the woman driving out of here in a white pickup. Could be the same pickup from the park security footage. The clerk didn't see a passenger—"

"But Gilly could have been inside, lying down. He get a license plate?"

"No. He says there was a guy parked in front who saw what went on. Drove a black Lincoln Navigator. The clerk didn't get his plate either, but Mark Riley drives a black Navigator."

"You think he's in this with Karen?"

"I don't know what in the hell is going on. We got a report, too, of a white pickup that was stolen from Burley's yesterday morning, early."

"Where the blue sedan was with Zoe's backpack inside."

"Yeah. The driver left his truck unlocked and running while he went in to get bait. Can you believe it? Dumbass. He said he figured jacking cars didn't happen in the country."

"So Karen saw it and decided it was time to trade—"

"The idiot couldn't have helped her out any more if he'd handed her an engraved invitation. She's got to know law enforcement is on to her."

"This is just unbelievable." Jake's head felt light.

"There's more. I spoke to Roger Ames, Karen's husband. He's a long-haul trucker. He's been on the road for more than two weeks. He didn't know she'd left home, but he's kind of suspected something was going on the last several months. He's noticed she's been putting miles on her car, a lot more miles than if she'd just been doing routine stuff around town."

"Did you tell him she was here, that she's got Zoe? Can he get hold of her?"

"She's not answering her phone. Gilly's phone is here, busted on the concrete by her car. Look, from what Ames said, Karen's in some serious trouble mentally, emotionally, legally—you name it. Last December she was fired from her job at the hospital. She's an RN, and she was caught stealing drugs, using some, maybe selling some. Roger wasn't sure. He said she's had problems over the years. Been off and on prescription meds for depression, bipolar disorder—"

"No surprise there."

"Yeah, well, it gets worse. Around the same time she was fired, her folks were killed in a car accident up in Illinois, where they'd been living since they moved from here. Roger said she hadn't talked to them in years, and it tore her up. She blamed herself."

"He know her history? Does he know about me?"

"Yeah. He said he picked her up off the highway when she was nineteen. She'd broken out of the psych ward at the state hospital in Austin. I guess you know this?"

"Somebody from the hospital called us. I kept waiting for her to show up." Jake remembered how scared he'd been—for Karen and himself—when he found out she was on the loose. He'd been dating Courtney then, but the hell of it was he'd missed Karen, had a god-awful craving for her, deep down. He never told anyone, and finally it had gone, leaving only the faint scrim of self-loathing and regret. Until now, when she'd taken Zoe, the only thing in his life that mattered. She still wanted to hurt him, to make him pay.

"Ames said all she could talk about was you, how your folks got her arrested and charged with arson and attempted manslaughter. How they caused her to end up in a mental hospital, and you let it happen."

"Ha! My folks went to bat for her, Clint. The DA wanted her to do hard time in a prison cell, but Mom and Dad went to the judge and said she needed psychiatric help."

"Well, it took a long time, but Roger said she finally settled down. I guess there were some good years in there, riding with him. But that's over. The guy's shook up, Jake. He's on his way home now. He said he had the Lubbock police do a welfare check at his house yesterday. They didn't find her, or any sign of her car, which turns out is a rental. Ames said her car's in the shop for some transmission work. He rented a car for her to drive while he was gone."

"Don't tell me—it's a light-metallic-blue Toyota Corolla like the one Gilly dreamed about. The one the neighbors saw outside my house."

Clint didn't answer. He didn't need to.

"So where does he think she is?" Jake asked.

"I told him she was here, but not the circumstances. I didn't mention you. He's freaked out enough as it is, worried she's on something. Self-medicating, he called it. He told me the first time she took drugs from the hospital where she worked, no charges were filed. They didn't want the publicity. But after she got the news about her parents, Roger said morphine and some other prescription meds turned up missing, and when hospital personnel looked at security footage, they identified Karen as the one who took it. And this time, they did file charges."

"So not only is she crazy, she's a damned dope fiend?" Jake had heard enough. Adrenaline pumping, he wheeled back onto the deserted highway. He wanted to floor it, leave the road and cut across the roughened countryside toward the Ameses' house. It was only cold logic that kept him on the pavement, searching the weed-choked shoulder for the turnoff. He could feel the panic heating up in his gut, but he couldn't look at it. Couldn't feed it any of his attention.

"The drugs concern me, too, and there's one other thing. Roger said the Glock he carries in his truck for protection? It's missing."

"You're serious."

"As a heart attack. That's why you need to let law enforcement handle the situation."

"She's got my daughter, Clint!"

"You don't know that, Jake, and goddammit, if she does have Zoe, do you want to get her shot?"

Jake found what he thought was the right highway turnoff, and going another hundred or so feet, he spotted the second turn—the dogleg that led to the Ameses' private drive. He knew he was close. He would have missed it if another vehicle hadn't already nosed a path through the tangled growth of grass and weeds that had overgrown it. He bumped down a shallow hill, rounded a curve, and caught a glimpse of the old metal roof, a rusted silver sequin blinking in the dying sunlight. His pulse ticked.

"Jake? Talk to me. For God's sake, it's already getting dark—"

"There's nothing to say. Karen's got Zoe—"

"Where are you?" Clint asked. "On 1620? Just stay there. I'm on my way."

"Sure. Okay. Will do," Jake said, and cutting Clint off, he tossed his cell phone onto the passenger seat. It rang again immediately. He ignored it, hands gipping the wheel, bent over it, stare fixed on the tire tracks of the vehicle that had preceded him. They led down from the limestone ridge that rose along the east side of the house. Pieces of it flashed in and out of his view: a bit of the eave, the darker rectangle of a window, one end of the deep front porch. The drive had been pretty back in the day, winding its way along a gentle decline, curving beneath an archway of oaks and sun-reddened maples. He remembered the light filtering through the leaves, the way it had dappled the grass in shifting shadows. He remembered Karen's dad had been religious about keeping up the property. It had always been tidy, welcoming. He remembered if he kept going now, he'd soon emerge into full view of the house, and he slammed on the brakes behind a screen of juniper.

He needed a plan.

He had no idea in hell what it should be.

He got out of his truck and pushed the door closed without latching it. It was dusk, and the light was uncertain. He could still make out the tire-flattened grass trail that looped around to the south-facing back of the house, but rather than follow it, he angled west, making his way down a gentle slope toward the side of the house where Karen's bedroom had been. He thought of the nights when he'd wait for her near where his truck was parked now. She'd climb out her window to come meet him, naked beneath a thick quilt she'd bring to lie on. Sometimes they'd share a pint of something they managed to get their hands on. Jake remembered a bottle of peppermint schnapps they'd passed back and forth, drinking until their lips were numb. He remembered pouring some in her navel, the minty taste, dipping it out with his tongue. He remembered having to cover her mouth when she came, lest her cries wake her folks. *Hormones*, his mom had said in no little disgust, looking in at the wet, charred mess of his room after Karen had set fire to his bed. *Nothing but a lot of teenage hormones.* They'd known it was more, that fire and police involvement were inevitable. Karen's fate had been out of their hands after that.

Jake beat his way through the near impenetrable growth of juniper, impervious to it even when it tore his flesh. Reaching the foot of the slope, he paused to get his bearings. The outline of the house, the east side of it, rose in front of him. There were three windows, all of them dark. Boarded up, Jake thought, from the inside. A feeling of dread uncoiled in his gut. The air, heavy with the silence of desertion, was broken only by the drone of cicadas, the stir of a fitful breeze. His pulse wouldn't settle. It was like an unfleshed bone, tapping his chest.

Staying low, he left the relative protection of the juniper thicket, heading toward the back corner of the house, taking a quick look around it. The truck—the white pickup with a camper top, the one he'd seen on the park security footage, the truck Karen had stolen—was parked steps away. Its bumpers glimmered in the lingering twilight. Jake withdrew, flattening his back against the house wall, trying to think.

He felt for his phone, but it wasn't on him. He'd tossed it into the passenger seat, left it in the cab of his pickup.

Because he was one smart cookie, wasn't he?

Jesus.

You idiot!

He risked another longer, more thorough look, and he almost shouted out loud when he caught sight of Karen, sitting on the back stoop. Light from a source he couldn't see picked out her huddled form. He recoiled, hard enough that his head slammed into the stone wall.

Behind his closed eyes, he saw pinpricks of light. His heart heaved in his chest. Where was Zoe? That was the million-dollar question, and there was only one way to find out.

"Karen?" It was a moment before she looked his way, and something in her posture warned him to take care. As he walked toward her, he held his hands up, palms out, a gesture that said *No worries.* Stepping closer now, he saw that the source of the light was a pair of camp lanterns sitting on the step behind her.

She peered up at him. "Jake? Are you really here?"

"I came for Zoe. Where is she?"

"Gone."

"Gone?" Jake took another step.

"Don't come any closer." Karen reached for something beside her.

Jake's heart paused when he saw that it was a gun, a pistol. The Glock Clint had mentioned?

She waved it at him, a warning.

He did the thing with his hands again and hoped she didn't see how badly shaken he was. "Where is Zoe?" he asked again.

"Gilly took her away."

Thank God—that was his thought—if it was true, if Gilly had gotten Zoe out. "Where did they go?"

"There." Karen gestured with the gun toward the dark wall of underbrush and trees that encroached from the side of the house opposite him. "I told her not to go in those woods, that there were snakes in there and God knew what else."

Jake looked, but he couldn't see farther than a couple of feet. Zoe's name, and Gilly's, were hot in his mouth, but if he yelled for them, he was liable to get a bullet in his head, and what use would he be to them dead? He looked at Karen. "Are they all right—Zoe and Gilly? You didn't hurt them?"

"Of course not. I'm not like you, Jake. I don't hurt people." She raised the gun muzzle casually to her temple.

"Whoa." He took a step. "Don't," he said, taking another step.

"Why not?" She held his gaze, waiting for his answer, lowering the weapon when he couldn't supply one. "Zoe's fine. Gilly, too," she said. "Sleepy. From the morphine. But probably even that's wearing off now."

"You gave Zoe morphine?"

"I bought her some new clothes, took her to the lake. We waded in the water. She loved it."

"Have you been doping her this whole time?"

"Just to make it easier on her. Don't worry. I'm an RN. I know how to gauge the dose."

"That supposed to comfort me?" Jake went toward the tree line. He shouted for her now. "Zoe? Can you hear me?" At a noise from behind him, he wheeled.

Karen was holding the gun, looking down the barrel at him. She kept his gaze, and his head emptied of thought. The moment held. There wasn't language for what passed between them, a history of old love that had ended in anger and sadness, her accusation, his bitter shame. But now, with the jerk of her hand, she raised the gun to her own head again, pressing it to the place above her right ear, and before Jake could react, she pulled the trigger.

Nothing happened.

Tears brimmed her eyes, tracked her cheeks. Slowly, she lowered the gun, laid it in her lap, brushed her face. "I can't even get killing myself right." Her voice was barely above a whisper.

"Jesus, Karen." Jake's words came on the rough gust of his breath. "Why are you doing this?"

She didn't look at him, didn't answer.

"You want to give it to me?" Jake took a couple of steps but stopped when he saw her fingers close over the gun's grip. Who knew if there were bullets in the other chambers?

"When I saw you earlier at the school, you remembered, didn't you?" She raised her gaze.

"Of course—"

"I don't mean it was like I was just some old girl you used to know." She interrupted, sharply annoyed now. "Your heart, your gut, your skin remembered how we used to touch, how we loved each other. I know. I felt it when you took my hand. Don't—" Her voice broke on a half sob. "Don't shame me more by denying it."

"No," he said, and there was a part of him that knew it was the truth. But his desire for her—that odd current he'd felt ricochet between them—it was only memory, a boy's memory, and he wasn't that boy anymore.

"I've been waiting six months for this—for you to see me."

"Six months?" Jake was at sea.

"Did you know Mama and Daddy were dead? Last January, in a car wreck. Both of them gone. Poof. Like that."

"I heard about it, and I'm sorry." Jake was barely aware when he took a step toward Karen and then another. She didn't seem to notice either.

"You know, one of the last things Mama told me before she cut me out of her life was that I needed to get a grip and move on. That's what she and Daddy were doing, and if they could, so could I. I really tried after I met Roger. Tried to be a good wife and nurse. Tried to have a life and not mind that we had no children. But there was always this place inside me, this empty lonely place, where you used to be, and Cassie. Remember Cassie?"

He shook his head, unsure, and yet somehow certain of what she'd say next, frightened of it, wishing he could stop her. He glanced to his right, in the direction he'd come from. His truck was up on the ridge. Clint would see it, maybe come down the same way.

"She was our little girl, Jake." Karen's voice slipped and caught. "She was the baby we made. I never got a chance to tell you the way I wanted to, just you and me. I was going to on prom night. I had this made. I was going to put it around your neck, make you guess what it meant. I had it all planned."

Jake watched as Karen pulled a slender chain with a locket attached to it from the collar of her hoodie. She fumbled to open it, and meeting his gaze, her eyes filled with fresh tears. Her fingers trembled as she extended it toward him, a gesture that begged him to come closer.

"It's engraved with her initials, and this is us, see?"

The insanity and panic were gone for the moment, eclipsed by anguish, a mother's grief. Jake felt overcome by it—the sense of what had been lost all those years ago. He went to Karen, bent over the tiny locket, touched his fingertip to the image.

"I cut our faces out of that pep rally photo in our annual. Remember it?"

Jake did remember. The picture had been of a larger group of their friends, taken in the gym, in the fall of their senior year, before she'd gotten pregnant. That had happened the following February, although for Jake the scare hadn't turned real until after they graduated. It had been in late March or April when Karen had told him about her missed periods, that she was worried, but he'd blown it off. By then he'd begun to feel there was something not right with her, something too intense in her devotion. He'd wanted out of the relationship, and he'd tried telling her that it was over. He'd insisted their prom date would be their last. After watching her tear up her corsage on prom night, he'd figured she'd finally gotten the message. Karen hadn't returned to school after that weekend. Jake hadn't seen her again until sometime in June or July, when she came to his house with her parents to inform him and his parents that she was having his baby. Karen's folks had insisted on a wedding. His mom and dad had been equally adamant against the idea. It wasn't the Dark Ages, they'd said. There were other more sensible options for a couple so young.

"I was eighteen," Jake said softly now. "You were seventeen."

"We were old enough to make her." Karen jerked the locket away, shoving it inside her hoodie, eyes flashing, incensed. "She was born in the state hospital, Jake."

"We—my folks didn't want to press charges. That was the DA—"

"You let your baby be born in a nuthouse, and she died there—"

"No." Jake extended his arms, turned up his palms.

Karen slapped them away. "She *died*, Jake, our little girl, because of you. Because you didn't want her."

"That's what you meant. What you said when you called, what you wrote in your note, that I didn't want her, didn't deserve her . . ." Jake trailed off, seeing it now, that Karen couldn't have known there had once been a time when he hadn't wanted Zoe either.

"Cassie." Karen's voice broke on her name. "How could you not want Cassie?"

Jake sat beside her, taking her into his embrace, despite how she fought it, beating against his arm uselessly with her fist. It galled him that he felt pity for her, but he held her until she grew quiet. He felt the press of her face against his chest. The dampness of her tears soaked his shirt there.

"Why didn't you come, Jake?" Her voice was muffled, hoarse.

"My folks—"

"Your folks were meddling assholes."

"Your psychiatrist agreed with them that we shouldn't see each other."

Karen's head came up. She looked at him wide-eyed. "You wanted to see me?"

"Yes, I felt horrible. I still feel horrible."

"Cassie would be twenty-one."

A beat.

"I couldn't have any more babies after that."

Jake looked off into the sky, heart tight, throat constricted.

"Now that you don't have Zoe, you feel how I have felt all these years, don't you? Like someone ripped out your heart."

It was the eerie remoteness in Karen's voice that stalled Jake's breath and brought down his glance. The emotion, the intimacy of moments ago, had vanished. He watched as if in a trance as she picked up the gun that had somehow slipped from her lap to the step below them by her feet unnoticed, at least by him. She pointed it away from herself, sighting down the barrel, talking away, as if they were involved in the most ordinary of conversations.

"It's what I wanted, for you to know how it felt. So I took Zoe."

"What about Gilly?"

"What about her? She was in the way, trying to start something with you and Zoe. All wanting to be Zoe's mama. Gilly lost a baby, too, and I'm sorry for her, but she's got no more right to raise Zoe than you do. But you—you don't deserve even to be happy after what you did. There's not a day that's gone by that I haven't thought how Cassie might have lived if only she'd been born in a real hospital. I've torn myself apart thinking about it. But thanks to you, she wasn't. Thanks to you, she never had a chance." Karen swiped her cheeks, shoved her hair off her face. She still held the Glock loosely in her free hand.

Jake was thinking—wondering if he were to grab for it—

She raised it suddenly to his eye level. "Something happened today at the school." She declared this as if it were an ultimatum. "We both felt it. Don't say you didn't. We could still do it, you, me, and Zoe. We could still be the little family that we planned."

Her gaze was locked with his, and Jake saw any normalcy she'd managed to recapture was gone. Her eyes were alight with something spectral, unhinged. Her tone was different—edgy, truculent, somehow wild. It made him afraid to move, to speak. He looked toward the ridge. *Where in the hell was Clint?*

"I still love you, Jake." Karen brought the gun barrel closer to his face. "I love you with everything that's in me. But I hate you, too. I hate you just as hard."

"I understand," he said softly. "But if you shoot me, you know the police will arrest you. They'll send you to prison, or back to the hospital. You don't want that, do you?"

She held his gaze, and the moment lingered, brittle, frozen. If there was a sound even of breath, Jake wasn't aware of it. Karen moved first, dropping her glance, lowering the gun. Jake started to breathe but then she brought the Glock up again, thrusting it at him.

"You do it," she said. "You make it work. Mercy killing," she added. He shook his head.

"Please, I can't do it anymore. Can't fight. Fight all gone." Her voice trembled.

"Hush." He put his arm around her again, hooked the crown of her head with his chin. She was smaller than he remembered. She felt fragile, the way a bird might feel if he were to hold it in his hands.

"Do you remember the fox we found in the woods here?" she asked.

"The one with the broken leg?"

"Yes. He was crying, and you told him to hush. You were so calm and gentle. He let you pick him up. I was so scared he would bite you, but you talked to him. We named him McTavish. Do you remember?"

He did. He'd ridden shotgun in Karen's dad's truck with the fox on his lap, and Karen had driven to Hester Blankenship's house, a few miles away. Hester was the local certified wildlife handler. She'd set McTavish's leg, kept him in her barn until the limb mended, then released him back into the woods. Jake remembered that months later she'd told him McTavish still came by on occasion looking for cantaloupe, the treat she'd fed him while he'd been with her.

"If only you had loved me, stayed by me."

"We were kids," Jake said.

He would never quite remember the sequence of what followed after that, whether he first saw Clint coming around the corner of the house, or saw his chance to grab the gun. It was almost as if the two things coincided, followed by the crack of a single shot, a tiny flare of light, then everything went dark.

26

It was dark. Darker still in the thicket of trees where Gilly sought cover. She couldn't run any farther, and she collapsed at the base of an oak tree, pulling herself close to the trunk with Zoe in her lap, comforting the child when she whimpered, murmuring nonsense. "Ssh, ssh, it's okay. We're okay."

She had no idea if it was true, or if Zoe could even hear her. Her own ears were still ringing from the gunshot Liz had fired, the one Gilly had waited to feel tear into her back, the one she had feared would go right through her to hit Zoe. Lightheaded and breathless, still buzzing from the waning effect of the morphine, Gilly balanced her cheek on the crown of Zoe's head, rocking her slightly, fighting tears and a hard tide of panic. But there was jubilation, too, a silvery thread of joy, at having rescued this small treasure she held in her arms.

Please help us. She offered the prayer even as she listened for the noise of pursuit above the thud of her pulse, the whish of the wind. But in the oncoming night, there was no other sound, not the song of birds, nor the chirr of insects, nor the fall of human feet. Gilly held her breath, listening harder. Nothing. It didn't seem likely Liz would let them go.

But neither did it seem likely that Gilly should be sitting here now, still alive. Tucking her chin, leaning slightly away, she looked down at Zoe sucking her thumb, pulling on it for all she was worth, eyes open, breath coming in short pants. She was so quiet. Lifting Zoe's chin, Gilly found her gaze. "Are you okay?" she asked softly.

Zoe took her thumb from her mouth. "Where's Daddy?"

"He's been looking for you every minute."

"The bad lady let me talk to him on her phone. He said he was coming. Does he know I'm here?"

"You'll see him soon, I promise." How fervently Gilly wanted this to be the truth.

"Is the bad lady gone?"

"I don't think she knows where we are."

Zoe leaned back in Gilly's embrace. "How did you know she took me here?"

Her query caught Gilly off guard, but she was too weary to make up a story in any case. "I had a dream," she said.

"A magic dream?"

"Yes. It showed me where to find you."

"Did you tell Daddy?"

"He'll know." Gilly said what she believed, that by now Captain Mackie would have told Jake about her dream and somehow they'd figure out the location.

Zoe aimed her thumb at her mouth again, then shook her head. "Daddy will be mad," she said to it.

"Why?"

"Only babies suck their thumb. I'm not a baby anymore."

"He won't mind. These are special circumstances."

Zoe poked her thumb in her mouth again and laid her cheek against Gilly's chest. Her other arm was hooked around Gilly's neck, and her legs were fastened around Gilly's waist. It was hard to say which of them was holding on to the other one tightest. They were stuck together, a foul-smelling and sweaty mess. Gilly looked back in the direction they'd come from. She'd run maybe fifty or sixty yards before she'd dropped down here. She and Zoe were both scratched and bloody from the juniper. There was only more of it, whole packed scrubby brakes, going away from the house, but to go back in the direction they'd come from would be suicide. Even if the keys were in the cab of the truck, it was parked in plain view. Gilly had looked at it when she'd run out of the house. Its bumpers had gleamed in the light from the porch. Liz might have missed her first shot, but Gilly doubted she'd miss the second time.

"Is it a real gun?"

Gilly looked down into Zoe's upturned face.

"Yes."

"Why is she shooting at us?"

"You see where we have these scratches?" Gilly tapped the angry red lines on Zoe's forearm.

"Uh-huh."

"Well, sometimes people get their brains hurt, and it makes them do things they wouldn't ordinarily do."

"They get scratches on their brain?"

"Sort of like that."

"I wish I would have done what Daddy said."

"What did he say?"

"That if a stranger comed up to me, I haf to yell my head off, but the lady said she was Mommy's friend. We were going to see her."

"That's why you got in the car?"

"Yes." A beat. "The lady lied."

"Yes, she did."

Zoe toyed with the button on Gilly's shirt. Tears brimmed in her eyes and spilled, making fresh tracks through the history of tears that had already dried on her cheeks. "She threw away my skirt with butterflies on it."

"Maybe we can get it back."

"She gived me shots, too, and it hurt."

"I know, baby. I'm so sorry." Gilly loosened a corner of her shirt and wiped Zoe's face, under her nose, pushing away her anger. It was useless now.

"She said it was medicine to make me feel better, but it didn't. It made me dizzy. I threw up in the bed, and she wouldn't let me go to the potty, and I wet myself, and I smell bad." The words broke on Zoe's sobs of remembered terror and current humiliation, and Gilly gathered her more closely to her breast, murmuring comfort. "It's okay, it's okay." And she waited to hear it, any second, the sound of Liz coming through the woods. But there was no sound of that. Liz didn't appear, although she must have heard Zoe crying. Where was she? Could she have left? But Gilly would have heard the truck, as close as they still were to the house.

Zoe's sobs subsided into tired hiccups. She laid her head down again on Gilly's chest, and Gilly stroked her hair. *"There was once a king . . ."* She began the opening line of the fairy tale Zoe loved so much, and Zoe sighed.

· · ·

Gilly came to herself with a start, looking around wildly. The trees loomed overhead; moonlight silvered their branches. She had heard someone—a man—shout, or had it been a dream? Zoe was still stuporous against her chest, but Gilly's head felt clearer, as if the morphine had finally worn off. She must have dozed, but for how long? The last thing she remembered was beginning the fairy tale. She shifted uncomfortably. Her body, her arms and legs especially, felt weighted with exhaustion, and her mouth was drier than dirt. She needed to get up and get herself and Zoe out of here. But how? No way could Zoe walk far under her own power. She would have to be carried. Gilly pulled Zoe's hair off her cheek, tucking it behind her ear. She said her name. "Zoe? Can you wake up?"

"Are we going home now?"

"We're going to try. Do you think you can walk a little way, and when you get tired, I'll carry you? We'll have to go through the woods until we find the road—"

"What if the eyeball-eating monsters get us?"

"I won't let them," Gilly said.

"Maybe they ate the bad lady."

"That is a thought," Gilly said.

"Can we go to the calf and eat pancakes after we find the road?"

"Do you mean the café? Cricket's?" Gilly asked, smiling down at Zoe.

"Next you were going to make a g'raffe, you said. Will you?"

"Yes," Gilly said. "We'll go there, and I will make you a giraffe pancake with blueberry eyes and a chocolate chip nose. How about that?"

"Promise?"

Gilly was on the verge of it, making that promise, when the gunshot sounded. She clutched Zoe to her, worked her way to her feet, ready to run deeper into the woods. But now she saw lights. Sparks of red and blue flashed through the trees. She heard voices, men's voices. One in particular rose above the others, shouting, "Zoe? Where are you?"

Her head came off Gilly's shoulder. "Daddy?"

Gilly waited, hardly daring to believe it, but then he was there. She thought—believed with her whole heart—it was Jake, in the flesh, coming toward them.

27

"D addy! Daddy!"
He heard Zoe calling, and he ran, breakneck, mindless, swinging the beam of the flashlight Clint had given him across his path. On catching sight of Zoe, seeing her in Gilly's arms, he staggered, weak from relief, an engulfing wave of jubilation. Gilly set Zoe on her feet, and he went to his knees, gathering her tightly against him, burying his face in her neck. "Boy, am I glad to see you." Tears wet his face. He couldn't stop them.

Standing back, Zoe touched his cheeks. "You're crying, Daddy." Her own blue eyes filled and brimmed over.

"It's because I'm so happy to see you." Setting the flashlight on the ground, he pulled her back against his chest, reveling in the warm, living, breathing sense of her. He would never let her out of his sight again. It was impossible, he knew that, but he made the promise to himself anyway. "Are you okay? Did she hurt you?" He stood Zoe out of his embrace, looking her over.

"Miss Gilly got me away, Daddy. The bad woman had a gun. She shot at us—" Zoe's voice broke, and she was trembling.

"It's all right now, ZooRoo." He wrapped her in his arms again. "Captain Mackie and some other policemen are taking her to jail." Jake glanced up at Gilly. "Thank you," he said, and it was hard pushing the words, small and so inadequate, through the narrowed channel of his throat.

"I'm glad you found us." In the flashlight's glow, Gilly's eyes, too, were shimmery with tears. "I didn't know how we were going to get out of here."

"I'm so sorry you got pulled into this."

"Well, I kind of asked for it."

"The dream."

"Yeah. And for once it worked—sort of." She smiled again.

"It took me a bit, but when I figured out it was Karen's house you'd described—"

"Karen? I thought her name was Liz."

"Elizabeth is her middle name."

"Ah, yes. She did say something about going by Liz." Gilly's hand settled gently on the crown of Zoe's head. "Well, this little one is very brave."

Jake's eyes teared again. He pulled Zoe to him. "What do you say, ZooRoo, you ready to go home?"

She nodded against his neck.

He scooped her into his arms, and together with Gilly, they walked back toward the Clayton house, brightly lit now in the glare of head-lights from a half dozen emergency vehicles.

• • •

It turned out they didn't get home until the following day, Sunday.

While Zoe's vitals checked out within normal range at the scene, the paramedics, and Zoe's pediatrician, whom they contacted, wanted her transported to Wyatt General for a thorough examination. They kept her there overnight, rehydrating her and monitoring her for any sign of trouble from the morphine she'd been given.

Jake's mom came with a shopping bag, and Jake grinned, seeing her peep into the room. She looked from Zoe, lying in the small bed, blissfully unaware, to Jake, where he was stretched out in an uncomfortable orange cushioned chair.

"She's asleep?" His mom mouthed her query.

He nodded and went to join her in the hall.

"I went by your house." She opened the sack. "I've brought her some pajamas and clean clothes to wear home, her hairbrush, your toothbrushes. They'll release her tomorrow? She's really okay?"

"Yeah," he said. "She's fine, or she will be."

Setting the sack down, his mom wrapped her arm around his waist. "Thank God."

"The doc said the effects from the morphine won't entirely wear off for twenty-four hours, and we don't know the last time Karen injected her."

"Did anybody ask Karen?"

"She claims she doesn't remember. She shot herself up with it, too, and Gilly."

"Is Gilly here?"

"No. The paramedics wanted her to get checked out, but she refused. She went with the detective who's working her husband's murder case, Carl Bowen—"

His mother frowned, and Jake told her what he'd heard about Warren Jester from Clint—who'd heard it from Detective Bowen—that Jester had been spooked when he'd heard the news story about Gilly being the psychic hired by Jake to find his daughter. "According to what Jester told his sister, he's been scared ever since the night he shot Gilly's husband that she was going to ID him somehow, either because she was there and saw him, or through a dream, or one of her visions, but it was seeing her photo and hearing the story about Zoe on the news that put him over the edge. He figured he had to do something, stop her somehow."

"The police don't know where he is? Are they looking out for her?"

"I think that's why Bowen's here," Jake said, although he thought it was more than that. He'd seen how Bowen looked at Gilly. Jake thought he should be grateful to the detective. It meant Bowen would stay on his toes. He wouldn't let anything happen to Gilly. "I feel bad Jester found her because of the situation with Zoe."

"You couldn't have known. It's just one of those unfortunate things. Life can be so strange."

Jake hooted softly.

His mom looked up at him, searching his gaze. "Are you all right?"

He knew what she was asking. "Yeah," he said. "It's like somebody took a boulder off my chest, and I can breathe. I don't want to let Zoe out of my sight, though, and I know I'm going to have to."

"We'll both have to work on that. I was thinking of asking if I could move in with you, sleep in the hallway outside her door."

Jake laughed, not hard, or long, but it felt good. "Might not be a wide enough fit for both of us."

A beat.

"I thought I would be mad as hell."

His mom looked at him, brows raised.

"When Zoe was missing, when I had to face it that some stranger had her, I wanted to kill whoever it was. I imagined it. Strangling them with my bare hands. But when it all went down at Karen's house, there I was, sitting with my arm around her. She was so pathetic, Mom."

"If only she'd gotten help when you were teenagers—"

"She blames me for how the baby was born in a mental hospital. She thinks if it had been a real hospital—maybe she's right, Ma. If I'd been there for her, maybe this wouldn't have happened."

"It wouldn't have mattered, Jake. The baby had died some time before they induced labor."

"How do you know?"

"I had a friend, a nurse who worked at the hospital. She told me. It happens sometimes when a girl is very young."

Jake stared into the middle distance, not comforted. He thought he would always feel responsible now.

"I remember feeling so frustrated then, with her and with her parents. Karen's issues, her emotions, the attachment she had to you—it was over the top. The times I tried to talk to her mother, she was as bad as Karen, going on about a wedding and grandchildren. That is not what your dad and I wanted for you. Not at eighteen."

"I had it bad for her, too."

"Yes, but you woke up. You saw that the relationship wasn't healthy. You two weren't bringing out the best in each other."

"It was too late."

"You aren't to blame, Jake."

"She hates me, truly hates me. It's hard to take, that kind of hate."

"Oh, honey." His mom took his hand. "I could say that's not your burden to bear either. I could say she's projecting, but I know you aren't ready to hear that any more than I am ready to forgive her for the pain she's caused you and Zoe." Giving his hand a bit of a shake before releasing it, she said, "I guess we'll have to work on it."

"I really hope never to see her again."

"How would you? Unless there's a trial—"

"According to Clint, she doesn't even want an attorney."

"That's—I guess she'll end up back at the state hospital then, or maybe she has better insurance now."

Jake didn't answer. What was there he could say?

"I had to dodge a bunch of reporters outside the hospital," his mom said after a moment.

"I gave them a statement and asked if they'd leave Zoe alone," Jake said. "I don't want them questioning her. It's going to be hard enough for her to talk to Clint."

"What has her doctor said about the morphine? Any lasting effects?"

"He seems to think it might be good in the long run, that it'll blank out her memory, or the way she remembers—it might just seem to her as if she took a long nap."

"When I think—if it had gone on any longer—" His mom's voice was rough. She cleared her throat. "Thank God for Gilly and her dream."

"Yes," Jake said. "I'll never be done thanking God for her."

28

After Jake left with Zoe in the ambulance, Carl drove Gilly to the police station, where Captain Mackie took her statement. They sat down in his office, the captain behind his desk, Carl and Gilly in the two chairs in front of it.

"I'm not going to keep you." Captain Mackie glanced at Gilly. "I just wanted to get your impressions. Did Karen talk about her intent? Was this something she'd been planning?"

"For six months, if you can believe what she told me. She's been coming here for weeks, waiting for her chance. I thought she was my friend, but everything she told me was a lie. She built this whole persona, this life, and I bought into it, every word." Gilly shook her head. She was angry at the way she'd been used, but it was astonishment at Liz's nerve that made her feel lightheaded. "She wanted a family," Gilly said, "attention—someone to know she was unhappy. She saw me talking with Jake and making the pancakes for Zoe, and she thought—wrongly—that I was competition."

"She targeted you? It was part of her plan to befriend you?"

"That's what she said. The first time we met she was at the park where I walk my dog. She didn't even have a dog, but I didn't question it." Gilly swiped her hair behind her ears. How pathetic it sounded now. Had she been—was she that lonely, that desperate for a friend? "I was in her way, or that was her perception. When I remember—I mean the day before Zoe disappeared, I went with Liz—Karen—to look at a house she wanted to buy. That Friday, she was supposed to come to my house for dinner. I can't get over it—how she faked everything. Her concern for Zoe—my God, if you could have heard—but she told me she's had issues, mental and emotional issues before."

"She was high school age when the trouble began," the captain said. "She ended up being sent to the state mental hospital. Did she talk about that?"

Gilly answered, "Yes. It's a wild story, but from everything she said, after she escaped from there, she was stable for a long time."

"Something must have changed, set her off," Carl said.

"It was a locket she found," Gilly said, and she related the details about it that Karen had told her. "It's awful, what she's done, but on some level, I can understand it, too." Gilly paused, fighting the confusion of her emotions. "It's a horrible experience, losing a child."

"I think you've had enough, been through enough, for now." The captain pulled papers on his desk into a stack.

"What will happen to her?" Gilly asked.

"She'll be arraigned. The judge will decide on the issue of bail. He'll appoint a public defender, although she's saying she doesn't want an attorney. I would imagine a psych exam will be done at some point."

"Will she get out—on bail, I mean?" The prospect made Gilly anxious.

"There's a good chance she won't. Even if the judge grants bail, I doubt she's got the resources to meet it. In any case, we'll be running surveillance on your house."

"I'll be around, too," Carl said.

"I'd like to go home, if that's all right." Gilly stood up. Her legs were trembling, and she locked her knees.

Captain Mackie came around the desk and put his hand on her shoulder. "What you did today took some kind of courage," he said.

"Anybody else would have done the same."

"I don't know. If you hadn't called in with the details from your dream, we might not have found Zoe in time. I might want to call on you again." He smiled.

Gilly didn't. She wanted to say he was giving her too much credit. But even had she been able to form the words, she didn't trust herself to speak. Her tears were riding too close to the surface. She was still shaky with the receding effects of panic and morphine, and with growing joy over Zoe's rescue. She doubted she would ever forget the look of pure elation on Jake's face when she'd set his daughter on her feet in front of him, safe and mostly sound.

But as thrilled as Gilly had been, her own heart and arms felt Zoe's absence. It was unreasoning and pointless—her longing. Zoe didn't belong to her any more than she belonged to Liz. Gilly had told herself that while she, Jake, and Zoe had still been in the woods, and once they walked out, she'd lost sight of them in all the chaos. The place had been swarming with emergency vehicles, every flavor and variety of law enforcement.

"Zoe's going to be okay?" Gilly asked the captain as they walked out of his office. "Have you heard from the hospital?"

"She's a fighter, like you." He patted her arm. "Go on home now, get some rest. Detective Bowen here is going to keep an eye on you. I'll give a shout if we hear anything about where Jester is. Until then, keep your doors locked, okay?"

"She'll be fine with me," Carl said, and Gilly let him take her arm.

"Oh," Gilly said, turning back to the captain at the door. "I thought when I was at the gas station earlier, when Liz came up to me—I thought I saw Mark Riley. Was he there? Do you know?"

"No. When an officer with the DPS caught up with him, he was just west of Houston, too far from Wyatt to have been here during the time you were at the Quick-Serv."

It had been a product of her fear, her imagination working overtime, Gilly thought, and she was relieved.

"You let me or Detective Bowen know if you hear from him again."

Gilly told the captain she would. She let Carl steer her to his car. It took a brief heated argument, but when she insisted, Carl took her to get her car at the gas station, then followed her home and checked every room of her house before leaving to pick up hamburgers for dinner.

Bailey was ecstatic to see her and relieved to get outside. Once she brought him in and fed him, she called the hospital to ask about Zoe. The nurse who answered recognized Gilly's name. "You're the psychic. You found her."

Gilly cringed at the awe in the woman's voice. "How is she?"

"Doing wonderfully. We're keeping her, but it's erring on the side of caution, you know? She's been asking for you."

Gilly's heart rose. But no. It would only confuse things if she were to visit Zoe. She didn't know what things, or in what way—just something in her head warned her to stay away. It was a feeling similar to the one she had about Carl. He and Zoe, and Jake, too—they were better off without her.

"Can I tell her you're coming?" the nurse asked.

"No," Gilly said. "I'm sorry, I can't." She thought for a moment. "Tell her sweet dreams."

The nurse was disappointed, her goodbye clipped.

Bailey was curled at Gilly's feet, and setting the phone on the kitchen table, she dropped down beside him and buried her face in his fur, breathing in his earthy, doggy smell. She thought of Liz, how sad it was that she'd carried her sorrow over losing Cassie for so many years, how it had festered and flickered back to life when she'd found the locket. Gilly couldn't let it happen. She couldn't hold on to her memory of Brian and Sophie, letting it chew her up from the inside until she had nothing left of herself. She wouldn't ever forget them, but she had to let her grief, the debilitating sadness, go. She had to move on. Hot tears seared the undersides of her eyelids, but she held them in. She didn't want Carl to catch her crying.

•   •   •

"Jester's got no record," Carl said.

They were sitting at the table. Carl was wolfing down his burger.

Gilly hadn't done more than cut hers in half. She cut the half into quarters. *Stop playing with your food.* Her mother would say that if she were here.

"We're pretty sure he's responsible for a string of armed robberies that were committed in your old neighborhood around the same time. The guys in the bar down the street from the convenience store—"

"The witnesses you told me about?"

"Yeah. They ID'd Jester from a photo lineup. Said he came into the bar a couple months after Brian was killed, looking to trade a gun he had for another one that was clean. They said he was shook up, talking a blue streak." Carl wiped his mouth, set his napkin back in his lap. "We would have got him without his confession to his sister, but it damn sure doesn't hurt." He looked up at her. "You realize he's not going to let this—let you—go? You do understand that? He's got too much to lose."

"He was a family man," Gilly said. "A fireman. He told me it was all he ever wanted to do."

"So?"

"So what happened to turn him into a robber, a killer?"

Carl shrugged. "Human nature being what it is, even the most ordinary person in the street is capable of murder under the right circumstances. Give them a gun, put them in a desperate situation and— boom." He wiped his mouth.

Gilly dipped a french fry in ketchup, thinking about it. That afternoon, when she'd served Warren his coffee, when they'd chatted, she'd seen something in his expression that had unsettled her, but her mind had been on Zoe, the idea that she might find the child. Gilly hadn't really given Warren, or his demeanor, much attention. Even now, looking back, she realized he hadn't made her uncomfortable in a way that worried or frightened her. "You're sure it's him?"

"You're having doubts now? You said you remembered his face. He's wearing the same Rockets cap. You saw the gun." Carl's look was contemplative, possibly dismayed.

Gilly toyed with her iced tea glass, turning it in a circle. She had told Carl how it had come back to her, Warren's image—that she had seen it vividly in the moment when Karen had aimed the gun at her. People in near-death experiences often said they saw their lives pass before their eyes. That was how the vision of Warren, that moment of utter desperation and terror they'd shared, had come back to her. There wasn't a doubt of his identity in her mind, and yet . . .

"What if I'm wrong?"

"He's confessed, for Christ's sake."

Gilly allowed the tight pause.

In a softer voice, Carl said, "The guy is on the loose. There's no telling what's going on in his head."

She folded her napkin, ran her fingertip down the crease.

"You're a threat to him, Gilly."

"But there's no sign of him since he left Cricket's this afternoon. If he's been in touch with his sister, he has to know there's a BOLO out. He wouldn't stick around now, would he? Take that chance just to—what? Is he going to kill me?"

"Not as long as I'm here. Not as long as every cop in this state is looking for him."

"But you can't stay with me forever."

Carl locked her gaze. "I could, and you know it."

"You would leave Houston." She sat back. They were talking about something else now, a future she couldn't conceive of. She knew, anyway, that he would never leave the city, his job there, his brothers in blue, or however they referred to themselves.

"You're not meant for this," he said.

"What this?"

"Life in a burg like Wyatt, a job as a waitress. You're an architect, Gilly—a damn fine one, from what I've seen of your work."

"It wasn't only my work, it was Brian's, too." They had been two halves of the same whole. "I'm not even sure I can or want to design buildings on my own."

Carl left the silence alone. What could he say? She felt it, too, that she was still as married today as she had been when Brian was alive.

"I like it in Wyatt." It surprised her, hearing it aloud, feeling the truth of it. "Waitressing is fine for now. If I even have a job anymore." Gilly still hadn't spoken to Cricket.

"You've been here six months and haven't unpacked." Carl's gesture included a stack of boxes against the kitchen wall. "I could rent a truck. Wouldn't be anything, hauling your stuff back to Houston."

Gilly imagined it. She wouldn't have to move in with her mom. She could find her own place. There must be plenty of waitressing jobs in a city the size of Houston.

"I know you think the times we were together, making love, it was a mistake, but you felt something, Gilly." Carl pressed his cause, encouraged by her silence. "We both did. You can't deny—"

She shook her head, not in denial of their attraction. That had been—was—real enough. But she couldn't allow herself to lean on him, to use him as a crutch. If she went to him again, it would be because she was whole.

"If you aren't ready, that's okay. I can wait."

"I don't know that I'll ever be ready," Gilly said, and she had to look away from the lance of disappointment that flashed through his eyes.

Gilly had said as much to Julia when she had called her sponsor earlier, badly in need of guidance. She hadn't willingly sought to be injected with morphine, but still she had needed to confess—had badly needed Julia to hear that the thing inside her, the monster of her addiction, that monkey, bless him—had been ecstatic at the opportunity to get high, yapping how simple it was to forget it all. *Sobriety was too hard*, he'd said. *Just let it go*, he'd begged. Oh yeah, she had miles to go on this journey before she'd feel safe from that animal. Maybe it would never happen.

Carl stood and gathered his dishes. "You going to eat that?" he asked.

He slept on her couch that night and left the next morning for Houston. There had been a break in another murder case he was working, a triple homicide in a quiet, well-to-do neighborhood, and everyone from the governor on down was pressuring for a resolution, justice for the family.

"I wish you'd get a gun," Carl told her when she walked him out.

"I'd only shoot myself, or Bailey," she said.

"Not if you'd let me teach you."

They shared a moment.

He said, "I can be here in no time."

"Thank you."

"If you need me, just call." He slid his palm down her bare arm, took her hand in his, and bending swiftly, he kissed her, the tip of her nose, her lips, the inside of her wrist.

She started to speak, but he placed his fingertip against her mouth, and then he left her, got into his car and drove away. He didn't look back, although she stayed there in her drive waiting until he turned the corner and disappeared.

• • •

It was the third Wednesday, eighteen days since Zoe had been rescued, and Gilly went early to the café again. Much earlier than necessary. It was barely light outside when she arrived. The alley where she would ordinarily have parked was being resurfaced, so she parked in the next block and walked back, letting herself in the café's front door. She didn't flip on any lights in the dining area. It was a full hour until they opened. Stowing her purse in the office, she tied on an apron and got out the ingredients for pancakes. She'd gone through the same preparations the last two Wednesdays in anticipation of making Zoe her "g'raffe" with blueberry eyes and a chocolate chip nose, but Jake and Zoe hadn't come for breakfast.

They hadn't resumed their usual routine. Gilly tried not to mind, to ignore how it deflated her. She tried not to remember the way Zoe had felt in her arms, how reluctant she had been to relinquish her to Jake. She had thought she would hear from him. She realized she wanted this, a connection, and her wanting disheartened her.

She thought she would never learn.

She might have worried about them, Jake and Zoe, had she not known from the town talk they were okay.

Working through it, Cricket said.

"I saw them at the grocery store, and they both looked great," April said.

At least Gilly still had her job. Cricket had been amazed.

Do you still have a job? Cricket had repeated when Gilly called to ask her. *Of course you do*, she'd said. *You're a hero in this town. Don't you know it?*

The customers had echoed Cricket's praise. Gilly had been embarrassed. She'd insisted she hadn't done anything. It wasn't happening so much now—the accolades, the impromptu hugging, the sidelong looks. Regular life was carrying folks forward, thank heaven. The Little Acorn Academy had resumed its regular schedule. Marley, the assistant who had allowed Zoe to go with Karen, had been given back her job. Gilly had heard Jake was the one who'd put in a word for her. Cricket had said he felt bad for how hard he'd been on her and on Kenna. Gilly admired him for it, that he seemed to be putting the whole ordeal behind him.

Folks were still asking her about her so-called skill, though. No matter how often she said, "It doesn't work that way," people acted as though it was a faucet she could turn off and on. On a recent visit to the café, Captain Mackie had mentioned that he wished he could call on her sixth sense, or intuition, or whatever it was, to solve other crimes. He had a boatload of cold cases, he'd said. *Maybe you could take a look one day, see if you'd get anything.* Have one of your visions, he'd meant. She didn't think he was joking.

When Gilly had asked, he'd told her it was unlikely that Karen would see the light of day as a free woman again. Kidnapping was a felony offense, one that carried the possibility of a life sentence. He'd said she'd waived her right to a trial and would likely be remanded to Mountain View, a prison near Waco that housed women who'd committed more serious offenses. Female Texas death row inmates were incarcerated there. It had given Gilly chills. But she agreed with everyone else in town that it was the right thing. No matter how experienced Karen was as a nurse, she might have killed Zoe, shooting her up with morphine. It was no better, no different than giving someone heroin. In fact the only difference Gilly knew was that morphine was legal to use under medical supervision.

But what good did it do, locking someone up who was as obviously disturbed as Karen? Gilly could be her; she could have gone the same way as Karen. Their stories, their wounds, weren't identical, but they were similar enough. She and Karen had both self-medicated. They had entertained delusions, been unable to tell the real from the imagined.

They'd both taken someone else's child.

Gilly didn't know why she'd wakened out of the hell into which she had disappeared. But it was the horror she had felt looking down at little Anne Clementine Riley lying in Sophie's crib that had brought her out of that hell. It was that same image that kept her from slipping back. Kept her going to meetings, kept her looking forward.

She made a well of the dry ingredients in her bowl and poured in the combined milk and eggs. She would make a few practice giraffes. Maybe she would try a monkey, make him, and eat him up. Consume her own monster. Maybe then he would shut up—

"Anyone here?"

Gilly froze at the sound of the man's voice. Setting the handle of the whisk against the side of the bowl, she turned, wiping her hands on her apron. Her heart had fallen almost silent. She could not feel her breath. She knew who it was before she opened the swinging door and saw him.

Warren Jester was standing a step or two inside the café's entrance. The light behind him cast his face in shadow, but she would know him anywhere. She realized she'd been waiting for him.

"It was unlocked," he said, hooking a thumb toward the door.

"I must have forgotten. I don't ordinarily come in that way." Gilly smoothed her apron.

He swiped the red Rockets cap off his head, and held it in front of him in both hands. It was a peculiar gesture, somehow abashed.

Gilly felt a stab of something like pity. *For the man who murdered your husband? Really?*

"I know you aren't open yet, but could I trouble you for a cup of coffee?"

"It'll take a minute to brew."

"That's okay. I've got nothing but time these days. Mind if I sit?"

"Help yourself." Gilly went behind the counter.

Warren slid onto a stool.

She filled a carafe with water.

"You must wonder why I'm here."

She glanced at him, said nothing.

"I told you before I was a fireman, into search and rescue. Helping folks was my life. I had everything—a great wife, two kids, the works.

We couldn't have been happier. We weren't rich or famous. We didn't live in a McMansion, but you don't need that crap to be happy. You know what I mean?"

Gilly measured grounds into the basket. She flipped on the machine. She didn't answer Warren, didn't turn to him when she finished. She watched the coffee begin to drip, and for several moments, its sighs were the only sound she heard over the paced and heavy hammer fall of her pulse.

"Maggie and me—she's my wife—we didn't care for stuff. We raised our kids to know what was important. They didn't whine because they didn't have a PlayStation, or whatever, or a TV in their room. It was good, a good, solid life."

Gilly turned now to see that Warren was shredding a napkin. "What happened?"

He looked up at her, and his eyes were dark with loss, the kind she recognized. "Maggie got sick," he said. "Uterine cancer. She suffered so, was in agony. We tried everything. Went to Europe, then Mexico, a hospital across the border from Yuma. Insurance doesn't cover alternative treatments. Then I was taking time off to be with her, to travel with her. The kids didn't agree with what we were doing. They're in their twenties, think they know everything—know what it's like watching the love of your life—" Warren stopped.

Gilly dropped her glance. She knew where his story was going.

"We were losing the house. Where would we stay? A shelter? Maggie was end-stage. No shelter was going to take her."

"So your answer was to rob people to make your mortgage payment?"

"Stores. I robbed stores, not people."

Gilly laughed, an ugly sound.

"I was desperate, and I know it was stupid. It was fucked up, but so was I. I wasn't thinking straight. Don't you think I know that?"

"I can't listen to any more—"

"Okay, okay. You don't have to. God knows I've done enough damage—"

"What do you want? Are you going to kill me, too? Is that it?" Gilly was shaking and crossed her arms. She thought how even as little as six weeks ago she might have wished for it—to be not so much dead as not here. Gone. But she didn't feel that way now, and it confused her. She didn't know what had changed, or when.

"I'm not here to kill you," Warren said. "I need a favor."

She stared at him, incredulous.

"Will you call the police? I would do it myself, but I don't have a phone, or you could let me borrow the phone here, if you prefer, and I'll call them myself."

"You want me to call the police." Was this for real? Was she dreaming? She glanced toward the front of the café. Outside, the new day was oncoming. The large plate-glass window framed light that was translucent, shimmering.

"I wanted you to know what happened," Warren said softly. "It's probably nuts, but I thought it might help. That night—your husband—it was an accident. The clerk pulled a gun on me—"

"I know."

"Yeah, but what you probably don't know is that your husband stepped into the line of fire. He took a bullet for that kid. I had no idea he was going to do that. I didn't shoot him on purpose. I wouldn't have, not someone unarmed."

"That isn't how the police say it happened. Where Brian's body was found—"

"I moved him. For a couple of seconds I had this idea I could hide his body, get away. Like I said, I wasn't thinking. I never shot anybody before." Warren's gaze was locked on hers. "Your husband tried to save that kid's life. It's what I used to do, how I knew myself once."

Gilly couldn't speak.

"My life's not worth shit now. Maggie's gone; my kids hate me. The rest that was left, I took down myself. So I'm done, but before they lock me up, I wanted you to know the truth about that night, about your husband."

"Did he say anything? Brian? Before he died, did he—?"

"No, I'm sorry. I mean he could have, I guess, but I didn't hear—no."

Gilly walked to the cash register, and opening the drawer beneath it, she lifted out the revolver, a 0.357, that Captain Mackie insisted Cricket keep on the premises. It was loaded, and pulling back the hammer, she walked to where Warren was sitting and raised it until it was level with the center of his face.

"Go ahead," he said. "You'd be doing me a favor."

The moment held, and it was as if time, even the world turning on its axis, stopped. *Don't you want to take something from him? Like his life? Don't you want to kill him?* Karen's query rattled across Gilly's mind. Jake had expressed similar feelings, but when he'd had the opportunity, he hadn't acted on them. Now it was within her power. *An eye for an eye . . .*

And then what? The voice that was different from the monkey and Miss Two-shoes was asking. *Who will feed Bailey after you go to jail? Who will make Zoe's pancakes? Tell her silly stories? Brian wouldn't want this, you taking revenge.* The voice was shouting now. *Think! You found Zoe. Your dream found her. What if there are other times, other people's lives you could impact if you focus on the gift you've been given and the good you might do?*

She didn't know if she believed in it, the good she might do. But somehow she understood she wasn't a killer.

Gilly lowered the gun, and disengaging the hammer, she returned the revolver to the drawer. She felt Warren's eyes on her. She thought she sensed his disappointment. She pulled her cell phone from her apron pocket. "I've already given you—what you did, what you took from me—too much time, too much of my *self*—my soul. No more. I'll let the justice system take over now."

He flattened his palms on the countertop and nodded once.

Scrolling through her directory, she tapped the entry she needed.

"Captain Mackie," she said when he picked up, "could you send someone over here to the café? Warren Jester's here, and he wants to turn himself in."

. . .

She was unpacking a box of dishes, the set of plain white with the gently scalloped edge that she and Brian had bought from Pottery Barn, when the doorbell rang.

Bailey, lying at her feet, stood up and barked, looking up at her expectantly as if to say, *Oh boy, company!*

She tousled his ears. "Some watchdog you are."

Leaving the kitchen, she wondered if it was April, or possibly Cricket at the door. They'd both been concerned for Gilly, her state of mind, when they had arrived at the café earlier to find several police cars, and Warren Jester being led to one of them in handcuffs. Cricket had insisted Gilly take the day off, go home, relax.

But Gilly was too keyed up to relax. She felt different, less weighed down than she had in months—years, maybe. She felt free in a way that seemed distantly familiar. In her mind, it was as if she saw herself coming—back? To herself? She wasn't sure. In the past people had spoken to her of closure. They had suggested—some had even promised—that when the man responsible for Brian's death was caught, when justice was done, there would be closure. *At least you'll have that*, they had said.

Really? Would closure be there when she was scared? Lonely? Sick? Would it grow old with her? The questions, unasked, bitter, had stacked behind her teeth.

What she felt now, the lightness, the tingling sensation in her veins and through her bloodstream—rather than a closing, it felt more like a sort of settling. A coming to terms.

Acceptance. That was the word Gilly had used when she'd called her mom a bit ago to tell her that Warren was behind bars.

"I feel as if I can accept it, that Brian and Sophie are gone," she had said. "I know—I really understand now I can't change it. It came over me when I held the gun on him, you know? I realized killing him wouldn't change anything. I would still wake up every morning, breathing, alive, free or in a prison cell, and Brian and Sophie would still be dead."

"Yes," her mom said. "But having him locked up will keep him from harming others."

If only it could have been prevented in the first place. If time could be rewound, Gilly thought, farther back than the night of Brian's murder, to the moment before desperation drove Warren across the threshold of the first store he'd robbed, to when he'd still been a man with self-respect, a man of integrity, one who prided himself on serving others, not robbing and killing them. If someone had intervened then, stopped him, offered compassion, meaningful help for his wife and family . . .

"He isn't a monster," Gilly said, and it was almost a lamentation. It would be easier if she hated him. Now she was confronted with the difficulty of finding a way to forgive him.

"But it's a relief he's in jail, that he'll go to prison, hopefully for a long time."

Gilly didn't speak into the momentary pause her mother allowed for a response.

"You left Houston to get away from the memories, the—the drama—but you ran smack into it again with that woman, the little girl who was kidnapped." An element of protest thinned her mother's voice. "When I think what might have happened to you—"

"But nothing did, Mom. It's fine—"

"It's the dreams, Gilly. It's useless, I know, to tell you to stop having them, but you have got to stop talking about them. They go against the norm. People are disturbed by them—"

"Mom?" Gilly interrupted. "Why does my dreaming bother you so much now? I can understand why it might have when I lived at home, but even then it was no reflection on you. It isn't as if you're any more responsible than me for what I dream."

Her mother sighed, and the sound seemed to convey reluctance and regret.

Gilly waited, feeling herself on the cusp of understanding, of revelation, but it was almost as if she knew beforehand what her mother would say.

"It's no blessing, no gift, is it?" her mother began slowly. "From the moment you came to me the first time with the first dream—you were a little girl, no more than two or two and a half. You told me Daddy would be in a car accident that day, a fender bender. You said those exact words. I wondered where on earth you'd heard them, and not an hour later he called to say it had happened. Then I knew I'd passed it on—"

"Passed it on?" Gilly struggled to get her mind around it. "Are you saying you dream, too? That you see things?"

Her mom started to answer. Gilly cut her off. "All this time, all these years you've lectured me, cautioned me—you never once took my side when Dad criticized me, when he accused me of making it up to get attention, when he called me a freak and said I was trouble."

"I didn't want you to have the stigma, Gilly. I thought I could— I don't know—spare you? Talk you out of it? If I didn't approve, if I treated your dreams like the curse they are—"

"But you just said you knew you couldn't stop my dreaming." Gilly paused. "Do you still dream? Do you see things?"

"Your grandmother—my mother—encouraged me. She had it, too, the ability to see the future through her dreams. She said it was a gift, passed down. She didn't know how far back it went. She said I should embrace it, but I never wanted the awful responsibility. I don't want to know the future."

"You don't have the dreams now?"

"I don't remember."

Whether you have them, or the dreams themselves? Gilly might have asked, but from her mother's tone, she knew the door was closed; there would be no further discussion.

The silence between them lingered, becoming complicated with the number of other questions Gilly would likely never know the answers to: Why didn't you tell me? Why did you let me grow up thinking I was weird? How could you pretend you didn't understand? She felt the prickle of anger, of frustration, but it soon fizzled. What use were her feelings?

"You aren't coming home, are you?" her mom had finally asked.

"No," Gilly had said. "Houston isn't my home. Not anymore."

The doorbell rang again now, and Bailey looked back at her, *hurry up* written all over his expression.

"Okay, okay," she said to him. And she was thinking if her visitor was April, she'd just get Bailey's leash, and they would walk him to the park. But when she opened the door, the suggestion died on her tongue.

"I hope we didn't wake you," Jake said.

Gilly touched her hair at her temple, and higher up, where her messy ponytail was fastened with a rubber band she'd found in one of the boxes. She was barefaced, barefoot, and dressed in ratty cutoffs, and her heart was pounding in her regret over it. But why did she care?

"I told Daddy we should have called."

Gilly looked down at Zoe, adorable in yellow shorts and a lime-green T-shirt centered with a yellow daisy. A halo of words around the flower read: You are my sunshine. Her pigtails were tied with green ribbons. Gilly was glad to see the faded blue ribbon circling her wrist. She had wondered if anyone had thought to retrieve it. Kneeling, she drew Zoe into her embrace. "I'm so happy to see you."

Zoe's arms tightened around Gilly's neck. "I told Daddy we had to come."

"I'm so glad." Gilly sat back.

"He didn't think you would be home, but I knew you would be."

"Oh?"

"Sometimes I have magic dreams, too."

"Really?" Gilly looked up at Jake.

He shrugged. "Her dreams seem uncanny sometimes. I never thought about it before, but now, since everything that's happened—"

Gilly opened the screen. "Would you like to come in?"

"If you feel like it. I heard what happened at the café this morning." His glance dropped to Zoe.

Gilly understood; they wouldn't discuss the details while Zoe was within earshot. She said, "I've unpacked the rest of the glasses. I could make lemonade."

They went into the kitchen. Gilly introduced Zoe to Bailey, and she knelt beside the table to coo to him and rub his ears. Bailey rolled onto his back in ecstasy, making Zoe giggle. Her laughter was a tonic, a boon.

Setting the sack of lemons on the counter, Gilly turned to look at Zoe, reveling in the sound. She exchanged a glance with Jake.

"I should have come before now, should have at least called to tell you she was—" He stopped. "God, when I think what could have happened if it hadn't been for you—" His voice broke. He cleared his throat.

They looked away from each other, as if by mutual agreement.

Gilly said, "I don't know where the lemon press is, but I did find a pitcher."

Jake said, "I know how to squeeze lemons."

Smiling at him, giving him a look, Gilly said, "When life gives you lemons . . ."

He hooted.

Bailey found his ball and brought it to Zoe, and the two went into the backyard to play.

"She looks wonderful," Gilly said. "Back to herself. Is she?"

"Well, she's quit asking me so much about the lady with the scratches on her brain."

Gilly was at sea.

"Zoe told me you said that's why Karen was shooting the gun. Because her brain had scratches."

Gilly laughed. "I'd forgotten. I didn't know how else to explain it so she'd understand."

The light of humor flared, but only briefly, in Jake's eyes. "I'm having trouble finding an understandable way to explain about her mother. Zoe wants to know where she is, when she can see her."

Gilly had wondered about Stephanie, but it wasn't her place to ask.

"She's still in jail," Jake said as if he'd read the question in Gilly's mind. "She hasn't got bail money, and I'm not helping her this time. Maybe if she's in there long enough, where she can't drink and do drugs—"

"She'll wake up." Gilly paused. "I did," she added quietly.

"That's what I hope for." Jake kept Gilly's glance a long moment before turning back to his task. He squeezed the last of the lemon juice into the pitcher.

"Stephanie wants me to bring Zoe to the jail to visit, but I can't decide if that's a good thing. What if it only scares her or confuses her more than she is already?"

"Maybe if you let a little time go by, you'll see what to do. Zoe herself might tell you. She's a strong little girl. She has a joyfulness about her, a kind of irrepressible spirit."

Jake washed his hands.

Gilly handed him a towel.

He kept her gaze. "I've wanted to bring her to see you. She's asked, but we haven't been out anywhere, really."

"It's all right." Gilly smiled at him. She didn't say she'd gone early to the café every Wednesday since Zoe's rescue in anticipation of seeing her and her dad.

He folded the towel. "Folks in town have been great, but, you know, they want to talk and talk, and the press—I don't want Zoe exposed to it. All the questions, the gossip and speculation. At least the media seems to have finally given up. I was surprised not to see them here, after this morning."

"I had a little help from a detective in Houston."

"Carl Bowen?"

"You know him?"

"We met briefly at Karen's house."

"Ah. Well—" Did she imagine the sardonic edge in Jake's voice? "He called in a favor. It must have been a big one. There've been no reporters here."

Jake leaned against the countertop, close enough that Gilly could smell his aftershave, something fresh and citrusy.

"Warren came because he wanted to explain." Gilly spoke after a beat.

"He just showed up?"

"Yes. I wanted to shoot him."

"We talked about that, didn't we? I thought I was the one stoked for revenge. You only wanted to forget."

"I know. I never imagined I was capable of taking someone's life, or even wanting to, but for one awful, horrible moment, I could truly see it—see myself—" Gilly looked away. "It's disturbing, knowing I have the capacity."

"I think everyone does in the right circumstances. If someone you love is in danger, if their life is destroyed, and yours, too, because of what they did—"

Gilly met Jake's gaze. "But you didn't do what you said you would do."

He frowned.

"You got the gun from Liz—Karen—that day. That's why it went off, right? But you didn't shoot her."

"It was totally unplanned. She was talking about us, the way we were all those years ago. I guess you know she was pregnant. It was our baby, and she—the baby was stillborn."

"It's not something you get past easily."

"No. I wish I'd been a better—a better person, a stronger guy for her then."

"You were a kid."

"That's what my mom said. Somehow it doesn't—maybe it's an explanation." Jake wiped his face. "It was rough, listening to Karen. I felt bad for her, but at the same time she had the gun, and I had no idea what she'd do. Her state of mind—"

"But then you got the gun. You could have shot her the same as I could have shot Warren, and you didn't."

"I thought of Zoe, that she would be without her mom and her dad."

Gilly took the pitcher of sweetened lemon juice to the sink and added water.

"She's talked about you every day. Miss Gilly this and Miss Gilly that."

She looked at Jake.

"From the first pancake you made for her, the first fairy tale you told her, she's talked about you. And I—I don't mind. I like it. Even when she isn't talking about you, I'm thinking about you." Jake cupped her elbow, and Gilly looked at his hand there, feeling the warmth of his palm. She tried to resist it, to pretend she didn't feel the tiny thrill run on little mouse feet up her spine.

He raised her chin so that she had to meet his eyes. "I don't know what this is between us, and I can feel how you don't want it to be anything. My head is telling me the same thing. But maybe we should ignore those voices—" He paused, looking intently at her. "What?"

Gilly knew it was the way she was smiling that made him ask. "It's just I have quite the circus of voices in my brain."

"Do you?" He grinned. "So what are they saying? You think we could see where this goes? It doesn't have to be more than we make it, right?"

"No," she said, and the surge of her trepidation was threaded with the crystalline lightness of new possibility.

"Good," he said, and she shivered slightly when he slid his palm down the length of her arm and twined his fingers with hers.

Zoe clattered through the back door, Bailey at her heels. "Miss Gilly, when we make pancakes again, can they be in the shape of Bailey?"

Gilly looked down at her. "Absolutely," she said.

"Can I help? Can I make the dough?"

"It's batter," Jake said. "Pancakes are made from batter."

"Well, I think we'd have to mix it up here, and not at the café," Gilly said.

Zoe bounced. "Now? Can we now?"

"It'll be dinnertime soon, ZooRoo."

"We have pancakes for dinner sometimes, Daddy."

"Miss Gilly might have other plans." Jake held her gaze.

"No," she said. "I can't think of anything else I'd rather do."

ACKNOWLEDGMENTS

With each book my gratitude to my core support group gets bigger and warms my heart more. Thank you forever to my fabulous agent, Barbara Poelle, for opening the door. I am indebted to my interim editor, Danielle Marshall. Even though her desk must be piled to the sky, she is always there with an answer or encouragement, ready to cheer us all on. As I was nearing the finish line with this book, Barbara and I got a call from Danielle and my former Lake Union editor, Kelli Martin. Barbara and I had guessed the reason for the call, that Kelli was leaving, and we were both in dismay until it became clear Kelli was going to freelance; she would still be my developmental editor. Danielle calls Kelli and me a dream team, and we truly are. Kelli has such an uncanny ability to guide my vision, to help me find the beating heart of the story I want to share with readers, and it means the world to me. She is a gift. Thank you so much, too, to Alicia Clancy, my new Lake Union editor, for her guidance as we have gone forward with this book.

Huge huge thanks to my copyeditors and proofreaders: Ciara, Elise, Albert, Claire, and Nicole. I am in hope that I have included everyone. I am beyond grateful for the gift of every sharp eye that has gone over this story. In particular, I'm grateful to Ciara for her careful and insightful commentary throughout. The story is so much better told because of her thoughtful reading and attention, and that of the others.

Thank you so much to Derek Thornton for the fabulous cover. The image so beautifully captures the mood and atmosphere of the story. It's eerie and lovely all at once. Simply perfect.

In doing legal research for the book, I again turned to my neighbor, John "Chip" Leake. I can't even say how cool it is to have his wealth of experience—thirty-four years as a Texas law enforcement officer—to draw on. Any inaccuracies in that area are my own.

Thank you to my street team of early readers. You guys are fabulous in the effort you make to read advance copies and then post reviews. It's an invaluable resource, connecting authors with readers, shouting out praise, getting a buzz going. Pauline Tilbe, you are the best. You've been with me from the beginning. Jink Willis, you've shouted about my books and shared them with your book clubs—your support and enthusiasm means the world to me, and it is such a boon. Thank you to Lynette Burnette. I was so thrilled when you invited me to meet virtually with your book club! It was such an honor. Thank you to book angels Mary and Amber Blackburn, Susan Roberts Peterson, Barbara Bos of Women Writers, Women's Books, Mary Lazon of *Linda's Book Obsession*, Deborah Blanchard, Kristy Barrett of A Novel Bee, Holly Casper of the book review blog, *Country Girl Reads*, and Cheryl Masciarelli of *C Mash Loves to Read*, and to the many members of the wonderful Facebook reading and author groups, in particular Great Thoughts, Great Readers, Reader's Coffeehouse, and A Novel Bee. I am forever grateful for everything you do to shout out and spread your love of books everywhere!

Thank you to my Amazon/Lake Union marketing and author liaison teams, naming just a few members, Dennelle, Gabby, Michael, and Gabe. It's all of them—and the countless others who work behind the scenes—who give books their wings. I'm so grateful for all you do to get my books into the hands of readers!

And yet again, a huge and heartfelt shout-out to my readers and to readers around the world. Sending love, joy, and gratitude to all of you. Thank you!

WHAT LIES BELOW BOOK CLUB QUESTIONS

1. Early in the story we learn that almost four-year-old Zoe has disappeared, that she may have been taken from her preschool by her mom, who is the noncustodial parent. According to Child Find of America, 78 percent of child abductions in the United States are committed by the parent who doesn't have custody. Are there circumstances where you feel such extreme action might be justified? In the story, do you feel law enforcement should have acted more quickly? Should the FBI be called in immediately when a child is taken, even though strong evidence supports it is a domestic matter?

2. When Gilly dreams of Zoe's abduction before it happens, she's reluctant to approach anyone to warn them of the danger Zoe might be in. Have you ever had a precognitive dream? Did you share it? Do you believe people have the capacity to see the future? Do you think psychics should play a role in law enforcement?

3. Gilly's parents have encouraged her from childhood to ignore her visions and dreams. She was punished for sharing them and feels that her father abandoned her and her mother because of them. Her mother's motive was to keep Gilly from being stigmatized. Was she right? If your child had such experiences, what would your reaction be?

4. If someone warned you of a future calamity they'd visualized happening to you through a dream, would you listen and act accordingly, or ignore it the way Gilly and Brian did?

5. Have you, or would you ever, consult a psychic in regard to your future? Discuss the circumstances that might lead you to such a decision. Or if you can never see yourself doing that, discuss why.

6. While Jake's parents are willing for him to be responsible for his role in Karen's pregnancy, they are adamant that marriage for their eighteen-year-old son isn't an option. How would you advise your son or daughter in a similar situation?

7. After Gilly witnesses her husband's murder, the shock brings on labor, and she loses her prematurely born infant daughter only hours after her husband was killed. Grief causes her to spiral into addiction. Is this understandable? Is her own criminal act forgivable given the circumstances?

8. Gilly assumes it isn't possible to find a second soul mate. What do you think? Is there more than one person who

can fulfill this role? If you were to lose your life partner, would you seek another, or like Gilly, would you retreat into yourself?

9. Jake blames himself for the emotional and mental issues Karen has dealt with in her life. Is he right to assume responsibility? Was there anything more he or his parents could have done, or should have done, to help her? What do you think of the two sets of parents and their varying opinions and reactions to Jake and Karen's relationship, and their unplanned pregnancy? What are your ideas about parenting teenagers when it comes to their romantic relationships?

10. Both Jake and Gilly suffer harm as the result of the criminal actions of others. Initially, Jake voices his vow to seek revenge, but Gilly demurs. Revenge won't bring back Brian or Sophie. In the end, though, when both she and Jake are confronted with the opportunity to take their revenge, it's Gilly who comes closest. What would you do in her circumstances? In Jake's? Would you be able to forgive a perpetrator who had cost you the life and the people you loved?

ABOUT THE AUTHOR

Barbara Taylor Sissel writes issue-driven women's fiction threaded with elements of suspense, which particularly explores how families respond to the tragedy of crime. She is the author of eight previous novels: *The Last Innocent Hour*, *The Ninth Step*, *The Volunteer*, *Evidence of Life*, *Safe Keeping*, *Crooked Little Lies*, *Faultlines*, and *The Truth We Bury*. Born in Honolulu, Hawaii, Barbara was raised in various locations across the Midwest and once lived on the grounds of a first-offender prison facility, where she interacted with the inmates, their families, and the people who worked with them. The experience made a profound impression on her and provided her with a unique insight into the circumstances of the crimes that were committed and the often surprising ways the justice system moved to deal with them. An avid gardener, Barbara has two sons and lives on a farm in the Texas hill country outside Austin. You can find her online at www.barbarataylorsissel.com or on Facebook at www.facebook.com/BarbaraTaylorSissel.